D1563700

ASHE OF RINGS

AND OTHER WRITINGS

RECOVERED CLASSICS

Ashe of Rings
and Other Writings

Mary Butts

Preface by Nathalie Blondel

McPHERSON & COMPANY

ASHE OF RINGS AND OTHER WRITINGS

This edition copyright © 1998 McPherson & Company, Publishers, by arrangement with The Estate of Mary Butts. All rights reserved. Preface copyright © 1998 by Nathalie Blondel.

Published by McPherson & Company, Post Office Box 1126, Kingston, New York 12402. All rights reserved under International and Pan-American Copyright Conventions.

The publisher gratefully acknowledges the assistance of a publishing grant from the literature program of the New York State Council on the Arts.

Library of Congress Cataloging-in-Publication Data

Butts, Mary, 1890-1937.
    Ashe of rings, and other writings / Mary Butts ; preface by Nathalie Blondel.
        p.   cm. — (Recovered classics)
        Contents: Ashe of rings — Imaginary letters — Warning to hikers — Traps for unbelievers — Ghosties and ghoulies.
    ISBN 0-929701-53-4
    I. Title. II. Series
PR6003.U7A6   1998
823'.912—dc21   97-49604
                                              CIP

Printed on pH neutral paper.

Manufactured in the United States of America.
1 3 5 7 9 10 8 6 4 2   1998   1999   2000   2001

PR
6003
U7
A6
1998

CONTENTS

PREFACE

W hat Mary liked most," the American composer Virgil
Thomson once declared about the Mary Butts of 1920s Paris,
"was a long pub crawl—going with loved ones from bar to bar,
dining somewhere, then going on, tumbling in and out of taxis,
fanning youth into a flame. Come midnight, she would as leave go
home to write."

Even when she was alive, the image of Mary Butts as a flam-
boyant socialite tended to overshadow the publications which resulted from her daily routine of *going home to write*. The watershed
of the Second World War, coming soon after her sudden death at
the age of 46, contributed to her work going out of print. Her
existence became mythologized, recorded mainly in the memoirs
of the Long Weekend, as the inter-war period came to be known.
In these accounts, superficial facts about Mary Butts tend to be
exaggerated: her larger-than-life personality (Sylvia Beach, Aldous
Huxley), her interest in magic (Quentin Bell, Aleister Crowley,
Douglas Goldring), her vivacious socializing (Evelyn Waugh, Harold
Acton), her striking red hair (E. M. Forster, Robert McAlmon,
Wyndham Lewis). But Mary Butts had more serious sides to her
personality. "I have always thought," declared the Australian painter
Stella Bowen, who first met Mary Butts during the Great War,
"that if ever one were ill, destitute, a refugee, or in any really
spectacular mess, Mary's doorstep would be the right doorstep on
which to be found in a fainting condition. She would receive you
and your woes with open arms, without question and without cau-
tion."

Mary Butts also possessed a social conscience. She worked, for
example, for the National Council for Civil Liberties during the
First World War. After she had been called for jury service in 1922 on
the case of Nelson vs. Moir, Mary Butts gave a newspaper interview
explaining why she declined the judge's suggestion that she (and

two other women) retire from the case: "To begin with," she declared,

it does not at all follow that because a woman knows and hears many of the unpleasant facts of life she is thereby coarsened. In any case women know a great deal more than they are credited with knowing, and are quite capable of forming a reasoned judgement on the facts.

... I consider it most necessary that there should be a frank and adequate knowledge of moral and criminal questions. The law's decisions will be hampered and woman's usefulness will be rendered abortive unless all obscurantist prejudice is done away with.

Yet it was writing, not politics or social work, that was her "raison d'être." Mary Butts kept a detailed and voluminous diary for most of her adult life, and from those pages emerges a very different person from the ebullient party-goer of her friends' memoirs. Here she is less confident, and subject to truthful introspection. In the spring of 1927, aged 36, she remarks: "...up to now, I am an unsuccessful writer, lover, dubious mother, of no social distinction—well liked, but my looks are going and, to a certain extent, my health. Well, I can write and I want to, should never want to do anything else." While she was regularly published in these years, she was never complacent, noting in the summer of 1929 how "it has taken me all my life to fix the little of which I can be sure, arrive at such poor theorisings from them as I have, while I am haunted that they slip by me each day in millions."

Notwithstanding the intensity of her social life and the quantity of private writings (she was a prolific letter writer), Mary Butts was tireless on the literary front, publishing five novels (two of which are historical narratives), three collections of short stories, a childhood autobiography, and an epistolary novella, all within a mere fourteen years. If the steady republication of her work in recent years has meant that she is no longer the scandalously neglected writer she remained for too long after her death, Mary Butts is still known mainly as a novelist and short story writer, and to a lesser extent as a poet. So before turning to the present volume, it is worth noting several other areas of her oeuvre and paying proper respect to Mary Butts the essayist, the critic, the reviewer, the translator, and not least the gardener. She published one of the first recorded critical appreciations of the ghost tales of M.R. James, and she wrote lengthy articles on Aldous Huxley, Baron Corvo (F.W. Rolph), and the Bloomsbury group. She wrote over a hundred reviews for newspapers and little magazines, including *The Bookman, Time and Tide, The London Mercury, The Observer,* and *The Sunday Times.* She helped translate Jean Cocteau's play, *Orphée* (1926), into English. As for her love and knowledge of gardening, consider her description of this coastal Cornish garden in 1935:

...in an island of garden, hollowed out and protected by turf walls and hurdle and stone, growing hedges of fuchsia and veronica, and young sycamore trees just breaking into their gold-beater's green leaf. There are lilies whose green towers the Florentine artists copied in marble and bronze; lupin and honesty and columbine, alison and sweet william, pansy and peony and carnation. At the back a great rock with the herb patch round it, thyme and tansy, parsley and rosemary, garlic and alisanders, mint and Corsican carroway. The vegetable garden round the herbs, raspberry, and broad bean and green pea. All divided by rock walls where the ice-plants crept, the saxifrages, while between each plant-ing, like a corbel, a knob of house leek, blue and bloody-thorned, its flower beginning to rise like a feather in its cap. All are rather behind, what with the late winds, but 'coming along handsome'.

The present volume displays the impressive eclecticism of Mary Butts's talents and interests, for here we have a novel, *Ashe of Rings*; an epistolary novella, *Imaginary Letters;* two lengthy pamphlets, *Traps for Unbelievers* and *Warning to Hikers;* and a study of supernatural fiction, "Ghosties and Ghoulies." Written between 1916 and 1932, each illustrates Mary Butts's lifelong desire to create texts which act as remembrancers, evoking and invoking "spiritual" aspects of human existence.

Ashe of Rings

Begun during the First World War when she was in her mid-twenties, *Ashe of Rings* became Mary Butts's first published novel. It was praised by May Sinclair, partly serialised in *The Little Review* in 1921, and taken up enthusiastically by the American writer and editor Robert McAlmon, who issued it in 1925 as a Contact Edi-tion alongside works by James Joyce, Gertrude Stein, Djuna Barnes, H.D. (Hilda Doolittle), Ernest Hemingway, and Ezra Pound—authors Mary Butts knew personally. The following year *Ashe of Rings* was published in the United States, but a British edition did not appear until 1933.

Ashe of Rings is a Modernist work. It combines realistic and fantastic elements in a linear narrative which defies temporality by aspiring to a condition of myth. Part I is set in 1892, Parts II and III in 1917. Mary Butts describes the novel in her 1933 Afterword as a "War-Fairy-Tale." Early in the story, Anthony Ashe asks his wife, Melitta: "Can you feel how time is made sound and we listen to it, and are outside it? Have you thought what it is to be outside time?" Later, another character declares: We are spectators of a situation which is a mask for another situation that existed perhaps in some remote age or in a world outside time."

The Rings of the title refer to Badbury Rings, a set of prehistoric concentric earthworks in south Dorset. Mary Butts visited these Rings throughout her life and felt them to be her spiritual home. Their "grounding" power was such that she claimed in her memoir, *The Crystal Cabinet* (1937): "Without the Rings I know what would have happened to me—whirled away in the merry-go-round of the complex and the wish-fulfillment and the conditioned reflex, with Jung and Pavlov, Julian Huxley and Bertrand Russell, in group-consciousness of my group." Instead, her work retrieves what was destroyed by First World War. As the poet John Wieners observed, "she...called around her, called down the finer spirits, whose every book is a re-affirmation of life, who says in every book that that other thing has to be fought."

Ashe of Rings is an allegorical contest between those who understand this prehistoric landscape (and who thus see themselves as the Eumolpidae, inheritors of the Eleusinian Mysteries) and those antagonistic to it. These forces are portrayed through the "masks" of the characters. Anthony Ashe and, upon his death, Vanna, his daughter, become guardians of the Rings. Ashe's wife, Melitta, is indifferent to their power, so much so that she defiles them by having sex with her lover upon the Rings. Vanna's friend Judy Marston personifies the ruinous First World War, which hangs over the entire novel. While Serge Fyodorovitch, a Russian artist, tries yet fails to grasp the significance of the Rings, unable to see beyond their surface appearance of "wet grass and high trees...a cold wet place... [where he] chewed on wet leaves and laid on stone."

In First World War London, Serge and Judy are locked in mutually destructive sexual combat. When their relationship breaks down temporarily, Vanna rescues Serge from near-starvation and encourages him to resume his painting, removing him to the countryside of her birthplace—and the Rings. No personal or physical relationship is possible between them: Vanna is preoccupied with regaining possession of Rings after having been disinherited by the birth of her brother, born of the sexual relationship of her mother and her mother's lover. Meanwhile, Judy becomes involved with Vanna's neighbour, Peter Amburton, a soldier discharged because of shell-shock. Blinded by (misplaced) sexual jealousy of Serge and Vanna, Judy convinces Peter to rape Vanna on the Rings by night. Vanna thwarts this plan by lying naked on one of the stones so that Peter is terrified by the sight of her and flees. Vanna thereby atones for her mother's earlier defilement of the Rings, and the novel ends with a reconciliation between mother and daughter which re-establishes Vanna in her rightful place as guardian of the Rings.

While contemporary in its wartime description of London, *Ashe of Rings* is written in a evocative style that draws on a range of imagery from ancient classics to Sir James Frazer's landmark study of myth, *The Golden Bough*. As a small child she had acted out Greek fables and historical events with her father in the garden of Salterns, her home in Parkstone on the Dorset coast. Perhaps not surprisingly, classical images and references to the Dorset Downs of her childhood recur in Mary Butts's writing. Once in a book review she made the case for the "profound familiarity" she felt toward classical mythology:

One reason why we study the classics, why we assume, or used to until lately, that whatever an educated man did or did not know, he must know something about the language and thought of the antique world, is because we feel that we are dealing there with men who had the same assumptions as our own. That this in itself is a very large assumption, does not trouble the intuitive conviction. We feel that their delights and desires and difficulties were in the same terms as ours: they were examining, shaping, using and being used by life in a way we understand: and when all allowances have been made for varieties of custom and speculative belief, what they did and were is recognisable; has a profound familiarity—and not of the kind that breeds contempt for us.

Indeed, her friend and admirer, the writer Hugh Ross Williamson, thought highly of Mary Butts's "scholarship [and] her knowledge of Greek life," which sprang from her early experiences. In his "Portrait of Mary Butts" (1931), he writes:

She was the heir of Hellas. It was on a hill that Endymion slept; Aphrodite had risen from the sea and in the woods Adonis died: Persephone haunted the meadows and Pan the pursuer still lingered by the reeds in the marshes. She had inherited their land. Gradually she came to understand them. If they began as real people, they ended as equally real forces, which refused to be moralized over but demanded acceptance.

So powerful was her imaginary world that Mary Butts declared in her journal: "We do not escape the dead: stronger than the living the dead surround me; figures and men-gods and I hardly need say, *distinguo.*"

Imaginary Letters

Imaginary Letters is the only prose piece in this collection to have already been reprinted since Mary Butts's death: it was republished by Talonbooks in Canada in 1979 with an insightful afterword by Robin Blaser. The original edition of 250 copies was published at her own expense by Edward Titus's At the Sign of the Black Manikin Press in Paris in 1928. Printed on hand-made paper, it was beautifully produced with six illustrations by Jean Cocteau, including a striking line drawing of Mary Butts. Titus claimed that this was the first time that Cocteau illustrated the work of another writer, but it is omitted from the major bibliographies of his work. Although the narrative is dated Autumn 1924 (when Mary Butts started to write it), *Imaginary Letters* was extensively redrafted in September 1926 when she was reading *Science and the Modern World*. This was a collection of lectures by the English philosopher Alfred North Whitehead which came out that year and which she cites in the epigraph to *Imaginary Letters*.

As the title implies, this 60-page novella is an epistolary fiction in which the female narrator addresses a number of letters to the mother of her lover, Boris, a Russian emigré, who, as Blaser points out, "will not stay still...[being] unstable, lost, homosexual, unavailable." "God forbid that I should give away the young to the old," the narrator declares in her first letter, adding: "but as you will never read this...I do not think it will be impertinent of me to talk to you, as if you were a living ghost." These never-to-be-sent letters are in fact a kind of diary in which the narrator tries to understand the magical, incongruous and inescapable power of love, however hopeless it is. *Imaginary Letters* is a lyrical prose sequence, evoking all the qualities, faults and mysteries of what Russia meant to Mary Butts, who repeatedly peoples her fiction with Russian "emigré boys" of 1920s Paris.

Traps for Unbelievers and *Warning to Hikers*

If she looked to the past for inspiration, it was because Mary Butts felt that the present lacked (because it had lost) a resonant quality which past cultures possessed. This makes her work somewhat more difficult for a reader unfamiliar with the classics, but it is worthwhile persevering, since her use of myths provides access to other dimensions of experience or imagination. As Ezra Pound once remarked: "speaking aesthetically, the myths are explications of mood: you may stop there, or you may probe deeper." When you read Mary Butts's work, you always get a sense of probing deeper. Thus, the poet Robert Duncan described his introduction to her work in 1941 as an "initiation." The term is not used lightly; by 1947 Duncan and his fellow poets had "collected signs and rumors" because of her writing which, he explained, "incited us to traffic in myths and to derive a 'scent' by charging every possibility with overtones and undertones, to make thunderheads, storm weather—but to hold it unreleased—for the power's sake, living in actual life as if it were a dream."

Warning to Hikers and *Traps for Unbelievers*, the two pamphlet essays included here, were issued by different presses in March 1932. They are very much companion pieces, directly addressing the need for preserving the land and retaining or restoring some sort of spiritual consciousness.

Developed from an earlier unpublished article entitled "Vision and Belief," which Mary Butts wrote in May 1928, the theme of *Traps for Unbelievers* is stated at the outset: "It is continually being brought to our notice by different people in various ways that for about the first time in history, the Western World is going about its business, to a great measure without the belief or practice of religion, organised or private." This "strident indifference" to belief which Mary Butts discerns, includes not only Christianity but all religions; life without God(s) arising, she maintains, from the misconception that to discard God(s) will free us from the constraints of social morality. Actually, this banishment of belief has repercussions which extend far beyond the physical and social realms of life. Mary Butts agrees that gods are not needed when all is well, but *the time comes when something disagreeable happens, quickening often with secret and horrible vitality into tragedy; and one begins to notice what happens to natures who have only human nature to fall back on; not strengthened to meet pain by any of the old receipts and for whom no new ones are available. Receipts which linked the phenomenal world to the eternal, condemned events by reference to concepts not affected by change or by any vicissitudes of man.*

In other words, by focusing on and giving priority to "human nature" at the expense of the "phenomenal world" (i.e., Nature: that realm within which the human exists but which is other than human) and the "eternal" (i.e., the supernatural: that realm entered through religious belief), an anthropocentric interpretation of existence has been formulated which cannot bear the tragic, the unordered, unnameable sides of existence. What is now absent, because it has been lost, is "a very peculiar kind of awareness" which Mary Butts locates not only in religious belief, but in primitive mysticism and the occult. While regarding the practice of magic as "very largely primitive science," she discerns "behind" magic a kind of awareness which

has something to do with a sense of the invisible, the non-existent in a scientific sense, the relations between things of a different order: the moon and a stone, the sea and a piece of wood, women and fish. Its appellation by means of primitive guesswork is one of the most shocking records of human trial-and-error in history, but it is by no means quite so sure that all of the original guesses were unscientific or the original "awareness" quite such nonsense.

This perception has no more died in man than has his sight or any other of his senses; only he does not now try it out or at least not often...

This awareness or "perception" is not, as far as Mary Butts is concerned, a luxurious sixth sense which enables a richer, more complex life—we are not presented in her writings with an aesthetic consciousness like that of Henry James who explores the never-ending "beautiful difficulties." Rather, it is a crucial filtering process through which we can see how things *are*, and without which life under its disabling aspects is intolerable. It is significant that Mary Butts should attempt several descriptions: "a sense of the invisible, the non-existent in a scientific sense, the relations between things of a different order." Her inability to put this awareness exactly into words—to define it, to pin it down—reveals not her inarticulacy, but the limitations of articulation itself: that there are areas where language cannot go, or at best only go "around" by a series of metaphors or paraphrases. We have bodies, we live in space, and we have language. These are not of the same qualitative order. Mary Butts's works try to link up the phenomenal world to the eternal one: "Holy, holy, holy sang our fathers and they felt better. What they were doing was very ancient magic."

* * * * *

In the past, it was to points of nature that men were sensitive; spring's return, daisies white on dark grass, the "klange" of cranes that fly across the sunrise; but these are noticed with the kind of surprise that comes when the attention is caught by a detail of the familiar. Gilbert Murray, in contrasting our nature sensibility with the Greek, says in effect that we rhapsodise about the state they breathed: that "we talk about worshipping a sunrise, while they trudged to the top of a mountain and did sacrifice."

—FROM *Warning to Hikers*

Mary Butts completed *Warning to Hikers* in London in October, 1931. She had just spent several months with Gabriel Aitken (whom she had married the previous year) visiting his aunts in Newcastle-upon-Tyne. The setting for the fifth part of the pamphlet is the countryside around Newcastle, rather than her beloved Dorset. Written partly in response to the tremendous rise in popularity of hiking in the 1920s and 1930s, it warns against the increasing prevalence of a "cult of nature," the use of the countryside not as a place to live in, but simply as another source of "free" leisure. Mary Butts writes (with respect to her own experience):

If it has been one's fortune to be brought up among physical beauties, natural and created, if one's sense and tastes have been formed on them; if also one was taught their use as a standard and to reject passionately all that was not like them, adult life becomes a greatly enhanced but not an easier thing.

She compares this with "a kind of psychic shock or rather strain" which is endured by the dwellers of "the majority-home of England, in a town or a suburb of a town." Interestingly, the people inhabiting her fictions are correspondingly divided between those who are "town-tuned" (e.g., Judy Marston and Serge Fyodorovitch in *Ashe of Rings*), and those who respond to the mysterious forces of nature (e.g., Anthony and Vanna Ashe). In view of present-day concerns for ecology, *Warning to Hikers* seems both prophetic and pertinent.

"Ghosties and Ghoulies"

It is curious. Up to our age a writer, even the most detached artist, was allowed to teach. Having special love or knowledge of something, he was supposed to hand it on. The present world, its majority suddenly become literate, unless the subject is technical, faints at the thought. Until it is noticed that, having read any imaginative work from Aristophanes to Ronald Firbank, and taken pleasure in it, something of the quality has entered in and become part of oneself. Has made one more aware and sensible, using the writer's eyes. So that one finds out that, after all, one has learned.

—FROM "Ghosties and Ghoulies"

From ghosties and ghoulies and long-leggety beasties
And things that go bump in the night,
Good Lord, deliver us!

Throughout her writing career Mary Butts often uses the term "supernatural" when referring to a quality embodying something more and other than the natural, and underlying it. In "Ghosties and Ghoulies," her study of ghost fiction, she defines the term in more detail as "a stirring, a touching of nerves not usually sensitive, an awakening to more than fear—but to something like awareness and conviction and memory." Such an atmosphere of heightened sensitivity forms the criterion by which she assesses this fiction; it is also evoked particularly strongly in two of her own short stories, "With and Without Buttons" and "Mappa Mundi." Like *Traps for Unbelievers*, "Ghosties and Ghoulies" was developed from an earlier unpublished article which Mary Butts worked on in Paris in August 1928, and which she called "Use of the Supernatural in Fiction." The rather more tantalizing final title comes from the anonymous Scottish prayer. Published in *The Bookman* in four parts between January and April 1933, this study is extraordinarily thorough, ranging from Shakespeare to M.R. James, from Paracelsus to May Sinclair, from Thomas the Rhymer to E.M. Forster. Mary Butts takes us on a literary tour round stories, songs, poems and ghost-anthologies from all over the British Isles and beyond, providing, into the bargain, an account of the supernatural fiction being published in the early 1930s. There is something here for all tastes: not only does she praise such well-known writers as E.F. Benson, Rudyard Kipling and Joseph Conrad; she also draws attention to that far less well-known "masterpiece of sober loveliness" by Mrs. Oliphant, "The Library Window," and to Branch Cabell's "The High Places." Mary Butts is drawn to supernatural fiction, she tells us, because she is interested in the "mysterious links and repetitions of history...[which are] reborn, now here and now there, making one feel that such happenings and such repetitions are not fortuitous." She is not convinced by the "point of view which is a legacy from the dogmatic materialism of the last century and still unconsciously powerful; whose influence to-day leads us to describe the beliefs and faiths of our ancestors as science misunderstood; or the visions of saint or artist, profound or fruitful, curious or bizarre, as nothing more than a way of externalising the unconscious."

* * * * *

The underlying aim is the same across Mary Butts's writings. The title of one short story—"From Altar to Chimney-piece"— epitomizes what she felt was happening in the modern world. Throughout her work she strives to arrest this drift from the numinous to the mundane by reversing it; that is, by evoking the sacramental quality embodied in seemingly ordinary situations and social exchanges. In *Warning to Hikers* she praises Havelock Ellis's *The Dance of Life*; and in one sense his title is the unwritten subtitle of all her writing, each text a "separate dance," the whole attempting to recreate "the Dance, the Ballet of the World." When she succeeds—when, as often happens, you are drawn into her visionary atmosphere—then you may in fact undergo a rite of passage whereby reality is modified and some new "quality has entered in," has become a part of you, and makes you "more aware and sensible." More enchanted.

—NATHALIE BLONDEL

Ashe of Rings

To J.A.C.M.

I

CHAPTER I

RINGS lay in a cup of turf. A thin spring sun painted its stones white. Two rollers of chalk down hung over it; midway between their crest and the sea, the house crouched like a dragon on a saucer of jade.

In the walled garden behind the house, the air was filtered from the sea wind, and made a mixing bowl for scents, for bees, coloured insects and noisy birds. A gardener, picking gooseberries, straightened his back to spit. The great drive, up which the countryside crawled like flies, swerved to the right where a stream ran into the sea. There the cliffs parted, and the hurrying surf beat into a round cove full of rocks. The waves rang within earshot of the lodge. In storms they covered it with spray. There Rings ended and the world began.

The station fly ground round the corner by the shore. Anthony Ashe poked his head out of the window and smelt his strip of beach. Half-way up the avenue he stopped the cab and got out.

"That will do, Houseman, thank you. Good afternoon."

He passed under the trees whose quickening buds broke the light, and walking fast, took a footpath across the park. *The house has a thousand eyes.* —He turned his head to the sea under their scrutiny, till a straggled wood of black pines hid him, and the path turned red.

Anthony Ashe of Rings remembered that he should have insured the driver's silence. But he could not think what to say, and to a squire even of the last century tongue slitting had gone out of fashion. The house would know already—a small child was running up the drive with the news. It did not matter.

5

It is said of this place that in the time of Arthur, the legendary king of Britain, Morgan le Fay, an enchantress of that period, had dealings of an inconceivable nature there. Also that it was used by druid priests, and even before their era, as a place for holy and magical rites and ceremonies. A battle of the Danes and Saxons was fought there. To-day the country people will not approach it at night, not the hardiest shepherd. There is a tradition that in the barrow above the earthworks is placed a box of bright gold.

So much for the County History.

The first Ring raised its thirty feet of turf. A ribbon of chalk path ran along its crest, a loop a mile round. Inside was a second wall and within that a third. On the plateau above them was a round barrow, irrelevantly placed, and a dewpond, full of mud. Behind the pond and the barrow, there was a grove, ragged trees, exceedingly tall, pines and beeches, knit at the feet with hazel and bramble and fern. On its skirt a pleasant wood; its centre was a soggy thicket full of white marsh grass. Year in, year out, the wind rang in its crest with the noise of a harp.

From these rings and this grove depended the fantastic house, and the generations called Ashe, which were born there and pattered through its hall and bright passages like leaves. Its triple circle was the sole device on their shield, represented from the hatchment of their dead to the coral and bells each baby chewed and shook. An old drawing represented the Rings, come down from their hill and sitting like an extinguisher upon the house. It had been calculated that, allowing for all projections, the house would fit exactly into the inmost ring.

A British camp, but of pre-British—possible neolithic origin, used by the Romans; a refuge for Celt and then for Saxon, a place of legend and consequent aversion to the countryside ever since; it is well that so interesting an historic site should have remained in the preservation of so ancient a family.

Anthony Ashe stamped his arms on the presentation copy of these sentiments and knew better. The Rings preserved him. His son Julian had died, and that night he had gone up to them like a blind beast. After three years in the East he had come back, without mate, without heir, to present his accounts and their deficit.

He went through the gap in the first rampart, crossed the fosse and mounted the white chalk steps over the second ring, and the third. The wind ran along them shivering, and a thistle tapped his boot. He climbed the barrow, sat on it, and looked back down the valley to his house.

The Rings kept the valley head. From them a road, green, white and faint ran into a birchwood, and through the delicate trees to a door in the kitchen garden wall. Thus no one but shepherds came to the Rings except through Rings. At the valley head the road was lost in a powdering of flints.

Thick white smoke rose from two chimneys below. The fire was lit in the library and in his dressing-room. The news of his return had come. He dragged at his short beard with his hands till his chin ached. These were his thoughts. There must be children. And for that some strong girl. His name would obtain him one. What was left of his life could be given to her training. A livery sacrifice to this place. It did not matter whom. *"I'd be daft to refuse him, the laird of Cockpen."* An old tune. That's it. Soon to find. Easy to keep. But a stale business. What had been a duty would remain one. The carved bed frightened them. Chinese. The Imperial Court. A girl slung across the back of the chief Eunuch. Left to crawl up from the foot of the dragon-bed. Would Clavel like the job? …All the solemn county to placate. Cruets….

Oh God! Let me see it through. Rings, it's been a labour following through the centuries your eternal caprice. Yet it comes again… I don't doubt that it will come again… I do not know what it is… To every Ashe in turn it happens… You…*sing, and singing in your glory move…* Then he said aloud: "Julian—my son Julian."

It's a specialists undertaking. The things that one foregoes to set a feather in Ring's cap. You could cover a broader skull. My old head aches with you.

7

He wrote with his stick upon a patch of chalk. Anthony
Ashe 1892. *Iste perfecit opus.* He said:

"I must go down and see about that child." He stood up,
resetting his grey top hat. A breath fluttered through the tree-
tops and ran through the grey hair fringes on the back of his
skull. He shook his head.

"Caprice—Caprice—stop tickling my neck. I tell you one
thing. Not one of the girls who want it shall have it. I'm an
old man. The strain needs crossing. That's it. Dance round.
Tickle my chin. So Julian wasn't your fancy.... If I stopped
calling you pretty women, Lesbian-dryads—I couldn't stand
it. Is that why my son died? Did he see in you what I dare not
see? So that he died.... *Good night, sweet prince.* You were a
young dog to turn up your nose at the pretty ladies of Rings
Hill.

"I suppose I had better go through." He ran down the
side of the barrow and walked into the wood over a light
shell of turf, and springing needles. Then mud curled over
the toes of his boots. A springing bramble reversed its hooks
across his nose. The blood dropped through the thin skin.
Another curled across his waistcoat. He loosed each hook in
turn. High up the wind sang with seraphic lightness; a transparent feather fluttered onto the crown of the grey top hat.
With lovely lightness the wind fell, the last sigh ran down the
shafts and scattered in minute touches... He thrust on slowly
into the clearing where there was a large stone.

Light women. Light women. *Light things and winged and holy.*
He stood five minutes with greedy eyes. Then he struck
through the wood, hurried over the rampart and down the
rabbit-darting hill.

8

THE library had sixteen lancet windows to enclose a quartering of Ashe. At the east end, in the wall's angle, seven stairs led up to a round room, the floor of a tower, called Rings Root. Anthony Ashe ran up. He stood inside the curved panels like a man inside a barrel. The sun lay in ochre strips on the floor's deep brown glass. Across each window the sea sparkled, but no breeze followed through the great depth of stone. A fire of fircones charred to a chalk-red ash. He stretched and straddled in his quintessence of privacy, a handsome daimon inside a chinese ball. The room was in the heart of Rings. There Ursula Ashe had declared herself a witch. There there appeared at uncertain times a sphere of pure light. On the wall hung a lead hour-glass. He reversed it and sat down at the open cabinet. He drew a trail of little beasts, cats, cows, occasionally birds; but the head of each was that of a marriageable girl of the place.

"The Landlady's girl at the Crow. We might do worse. She'd fill the gilt cradle, and the oak cradle, and the ivory box that held the Italian brat." He looked up at the red trickle.

"Do it by the alphabet. A for Anne. Anne Avebury. She's a sweet maid. I like her too well. Let her keep her innocence. B. D. Damnation. Deirdre—Doris Benison of Phares. No.

"H—there's Hilaria Lynde—name's the best part of her. I. J.—Jocelyn—bad little bitch that. K.L.N.M. Marion Mangester. God forbid—Muriel Butler. What made me think? They live at Gulltown. Blind father, black satin mother. Sprigged muslin girls—Two. What a name! She's neutral. She'd do. Body like a tree—Head like a daffodil—The name—Terrible name—what can she be called? Mavis, May,

Millicent. Oh, Christ! Melitta, that's better. Melitta Ashe."
The sands ran out.

*   *   *   *   *

At Gulltown, two young ladies talked:
"A frill of saffron muslin, goffered small. Nancy would do
it. You ask her, Ver'?"
"Did he pay you much attention, Muriel?"
"They did say he's engaged to Norah Clancey, but it's a
secret—"
"Then don't mention it," said the younger sister, gently.
"Poor young man. I pity him if it's true."
"He is old enough to know his own mind. I believe it's
a case. Haven't you finished. Mother wants us to go shop-
ping—" She added suddenly—
"—Have you heard that old Mr. Ashe has returned to
Rings?"
"If I meet the Morton boy I shall ask him about Norah."
"Muriel, that would be abominably inquisitive."
"Ver', Ver', what else is there to talk about? What else is
there to do?"

Gulltown hung on a cliff—white houses hung with flowers on a white cliff. A breeding place for fishermen and shepherds, there was also a snail's nest of little gentry hanging on
its terraces.
Anthony Ashe was saying to Mrs. Butler:
"Tell her that I will come for her answer to-morrow. Give
her these roses. Tell her I will wait a week longer, if she
pleases."
Muriel Butler had not seen the scarlet sands run out, nor
a piece of paper covered with sketches in the round room at
Rings.
A ripe virgin, she wept into her Tennyson and combed
her rich hair.
"Ver', how can I? Ver' what shall I do?" Her sister said:

"Ask yourself, Muriel. You like him, you esteem him. Do you love him?"

"I cannot believe it's true."

"Marriage is holy. Don't forget. It cannot be undone."

"Mistress of Rings," said Muriel.

"The wife of Mr. Ashe," said her sister. "Who could have believed that when poor Julian dragged him over for tennis it would ever come to this? He was very kind to me."

"So he was to us all." She was thinking: Jealous of me already. "How shall I manage that marvellous house?"

"You mean to accept him?"

"Accept him. Oh yes, yes, yes. Refuse Rings?"

"My dear Muriel—remember—you are not marrying his estate, you are marrying Mr. Ashe."

"Who marries Ashe, marries Rings. You silly woman, don't you know that?"

Her eyes crawled over her sister, scissor-point to scare the unchosen. Vera looked steadily over her sister's shoulder.

"Have you thought. There may be babies—that would make up—"

"Children—I hope not. I mean—I don't quite know. It's a nasty subject. Oh I wish Mr. Ashe had never called."

"Look here, young lady, do you want to become Mrs. Ashe, or don't you?"

"You know—Anthony, you know—"

"Then you will not be called Muriel. When you understand things rather more, you will know why. You shall be called Melitta, see?"

"Very well. Then I shall call you Tony."

"As you like, puss. Now you had better find out what Melitta means."

CHAPTER 3

IN the well of the library, Melitta Ashe summoned her courage. It did not come as an elemental to the word of power, as angel, socratic daimon, or noble beast. She urged, she whimpered, commanded as her bully commands a resentful, sensual girl. Una mounted her lion. Anthony Ashe came down the seven stairs.

"We were told not to strike a woman with a flower, but what am I to do to you if you poke your brassy head into my room?"

"How am I to know if the servants do their work?"

"There is no need. They know their work. Part of which is to tidy the room and leave me alone."

"Where is the crystal ball you promised to show me?"

"Ursula's? I have it. Do you want to understand these things?"

"I thought that one saw pictures—and the future—and—"

"Go to any Bond Street hag for that."

"Tell me about your great great grandmother."

"Ursula Ashe?" He led her to a seat and placed a footstool for her. A snake was carved on it, reared in loops about a bee-skep. Her feet shifted in their lace stockings. Anthony Ashe said:

"You spoke of Ursula—she was earlier. It was she who brought into prominence the practice of magic to which our family has always been liable."

To Melitta it seemed that the slow pencils the sun laid across the floor moved on.

—"She travelled to Italy. She lived here as a girl. She

came back, and you can imagine the contacts. Up there I keep her book. Every Ashe in his turn lives to read it. None of us has done so entirely. I no more than the rest. I sometimes dream about it. If you live here long, you will dream."

"Does it make nonsense?"

"No. Part is in reference to an occult book, the Enchiridion of a Pope. To us conventional hocus pocus. Then a diary full of morbid psychology. Then a section in cipher which, so far, no one has read."

"What was she like?"

"Her son destroyed her portrait. He was on Cromwell's side. He saw chalked on his bedroom door a curse *because of the whoredoms of thy mother Jezebel and her witchcrafts*. He cut off his hair, turned the gilt chapel her Italians had built her to celebrate the black mass into a still room, and celebrated the beheading of Charles instead. Plus ça change."

"Oh, how dreadful."

"But romantic, girl, romantic. I should have thought romantic enough even for you."

"But to behead King Charles, it was a crime. *He nothing common did or mean.* I've loved that verse. And you speak as though it were any common execution."

"My dear silly girl."

Over the house, through the sparkling air, the bronze note of a clock rang, like a body falling bound into deep water. Within the house followed a burr, a tinkle, a humming, breaking with cross beats into the same sequence.

She sat still.

"Can you feel," said Anthony Ashe, "now time is made sound and we listen to it, and are outside it? Have you thought what it is to be outside time? Turn again, little Melitta."

He took her on his knee.

"Melitta, Paphian.

"Mother and Courtesan—

"Virgin—I'm sorry, but there are times when every Ashe tries to make a verse."

"But it sounds—it sounds."

"Like the Ephesian Artemis. She of the Hundred Breasts."

"But Anthony, it is coarse, and disrespectful to me as your wife."

His fine hand smoothed away his sneer.

"Try to understand." Silence. "Do you not understand the link between yourself and a great goddess—the type of all things which a woman is or may become?"

She wriggled and sprang down from his knee.

"I've been trying to tell you all the morning. And you make it harder with every dreadful thing you say. I am going to have a child. I know I am going to have a child.

"And there is something vile about this house. I don't know what the things in it are. I feel its memories watching me.

"It is much to beautiful. Only wicked people would have cared about it so much.

"I don't know how you can sit there. Don't you care for what is going to happen to me?"

"Why, my dear little fool, what do you suppose I married you for?"

She ran out wailing. He told himself:

"Take it quietly; it's all in nature. My God, does she want every servant in the place to know her condition?"

She was gone, and from under a cloud the sun rolled into the room. A crowned globe, a poppy head burst and scattered, it enriched the gilt and the glass and the waxed floor the colour of old beer. Outside the birds struck up and the bees thundered. The letters on the books sparkled, his cigarette lit at a puff. He was comforted. If he had laughed her out, it was to give the room its turn. Why didn't she meet its challenge?It could be hers. He remembered. Why had he not got him a mate? Rings saw nothing but the soul. This pink and white shepherdess, not three months married, raised her moralities....

And to his estate, aloud, he said—"O, thou delight of the world, may my child be equally delightful, to thee." He surrendered himself. The long glittering room blessed him. He followed Melitta out of the house.

*　　*　　*　　*　　*

On the valley path she struggled with the sun. The sphere which had broken and bubbled in the house shot out and beat her with golden rods. The turf closed round empty shells. The path was sharp with flints, the heat like an army with banners. She thought. Get up. High, ever so high. Up there over the earth-works there will be a cradle, long grass and clean and light. Only sun and butterflies, and over the rampart a peep down into a world like tea-things set out on a lawn. All the way over to Gulltown. She was a great lady now. She despised Gulltown. She was ashamed to remember Gulltown. Her obscure initiation was concluded. By a process equally misunderstood she was to produce a child. A long way to the top of the hill. Of course. That was why the place was called Rings. Mrs. Ashe of Rings. They belonged to her. One might put a summerhouse there, and have the stones picked out of the path.

People were coming to lunch. There was just time to let the wind blow through her hair. Wear a string of yellow topaz, but not round her neck. Slung across, on a white gown. Pretend to be ill. No good. She would make excuses and cry. *He* would never do anything he did not want to. Horrid, horrid, insolent old man…. We're married. We're married. Till death do us part. It will part us. Not for years and years. It was a long way to the breeze. Anthony Ashe found her quiet on the grass.

"The sun was making a burning glass of your hair."

"Was it?"

"Aren't you coming back to lunch?"

"I suppose so."

"Would you like to go to the South of France this winter?"

"Monte Carlo?"

"If you insist."

"Ought I to—when—Anthony, don't laugh at me like that."

"Don't cry at me like that then with greed in your eye… Coming?… Don't forget the topazes on your dress?"

15

"No."

"On white, mind...."

Later in the day. "What made you run up there?"

"I don't know. They seemed so high, up and away from the pettiness of the world."

"Do you know that if it were not for that place there would be no Rings. And no Ashe of Rings."

"I don't understand."

"That you are my wife—and your life is bound up with the life on that hill. Your child's life will be bound up with a life outside your own. Like the mother of Meleager."

"It sounds heathen. I don't understand."

"You must become a brave woman. You must learn. You must be a brave woman. Before we go abroad I will take you up there."

"Oh, Anthony—"

"Ursula Ashe was carried up there to be delivered of her children—"

"Because your people were as hard as flint and as wicked as hell, why do you expect me—?"

"That's better. That's my brave girl."

CHAPTER 4

"WHICH is it—which is it?"

"It's a girl, Mrs. Ashe, now don't excite yourself."

"A beautiful little maid. Her head be covered with red, and she do kick and squeal."

"I didn't want it to be a girl—let me go to sleep."

The red baby slept in the Italian cradle. The cycle of existence run round again. Flat on the ebony hood the young Apollo, the young Artemis raced their ivory bodies round the Delian palm.

Anthony Ashe came into the nursery, whistling.

Vera Butler counted napkins, soft linen squares in dozens. She said:

"You are not sorry, Anthony, that it is a girl?"

"I had a son and I lost him. That will do."

" — Ten dozen. I'm glad you feel like that. I'm afraid my sister expected you to want a boy."

"Melitta will get to know me better in time."

"You will be patient, Anthony?"

"I don't know if you are wise to ask me that."

"Oh well, a sharp tongue like yours needs watching. But now this little darling has come—"

"Was it a difficult birth?"

"Perhaps worse than we expected—her resistance."

"Her courage you mean," said Anthony.

"Don't say that. She is now sleeping quietly."

"I hope we shall see you often at Rings."

"You may be sure."

"I set great store by the child's education."

"I'm very glad to hear you say that."

17

"You must help us."

"I will," said the sister.

"I hear the luncheon-gong. Shall we go down?"

A stern Madonna nurse from London stood at the cradle's foot, beside the tanned peasant who would take the child from her at the month.

"Well, my little lady."

"I tell you, he's glad it's a girl."

"He lost his first son did he not?"

"That's an old story. But I'll tell you one thing, nobody ain't going to give her much change."

"Mrs. Ashe?"

"Clavel, he's from the north, he do call her the wreckling of Rings."

"What is a wreckling?" said the London nurse.

"Out of a litter of pigs the one that do die."

"Is Mr. Ashe kind to her?"

"He could melt a peach stone, maybe he's no teeth to chew an acorn."

"Well—I expect there's her side to it if we only knew."

The two women left the nursery.

The red baby moved and then lay, dark eyes open, gathering life in pure form without constituent of pleasure or pain. A fist stirred and a foot; imperceptibly it took possession.

"Anthony, I've been staring at it all the afternoon? What is the green hump on the lawn?"

"There was a tower there once. You can see stone sticking out of the turf."

"Is that a bush growing on it. It seems a pity that it should break the green sweep to the sea."

"My dear, once one starts disturbing old things, one raises something one did not know was there to be disturbed. I know what you mean. You would like one opposite to match it, two grey nipples on a green breast?"

"Why not finish it off with a rustic seat?"

"No."

"You'd better tell me about it."

"Why do you want suddenly to know all about the place?"

"Isn't it better to know than to go on imagining?"

"Look it up in the Book of Ashe."

"I'm no good at books. —Please Anthony, I can't be left to find out. I'm afraid not to know. I have tried to be a good wife. Tell me. Tell me. I'm afraid not to know."

"Stop distressing yourself."

"Why is there a bush on the mound?"

"Well observed. Eat some more nougat?" Her sticky milky teeth shewed in a smile. He drew the curtains, embroidered with the birds and apples of paradise, and lit the candles at the foot of the bed.

"The bush is the stump of a thorn. When there was a tower there, the parent tree grew beside it under the wall. There was one of us once who was hated. They came and found him there. They took him and made him wear a crown of thorns."

"Yes."

"There they crucified him—or rather they nailed him onto the wall. He died looking on the sea. He was a long time dying. It is because of that, and not because of Charles II, that the remark is a family joke."

"How can you joke about it?"

"Because we are like that."

"When did it happen?"

"Once upon a time."

"I don't believe it."

"It is in the Book of Rings."

"I was never much good at lessons. We were so badly taught. Won't you translate the interesting bits?"

"I will teach you Latin, and courthand. Then you can do it for yourself."

"There are late bits, your own and your grandfather's."

"Since the decline of our Latin. You can manage them."

"Anthony, what is it all about?"

19

"Go on."

"What is this place about? What has the house to do with the Rings and what have the Rings to do with me, now I've married you?"

He considered and said stiffly: "We are a priestly house, like the Eumolpidae."

"You know I know nothing about your classics."

"I'm sorry, but what I've said is the answer. If you really want to know more, you will find out for yourself."

"Anthony, you pretend that there are ways of looking at things which have nothing to do with Christianity."

"Little Melitta, Christianity is a way, a set of symbols, in part to explain and to make men endure the unutterable pain that is the world. There are other sets, like chessmen. But only one game."

"Do you believe in the heathen gods?"

"Yes."

"But not that Christ died for us?"

"Yes."

The curtains bellied, the fire-tongues darted out. Melitta sat up and drew a wrap across her breasts.

"Tell me more about the man they killed at the tower. Is his portrait downstairs?"

"He was too early."

"Right back in the Middle Ages?"

"Yes. In the book there is a miniature of him. There he is a saint, and the tower is a tree."

"A stiff thing all angles and thick gold?"

"It was before people wished to paint realistically."

"Yes, you've told me, but please make him a person?"

"He was Florian Ashe. He lived in Henry VI's reign. He made a pilgrimage to the Holy Land. He must have been young, brave, and amusing. His wife disliked him. One day her people came and nailed him to the tower."

"How irreverent. Did they—did they—make it quite like the Crucifixion?"

"Like enough. He said to them. *You have nailed me up here*

20

like a kite, to be an example to birds of my kind. And they said. *We are to make an end of you, so that you cannot laugh or pity any more.* And he said. *You have forced on me the likeness of our Saviour; so in my own name, I forgive you.* Then he looked at the sea and refused to speak."

"Did he say anything else?"

"Just before he died, he strained about and said: *I cannot see the Rings.* A shepherd threw a flint at him and killed him."

Melitta said: "You make me as though I saw it in a glass."

"But not darkly?" he answered. "That's good: We are a united family. He is our young brother. We have never got over his dying like that."

"I'm sure he went to heaven."

"May be. But he left a question behind him no one has answered. It is asked again in some Russian books you should read.... And at the foot of that tower, I tell you, every Ashe will weep."

"There is a new Ashe, Anthony, even though it's a girl."

"Silly one, must I explain again that I am glad of it."

"What are we to christen her?"

"She should be Melitta, but you do not really like that name. A red brat. Let's call her Elizabeth. It is one of our names also."

"Yes. I like Elizabeth."

"Add anything you like."

"My mother's name was Cicely."

"It doesn't go with the rest."

"All right. What is yours?"

"Vanna. After Monna Vanna, an Italian lady I admire —Vanna Elizabeth Ashe."

CHAPTER 5

"THAT is how we christen them at Rings."
"But, Anthony—?"
"You can have it done again, in a church—in Ursula's
chapel—by a parson if you like. That's your affair. But ours,
I tell you, is the one that lasts."

They were in the walled garden, a square produced from
the library wall, emerald grass pegged with yews and impaled
by a stone well. There he had caught Melitta, playing Nar-
cissus to the star-filled water. In one corner stood the tower,
Rings Root, filling an angle. A path of slimed pebbles ran
round the walls. In the outer wall a door opened on the terrace, and there flowed the great space to the sea.

> *"Toreador,*
> *Toreador,*
> *For thee love waits!"*

Melitta looked at Anthony Ashe as he opened the terrace
door. Through its square there rushed into the dim heat a
breeze and a blaze of light. His grey suit fluttered. Round the
well grew bushes of lad's love. She arranged the train of her
dress. A flock of fantails hummed over the rich sky, and
mounted crooning on the tower. So long as there were no
more babies....
The red child slept in its nurse's arms. In the library, on a
slab of blue marble, stood a winnow-corb of wicker, black
with age. Tied on it by wool-threads were dried ears of corn,
figs and fircones, dolls' cups and cylinders of baked clay.

22

Anthony Ashe shook down into the basket a bed of tiny coloured feathers.

"Melitta, Queen Bee," he whispered.

The servants of Ashe stood round acquiescent, friendly. The nurse unwound the child and laid her naked in the basket.

"Now." Anthony lit a tall candle and placed it at the baby's head. Melitta on the right laid a jar of fresh earth, and a bowl of water on the left.

"Earth and water and fire," he said.

"They are all round her."

"Breathe on her then with your maternal breath." Her eyes brimmed. She kissed her baby. They both stood back. It opened its eyes, and an uncertain hand grabbed the feathers.

"Vanna Elizabeth, daughter of Melitta, bird of Rings! The elements composed you, the elements surround you; so may their harmonious properties sustain you."

But Melitta, bold with feeling, cried after him—"In the Name of the Father, of the Son and of the Holy Ghost."

$$* \quad * \quad * \quad * \quad *$$

An hour too soon, Melitta dressed for dinner.

It was all right. Everything was all right. She had got over having the baby. Nothing in the bargain could be worse than that. It was her baby. She did it. There is a God. That christening might be blasphemy. There was her duty to Anthony: she was learning to manage Anthony.

God had been good: He always is if we are only patient. There was Rings. To-night she would sit at the table head. A young madonna—Friday night at home in Gulltown, fried fish and raspberries—cream for a treat. Ought she to have fed Betty? She was thriving. Had anything been said? Horrid, but people did it now. That christening couldn't count. It ought to be done again: such a pretty idea. But what did it mean? Sir Frederick Leighton. *Wedded.* Oh his horrid, clear, contemptuous mind. He's given mine up. Thank goodness.

Bits on that greasy old basket? Queer things put away in

23

the gallery that ran out of the tower to the locked rooms. It meant something. find it out for yourself? Too much trouble. She wasn't going to be bullied. Men do not want women to understand. Look at old Ver' pretending to be a blue-stocking: what good would it do the baby?

The house was different. One would have to understand its things. She had always had taste. Always a success. *Uneasy lies the head*—I don't care—I'd sooner wear it than a home-trimmed hat. I shall be a young woman when he dies.

"Mrs. and Miss Butler, ma'am."

"I can't see them. Tell them it's impossible. I'll come down. Where are my rings?"

She made along the corridor to the head of the stairs, head forward, bottom to balance, train over arm, like a charging cockerel.

From the door of his dressing-room Anthony saw her pass. He had brought her to this house. Well, she was not so insensible as at first. He was surprised at the remodelled body, uneasy at the sharpened wits. She had bred quickly, but the red baby ignored her, and Clavel and the old servants, the horse Aldebaran, and the rhythms of the house. The pearls he had bought her in Paris were china beads on the milky skin. Only her gowns obeyed her.

He had called it eugenic impatience. It had but masked his slackness. In his last woman he should have sought for peace, and he had established beside him this intelligent and developing greed... He had heard her cry for her rings. God! It was complicated.

"My last duchess?" He followed her to the stairs, saw her prance down and cross the hall at a run.

"In the library, ma'am," said Clavel forestalling. She did not want Clavel to see her people. They were plain ladies. Was her dress a sufficient indication? Not to her sister.

"My darling—how is your Betty. Your note of yesterday said she had a cold. One cannot be too careful, even in summer."

"Betty? She is very well." Vera recognised Anthony's intonation. Her mother said:

"As we were going for a drive this afternoon, I thought we would call here and ask. Vera cannot endure—"

"I am glad I can reassure you. Would you like to see her before you go? We have several people dining to-night."

"May mother have a cup of tea?"

"Won't you help yourselves?"

"If you don't mind, I will run up and see her?"

Clavel interposed: "Shall I tell the coachman to put up, ma'am?"

Vera had gone to the nursery. "I am afraid the stable will be very full to-night. It is rather late, Mother."

Anthony came in.

"I thought Vera was here."

"She has gone up to see Betty."

He turned to the mother. "Will you join her with me? I must show her off before she sleeps. I have told your coachman to put up."

"Oh, my dear Anthony, we must go."

"Why? Stay and dine. We have people coming. Can't you see Melitta's war paint? She can lend you things."

"We must go home."

"This day week then—I will send over early for Vera." He turned the door. But Melitta said:

"Please Mother, do come. So long as you let me know before." Now let Anthony go to the nursery with them if he liked.

His face shewed in the mirror from over the back of her chair. An earring fell like a star.

"Since when have you thought it unlikely that I should welcome your mother and your sister to Rings?"

"It wasn't that. It is so inconvenient of them to turn up when we are busy. They felt out of it themselves. They would not have liked to have stayed."

"I did not know that you were occupied with cooking dinner."

"No, I've had enough of that on the cook's evening out."
He laughed.

"You wicked, intolerable child. If you were anything but
a schoolgirl, an inquisition could not punish you. However.
No diamonds to-night. Off with them! Not an ornament.
Quick! If you cry, you shan't appear at all."

"Ver'—Ver'. Vera has been telling you—nonsense. I
minded, I minded because she is jealous of me."

"That may or may not be true. But you'd like her to be.
More powder on your shoulders. Now come down... You're
smiling. That's better. There's a brave girl... Why are you
smiling like that?

"You have remembered that when I am dead you will be
a young woman able to have a young man for your mate.
Have you just remembered? No protests. You should never
have forgotten it. Let us wait in the library.... There is only
one thing, girl. When your beauty has waxed from rose to
peony, there will be Vanna, coming up immaculate to take
your place."

So they lived for five years.

CHAPTER 6

THE head of the house was the guardian of the Rings. Assuming that, thinking of them as potencies if not persons, whose sanctity could be violated, for five years Anthony Ashe guarded them from his wife. At the end, they were inviolate, the great girdles, the wood, the stone. She had not been there. This was the outward sign. He had not explained, he had insisted on it. Principally he had interposed his hard, elegant body between her and the valley road.

He had seen how the house, like a hive of quintessential bees, had enclosed her, not with honey, but with wax as though she were some insect trespassing. Pity and wisdom—his people had kept the Rings, guarded the house, the humanities, each in his age's formula; and if they had preferred wisdom, it was because wisdom is easier than pity. But Melitta, a mother of Ashe, would have neither pity nor wisdom. (He had shewn her Ursula's book, and in Florian traced a Christ.) He would die, and she would be left with the bird of Rings. While he lived he could separate them as he had separated his wife from the hill. He was not ill, but he knew when he was likely to die. It was still a great lord of the world who took the air at Rings. Meanwhile there was the child, Van, before whom the house laid down its subtle spears. Before she could walk, the arrows of the sun, the arrows of the moon and rain, were ribbons to keep her upright.

Melitta had her idea of the accident that had brought her to Rings. She believed also that Anthony might attempt to be rid of her once she had born a child. She intended to stay. Envied only of fools, she would remain, mistress of the house. Her family did not trouble her; only Vera, who came often to Rings.

27

The county subscribed to her legend. Anthony's friends from town did not. If it were not for her child... The baby did not like her. There were no more babies. Thank goodness. Only wicked women prevent babies. She had nothing to do with her education. Anthony knew what he meant by education, and she was not sure. It was wrong to bear his death in mind, but he had an awful way of reminding her that he would die. Later she would feel relief, like a puzzled child who rediscovers its toy.

Anthony, the only acknowledged sign of his age, would remain at Rings. A month abroad, a month in town he would be back. She was lost without him. One thing she had done. She had instructed herself in plate and china, in the periods of furniture and portraits, and the history appropriate to each. Dress was her success. Wine and food were beyond her, and such things as Anthony added to the house.

"Why buy anything new when you have so much old?"

"There is a change coming," he said. "Designs are beginning to interest me again. In twenty years there will be something good. God is not left without witnesses."

Through the seasons, the sun's light fell pure and hard, alternating with the sinister moon. The wind rang across the sea, the rain orchestrated itself on the flats of the roofs. These worked upon Melitta's nature, without any necessity for ghostly tamperings with sound or light.

Vera had learned to bicycle. She must learn. Vera was coming to lunch. She left her writing-room and saw Clavel go into the library with a glass of port. Anthony would be in his room up the seven stairs. She followed the butler. Black wings folded tight, like a tall beetle. A hieratic scarab, made of stone, whom Anthony had made a friend.

She stood in a corner of the dais where she would not be seen. A child's naked feet padded over the burnished floor. Clavel's black trousers bent at the knee-joint alongside a blue smocked shoulder. Anthony came out.

"I want to play with the red sand."

"I'll fetch it, Betty."

28

"No. Play in the round room."

"I'll carry you up."

"If I shut my eyes, I'm there."

"Good."

"Thank you, Clavel, for bringing me."

A bambino between the saints. Clavel turned the length of the room to make up the fire. The mistress of Rings pressed back into a corner and shut her eyes. . . .

"Van put one alley in mouth. Van put two alleys in mouth. Wob. Wob. Wob."

"Van, take them both out at once."

"Daddy, shew me more."

"Tell me when are you called Van?"

"Here and up there?"

"What have you seen up there?"

"A wall and a wall and a wall."

"Then?"

"A green hump and a pond and a wood."

"Who goes there?"

"You and I. Then I am called Van. Pull open drawers."

Melitta thought about governesses and duty. She owed it to the child. The child could read—soon she would get the use of books. She cast out her thought over the deep floor. The room received it, and for answer a sheet of clear glass dropped between her and the will of her world. She crossed the room, a noise of water in her head.

"Anthony, may I come up?" She ran up. "I want to consult with you."

"Well?"

"Isn't it time we had a governess for her?"

"Plenty of time yet. Next year we might think of a tutor."

"A man?"

"It would be best."

"Is it suitable?"

"It can be made so. She must know Greek and Latin. She speaks a little French with me. She has taught herself to read. My dear, don't worry. She won't be the less marriageable for it."

"You never shewed me what was inside that cabinet."

"You were not interested. Do watch those brown paws. That green man, that's a Lar. A Lar is a little god of indoors. He sees that the fire stays in, and warns the mice when you are coming back. The Chinamen with the fat stomachs in the drawing-room are Lares."

"Have this Lar."

"Treat him carefully and kindly. Remember he's a god. There is you nurse." Cool brown legs hung from the little body gathered up in Anthony's arms.

"Anthony, do you think it is right to muddle the child with superstitions?"

"They are what she can take in."

"You do not take her to church."

"I do not go there myself. Why should she? It's all right. *St. Bride and her brat. St. Colme and his cat. St. Michael and his spear.* She knows about that."

"Does she know the simplest prayer?"

"Does she know the simplest fear?"

"So I'm to be kept out of my own child's education. Besides you are wrong. I don't care what you say. The women of Ashe have been bad lots. And men hate learned women, and if they are learned and loose-lived as well—"

"Ah, that was what made it amusing."

"I've never needed to know things."

"Is it possible you can still think that—?"

A servant called her away. He followed her to the stairs, and stood there, looking down. It seemed to him also that the house dropped behind her its sheet of crystal, and the floor of the library might have been a pool of the unstirred sea. He would look down and one day his bones would dissolve and he would dive forward into its glimmering well. *Full fathoms five.* Tell that song to the child. The red lozenge from the window threw a red stain on the floor like a patch of blood.

CHAPTER 7

ANTHONY asked Melitta if there was anything she wanted. She sat still, her brassy head down, plucking at a ring on her plump hand. He had gone out into the walled garden with the child, to play Phoenix persuading Achilles. He had come in to find an instrument that would do for a lyre. All his life he had played at games and now with his imp of seven years—a girl of that age makes as good an Achilles as another.

It would soon be time for him to fall down into the room that was like the sea. He had reminded Melitta more than once that he would die. He thought:

"Well said, old tongue. You've had your turn—licked and stabbed the world's wound."

The sun was warmer than Clavel's brilliant fire. A whiff of old age. It passed. A good game. Evans was right to go straight to Epic.

They played round the carved well. Out came the tutor to play Patroclus. Out came Melitta, still turning her rings. She ran back into the house. A great vacant afternoon to tea. Who would notice if she was not back? Would they notice if she never came back? A rush garden hat, a shagreen cane tasselled with blue silk, their incongruity distressed her. A door into a cobbled court, hung with washing blown like full sails, let her out past the stables, and by a detour into the pine wood Anthony had crossed eight years before. She stepped off the muddy path. Behind a tree, lifting a welling skirt, she produced from the dark triangle of her legs, a marquise hat built of curled feathers and looped with a pale rose wreath. She put it on, consulting a tiny mirror, and hid its

31

predecessor in a bush. A vigorous walk succeeded the modest trip. In the black summer house in the wood, Morice Amburton sat and smoked. Dogless, on scaifed feet, he waited for her to come and melt before him like a neglected ice.

"We might walk across the valley," he said, "then you could bring me back and give me dinner. As a matter of fact, a greyhound of mine got lost over there last week."

She answered:

"I might have been in the grounds and seen you come over the hill." It had got so far— "When there is so little wrong, don't let's give people any cause to talk. You understand."

They looked down into the valley where once she had fallen down—a wingless, sulphur bird. Now lightly, silently, holding one another's hands, they came out of the wood. From behind the last tree they looked down and back. A mile below, Rings' chimneys lifted crooked fingers and a copper cowl winked in the sun.

A sheep-flock straggled on the hill. The earth danced. Morice Amburton turned his head left and right.

"We might go up further."

"Up where?"

"Up to these earthworks of yours, the Rings."

"Oh yes."

"Will you find it too hot? It's precious sultry."

"No. I remember. I wanted to go up there once. Anthony fetched me back."

"You've never been there?"

What did he know? Amburton Hall was twelve miles away. The two estates could not touch. Their moderate shadows preceded them. The pleasure left her.

She was going up there to commit adultery. On the Rings. She wondered if there was a chance for her to come down reasonably virgin. What do I want? This man, and to be quite pure. Go on, and get it over.

She charged the first circle, her body flattened against the rampant. She peered over the top. A thorn caught her skirt and bared her strong leg to the knee. She posed there an instant. Morice, eyes on the tree-tops, gave her his hand. To climb down he forced her to lean on his shoulder. She felt his fingers through her corset bones.

"Stiff work," he said, "we're on the wrong side. If we try round, we'll find an opening."

They went into the wood. A bee was attacking a foxglove. She looked away.

"The ground's dry. Shall we sit down?"

She slipped down and pulled off her hat. Courage. It's awful, but it's real at last. Pins complicated her gesture. They sat stiff, upright and apart.

They were on the further side of the wood, where an empty valley fell away into the limitless downs. A sun-shaft moving quietly through the wood picked them out. A jay shrieked. A light air woke in the tree-tops. Morice Amburton lit a cigarette.

She had not come for that. She would ask him for one, head aslant, and so proclaim the fast woman. Was he embarrassed? Were men afraid ever? A stainless gentleman. Perhaps he was despising her. Perhaps he would tell her to go home. Run for your life. Wait, wait. Crouch under his hand. Let him choose. That's best in the end. Please God let him make up his mind.

If he sends me away, I shall have kept my purity. I can tell Anthony. If he wants me, he wants me. This is my life. Here goes. He wanted her.

Morice Amburton was saying:

"I know it's pretty bad. But think of the rough time you've had, my darling. I've never stopped thinking about it. I suppose I've made things worse. How could we help it? It's all my fault. Try and forgive me. I'm yours for ever. I couldn't do without you any more. It won't hurt Ashe. Without you I'd have gone to hell." The formulae of an irregular situation in her convention. Nothing misunderstood.

They stood at the door of the kitchen-garden wall. It was locked. Fear rippled across her shoulders. Out at dusk with this man. The gardeners gone home, a tea-party abandoned, a hat in which she had not set out, a joy to lick over and no quiet, a need to shout and sing. (And if she were another sort of woman, Anthony would permit her to shout and sing.) But she had to face his smile. The wages of sin. An old man was standing under a sycamore tree. How long had he watched them?

"You'll be wanting a key, ma'am." Morice thanked him.

The house rippled with its currents. From the washed stones of the hall to the silent hearth, up to the lacquer cabinets under the mild chinese Lares, a wave of laughter ran, whose crest sparkled on the stair head…

"Shall we put off dinner for half-an-hour? But you have brought Amburton. We persuaded Vera to stay, and Betty is to sit up. Evans and I changed for coolness. Let us come in now."

She kissed her sister.

"I fell asleep in the wood. I woke up quite late and saw Sir Morice coming down the valley. We strolled back." Done. They sat down. "How did your play go this afternoon?

"We had the embassy to Achilles. Then the Doloneia—with a real wolf-skin."

Evans, the tutor, said:

"Miss Butler came. We had the parting of Hector and Andromache. I was Hector. Betty was Astyanax."

"Was she good?" Melitta asked.

"They said I was heavy."

"Only your person, not your impersonation, but she has invented a dreadful game, Mrs. Ashe, a dinner with the Borgias. We sit round a table and at intervals we die. Miss Butler and I, corrupt adults, were Cæsar and Lucretia. Mr. Ashe was magnificent as Leo."

"And Betty."

"She was a page and handed the drinks."

While they had been playing, she had been—?

Evans, the tutor, said:

"I shall cycle back with Miss Butler. Eight miles to Gulltown. Two of us together should cover it quickly."

After dinner they went out into the garden. Against the lustreless sky, the unlit house was black. Crystal black, and at midnight it would sparkle. Amburton's cigar made a hellish disk. But hell was more human than walls of crystal. "I must go," he said.

"The car seems to be running to-day. I will order it," said Anthony Ashe.

"So you've got one of those things?" said Amburton.

"When we enjoy it, we enjoy it very much. That is all that can be said at present. I am glad we have seen you. You make good company for Melitta."

Melitta thought: Old king toad. He knows. Of course he does not know. Don't give in to your nerves. The satisfaction in her body quieted her.

"You did not offer Ver' the car."

"A delicacy like your sister's must be appropriately handled. Don't you see, if she were not free to cycle, she would come less often? Evans has a delicate job as it is."

"Your tutor is good enough for my sister."

"Why did I say that?" She had cracked the tranquillity of Anthony's old face; the smile went askew. Oh god, she had forgotten. She was an adultress. If he knew, he would turn her out down the steps. She would wander away and meet the tutor returning.

She was going to be found out.

That night the moon climbed over the Rings. A bodiless shadow whipped round the barrow and skipped on its pale cone. The faintly clashing boughs accompanied it, and ceased as it darted into their shadows. To a light clapping it spun out, to reel and trip over a moon shaft, and gather, and prick the earth, and stab, and stab....

In the centre of the wood there was a large stone. It sucked the moon's white and gave back its own, a great egg at the point of cracking, so smooth, so blank.

The shadow flickered and darted deeper into the heart of the trees.

CHAPTER 8

THE Ashe-child's father was out of the house, Evans was out of the house, her nurse was busy and Clavel. Her mother was in the house. She heard her rustle in the hall. She stood on the back stairs, steep and black as a chimney. She jumped down, six stairs at a time, and thought there was a beast after her, jumping when she jumped. Her knees were weak. She rubbed her back against the wall. A clock struck. She ducked and listened and tore away.

She ran out onto the open terrace. The image of great skirts, the image of the jumping beast, contracted into the proportions of muslin rag or mice. She ran down the terrace and the steep lawn, and spun round, and threw back her head with its short, hot curls under the tower and the thorn.

Morice Amburton had not written. Melitta was sick in the throat. She parched and sweated, powdered her face, smeared it, stared into her mirror. In her bedroom Betty had left a bucket of shells. She could not find her to order her to take them away. She went downstairs. A steel flower from the scrolls under the bannisters tore a thread from her dress. The white stairs swept round the hall, and fell down into it, a rank of seraphic wings. She thought:

A house like this well lost? Never. Never. Of course, only for love. The house was laughing at her, the house was kind. "Courage," it said; "cheer up."

Why had it not been kind before?

It did not tell her that she had been wicked, it did not tell her that she had been good. It suggested that she should continue. She thought: *O most unhappy lady.* They would write her story gently in the book of Rings. *His young wife Melitta found to her cost.... The terrible old man....* There were horses at the front door. He did not ride alone now.

In the hall there was a head of Caesar. She was not an educated woman. Anthony had told her that there was a plan somewhere to include all these things. Hadrian and Clavel, and the Lares, and people like her. And men like Morice. The charity of God. She could not feel herself inside it, the taboo more potent than the faith. *"Clear, clear,"* said the house. *"You have hunger; satisfy it. Work from that. Make your danger bear you up."* She began to smoke clumsily as her thought spun round. Round and over the Christmas tree. Needles. Bundles of fan needles. Branches too green to break. Green cones to scratch you, and you'll never get it clear. Under the tree of heaven. Cry.

Anthony came in tired. "Young horses are getting too much for me." Taut and stiff, he stretched out in the tall chair.

"Cheer up. I shan't last long. You'd better marry Amburton. He's an honest gentleman."

Melitta thought: I have married Amburton. Song and dance about it like his Anthology girls. Heathen misses. I can't. I can't. Try and tell him. But with spirit. She unfastened her necklace and swung it. She began archly: "Anthony."

Evans came in. They would be off, shoulder to shoulder, thinking of games for Betty. Their games, and Betty's, and the pleasant servants'. She did not play. Her play was sin.

"We might see what Betty is doing." Off they went together over the wide stones. They did not ask her to play. She was not good at games.

She went again to her room, to ask herself what it was that made things happen like this. Or if ever the day was to come when the beast would turn into beauty, and Amburton into her knight. She would put on her Venetian dress and sit at her embroidery frame, till the men saw her and understood.

They did not return for some time. They were giving Betty her bath.

*　　*　　*　　*　　*

Next day the clouds stood round the world's edge, clotted mountains, honey-yellow. Each hour a storm hissed over the house. The thin air contracted the valley, the Rings overhung Rings, a crown on a hill, ready to rise and sail away down plump.

While the rain streamed over and sluiced the further valley and the sun spangled the wood on the Rings, Anthony found them. From behind he skirted them; came and stood and looked at them.

"Thank God you know," said Melitta.

"My God!" said Morice Amburton.

"Here?" said Anthony Ashe.

She snatched her hat. Morice said:

"We have nothing to be ashamed of, Ashe. You must see that. We owe you every apology, but I intend to make Mrs. Ashe my wife. Will you arrange for a divorce?"

"You've had her. You can have her. But why here?" It had seemed convenient.

—"Leave this place. Any other part of my grounds are at your disposal."

"You'll not stop being good to Betty?"

"*Stop being good to Betty?* Only leave the temenos of my race."

They got up, and went down the hill. He watched them over the Rings, and withdrew into the wood. They felt their backs naked while his eyes followed them. He brought clean leaves to cover the place where they had lain. A torn twig he broke off; two cigarette ends he scraped into an envelope. An idea made him pause. On a beech-trunk he scored a strip.

This, too, had its place in the cycles. He followed the history-makers down the hill.

The tutor joined him in the tower-room.

"I've caught her, man. Caught them both."

"Yes. Who? Where?"

"Amburton. He can have her, boy. Why did you ask me where?"

39

"It seemed important. I don't know."

"I tell you, it was on the Rings. Up there. In the wood itself. I tell you, this will draw down on my Vanna the anguish of Rings."

"Ashe, explain. Are you sure? What did they say?"

"Whimpered at me. I cleared 'em out."

"What will you do?"

"Divorce her. He can have her. Or tell her to be careful till I'm dead. It won't be long now. I don't blame young things with their lust. But I see I must hurry up and die. Too long on the stage. Dead cats."

"Had you expected it then?"

"Actually—no. So little, that, at the time, it did not seem natural. What did I marry her for? To be mother of Elizabeth. And Elizabeth is pure Ashe. But I'm old. It fatigues me to remember that it is in nature, and that in nature there is no shame—

—"But on the Rings, man, on the Rings."

"While we played Greek games with Elizabeth—"

"My lovely little bird. Your mother could have had the treasury of Rings. I tell you she had no pleasure in it. Stiff as a board in his arms. In her first passion. Grey when she saw me, and chattering. My sweet lass, you may have a thousand lovers. The world shall know what is due to so great a lady."

"She is not like her mother."

"Who shall not be known as her mother any more. Did I mate with one of my hill-girls to get the bird of Rings?"

"Ashe!"

"Too much for you, Evans? What is it?"

"If you do not mind, I will ride to Gulltown and ask her sister to marry me."

"I think you are quite right. Good luck! Don't take Aldebaran. I did my courting on him."

"*I* shall ride over on my bicycle."

This lyrical interpretation carried them through dinner. Melitta had stopped crying. The house knew. Clavel knew.

It had become almost an irrelevance. There was champagne at dinner, glasses leaping with the future.

"Shall we sit in the library?" He followed her. He did not catch her up at the door; he followed her, and placed her in her carved chair, and under her feet the footstool with the bee-hive and the snakes.

"Try and understand, girl, that I am not angry with your preference for a young mate. You are a vigorous, flesh-eating Saxon woman. It is to be expected."

"You are hard."

"I want you to comprehend."

"You make it just—just—an animal thing."

"As it is. You have nothing in common with Amburton but sensual ties, lusty youth, and in your case, I regret it, thwarted high spirits."

"That is not quite true. I don't know. It's more than that. To me, and I hope to him. You have been good to me. But I think you are wicked."

"While Amburton cheaply—or romantically seduces you, and you heroise him. But you are not altogether a fool. You are Mrs. Ashe. You will be Lady Amburton. It's a fine Georgian place, twice the stabling and no library."

"I shall be his wife."

"He thinks I'll kill him if he doesn't give you the chance. But I wouldn't."

She sprawled on the carved seat, and wailed and kicked off her shoes. He looked at her till Clavel came in with a bottle of salts. The old hands shook as they rubbed it on her nose.

"There is one thing you must attend to. Evans wishes to marry your sister. That must not be interfered with. He has gone now to get his answer. In six weeks they can be married. Till then can you behave yourself?"

"Yes."

"I shall make them Elizabeth's guardians. In some ways your action has not been inconvenient."

"Won't you let me have her any more?"

"You will have Amburton's brats."

41

"Anthony, I've been all driven and muddled; but if I were left in peace, I should love my baby very much. You are there to put her against me."

"My dear, your love is not the point. Evans and I have run our finest energies into feeding her imagination, eliciting her reason, and leaving her alone. Your sister no less. Left to yourself you would not have had her tonsils cut. Stop squealing, I tell you. You are going to get what you want; only I'm trying to make your pale maggot of an intellect realise our relative positions. Come, girl, shew some spirit. Can you do nothing but shiver inside that rich dress?"

The pearl cluster on her girdle clicked against the floor. She pulled up her body and lay back.

"You are spoiling it for me. You are spoiling it for me."

"Why did you not take your love in your stride and dare us all? It was sin. So you did not enjoy it. You did not enjoy it. So you call it sin. At which end do you work? All the same you went up the Rings for your adultery. Do you understand that? You climbed Rings Hill, and went over the first Ring and the third and into the grove. Have you no conception of them after these years?"

"If it is the kind of thing I think it is, it would not mind?" Feeble cry. She might be dying. Please God was she dying, away from that chilled, ecstatic voice.

"In the second fosse I found a gold bracelet. In the top tree, a honey buzzard nests beside a raven."

He talked on—names—people—beasts. Thrones, Principalities and Powers. What had they to do with the Angels?

"Speak up, can't you?" She was asleep; her mouth on the carved arm of the chair.

CHAPTER 9

THREE weeks later, Anthony Ashe died. Clavel woke the household as though it were some sort of formality. "I found Mr. Ashe by the well in the walled garden. He was lying on the edge. His head was hanging over. I have carried him into the library."

Melitta sat upright in the chinese bed, and tore at her nightgown and moaned.

Evans and Clavel took command. Vera came over from Gulltown.

Melitta lay in her room, a wounded cat in a cellar, licking, licking. She sent for her child. The second time her sister came.

"It is better for her to be in the garden. Little wandering thing. We have to remember his wishes."

"She is my child. Go and flirt with your Evans!"

"If it were not for Betty, we would leave this place and never enter it again."

"So you will, once it is decent for me to be seen."

"I think it only right to tell you that I know—"

"Oh, do you?"

"How soon do you intend to marry—him—Melitta?"

"Not yet. Over a year, I expect." She pulled a yellow curl. Grim woman, Vera, in black.

"Why?"

"I am going to have another child."

Clavel took command, constructing, with malicious formality, ceremony for death at Rings.

Melitta's pregnancy, her widowhood, Betty's reign, the raw ghost of Anthony—these were his motifs. Evans saved

43

the library for conversation, but Anthony's room was locked. Melitta took the air in the car with the side blinds drawn, and about the house her maid watched her with shawls and salts. A vigorous woman, she detested it.

She did not know. As well one man's as the other's. She did not know. She stood crying before Anthony's portrait. That might help. He looked down, smiling at her.

Vera and Evans talked in the garden.

"Do we spoil Betty?"

"She is not a greedy child. Better if she were. Your sister, once this is over, means her no good."

"I wonder that you should dare marry me."

"Anthony said—*Why let the jewelled one slip?* By the way—I shall have to find more work. Go back to Oxford. Turn don. Leave this place and this life; the secret pursuit I saw shaping, that the place kept profound, and the child sweet. You'd have been in it too. Our lives are switched back to the normal and the sad. Scold me, sweet friend."

"I don't know that I can."

"I see a great treasure withdrawn from us."

"It isn't coming our way, again. The winter, too, makes us sad."

"Oh, these long nights," he said, "every dusk I feel what we are waking—"

"What we are leaving for a child to explain. *And the Word was made flesh*—suppose—she were the word."

"I don't know what you mean. Or what any of it means. It is all too near the madhouse."

"I think we are living in an enchantment."

"I know. Everyone who comes here steps over the sensual ring."

"I mean that we are spectators of a situation which is the mask for another situation, that existed perhaps some remote age, or in a world that is outside time."

He stared at her. "There I don't understand. The masculine brain is not formed for speculation. And you make my spine crawl. And you don't know what you've implied yourself."

"We can pray God."

"There you are again. What has God got to do with it? You see, you don't know what you mean."

"Until the new one arrives, we have still to look after that child."

"After all, it is her funeral."

"Yes, my dear."

"Maybe it's as well—I have wanted to go into Parliament. Research is not the way. You would not be happy in the end, hidden here. Wherever one goes, one's way of life catches one up."

"Yes."

"Ashe is dead. Long live Ashe. This windless grey frost has made us sad. She'll never forget her Greek."

"No, she will not."

"What are you thinking?"

"I don't know. I'm only sad."

"We are escaping. Look at it like that. You will always see as much of Betty as you wish. You will have your own children."

"I wish I had been her mother."

"You're stubborn—why? I wish I had been her father."

"You are right. The classics you've taught her are the best you could have done."

"You see you are wrong to be unhappy."

"I see that there is nothing to be done."

"*But when even Bellerophon came to be hated of all the gods, then he walked alone in the Ælian plain—eating his heart out.* Is that right?"

"Right enough."

"Why does it end like that? What happened to Bellerophon?"

"There are two explanations. The rhapsodists had not time to tell the whole story, and so cut it short there. It was written somewhere else and lost. Or, it is just a story. It happened like that."

45

"Are there more people like Bellerophon?"

"I imagine so. Tell me who you think is like him."

"Mark Antony, Florian Ashe, two people called Spendius and Matho in a book of Dad's. People who had adventures, and then a horrible thing came after them."

"You mean that they were crucified?"

"Yes—but it's the same all through." She twisted and untwisted her fine, small hands, and said:

"You tell me. Does everything end like that? What makes it end like that?" He thought:

A fever runs in these people. If you nurse their imaginations, you raise insoluble terrors. "What did your father tell you?"

"Daddy said that there were things in the world, good and bad, and a thing called sophrosynê that helped you through both of them. On the road to Delphi, you know?"

"Yes."

"Is it any good for these things?"

"For what things?"

"For those people like Spendius and Matho and the things that happened to them."

"They lived a long time ago."

"Does that make any difference?"

"Betty, for God's sake, leave it alone. When you're older.... Look here."

(What shall I tell her. The truth. What is truth?)

"Go on. Evans." Impudent sweet smile. "Dad's dead."

"Betty, you want the world to be good. Like everyone else. I'm not at all certain that it is good. An Ashe has to learn that there is life outside good things and bad. Most people don't get so far. Confound you, child! You must learn to take it easily. You'll drive us all mad and yourself."

"Can't take it easily. There is a beast tearing inside me."

"Lots of stories end *and they lived happily ever after.* What about that?"

"Only fairy stories."

"What about heaven?"

46

"You don't believe in heaven."

"I don't believe in hell."

"Suppose hell is true and heaven isn't?"

"Suppose they are houses with open doors, that one can go in and out of as one likes."

"There was a bit in that book."

"You should never have read it. You can't know what it means. What was it?"

"The bit about the crucified lions when the men were dying. *The lions, he said, are our brothers.* I don't want it to be like that."

"Come on my knee. Try and be reasonable." (God help me.)

"Can't be reasonable."

"Pity, Betty. Remember what your aunt taught you. *Pity like a naked new born babe striding the blast.*"

The child considered:

"Say it again. Make a magic of it. I think I know what it is. It's in the tower on the lawn." He looked at her with great anxiety.

"No more Greek and games while you shiver like that. Come for a walk."

"Would the beast stop tearing your heart if you were sorry for people?"

"It might. Try it and see." He thought: I've shirked. Time we went. I'm no good. What answer can I make?

They went out by the walled garden, along the slimed pebbles to the terrace. The winter sea could be heard roaring. They could hear it running with the wind. Down the empty lawn, leaves raced and spun. A voice called from the house. They looked back where Melitta, big and spectral in pale shawls, followed them with cries.

"We must go back," said Evans.

"You go," said the child, dropped his hand, and spun down the lawn into the night.

47

CHAPTER 10

THE house stirred like rufled lake water. In the night, a son was born. Melitta, the skin of her face hanging in grey pouches, stared at him, and fell back smiling. She recovered, with no snatching at life, but a steadfast clutch. The boy was Ashe. It was over, the nine months expiation: enough to lift the sin of the world. Her first real child; not an idea made flesh, but flesh to be made into her word—Valentine Evelyn Ashe. A bishop christened him.

Evans and her sister married, and were dismissed. He went to his fellowship. Betty followed them for the second marriage. In three months, her mother became Lady Amburton. Morice was good to her. Amburton Hall was to her liking. There was one question for her—how much of the tradition of Rings she could deflect upon her son, how much she could ignore.

Amburton, propitiating, gave Betty a horse. They lived alternately at Amburton and at Rings.

The second baby throve, a fat crocus, but not one pushed up by a thought. His time spent at Amburton may have confused him. Six months after the marriage, Betty came home; for a year she ran wild. Melitta then meditated a governess.

The door onto the leads of the tower opened, and the greased hasp snicked. Outside the Ashe child shot the oily bolt. (Clavel and his bicycle can. Not returned.) She knotted a filthy handkerchief. Down under, in the walled garden, the well was ringed with narcissi. She ran to the other side. The house sprawled under her, about her rose cowls and weathercocks and crooked chimneys, a grey vegetation of roofs. The grit had spun on the leads, and sunk in little drifts. Another child had left there a pattern of broken tiles. She hung over the stable yard, bare, with water running in its cobbles, and the servants' yard a-swing with washing, and rosy with japonica. They had caught her. She was not to learn anything any more. That was for boys.

There was something queer about that baby. People were not pleased. Would Clavel tell? He knew a lot more than Morice called step-father.

Of what avails the sceptered race? There had been moments when Anthony had questioned. He was dead, and had left a child to be extinguished under the tiara of Rings. Her premature pains rounded her shoulders and hollowed her eyes. Her father was gone, the play of Rings, the words Anthony had made flesh, and Evans, the tutor, mind. She ceased to love her aunt; her gentleness had become a lie to a child driven to ferocity through unequal war.

Melitta had said: "You shall learn French and German and drawing and music and English history and embroidery. Things a little lady must know. How do you know that you will not have to earn your living some day? And suppose you should marry, you do not understand what that means, but men don't like women who learn things." They were setting a trap. A woman was coming that day. A long hour to tea. The pleasantness of nature, of which she was becoming conscious, kept her up there in the sun. The leads were warm under cheek. She listened to the tapping ivy, and rolled over on her back. Her mind fell through into the library. There the scared little animal drew life. The souls of letters slid off the books and out between their pages, clotted like bees in the air. The long room was thick with their souls. Up the seven stairs, an invisible brilliance streamed from the tower room.

There were the Rings also where she went, but only on clear days, a little shadow on that immensity of grass. There was the sea, a spectator. There was the house that watched her every movement. There were its beauties which made her laugh, a pleasure in the place that drew her into a kind of ecstasy.

49

The assurance for her sanity was Morice Amburton's horse; Aldebaran she called him from the black hunter gone to his peace, and rode him with confident timidity alone through the warm lanes.

It was only natural that her mother should have no influence on the dream-saturated brain, that she should try and immediately deflect it to the normal, and be irritated to find that what could not be done delicately, could not be done at all. *Olympian houses, imperishable, starlike,* she did not know that they existed to destroy. Her move was a governess, due to arrive that afternoon.

When she came, Melitta decided to treat her as a lady, and poured out her tea. Upstairs the nurse polished an alabaster neck.

"Maybe you'll get to like her, my lamb. Run down and see." Little Valentine screamed. She walked down the great stairs, chin up, her green frock tossed by her knees.

She did not drink her tea. Scent in a shallow cup. Dried jasmine flowers from a place of tranquillity. A sigh so deep and clear that her mother noticed.

"Cheer up, my darling. She misses her uncle and aunt. They have taught her till now. But I've explained that you won't be hard on her. I'm afraid she did not learn very much."

Humble smile for the great lady. The governess was led out of the front door, and round onto the terrace. Betty darted on, ran steadily a few paces, stopped, looked back. The governess saw two dark eyes flecked with cornelian, staring at her.

"Don't come with me if you had rather not."

"No. No. I don't want you here."

"My dear child—I'm not going to eat you."

"If you stay here, something will eat you."

"Don't talk nonsense! Why shouldn't we be friends?"

"Because you are here not to teach me what I want to know."

"Come, I must know more than you."

"More about Caesar, and Leonardo?"

In this demand was something final, fatiguing, useless. (Those are not the only things in the world.) The child's appalling relevance as to its own needs was a bore. Her profession was to be bored, but not in this way.

"I am sure you do not know French very well."

"Oh, don't I! Merde to you!" With a spit of laughter she was off.

The first crackle of wit. She raced, her ribs shaking and her curls. She ran round the house, and threw herself into a hydrangea bush under a wall beside a tall herm. Against the cool leaves, she kicked, laughing, her web of anguish broke into a million threads.

She understood, for the first time, amusement at others, and not to mind that they did not understand. A lesson she was to forget and remember, all her life; repeat and fail to repeat. What did that word mean? It was improper and people jumped. Jumped so much that they went away. Or you were brave enough to scoot yourself.

Say it again. Merde. That was what one said. Think of something else to say. Make that woman jump again. She rolled about with laughter, rubbing her face on the green silk drawn tight across her knees.

CHAPTER II

RINGS was shut up. On Amburton Hall a great covering of white paint was laid. Elizabeth Ashe went to school. Melitta had not planned this solution. It had shaped and fallen on her out of the grey heavens, whose canopy over her she did not forget. She was not very happy. There was Anthony who would have taught her, Amburton from whom she would have learned. She had dissolved before her second husband that he might send her back to herself, shaped, coherent. In his idleness and simplicity he had let her melt. Her yearnings and passions had trickled off him, cooled and congealed. She then became preoccupied with tracking his casual infidelities. The worst of these was his affection for Elizabeth; over the boy he assumed, without success, a father's authority. There were no other children. If the first child was a wrath of God to her, she hoped to make the second her slave. There began the seduction of Valentine Ashe.

Amburton accepted him, but not Rings. There he was shown to the people, hunted his black pony, was blooded, and seized of England. He was six. He hardly knew his sister.

His dreams, magical and delicious of a little child, were of Rings, a twisted house of spaces and curling ways, of rare objects, not to be touched, which were, in some way, his. All these things, and about the house, a tall, pale devil called Clavel, who followed him, obedient, implacable.

Then back to Amburton where one could boast of it. A very happy little boy, but he would have liked a proper father. He would have liked to be called Sir Valentine Amburton, and not Master Ashe. That would not happen.

"You shall have both, my darling."

"But why must I be called Ashe?"

"Well, when you are grown up, it might be changed. Ashe-Amburton. How do you think it sounds? You must wait though till then."

"When is Betty coming home from school?"

It was simpler to send her to Evans, for the holidays; and when they went to the Far East, not to send her anywhere at all. She had outgrown her beauties. An assistant mistress understood these things.

The school had fallen upon Melitta out of the obscure heaven she distrusted, and with which she sought to make terms. Evans and his wife, in despair, had localised it on the earth. Not a school for Young Ladies, but a place where she would play games and be solidly taught. Even girls of family were going to the universities. Melitta lifted her magnificent shoulders. She ordered a box of thick clothes, and sent her by a footman to the junior school. In this way she made a truce with God, and it became within her power to withdraw from Rings.

For seven years Rings curled round upon itself and slept. For months on end, a single plume from a contorted chimney marked the undying fire. Of the interregnum, Clavel was captain. From his stone lair, where outside the tiny window the starlings chattered, he came out and did his service.

His quiet rites were the funeral games of Anthony Ashe. The grave servant in his meditation first saw Rings as a temple built round a barrow of the dead. In his seven years contemplation he penetrated so far as to forget. What he learned he did not tell. Objectively he was servant to the children of the house; but it is to be doubted if anyone since Ursula Ashe knew more than he. When he dies, they hope to find that he has written something.

In the summer the house swooned, in winter slept like a bear. Through the afternoons it could be heard, sucking in its sleep, milky draughts, bubbles of quiet, drunk against the future when it should become a wrath. On spring nights there

53

became imminent the fantasy of Rings; when, on the screaming wind, the Rings went sailing, and hovered over the house and swooped and fanned, and skimmed away in the dark, a cap between the roofs and the blazing stars.

This at the equinox. At the solstice there was calm, a quiet of the siren's sea. The sun that fulfills all shadows and the sun that darkens them laid their gilt fingers across the empty rooms. The dust rose. Between the light rods, specks danced. Rings showed its teeth. In the library, in a crack under Anthony's stairs, lay a ring with a gem, long lost. It showed now, a coal of amethyst.

Clavel, huge, waxen, like a word of power, crossed the room. He took it from its crack and held it up. There appeared to him a hand which stretched up for it. A light blew out of Anthony's room and rolled down the seven stairs. It flew up to the ceiling, and broke in a storm of gold. The glittering points quivered into a mist, and dissolved again into the unspeakable quiet.

II

CHAPTER I

TWELVE years later. In a sitting-room of a small London flat, a young man and woman were disagreeing, bitterly, with each other. It was the year before the end of the war, when there was very little to eat; and along with the strengthless food and the noises at night, friendship had lost its generosity and passion turned *à rebours*.

Some essential oil had gone, a minute secretion, infinitely slow to replace, and without which anything evil between human beings is possible.

Bitterly poor they were, also young and handsome; in love, and the girl at the screaming point of rage, about everything, about nothing; and the tall boy weeping and spitting himself on the knife she held out.

"In payment for my meals."

"What a beastly thing to say——"

"You infected me. I am sorry."

"Now you mention it, even your partial board and lodging are expensive."

"Stop me as you stopped the cream."

"Going to whine about your lungs?"

"For God's sake don't," he cried. "I mean if you have to have this fury, get it over quick."

"I don't want your cheap psychology—I want my ornaments."

"I will do my best to get them."

"If you are really going to be ill again, you'd better tell me. I don't know what's wrong; you were never in the army to crock your health. You took precious good care of that."

"I'm not ill. Judy, chérie—I'll do what I can; but if they

57

were stolen, the police are not the only way. There are better ways. I'm going to try them first. Then I'll go to the police, if you like."

"It will be too late."

"My way won't take long. Agree. Tell me about this girl, and all that happened."

Respited he lay back, sensing her pacified. A crumb for his ravenous mouth to suck to rags. A little crumb, and he wasting and whining for a meal. To love the unhappiest thing on earth, who must be fed on blood. Poor girl, lovely girl. Forget the cream. Good while it lasted. Thick and rich and smooth in the throat. Cod-liver oil? My God no. Tramp round the bitter streets for her. It was bad to be poor. Judy had paid for the cream. To-morrow, go and work. Peel the misery off. Work till it skinned over. Contemplation and its pure technique. *To create a little like God.*

Kiss her now. He kissed her slowly, for pleasure, screwing up his eyes against tears. No response from the soft mouth he pressed back on her teeth.

She was twenty-seven, tall, sleek, restless. He was the same age, thin and tranquil with a quiet like death. He was a Russian painter and very poor. She was a poor gentlewoman, at work as a journalist. She would rehearse the turns of her screws on him at night. By day she would forget, because they acted exactly as she wished, but not as she had foreseen. Then her megalomania would reach a stage when she would peep through her furious climax like a tranquil young moon, and ask to be made to laugh.

They heard a latch-key grind. The glass-panelled door clattered and closed. A leather case flew in through the sitting-room door, and burst at Serge's feet. There scattered a fountain pen, a packet of gaspers, a dirty handkerchief, papers tied with string, and a copy of the Oedipus Coloneus. Serge leaned over in his chair and gathered them, stretching right and left. The girl, Judy, said:

"How like her to throw them in like that." Serge went on collecting.

"Have you two been together long?" he said.

"On and off for a year. When she has no money left she leaves her room to take care of itself and comes here. She heard there is someone here. I suppose she went to wash."

Van Ashe came in. Tap-water streaked black the cropped scarlet hair. Powder weighted the translucent skin and lay like pollen on the purple eyelids and bright fringes. She gave Serge her damp, thin hand.

"Pleased to meet you. That is what we say in the dressing-room. Who is going to get tea?" Judy said:

"I've had a long day."

"All right." She turned. A little later, Serge followed her into the kitchen.

"Tell me what has happened," he said, "and what this row of Judy's is about."

"I found a rather beautiful tart—she lived with a Jew dealer. He came from Smyrna. She said he'd given her some things. There was a leather box, all chipped and ragged, full of papyrus fragments, and some nice, blue Egyptian beads."

"Those you're wearing?"

She clutched a string under the rough, greasy collar of her coat. The hollows of the firm chest were yellow and bronze and rose.

"Yes. She gave them to me. Judy put her up for a week. I told her she'd get copy for London's underworld, and she did. But I liked the woman. I was to have had the box with the papyri. They were fragments. Lost fragments. I know they were lost fragments. She had only just let me look. She knew they might be valuable. She was rather a terror, but quite all right. Now, she's gone."

"You don't know where?"

"Of course I don't—she moved—casually and without malice I'm sure, with all our silk stockings, and the box, and Judy's powder-box and her stole—it's of rabbit, but she minds —and the apple which I had left—"

"Left?"

"Of when I was a child. It's a powder-box with Tè Kallistè on it, and a green enamel leaf."

The kettle spat. He leaned against the dresser frowning at it.

"Three of us. How much tea do I put in?"

"One, two, three, not one for the pot because of Judy's war," said Van. "Are you friends enough to have the china tea?"

He changed canisters quickly.

"Has she a lemon?"

"Here's one. She'd allow a Russian his fancies."

He cut it into trembling slices, and carried in the tray.

Judy said: "Well, have you settled anything?"

Van said: "The police are no good, Judy. Let's start with that."

"Van, you're hopeless."

"Where is she to be seen?"

"At Belmont the painter's in Gordon Square," said Serge. "I'll ask him. I must go now. He's giving a party to-night. Will you both come?"

"Yes," said Van.

A cobweb threaded them; a rope of bloody hair tied him to Judy's wrist. Now that he was committed to the party it pulled tight. Grubby little luggage. A delicate turn to her sloped shoulders. They would have to go now, and he would have to take his punishment. What a chance for Judy.

"I will go round now. Will either of you come?"

"I'll come," said Van. A man's hat of wide black felt, and under it those glittering curls. They went out talking. Judy threw away the cigarette she had lit for form's sake. She recalled what she knew about Van, the story which an impersonal generosity allowed her to accept; that she had been thrown out of a great house to live in cafés and cinema-studios, and exploit her curls and her laugh, and involute her mind with odd learning, and brood intolerable revenges for intolerable wrongs.

Her body made it credible and her manners. Illegitimate?

No. That was the situation's essence. She had been crowned, and her regent had died. She had been turned out by inches, till shame and futility had stopped her knocking. Her house had lost her so much as she had lost it. She had been in the garden where the lilies are and the fanged silken beasts. In it she had gathered wisdom through a set of symbols as commercial as the Kabbala.

These had been the transition from crude expensive school to University, from Oxford to London. Gradually Melitta had become definite. The girl was cretinous, eccentric, had religious mania, could teach. Evans was in Japan. The brother at Eton, elegant, indifferent. Melitta had written: "I see that you do not care for social life. You have grossly disregarded my wishes. You know that you inherit nothing. I shall not object to making you a suitable allowance." The hawk had wheeled away, dropped over London and shut its wings.

Judy had found her in a cinema-studio. She observed her shallow, sensual acquaintances with men and distinguished it from her own reserved concentration. Van did not care very much, but she knew the tricks. A Kirchner girl in boy's clothes, she had seen her intrigue a man to have the run of his library.

The woman who had robbed Judy was not at the party. The three left it early together. Outside the house Judy spoke to Van, in the raw voice Serge feared.

"I told you the woman would not be here. What did you make me come for?"

Van answered indifferently: "I didn't. It was agreed that we should try—keep your temper, Judy. He has thought of another place."

"Well, he can pay for the taxi." Van scowled and shifted her feet, chinked two warm pennies and swung a pace away.

In the square, the black box of the sky rested on their heads. Serge came up, swinging on a taxi-step. It ran away with them in the dark. He sat between, clasping them with impartial arms. Van lay back, riding the clear motion of the car.

He kissed Judy's neck, but she lay rigid. He turned and stared at the grey glass panels. On his right arm his tall mistress, on his left this child.

At a change of gears, he steadied her. She had slipped down and her chintz frock was heaped on her lap. His finger traced a ladder running over her strong knee. She went limp. He pulled her up gently. There passed that intermezzo in time between a significant event, and a succeeding significant event. Passive he waited. Judy registered it all in the pressure on her shoulder.

They leaned forward to read the meter, Van with shame for the thin boy, Serge with indifference, Judy with satisfaction. The numbers slid across, a menacing sum. The driver's shoulders were like a bowed mountain.

"What number d'yer want?"

"This will do. Stop," said Serge.

On Primrose Hill the trees, breathing like tall persons, fluttered their twigs. In Regent's Park a beast called. The sky had risen a few feet. Another mountain settled across their eyes, a house, with its roof wedged against the sky, its feet in the abyss.

"But it's empty."

"One can get in."

"I know. I know. She spoke of it. This is the place. She came here with her merchant."

"Other people have keys. I have not. But there is a back way in," said Serge.

A cat jumped out of the area. Judy skipped away from the charging eyes. In the mews behind, a window hung open and silent. Serge stood back to jump for it, but Van dived, a swallow into its eave.

Serge shaded a candle with his hand. They walked upstairs in the ring of light.

The torn paper hung down in ribbons from cornice to boards. In the brittle plaster dust they picked their way, always in the light ring that lit the ceiling, but round them left the dark to pour in.

"Who owns this house?"

"Hush; one does not know."

"We have no business to be here." He laid a finger on Judy's lip.

"Don't," said Judy. "It's a beastly, filthy place. I'm not going upstairs."

"But you shall." Van flew up the naked boards. Serge followed her, lighter and as quick. Judy hesitated. The candle-shine was running up the stairs. At their head a torn petticoat flapped from a gas bracket. Two girls' names were written in charcoal on the wall. A slip of plaster fell, and a window shook. A sheet of newspaper, lifted in the draught, sailed up behind and tightened across her legs. She followed them. The paper brushed against the third stair and sank.

In the back room they found a table, and two chairs turned from it at an angle for conversation. Van crept under the table and over it.

"This is the place. That's right. She has been here."

"Why? I don't see."

"Look," said Serge. In the corner, on the floor, a large Buddha in gilt bronze meditated at them.

"They pinched that from somewhere. Look at the cigarette ends." They followed each other round, peering into corners.

"There's a bundle."

Then Judy shrieked:

"That's my stole. Give it me."

Serge unrolled it. A dead cat fell out on to the floor. Van shrieked with laughter, sitting on the table. "That was her answer, Judy." Judy tore at her bitten nails. "Thank God— we've something now to tell the police."

"Come along. Let us talk outside." Serge led them, Judy striding, Van dancing, out of the house.

CHAPTER 2

S O you've settled something?"
"Yes." Serge rubbed the yolk of his egg off his knife on
to his toast, and ate it.

"Pig, aren't you? Have some more tea— And you might
be careful of the sugar."

One end of the kitchen table was laid with a cover of
drawn thread. The spring wind whistled above the gas fire,
the cold sun rolled in and poured out again, like water off
a cliff.

Judy went on:

"There are the cigarettes. You'll be sure to go before my
charwoman comes. Remember, I'm not like some of the girls
you know. Serge, can't you see that?"

"All right. I'm going. She will not be here for an hour."

"So long as you don't forget. Must you use the matches?
There—I'm not cross at all."

She was not. There was no underwhine in her voice. Her
interests were his. Affectionately he gave his attention. He
said:

"Well, we found your stole in the house. What else has
gone?"

"My stockings, I tell you, my gold shoe-buckles, my powder box—"

"Van's gold apple, and the manuscripts in a box. Van says
that if we go to the police, the girl will burn them out of
spite."

"I don't suppose Van's things were worth a penny. But
I'm so fretted. I'd go myself, but I don't like to be seen in a
police-court. The magistrate would wonder how I came to

64

know her. Oh, I do hate the shady character you and Van
adore. You make no allowance for a young lady's prejudice.
Now, Serge, do you?"

"I don't know. You need not have had her here."

"It was Van's doing. She makes things appear amusing
which turn on you once you admit them. But you understand
these things. Tell me, if your first plan fails, will you go to the
police?"

"If you insist."

"My dear man, I want my ornaments."

"Judenka, you must know what I have done in the past,
and because of that I want to avoid the police."

"But there is no risk."

"My papers are not in order, you know?"

"My dear boy, that is nothing to do with me."

"I tell you, I will go."

"If you are not quick, it will be too late."

"May I come back to-night?"

"Yes."

"Beautiful girl." She protested. Then she lay still. He heard
the clock beat like a hammer. He went out of the house.

He leant his face for coolness against Van's door. The
paint tasted bitter. He listened smiling. He heard her coming,
barefoot, and pass from scullery to living-room. The door
opened. She had covered her feet in strips of plaited purple
felt.

He followed her in.

Van said: "Forgive me. The room is none too tidy. I ought
to be at a rehearsal." She made him sit down. The room fell
into its positions, the raw material of a complicated life. He
looked for a focus, but the chimney-piece had no mirror. It
was a shelf for old books, leaning together and dropping off
onto the floor. The hearth was full of stale ashes, tea-leaves
and cigarette stubs and orange peel and a split bundle of wood.
Pinned on the wall was a plan of the Eleusinian precinct, a
Degas ballet, and a design for a ballet by Picasso. In the hollow
of the bed she had slipped out of, an orange cat was asleep.

On the table, stretched between loaf and tea-pot, was a yellow silk chemise and a pair of cherry silk stockings.

"These are to dance in."

"So."

"Tell me about Judy."

"She insists on the police."

"So." Van poured paraffin on the wood and threw in a match. "I like Judy's flat. It shines with wax and is dark with polish; clean, so clean. But I do not think that any of us had better have anything to do with the police. Do you?"

"No."

"I don't see why those papyrus fragments should be burnt. And they will. Please agree with me about that."

"I do."

"The girl could have the lot. But not the MSS. You see, if you could find her, she might be bribed. Give me the papyrus and she can keep the rest. The powder-box was real, and it was mine."

"What about Judy?"

"If I manage Céleste, can't you —"

"No. We each want a different thing—I must get Judy what she wants."

"Why not me as much as Judy? Serge, I don't know you, but I want to tell you —"

"Go on."

"Serge, I shall be impudent. Why is Judy excellent to you? You are not romantic—not playing at knight-at-arms? Yet you are prepared to evoke the police—an institution we despise; and don't tell me your papers are in order, they're not."

"What about it?"

"You are being an idiot. One does romantic things. One does not think romantically about them."

"I am not being romantic—I want to help you get your things back from this harlot, especially the manuscripts which do not belong to you at all."

"And Judy's jewellery because —"

"She wants it, too. It's good reason—"

"Judy is not an idealist—her reasons are real and bad."

"I thought you were a friend of hers."

"I like Judy because she is well-bred and feminine, and satisfies her limited reason and her unlimited instincts. Not my satisfaction, but I like to think of her doing it—I asked you before why you liked her, Serge."

"I don't see her like that—I see her instincts preying on her—worm gnawing worm."

"What an image." He became aware of misery, as he looked into the grey eyes.

"It is like a cruel thing I saw done at the foot of a tower."

"What do you mean?"

She answered delicately and carefully.

"Listen—You are asked to inform the police about our robbery—conduct the affair with them. Now you are either wanted for military service here, or for deportation back to Russia. I don't doubt that you have a political record. You are past those ambitions. You want to live quietly, and get on with your job."

"Quite so."

"The war is what it is—but Judy loves it."

"She does not. But all her people are in one of your services."

"So are mine, but she loves it. She wants to see it break you. She wants to break you herself. She is a microcosm of it."

"Perhaps I want to be broken."

"That's only a debauch. What shall you do if they get you?"

"My dear girl, I have been in prison, once, twice, before."

"In Russia?"

"Yes."

"Here?"

"Yes."

"Conscience?"

"Nearly."

"Political suspect?"

"As I was in Russia? Probably."

"And that's that. And you've picked up with Judy. Well. *Good can be attained; evil can be endured.*"

"Exactly. That's Epicurus."

"But, Serge, wait your turn."

"Little Epicurean." She turned away and wept.

"Van, what is it?"

"You said it with a sneer. This vile room I cannot learn to keep elegant. And you throw his adorable name in my teeth."

"I did not mean that—I think that what you said is true. But you must leave me to do my best with Judy."

"You haven't a chance."

"I have a daimon too, if it comes to that," he said.

"She is so tall— She affects the eighteenth century grace— Her glass is rubbed with chamois leather— She can be amusing."

"You think I am acquiring merit through a sexual and political martyrdom—It is not that at all."

"All right. But you must count me out. I do not want to go to the police. It is between you and Judy. I want to keep you out of it."

"I don't want to be protected."

"Do you want to go home and paint?"

"If I go back, I shall sleep."

"I am going out for the day. There is my bed. Would you mind? Move Thamar. There is food in the cupboard when you wake."

He rubbed his eyes. When she was gone, he undressed and slipped naked into the hollow of the bed. He drew the orange cat to him for warmth and turned over on his face.

CHAPTER 3

JUDY sat at her mirror, between the pure flame of two candles. The gas fire whined, but the twin flames were quiet; and the smoke of a cigarette rose straight off the table-edge. She sat very upright, and her hands moved steadily in and out, winding her hair. She swung her hand-mirror left and right, her free hand hollowing out a curl. She laid down the glass, and ran in a silver pin.

"My hat, please." Van offered her a great transparent disk. She put it on, and set it with its pins. She crossed her shoe ribbons round her legs, and deepened the purple under her eyes, and made her mouth blood-red. She stepped into her dress, and pulled it up her, setting it onto her body. Van, kneeling, fastened it, and with a broad puff dusted her back. Judy stared at her bright, ragged nails. She swung from foot to foot, judging the line of her body from brow to ankle. She ran round the room, the candles streaming after her. The bell rang. She flung herself again into the chair before the mirror.

"Don't start retouching. There he is."

"Suppose it is for the last time. Four days leave. My God!"

"Sentimentalist," said Van. Judy said: "There's that young brute Serge coming to-night."

"What shall I tell him when he comes."

"Anything. See if he's got the stuff."

"The truth might be the best." But Judy was running downstairs, and out into the glittering street.

Serge came to the door. Van spoke to him modestly, her eyes on the dun linoleum. She meant to go with him to the cinema. She saw herself a sweet-smelling bush for him among the thorns that were stripping off his flesh.

69

He asked her:

"What friend of Judy's is it, from what front?"

"Peter, from France."

"How long will he be here?" The wail was of desire pushed out of vigour and proportion into a monstrous order of insanity.

"Serge, my dear—"

"I will go and get her things." He spoke humbly. "Where is the police-station?"

"You blessed dear. You must not. What about your other plan?"

"It would take too long—I should have to watch. I must go."

"The English police aren't like the Russian. You'll miss spectacular martyrdom—but what you get will be just as bad." She danced before him, and stopped to watch his smile that quivered horribly, not with tears. "You are looking for your cricifixion. It is not sophrôn."

"Someone has got to die of pity for her."

"Maybe you have got to die of pity—but for her?" She spoke soberly. "But I have seen this before. I expect it is all the same. Come back to my place."

"I should like to."

"Did you sleep well there?" She thought: He is going to forget about the police. How wise I am. "Have you had a meal?"

"I have half-a-crown I borrowed from Judy."

They went out together. In her room he had banked up the fire, and made the bed.

Coffee-dregs and cigarette stubs floated in a red bowl. Van stirred it with a match. It bubbled between them in the ashes, a vent hole for infernal powers. She wished it had been ink for a mirror to show him the passion of Rings. She drew her figure through the ashes, and sat inside the circle, and recited the saga of the house and the tower. Contemptuous of his impassivity, she extolled the hill, the triple crown and the wood, impregnated by wind, which could be heard to laugh. She made an image for him of a cross on which every Ashe must hang, and every Ashe descend, a master of pleasure, and reascend of his own will. Then the facts of the case—

"The woman my father married is stronger than Rings. A bastard will have it. We may call him that."

"What will you do?"

"Live to plague him. I am Elizabeth Ashe, of Rings."

"Why are you called Van?"

"That is my secret name. If I am called that, no one will notice it."

"Is he a little boy?"

"He is seventeen. Morice Amburton gave me a red horse."

"How do you know that your mother is so powerful?"

"She has profaned our sanctities, and it has not hurt her."

"How could they hurt her when she did not know that they were there? Is there no one to watch for you?" She remembered Clavel, a cat's slit in an old door.

In the restaurant, Judy pushed forward her glass for wine. Preening she drank, and the hot bubbles stabbed her gullet, and she swallowed thorned steel. They ran down her body hissing, searing, and she gulped again at the warm air, diaphanous with smoke. The men in the restaurant were horned beasts plunging with locked heads. She might not relax her smile. She remembered the girl in the red shoes. But she prayed, no more than Van—*Cut off my feet in the red shoes.*

Serge and Van were still talking. Van said:

"What an adventure! How romantic! You are thinking like that, why don't you say it?"

"I do not think that."

"Go on."

"It is quite subjective of course, but it is a very moving story."

"That's only Russian for what I said. Judy knows more than you."

"That is another generalisation. It means as little as mine. But I should like to see Rings. Why are you crying again?"

"I have cheapened it to you. You do not understand at all." She wailed. He turned from her, because he could see here no need for compassion.

"Don't you see that it is because I admire you. How can one comfort when one should say—go on?" (I may mean that. Try the effect.)

"I don't want your bloody tact."

"It seems to me that out of what you have told me, anything might be made."

"You do not mean that, Serge."

"Perhaps not. But I think I do."

Van said: "It is time I began again."

"What do you mean to do?"

"I'm not insulated. I can't choose."

"Then I should find the boy, your brother."

"I despise him too much."

"Why?" Flat silence fell. The streets began to speak, louder than their thoughts.

"I am going," said Serge.

"Where?"

"To the police."

"It is not bearable—"

"Nothing is bearable. It is all an impertinence."

He took up his hat and went out.

CHAPTER 4

JUDY stepped out of the dark car at midnight, into the street, a stone flung out of marching heavens into a pool hung with mist. The car stole away. At the top of ten steps the door was set back between pillars like soiled candles. She turned her key in the lock and rushed in up the chill stairs.

Inside, a guttered candle was reflected in a cabinet, a mirror of oiled and waxed wood, the smell of a fir planting. Van had left the candle. It was the room of a poor gentle-woman, ivory work-box, candlesticks of brass. Judy thought: Damn Van for leaving that candle. But she cried when she lost the gold apple: she'd have pawned it if it had been real. Wastes my candles, does she? *On poverty this ill attends*—I am going to marry her cousin Peter. We will ask her down to Rings—perhaps. She shall decrease—I shall increase. Her mother did that: clever woman, Lady Amburton. My Aunt.

She turned on the gas fire, and struck a match neatly.

Why do I hate Van Ashe? What am I going to do to her? Born in the purple: wears it for a chemise. Skips in the gutter and straightens her tiara. Born, not made. Neither adoption nor grace—I am as well born. Not quite.

I like her. She's a spirit. I'm as jealous of her as hell. She shall decrease. If I could believe that. Can I make that happen? Peter, Peter, by Peter? There is a good second best. Her mother found it. We shall ransack Rings: A competence acquired, I might practise virtue. Make another Rings of Amburton. I should be another Ursula Ashe... Serge is after her. I've finished with him. Tie a tin can to his tail: and turn him out. Clatter. Whine. Clatter, clatter. He'll be a joy to Van.

73

It's the life. For women like me. Ours is the kingdom, the power and the glory. What's left over is for Van and Serge. Garden of the Hesperides. East of the Sun, West of the Moon. They say they like that sort of thing. I don't deny it may be the best. Now Peter and I are as good as engaged. What did he say to-night? "If I live through this." The reward of the warrior. Curse Van and her sneers. What is there for us if we don't back up our men? The war makes it easy. The war's going to make me Lady Amburton...

The drift into secular thought relaxed her. In a round, antique mirror she noted her beauties, dozing before the fire.

"*Come away, human child.* You are not to go there to-night. I've run after you. Oh how I've run. With the wind."

Van's fast breathing shook her body. Through her mouth's dark slit Serge saw her tongue, and felt in his own its ache and sting. He took her arm and led her to a coffee-stall by the police-station at the corner of the street. Its lights were tied up in blue paper, which made it like some large animal body, phosphorescent with corruption. He would come back in the morning. It wearied him that she should prevent him, but without impatience. Her sides were nearly burst. He held her arm, and she choked over the warm, greasy drink.

"There is a light in the window of that house again to-night. They are there. Come at once. I ran there first. That's why I'm so spent."

"It was lucky you found me."

"I would have tackled her myself; but if you must serve Judy, you shall."

Humiliated, he walked beside her. For martyrdom, a light whipping. He did not enjoy it. Arrogant little Greek. The trees closed over their heads. The window in the mews swung on its hinges, a little here and a little there. She hopped on to the ledge, and skipped back on to his shoulder, her arms round his neck.

"Tired. You go." He lifted her down, sprang up, crooked

74

his knees to his chin and dropped through. He opened the door and she passed him.

"In the room where we found the dead cat." He checked her pace, and they mounted at the goosestep. A rod of tawny light lay on the boards. He knocked. Silence. A voice said: "Who is there?"

"Two friends." They went in.

"We are not the police," said Van, "and we have nothing to do with them."

"But you have some ornaments that belong to this lady and to her friend," said Serge.

The dealer ticked a number off his list and sat back. Céleste crouched over the gold Buddha, on her knees.

"I should first be pleased to know how you got here."

"You are not the only people who have used this house."

Van said precisely: "Céleste stayed with a friend of mine. She quarrelled with her, a very natural quarrel. Then she went away and took some things with her. They were ornaments, and some of them were mine. We want them back. We hate the police as much as you do. The things were not of much value. Let us have them again."

The woman said:

"Little one, I've no quarrel with you: but your dirty friend she deserves what she gets."

"Judy can grumble in hell. But this man here is her lover."

"The poor child —"

"As a business formality," said the dealer. "What are the articles you accuse Céleste of having?"

"A gold powder-box, a fur stole, coral prongs for the hair, pink and black silk stockings; and also a golden apple that was mine, with a green enamel leaf."

"The stockings they were in holes—disgusting."

"They don't matter. Give us the rest."

The girl opened a bag on the table.

"They are here. The stole, I do not know where it is. She said my coat was made of cat, and it is made of seal lapin— So I put a dead cat in with it and now it is gone—"

75

"We took it when we came here to look for you before."
Serge filled his pockets. "That's all right," he said.

"It would be like her to leave you to get them back, little one. I did not know that the gold apple was yours."

"There is no bad feeling, chérie." The two young women moved up to one another, smiling. Their good will cut them off from either man, and from that half of the earth.

"Have a cigarette." Serge found some.

—"What about the manuscripts?" he said.

"Céleste, there was a box: you said I might have it. I understand these things. If they were valuable, you should not be the loser by it. But let me have it to examine. I want it so."

"The box, mademoiselle," said the dealer. "I have sold it to a museum. I am afraid you cannot have it."

"Ah God! I was afraid of that."

The men shuffled while Céleste kissed her. When the dealer saw that she was in misery, but not angry, he spoke with decision.

"Have you identified your articles?"

"Yes," said Serge. "Come, Van. You can trust us: we will say nothing. Good-night." He led her away.

"Serge, we've got it all back but the stockings that did not matter and my box that did."

"That was bad luck." His head was bowed in his personal acceptance of the stupidity of life. On the stairs she said:

"Count them. Think of Judy. Keep me from remembering.... But it isn't there. The gold powder-box. Judy's I mean."

"I took all that was in the bag."

"They did us in. Or perhaps they never had it. She may have lost it herself and said it was them.... Serge, take my golden apple. You must go with your hands full: it's the beau geste."

"But she'll know it isn't hers."

"She'll forget. Besides—*dôra adôra*—"

"What do you mean?"

"Take my gold box." She dropped it into his pocket. "Good-night."

Judy placed herself on her sofa, from breast to ankle transparent as a flame. A crystal glittered in each ear-tip, and under her eye, there was a patch, a death-point. In the kitchen, the charwoman cooked a rabbit. She beat up her cushions, blue and green, and one of them sewn with a scarlet pattern. The inner bell rang in the strip of dark passage. The charwoman shuffled to the door....

"Coffee, Serge? With milk? Is there anything wrong. Or is it the milk of human kindness you're wanting, as Van would say?...

—"Why do you insist on telling me the story of your friend who was a Trappist monk. I shall never meet him....'

"Oh!"... She thought: Perhaps it's the rabbit. Is it Peter? Is he going to ask me to marry him?... Serge said:

"Judy. Did you get the parcel with your things? I left it this morning. I am very sorry about your powder-box. They had not got it. Van says you must take hers."

"I couldn't. Still, she owes me something. What fools we've been. Here ends my sentimentality over prostitutes."

"She seemed a very nice person. Van and she got on well enough."

"Van's affection—"

He looked down at his fine ankles. That was over. Nice silk socks. The tiny, vivid pleasure was like a moment's rest. How to approach Judy, chin smooth and hair. The reward. To feel the steel-sprung body quiver in one's arms. Leda and she my swan. Marvellous throat. Sink into its plumes and sleep. *Free to be very hungry and very lonely.* Was that Van?

Judy asked: "Did Van get them back or did you?"

"We both did."

"Why you rather than the police?"

"Less trouble and less expense."

"Of course."

"Would you in reality have preferred a policeman?"

"I have no personal preference; but I like your cheek. Serge, I've been meaning to ask you for the last six months. Why aren't you in the Army?"

"Because I prefer to stay out. Or go to prison."

"Or back to Russia —"

"It's the same thing in my case."

"Speaking as an Englishwoman, it is not good enough."

"Can't you see that it would be as ridiculous for me to uphold this war as for you not to do so? No?" Oh my dear, your pretty dress is spotted with blood.

"The time seems past for these distinctions."

"What is life without them?"

" ine reasons to put before a man in the trenches."

—"Before a man who has seen all Europe." Quiet my soul. This is your firing party.

She looked at him. He had been her lover. Long, unnatural tale. He was made of wax. Men should be made of iron and flesh. He was of wax. Fat of dead men, melted and poured. Become flesh again. Out of a great torment. *The Word was made flesh.* The Word of a great torment. He'll melt again into his dead man's wax. Forever my floor will shine. Wax. Of no terrestial bees. Van, be quiet.... Love... Love, shake me out of this.

"Serge—it is time I was candid with you. I think our affair has come to an end." Excellent opening. She lay back.

"Why exactly now? Perhaps you are right."

"We do not seem to be winning this war. To people on the losing side, you are a luxury. Your dear Germans torture our prisoners. If I could I would send you over there. I'd hand you over to a Prussian officer. It's discipline you want."

> *How many miles to Dublin Town.*
> *Three score and ten.*
> *Can I get there by candle light?*

Three candles burned in the room.

"I'll go to Ireland."

"Go and squeal with those cowards. You'll find a change there, now we've shown them what their rebellion's worth." The sob squeezed out of him affected her sensually. She got up and looked down at him, and at his unsteady mouth, think-

78

ing. The woman that is the reward of the warrior. Silly. Why
do I do this?

He thought: Why do I endure this? Then he said: "I am
quite strong enough to rape you."

"You foul brute. You German. I tell you I've got a re-
volver." Good for him. Why doesn't he? I should have done it
long ago. Why do we treat each other like this? He said: "It is
women like you who instigate wars and extol them."

"Yesterday you said that we fought this war for coal."

"So we have. You go and be the reward of those warriors."

"I have been. Also I've told Peter about you. If he finds
you about here again, he'll pitch you into the street."

"It seems that I had better go." Then, "Judy, you will lose
your soul." Vile laugh. Squeezed scarlet gums. Blood down
the teeth. Red teeth. Red breath. Women were lovely; they
were gallant and quick and kind. Which was the hysteria?
They had a secret adventure. Judy, my love, you are an abominable hell. You are a pitiful, blind lamb. You are my peace.
There is no peace. He said:

"There is truth, but there is no peace." He looked round
for his stick.

—"We have been together, but now you know what you
want."

"I know this, that this is the last meal you will cadge from
me."

He took a feather pipe-cleaner from his pocket.

"Pin it in my coat."

"It's speckled. It should be dirty white." She giggled.

He shut his eyes. She watched, for the moment spent,
uneasy, sorry. He felt for his hat.

"Do you understand? You can come back in khaki or not
at all...."

—"I am sorry, but the refinement of your feelings is beyond me....'

"I should be quite glad to look upon you as a slacker I
had made into a man." Talked out.

He picked up his hat and walked into the passage. She heard the latch rattle and sprang out of the cushions.

"Serge!" The light grinding stopped.

"Serge! Come back.

"Serge, it is no good going on like this. Can't you see? Serge—Serge."

"Of course it is no good." He had come back to the open door.

"For God's sake say something. Make a decent defence."

"I have none. What is truth?"

She ran at him and bit his wrist. He threw her down on the sofa, and held her there. His blood smeared her face and her sleeve. He let her go and turned his back and went to the door.

She slipped onto the floor. He was not brave enough to look back; but he could hear her breathing as she lay on the floor.

He thought of the long pin in her hair. He walked along the dark passage, opened the outer door and looked back. She was still on the floor, sucking the blood from her sleeve, evoking an evil spirit.

CHAPTER 5

THE wind ran through the night. It tore through his thin clothes, and crawled over his skin. His hands hurt and his feet. He closed his flayed eyes. From the horizon, great clouds climbed up, thinning as they whirled over the pole star, into a dust of snow. Between their masses, the stars blazed and crackled. Born in central Europe, he could hear the travelling sky. He leaned against a lamp post. The shaded light fell on him, green and pale. The hushed, icy air gripped him. One by one, the stars were veiled. The pain drove in upon his chest and shoulders; soreness, the apprehension of a repeated blow.

He thought that this was what love came to, and the utmost sensuality of compassion. Nailed up by Judy to encourage no one—I can't bear it. She called up the deathless evil. It is riding my back. All one's life in the dark on the cross. In Russia, the heart was not broken. The war came and it cracked. You came with the war—you are inside me, playing its infernal tunes. You are the war's smallest doll. You are the war. Neither greater nor less—made on the perfect scale. I shall never be any good again, except for painting. That's your doing.

Truth to set one free. Love—Love, come into my arms. The hell in the world would end with the hell in our hearts. Just when you've nearly done killing me, to think of that. What you've done is your function. To insist on death, and preferably the soul's death. How dare you murder me? It's no good. I must have you. It is my function.

Driven by his pain, he moved away, crossing the street from side to side. The roads were silent, deep in snow, the houses transparent curtains, pierced by the wind.

81

Round a corner, the wind stood still and he met the snow. The air was still as midsummer and, he thought, as mild. He could feel scents touching him. The flakes whirled, and in each lamp's path he could see them, myriads falling, fluttering, rising, spinning, folding him. He moved slowly. They fluttered on his forehead and cigarette-stained hands. They mounted on his shoulders, and crystallised his hair. They cooled his face, falling on his eyelids, brushing his lips. He tasted them, and still they flew. Then they appeared to him as bees, white bees, comforters. They swarmed on him.

He stood still. They weighted him till he sat down on the curb. They hushed him, pressing in on every side. He clasped his knees, and saw, in miniature, on a Jesse tree, the pictures of his initiation into life. In Russia, a voice crying under a lamp, the lamp broken by a stone. A cat asleep on a prison wall, whose magical composure had taught him to sleep again. Cafés and meetings of the revolution. A miserable man shouting in a winter park. A wise man explaining in a splendid room the sequences of change. Oh! the cold, distinguished wisdom he could not despise. That he still despised. Then, in England, he had met Judy, a black rod tied at the top with a bunch of pale flames. She had walked beside him, and smiled and listened, and had not listened. A horse driven by a boy had fallen in the street.

"Come away. No, poor brute, go and help." Called back before he had done. Her rack of impulses became his rack. It occurred to him that she had been deliberate. Always she would be gnawing her nails. A drop of poison under each nail, and for them both death.

There might be one more chance. The Van child was amusing. She might kick death out of the room. Had death his eye on her? Faintly worth watching.

He sat up. It still snowed. "White bees, white bees," he said. A fresh spiral settled. He smiled as they built up a cap in his hair.

CHAPTER 6

A WEEK later, the dust film gathered. Under the bed, the sloven's fur piled in grey whorls. In the cupboard a dish of crusts turned blue. He lay in bed, thirsty, watching, amused, then frightened. His room began to live. Out of the unstirred quiet, life gathered. He grew weak. He saw it increased. There had been no life in the room that was not in terms of his own. But, as he lay there sick, the life of dust and scum multiplied without him. There was a tune for that. He learned sang it ten thousand times. He got up and took off the coat of his pyjamas and dusted the table. The small objects swelled, and the thin ones elongated until they met in a fan vaulting over his head. He went back to bed. In the fireplace were large, white coals, dead, lying on the ashes, and topped with orange peel. Van Ashe had orange hair. It was cold. He tucked the blanket round his throat.

He had thought he was dying. Now it seemed he might be in the passage of rebirth. The white bees came at evening, and when they flew there was no death. He turned over on his face and waited. They came, whirling in soft flights, swinging him on their wings. He would fall asleep on their wings and wake to find one walking on his rasped throat and dirty hand. A white bee. His hair would be full of them. A feather dipped in scent, they crossed his forehead and tipped the fingers of his hand. He did not see them come; but they hung over him, as though the roof were open, a Danaan shower. Then they went away. The great swarm passed, leaving only stragglers to sit on his hot eyelids. Days passed without them and nights. One evening they came as he had never seen them, and all night the bitter room had blazed and swung with their soundless ecstacy. That was the last time. Night after night he waited. One night he dreamed that he had found one dead and brittle on the blanket, and woke crying.

Mean and menacing, the life of his room closed in, the imperceptible worms of dust. Crossing the room weakly for water, he sensed a thickness in the air, specks marching, whose infinite ranks sank and stirred, and sank back and turned on themselves again. One upon another they swelled, binding one another, each a tiny death and a tiny life. They threw a light outpost on his pillow and scummed the milk in the green cup. The weight of the row pushed a book off the mantel-shelf. He felt the cinders score its leather. A pin dropped out of a drawing, and it slipped and fluttered a little and lay still.

Here is the sword with the roses about it. O Love! lead us home.

* * * * *

Judy was saying to Van:

"I am going down to stay with Peter's people."

"Am I to forward your letters?"

"The char will do that, thank you all the same."

"What have you done with Serge?"

"He's off painting somewhere."

"Is your affair with Serge over?"

"I expect so. You have a way, Van, of clearing up preliminaries."

"That gets rid of the irrelevant. Judy, my girl, he was a stupid lover for you."

"He did not think so."

"Stop being demure. What are you thinking about?"

…"Oh Serge, he's rather fine; but he could raise the devil in me."

"By what he did, or by what he was?"

"By what he was, of course."

"He made you feel mean?"

"Perhaps."

"Why did you have him then?"

84

"A year ago there were no men. I was bored. Van, you don't understand. Your treasure may be in heaven, but it is no good to me."

"You hoped he would paint you a flattering portrait? But he's not that sort of painter. I could have told you. You're right. Peter's your mark. Did you know he was my cousin?"

"What?"

"By adoption. He is Morice Amburton's nephew, the man who married my mother, Melitta Ashe."

"So I can give your family news of you?"

"Tell them that, with any luck, they can see me in the picture, *Fallen Lives*, at the Gulltown cinema."

"I will."

"Give me Serge's address?"

"I don't know it."

"You know your lies are no good. Judy, you've been up to your devil's tricks."

"What do you mean?"

"You have an evil power. Or else it is that an evil power has you. I am proof, nearly proof. It is something you suck out of the war. That boy might die. Tell me where he lives."

"I will not."

"It rests with me whether you go to Amburton. You'd like to bite me; but you won't. I stand between Serge and you. The extremes in your nature frighten me, but not your infamous tricks."

"I can tell them that you are the mistress of a Russian painter dodging the military authorities."

"I can explain, with added details, whom I may succeed. Judy, come off it. You have a clear head."

"He lives at 19, Swanhill Street, and much good may it do, you little toad."

"You have shut my mouth. Peace be with you."

"Are you sure you have shut mine?"

"I am Ashe of Rings. Open mouths and shut are alike to me."

"You mean me not to marry into your family?"

85

"You can marry whom you like. People belong where they belong. Peter will have Amburton."

"You think that is my sole motive for marrying him?"

"Scrutiny into your motives is the most shocking thing I've done in my life."

"Van! But they are not all bad. Be fair to me."

"When they are not abominable, they are silly. I'm sorry I can't say more. Smile. That's good."

"His cousin, your little brother, will have Rings?"

"If he can. It's a peculiar place. You get out of it what you put in. The same as with everything else, only more intensely. That is the first rule of magic, as you ought to know."

"Why should I be interested in rules of magic, whatever you mean?"

"Come off it, Judy. You've been mixing yourself up with some devil's hocus-pocus; going bad the way people do sometimes in the tropics. And the years we are living through have stirred the same thing up here. It's a state, a turn of the soul, people are making. But you keep bad company, if it's only your own thoughts."

"Van, you are being ridiculous. Van, you are unjust. Tell me, Van, why did your father marry Lady Amburton?"

"Maybe it was some crude theory of eugenics. He was an old man. Perhaps he was tired. Also it flattered his great pride. You know about old men, Judy. I don't know much about men at all."

"You get on with Serge."

"He's not a man. He's a spirit, casually sexed. You are a cruel, female principle with a flick of sentimental humanity."

"You don't spare me. But as to not knowing men, I think your cold sensuality abominable."

"Am I sensual? Am I cold?" Van put up her long cigarette holder, and ran her fingers up and down as over the stops of a flute.

"I say to you, *Know Thyself*— And Judy, I think, in parts, you do."

"There is no need to believe all one's own lies."

86

"That's good. It's the one good thing about you. I told Serge once, but he did not understand. He sees you when you are piteous and desirable, not when you are great."

"Leave me out of your discussions in future."

"You know that we are bound together till a further conclusion is reached."

"There isn't any need to tear it to pieces before it is reached," said Judy. "That is what you will never learn."

CHAPTER 7

NEXT day Van came to terms with her uneasiness and went to Swanhill Street. A temperate, brown March day, she shook the winter off. The sun was not a demon, nor the dance of air; nor were trees impelled upwards out of hell.

When the spring comes you shall have peace. Spring 1917. In the shadow of death, each one. And fairly comfortable. Or rather acclimatised to the unique monstrosity of life.

The bus leaped and swerved. She clung to the rail, pretending that it was a ship. She did not visualise what she might find. Life was moving. She rode its motion like a serene horseman who, on the horizon, sees spears. She dropped off at Theobald's Road and hung on the curb to watch the trams creep in and out of their hole.

Outside the door in Swanhill Street an old woman washed the steps. Van watched a line of filthy water rise against her shoe.

"Let me in."

"I ain't got the key." She looked at the bell-knobs, labeled, erased and labelled again. Mons. Duvanel, Picture Restorer. Two knocks. Mlle. Florence—bell does not ring. Knock loudly. Schiemann & Hamburger—very faded, scored with an obscenity. Joseph Smith. Universal Films. Bad firm that. Serge Sarantchoff. She loved him then. She had not known it till she read his name. Her eyes stung and her mouth trembled. If he were not there, it would be intolerable. The door's carved lintel was upheld by cupids. The brown sea of London's mud lay round her feet.

"Pouf! why doesn't he come?" She danced a little, and stopped, head low, hands crossed on her breast. A head stuck out of a window.

"Do you want Mr. Sarantchoff?"

"Yes. Yes."

"He's ill."

"Is he up there?"

"Yes."

"Let me in." Judy has done this. She is worthy of us. The door opened.

"Please, is he very ill?"

"I don't know. My wife's been up to him once or twice."

Van thought: Not Davanel, Mlle. Florence, the Germans, God pity them, or Joseph Smith. What places!

"Thank you. I'll go up." She mounted and knocked at his door.

"Serge, may I come in?"

"For God's sake don't."

"Why not? You're ill.

"Is that you, Van?"

"Yes."

"This place is horrible. It would disgust you."

"Not it. My dear, if it would not make you worse, unlock the door. Let me in."

She heard a faint, slow sound. She came through.

"Go back to bed." Was this grey creature, attenuated to famished points, that lean, subtle boy?

"I am going to get up."

"You are not. Go back." She saw the bed. Grey creases not fit for a sick beast. Judy had sheets and she should lend them. She was sleeping on embroidered linen at Amburton in the South. A broom and a mop and a dust-pan and brush. Then hot water, smoky and bitter with cologne.

"I will light your fire. You are not to fight me. Then I will go and come back with everything you want." She pressed him back on the bed and felt his chest like a hollow brick. She knelt and kindled the fire. The dry peel cracked and flamed, the raw ash lived as she swept the hearth.

"I'll be back in half-an-hour. Give me your key." She found it on the chimney-piece, under a cigarette packet, and rushed away.

MARY BUTTS

He sat on the edge of the bed, balancing himself with great difficulty till she should return. It became a point of honour to endure till she returned—when there would be no more endurance.

She came back, the linen balanced across her arms, clean pyjamas laid on it and a flask of scent. She shook the bed to pieces and spread it and swept the dust from under it. She knelt at the fire, holding the pyjamas to her body. The warmed wool smelt comfortable, and a light smoke rose out of it.

She bound more wool across his chest.

"Can you eat?"

"I've had breakfast."

Her eyes picked out each object for evidence.

"Good God, the milk's sour. You have eaten it solid with a spoon."

"That's yaghourt."

"But, my dear, it is very bad, I mean it is very Russian; but it is not yaghourt. I will get you food." She ran out. He lay back, smiling, then raised himself on his elbow and finished it, licking out the spoon.

On the gas ring she boiled water, washed him, and laid him down, a flying pietà.

"Suppose I have not been ill at all?"

"Why would you spoil my pleasure?"

She bent over the long broom like an oarsman, and the dust-pan followed the rubbish like a hunter's knife. The curtains, a wandering cat had clawed down, she lifted with their rod. He watched her shake their stuff and then her hair, and hang them again over the squat windows. The air filled them, the angular pattern crossed their folds, and he stared. The dust was afraid of her. A burrowing beast, she knelt before his cupboard. He would never see what was inside it again. The fire ate up the coal, briskly, delicately, and in the sink outside he heard the tap running like a song. A little dust for a specimen? Not a grain. Here was man imposing his will. Suppose he had died and the room had been left a month or a year longer? He was not to be allowed to die.

She threw scent from her fingertips about the floor. Bold girl. Sweet breath. Judy's scent, but Van's breath. Judy's linen, Judy's thick white blankets, Van's daffodils. All Judy's goods; but Van's hands and feet. Kourotrophos. Then he was the child-god and she the nurse-god. He had died and was reborn. Begin painting again. Go to sleep.

Before his spotted mirror, she combed her hair. It flew out, and in the scarlet glitter there was an essence of pleasure. She lit a cigarette. She was walking up and down the room, without shoes, because she thought him asleep. Slowly her chin lifted in contemplation, the gold plate of the moon in the window was fixed on the travelling head. *The moon endureth.*

It was night when he woke, and the gas was lit. There was food on a strip of coloured cotton, and the table rubbed and smelling of its wood. Fish fried in oil, and a froth of eggs beaten in wine, and weighted with sugar.

"Did these things come from Judy?"

"Yes."

"Did she send them?"

"No. She is at Amburton."

"She would not wish me to have them."

"She would not lend a blanket, not to Prometheus."

"So you took them from her?"

"The point at issue was your need of blankets, and I had none."

"So. You know that I shall not see her again?"

"I am afraid you will. Why do you want to?" She stood over him. He noticed how her body, in motion or in stillness, had a set pose that made her like a small, archaic statue.

—"Didn't you nearly die of what she has done?"

"She turned me out into the street, and I caught a chill."

"Serge, my heart, she used you vilely. You died and you are come alive again. You are born again." No answer. No answer for a celestial voice.

"Yes." He was faint as Melitta under Anthony Ashe, but with pleasure.

91

"I dreamt part of this when I was a child. What are you, Serge?"

"Prometheus had his sea girls. Oceanides?"

He caught her wrists.

CHAPTER 8

THE room smelt of Judy; but the body was Van's body.
He was very warm. The fire was a red wall, full of holes.
He smashed it and it leapt high. With the poker he scraped
the ash into patterns. This was peace. When could he begin
to paint again? That blessed girl had washed his brushes. Certain relations of forms he had not before understood were
now clear.

It was over; but directly he stood up his spine jellied. When
he thought of Judy, an image rose, inhibiting thought. He
was beside a grey brick wall and a furnace roared behind it;
a wall pierced with holes for the fire to stream out and lick
him in, to the end of his life's walk down the wall. That was
what could happen; but the interlude was delicious. Then he
thought of the streets—the hardy, mean life to begin again.
The talk. The cold, dirty streets. The talk. The coffee. The
talk. That invincible girl, asleep with her hair across her cat's
back, had her plans. Women to run the world. Men to lie
about in quiet and think. Not necessarily of anything.

We shall become lovers. Has she her eye on that? No. She
might seduce me for my good. She may know best. As a gentleman—ought I? He did not want to. He wanted nothing but
to walk warily along his furnace wall. And to be comforted
because of it. Perhaps to be led away. She understood that
also, and cool the grass would be where they laid them down
together. Sophrosynê—but Judy had indicated an answer to
the Delphian precept. Van swung up between the evil and
the good; but Judy had shown that the evil extremity was
God. Beside that, Van's temperance was no more than the bind-
ing-up of wounds and their wise avoidance; and for Serge

there was nothing to do but accept Judy and bear it. Was it because he loved Judy that he had to endure it? That was too simple. He must be a certain sort of man. He would not be another sort of man. His torment pricked him again. He sobbed and twisted and tore at his hands because of his shame, because he had been handled and held up to insult. Pharmakos of Hellas, scapegoat of Israel, a matted animal dead of thirst, a man and woman whipped with squills. Outside the city walls. Naked to the terrors outside the life of man. Van came walking through the desert, over the glittering sand, unscorched, unsandalled, Oceanid.

He was bearing the sin of the world. He had raised up Van to be a watcher of his passion. She might become its consolation. He was not sure that he wanted one. For a day or a month or a year it would be deep pleasure, and then the quality would go out of it. Then along the fire wall again, whose quality was the same to-day, yesterday, and forever.

Each morning she came in, with a string bag full of eggs and fire-bundles and cigarettes. There had been a bag like that in the Swiss Family Robinson. She made lists and scratched them off. Suddenly she would get up and run out into the street. He would have to give her a picture; and how, and when, and with what explanation and what grace, would Judy receive back from them her perfume, her blankets, her china tea? Careless, adorable courage that looted the she-wolf's den.

Her care for him quieted her sensuality. She worked to restore his beauty, as to bring out the grain in wood. She held up a glass while he brushed back his hair like dark feathers. The rooms's clean air had the stir and swing of the sea. The fire roared, the spring air puffed out the curtains.

"It is a night when I hear Rings."

"What does Rings say?"

"Come."

"Why don't you go."

"Because it is not time."

"Why not?"

"I don't know. It may be. But I can't go."

94

"Are you afraid of your mother?"

"Don't be a fool. Perhaps I am."

"I shall start work again to-morrow."

"Good. I think you're fit."

He lifted her hand and kissed it. She pinched his nose, and still sat on the bed, her chin on her chest. The brushing of his lips had moved her. He might tell her with his subtle smile that she had seduced a sick child. That would not matter. But at the back of her brain was a panel, written with the gilt point of the waxing sun. The sun was waxing on the Rings. *As the sun at noonday to illustrate all shadows, as the sheaves at harvest to fulfil all penuries.* As the sun increased, so would the love in their hearts. If it did not, the sun would still be there. She was three-score and ten miles from him then, off on her aerial horses. He caught her stirrup.

"You will not go out to-night."

"I should go. Shall I stay?"

"Tell me stories about Rings."

That was pleasant. His incuriosity could madden the artist in the girl.

"Think of Rings as a ship, full rigged, full of treasure, every sail set, plunging over the back of the world. The seas hiss and slide, and she cuts them; and crosses the horizon where the moon comes out of the sea."

It did not move him; yet he felt that he must respond for her relief.

"Serge, have you ever thought of the unused room in a house, empty for the sun to cross and the dust to gather in?" He moved a little. "The absence of one life makes room for another?" He shivered. "Sit in the chinese room at Rings. The men with round bellies sit on lacquer cabinets and smile. There are paintings on the wall a thousand years old, and a set of jade chessmen. There is a high gallery, that runs from the tower. Dusty, Serge, bare timbered floor, with a few old chairs between the windows. Tarnished gilt, so old, painted by the sun. It leads to rooms where no one ever goes. Perhaps the kêrês that our bodies in the great rooms are always disturbing, drift up there and become a kind of flesh. Serge, there is a tower in Rings. In the tower there is a lost room. I mean that in the old plans the room is marked. No one has added or taken away a stone. In Ursula's day the room disappeared. No one has found it again. Only once in a while we walk straight into it."

"Have you?"

"No. Have I had much chance?" He turned over on his side.

"You made me talk about Rings."

"I'm sorry, I can't live in fairy tales."

"Very well, you shan't." She would not cry. All men were like this.

To Serge it seemed that a situation had run out. Its tail wriggled and it should be cut off. One more twitch and it would disappear, or he would operate. He pitied Van. Nadir of Rings. Faint, ghostly talk. His life would become significant again. He had the memory of the bees to work on. She would not understand them. She might have something to remember. What do girls think about? They do all we do, and still we ask that. She was quite happy. He preferred to think so. An outlest for her immense energy, he had provided that. Women force us to do that. Not bad fun either. Little dynamo, toasting her legs at the fire. Thin legs, thin stockings with a ladder up the back. Ladders slip and run twelve inches and stick. Snags in the black web. Clotho, Lachesis, Atropos.

CHAPTER 9

VAN said: "Before you go to sleep I had better tell you what I've done." He drew his chin out of the bed clothes. He was on the trembling verge of sleep and delicious fancy. Van had swung round from the fire, grinning, a little ape.

"What is it?"

"I had better tell you since you may be in it. It seemed to me a joke. I've had some film work lately, and the lighter press is read at Amburton."

"You mean they know that you act for the films?"

"More than that. I wrote a scenario and I think it's going to be produced. A sort of *Shadows on my Life*. Rings, and Melitta, and the first baby and the second baby, placed in a gothic castle of squared board. There is a Sunday paper that does screen talks, and interviewed the producer of this all-British film, while I stood at his elbow and explained. They got it all in, down to Clavel. That should rouse Melitta. Ashe can stand such a thing. Amburton can't."

"Are you playing in it?"

"No such luck. And I don't know that I could have borne it. Serge, I threw you in as well."

"And Judy?"

"No. She had an axe to grind."

"Do you appear as my mistress?"

"Practically."

"I don't understand English etiquette. Will one of your family come and challenge me?"

"No, and you won't have to marry me either. They might try and buy you off."

"Is there money in it?"

97

"There might be."

"But you did not tell them what you told me of the ghosts and the lost room?"

"Not I. I've made an objective parody—a horrible mess."

"What did you tell the interviewer?"

"I reduced it entirely to terms of the cinema—the result was terrific. It was diverting to hold a mirror up to Melitta. She'd have been queen of the movies and a better woman if she had—"

"When will the film be produced?"

"I don't know."

"Then how do you know that they have noticed the interview?"

"Because I saw Morice Amburton this morning, on leave, walking along my street. He was looking up at the houses and down at a slip of paper, trying to divine which one I was in. He wore check trousers and a stick with a carnelian knob. But he hadn't got the number, and he went away."

"Do you want me to protest my chastity?"

"What would annoy them most?"

"This is voluptuous. Now you have enjoyed it you ought to think out an attitude."

"I can only laugh. It has added a richness to this poor life like a spread of cream... Is there so much pleasure in the world? Even this is smeared with futility and the bitterness of revenge. Another thing is that I am afraid to meet Morice."

"Is Judy at Amburton?" said Serge.

"Judy? Why yes. But I didn't think. She knew of it—"

"Then he will come here. Don't be distressed. I shall go down and be noble, and he will be sorry and make amends. Let us pretend—"

"We're kings and queens. And Serge, we are."

"You have said that before."

"So I have. Should I be so passionate about it were it not true? Don't ask me what is truth—"

There was a knock that rang up the stairs. He threw the blankets off saying:

"I am going. You'd better not—you must not. I'll tell him I'm away and have never heard of you. Make yourself beautiful." He put on an overcoat and ran down. She drenched her face with powder and rushed the comb through her hair, asking herself:

"Now why is he afraid? Because Judy is in it." She heard him come up slowly, alone.

"Who was there?"

"No one. The street was empty. I saw two cats following one another. Have you a banshee in your house?"

"No."

"You're trembling. Stay here. I will sleep on the sofa. Take the bed."

"No."

"Then we will sleep together, like brother and sister."

"No. I'm going home. Good night, Serge. Once we climbed up walled cities and made love to other lords' ladies. I will not seek to avoid one evil mind. Florian and Ursula should see me home."

He heard the street-door close below. He went to the window and saw a quick shadow pass out of the house and under the ring of a feeble lamp. It spun round twice, and vanished into the gulf of the street.

The next day was insignificant, and the next. He began to draw. When he went out in the evening, one of the two cats was there, a great beast writhing its way along a wall. There was a fury about it. When he came back, it was gone. A grey day, warm, stillborn. He fell into a heavy sleep.

On the third day he worked till mid-day, and then fell into meditation. Judy. Van. Serge. Three legs of a table dancing from foot to foot. His leg was in the air and Van's, Judy's the pirouett. A long foot down to Amburton in the South. Rings to supply diversion. He did not doubt that it would do its best. But that was a little thing.... Van was a heavenly girl, time spun into eternity, a fountain thrown up.

Suppose Amburton were to come upon Van, in a fury, or too amiable? Or Judy got the nephew, and was set on to hunt

99

by Van's mother. Then anything might be possible. In his concentration, he saw Melitta with Judy, a twin Erinys; Amburton an equivocal tool for them. Why should he be afraid of Morice Amburton? That man is what I am. The crease in his trousers seemed to separate them. A meditation followed on the price of trouser presses. Shop in the Euston Road, only seven-and-sixpence and a screw missing. Might wear them the other way. Out at the side. It would be as good. A stick with a carnelian knob, that's different. Bloody rot.

These people could do what they liked. Van was herself, her qualities and values pure. He disliked it that she was so linked to Rings. Rings had to be granted a unique life, and the right and potency to bloodsuck for itself. If that was not granted, a picture palace was as good as Rings.

Where would they end? Go to the stake together? And Judy's legs would straddle the iniquity of the world. The temple of the Carthagenian goddess. *Carthago delenda est.* Better go down to Rings and try our luck. That was Van's way. She would stand by her scholarship, her beauty; swallow them, affirming their reality and keep her head up to the death. Such candour, such modesty to support that insolence. He would affirm nothing as to the value of these things. He would creep off, still living, neither poorer nor richer, but entirely himself. And with his painting improved. That was what mattered. That was right.

The mid-day postman knocked with a letter from Van.

"Our treasure is back in Town, clinging tight to Amburton's skirts. We must send back her things. I think that I had better deliver them. Collect them. I will come at seven."

There was a tear in one sheet, a wine stain on a pillowcase and on a blanket. Four were in the wash. He had no money to get them out. At seven the laundry would be shut. Six sheets, six pillowcases, a dark green bottle, empty, but still sweet ot sniff. He must pawn. A bill came; a friend to eat his jam. He borrowed five shillings and went out. The sheets would not be ready for three days. Life would be always like this. The reward for painting. Worse for Van. Two onions, a carrot, four potatoes, and an oxo tablet. He fried the onions and boiled them together in a saucepan on a corner of the fire.

CHAPTER 10

V AN said: "You are certain you cannot get the sheets?"
"I don't see that it matters."

"Why not be brave, Serge, with me? We are like dogs not daring to howl together."

"What? I mean, why should Judy mind?"

"Don't try your cant on me. Have you the courage to face it. She was right when she said you'd none. That I had none."

"Why should it be cant? You said yourself that no reasonable person would mind."

"You dare call her reasonable?"

"I insist on believing that every person is capable of reason."

"You won't face a sickening fact."

"I can do it when I try. Now I would rather not try. And I think your sneers are ugly."

"They're true."

"Very well, they are true. But don't drag yourself in. You are a brave woman."

"Can't you see—you must see, that when you touch the property sense in Judy, you touch something as large as the world and as bad as the war? Serge, Serge, I'm sorry. Life is driving me into a corner. The fight I've trained for since I was born is to begin. Then there is Judy. But she is your burden."

"Then I have added to yours."

"And I, Serge, to yours."

"Let's share them. It may help." She crept close to him. His cheek on hers felt the warm spread of her tears, the weak movements of her mouth. For neither of them was there reinforcement. One extreme isolation met another. Blind she fingered his coat lapel. He rubbed kisses on her hair.

The end of the book of Rings. In an old room, a girl weeping, a man watching her. Only fatigue answering fatigue.

"Are you hungry?"

"Yes. I've brought two kippers and some coffee."

"Good. We'll have them after."

"Look in my bag. There's an envelope and some Turkish fags."

He took the saucepan off the fire. Two white plates, two spoons and a wooden bowl for bread. A morsel of cheese. The coffee rose in a slow foam. She watched him.

"Throw in a pinch of salt. I'm so hungry."

The end of the book of Rings. A girl watching a man cooking over a fire. In Theobald's Road, the trams clanged and passed. Her hair hung in rags. Sprawled over the arm of his chair. A crab groping over the floor of dim seas. Little crab, eat your supper.

This has happened to Rings before.

The moon endureth.

"Suppose that after the war there is a revolution," said Serge.

"Only a Jacquerie could destroy Rings, and the country people love us. There is not a bad cottage on the estate."

"Suppose the peasants want their land?"

"I know. And they ought to have it. Our kind have raised up trouble against them."

"Then Rings will go?"

"Yes, but I tell you there is such virtue in the place that it might give coherence to a new form of society."

"What would that be?"

"I'm not clear. Aristocracy and anarchy are the only two kinds for people of our sort. I mean a life fit for people who think and grow things, and for scholars and gentlemen and artists and pretty women. They made Rings. It dies with their death."

"All this presupposes a large income."

"Suppose Rings became a focus for the people who are proud."

"It would be an isolated one. And they would have to have money. Would Amburton do as well?"

"No."

"Or any other estate of the countryside?"

"Rings is different. It is a precinct, like Eleusis. We are its priests. It is because I may not initiate or be initiated—"

"Find the boy. There is a potency between brother and sister."

"His mother will have spoiled him."

"You cannot know that."

"How am I to find out?"

"Van, when we have any money, we will take a train to Gulltown. We will see what will happen. I know that you want to reign, not conduct a rebellion. But it will be amusing."

She looked at him, pleased. He would work for her, she thought, and something might come of it. Frog or pearl, life hid something at the bottom of the cup.

Sink twice before you strike for land. He watched her again, young fortitude leaning on its sword. Sunk into the one deep chair, knees apart, her stick following a cigarette-end across the boards. When she had come in that night, looking for food, there had been a significant moment. Zenith there might be, but no such nadir again. The nadir had met the zenith, but there had lain across the chair, that night, the dead slip of the moon. A good philosophy which gave this extreme nature freedom from the pair of opposites. Little Epicurean. There would be an ascent for her, till the courses of nature were checked, and in the quiet of their suspension—he did not know what would happen. The truth which may not be told, is the truth which cannot be told.

She drove the cigarette-end into a crack in the boards, and looked up for diversion.

"I have written to Judy: '*Serge has been ill. I nursed him and borrowed blankets, sheets, pillow-cases and cologne from you. They shall be returned to-morrow. Those which are at the laundry will take three days.'*—Now, we can't return the cologne."

"I have nearly sold a picture," said Serge: "Leave it to me."

The dead skin was thickening on Serge's wounds. It was for his sake that she hated Judy. He could not hate her, and so by Van a vacancy in nature was filled.

"Stay still and let me draw you." Again she became crustacean, her small hands gripped the stick. She would shake it at him and move off sideways. The ragged hair was like coral fingers. She was falling asleep. The last different thing she had done that day. He touched her to see if she were real, or a mood the mind made flesh. She stirred, and settled down. He made a parcel of the blankets, pinned a note onto it, and carried it out.

CHAPTER II

NEXT day, Morice Amburton took a taxi to go to
Swanhill Street. An age had passed when the driver
would have shown surprise at the address. Colonel Sir Morice
Amburton, in London on short leave, heaved himself into
the cab and slammed the door for himself. He watched the
unfamiliar streets. His thin, puckered eyelids showed a tension of nerves. His mind, soothed for years by inexhaustible
food and sleep and the great winds of Amburton, through
strain and abstinence had become capable of reflection. He
knew that he did not know what he wanted; and that he did
not think it possible to do as he had been told.

At Swanhill Street, tumbling with children, he got out
and walked to Serge's door. He selected his bell. At Georgian
Amburton there was a similar lintel of carved cupids. After a
silence, he struck with the great knocker. A head stuck out.
"The top flat says they can't hear." He had to stand back and
shout up. "Does Mr. Sarantchoff live here?"

"That's his name. I'll let you in."

He studied the names on the bells, glad he had come in
uniform. The voice added:

"If you go up to the top, when you can't get any further,
it's his door." Morice went up. Before Serge's painted door,
he had an involuntary taste of pleasure.

"Please come in. You are Sir Morice Amburton."

Gentleman's voice. He saw his step-daughter, fully dressed,
hair sleek as amber, for the young man's company. She was
writing in a note book, before a copy of Troilus and Cressida,
propped upon an idol.

"Betty!"

"Morice."

So her eyes had used to rag him over her clear smile.

"My dear girl—"

"What have you come about? This is my friend, Serge Sarantchoff."

A slight, stiff bow. Two children on their dignity. He had to make them see. Oh God! Where's Melitta?

Mary of roses…all young things

Am I to understand he is your fiancé?"

"He is not."

"What are you doing here?"

"My work."

"It's that damned work of yours, whatever it is, that I've come to see you about."

They nodded at him. Serge offered him a chair. And a yellow packet of atrocious cigarettes. Melitta had given him an important holder. He combined them, saw the young man's half-closed eyes, lost his social certainty, and his irritation distributed itself and became vague.

"Can't you see that it's a blackguardly thing to do, giving an interview like that. Rubbing your family's good name in the dirt."

"Wash its linen in public, you mean; and black it is."

Morice thought: Smart little devil. Now how much did she mean? Take her out. Show her what she's missed. Damned shame that. Sad looking kids. Cool and pure in the morning. She's not his mistress. Like young soldiers. She's grown a lovely girl.

"It's got to be stopped, that film. D'you hear?"

"Have you tried to buy them off?"

"Your mother and I intend to take action."

"I shall appear as witness."

"Betty, I didn't know about this, but you're a well-bred woman. You can't do that sort of thing."

"And I am to be well-bred to make it easy for you! Watch me."

"You are here, at ten o'clock in the morning, with this

young man, unchaperoned. What am I to think of that?"
She sang:

> "*Every tick of the clock,*
> *Every hour of the day,*
> *Every hour of the day or night, some woman is leading a man astray.*"

"It's impossibly bad form, I tell you, Betty. I can see you've
been here to breakfast."

"Come off it, Morice Amburton. You seduced my mother."

So that was it. Well, he had. *Long ago and far away.* What
was the young man saying? "This sort of repartee is no good
at all." Very sensible. He glanced up. Man to man, something might be done. So long ago. So sinless, so unimportant,
such a mistake. Serge said:

"I don't know, but from your voice, Van, one might think
that he had never stopped seducing her. But your father died.
They have been married for years. It is not relevant."

"Not relevant, my God!"

"Betty!"

"Van!"

"Link yourselves together with that cruel mother of mine."

"We're not!" They shouted it at her. She laughed. Relief.

"Look here, Betty, I'm ready to admit mistakes, I always
was. We should have looked after you better. You've never
had a proper allowance. We should have seen to it." He was
looking round the room, the proportions of whose poverty
were unintelligible to him, and said to Serge: "I suppose you
work here?"

"Sleep and eat, smoke and entertain my friends."

"By Jove!"

"Would you like to see my place, Morice?"

"I tried to the other day, but I hadn't the number."

"It is as well."

"Betty, a friend of yours is staying with us."

"We know. Juliet Marston."

"She is worried about you."

"That is her impertinence, not my fault."

One could appreciate that. The young man was of her own class, all said and done. That girl, Judy, had implied an outsider. Queer women. This one was a bit short, old Anthony's intensive cultivation of the brain. Seduced her mother. Fuss about nothing. Only the beastly silence. Nothing said from that day to this. The kid knows that. It's her only card. She's lovely. She shouldn't be sad. Young man ought to be in the army. Looks delicate. Well, well. Don't want her to despise me. He said:

"Look here. I want you to look at things without bias. I want to come to an arrangement for the good names of both our families."

Serge looked down. Van glanced at him, piteous, then stared away, her appeal glazing into contempt.

"I don't know."—Serge turned to Morice.—"You might come to an arrangement if a proper sum of money was settled on her, and her home shared on equal terms with her brother."

"My half-brother."

"Betty, you'll be sorry you said that."

"It will do for truth."

"For God's sake, tell us what you want."

"I have no terms. I will go on living to be a curse on you all."

"Van, can't you see? He means to do what he can."

"I do not want his offers. I do not hate him for himself. He gave me a red horse. He will remember how often we hid together from Melitta. But because of the woman he has married, Rings cannot happen properly which is the life of our race. And our race has become impure. And I, who am true Ashe, am hungry and lonely and thwarted. That would not matter. But Rings will pass away to his son—who is not Ashe but Amburton's child. An evil place, Amburton, and are you a happy man, Morice? Your son will have Rings. We are storing up futilities and adoring the past. I am not doing what I was meant to do."

"What makes you think that Valentine is your half-brother?"

"It is a matter of common belief."

109

MARY BUTTS

"What right have you to believe the servants' hall when it
suits you?"

"Clavel—"

"If Clavel ever thought so, he seems to have changed his
mind. Good God, that cub my son! I wish I'd his photograph
here. You'd soon see. You're hard people to deal with, you
Ashes, with your grand minds. You might add some common sense to them. You two are brother and sister. I've no
son of my own.

—"Look at the Slingsby baby. They called in a sculptor.
Your friend here, he's a painting chap, he ought to know about
faces. Ask him if there's a trace of Amburton in that boy.
Ashe to his toes. Won't play games. Acts in Greek plays. Keeps
Persian cats. All he can do is ride and sail a boat. Worships
your ghastly old manor. Goes in for science. Reads German.
Did a Salome dance for us in three red candle-shades.

—"He's taken to talking about you. I tell you, your mother
is dead set on keeping you apart." She considered this until
her lip began to tremble, and was silent for some time. Then
she said:

"If that is so, I said wrong, Morice."

"Betty, my dear. Don't stare like that. Here's a hundred
pounds."

"Morice, my dear, don't pretend to be a fairy."

He wished he was her father.

"Don't you see, it cuts both ways. Your mother and I have
no children. Your brother may have Amburton. There's no
entail. I don't want it to go to the only kin of mine the war's
left. It hasn't left him fit enough to keep cats."

"Judy does not know that. Rings will be enough for Valentine since he is my brother."

"Is Peter engaged to that girl who knows you? She's been
staying with us," said Morice.

"Do you like the marriage?"

"Got a touch of khaki-fever, hasn't she? You know I think
she's queer, and now I've seen them together, I think he's
queer. He was all right till he got shot in the head. Then he

110

met her in town. She's decently bred. No money—"

"She'd not be our friend if she had."

"She takes him for long walks. They talk and talk. I've met them in the High Woods, fairly screaming at each other. That wasn't like him."

Van was looking at her step-father with round eyes and lips that still trembled. She said:

"I remember him a sullen child, and I don't like to think of him with Judy. But you have made me happier, Morice. You have put ground under my feet. It's a pity you never had a child by Melitta. Then she'd have let us alone....

"Make it pax, Morice, between you and me, and the rest will work itself out in time."

"That's right. You keep the money and let me know when you want more. I'm back to France to-night. Come and dine when I get leave again. Good day, Sarantchoff. Take care of Betty." He went out.

"Serge—what a drawing you've made of him! You are a great man. Come out and spend that hundred pounds."

"We'll get Judy's cologne —"

"This moment. Then we'll have lunch."

"After that will you go straight down to your home? The time is now."

"Yes." A cry like a clap of wind. He wanted to go with her. Perhaps she would not want him now.

"What did you make of Morice."

"Quite a good sort."

"Another of Melitta's victims."

"I don't know. He didn't seem to like her much."

"Do you know—you are two extremely different men, but I saw you both alike."

"I know. It is because we are afraid of women."

"You edged together. You were ready to make common cause against me. I was watching you. I do not like you better for it."

"What would you have us do?"

"Not play into each other's hands, sex for sex."

"But you do that yourself."

"For sheer preservation. Men hold the cards."

"I don't see—"

"And you never will." He was a torment to her. She could have struck him and entreated. She would have torn off her skin to give him understanding. For her own relief. For the relief of all women. Break his little box of satisfaction. But not the instinct to rebuild it. A snail goes to its shell. Then she was a slug, to creep naked in dark places. She considered their reactions more coldly.

Both were free in their sorrows. Only they could not approach each other because of Serge's nature and her own. She could cry and fake a victory over him; but liberty did not allow that. Another stage in the association of two similar, slightly dissimilar animals. No need to make such a fuss. It was dreary. She loved him; but without the illusion that love would alter him. She also knew herself to be as unalterable. It was good perhaps that she should have vision and Serge detachment.

"I am going out," she said.

"It is a cheque. You have to cash it first."

"I know. Then I must pack."

"You won't want me for anything?"

"No; we might have lunch."

"Not to-day. I must see a dealer. No, I won't."

She thought that he wanted to come with her. Their adventure was still alive: he had let her understand that. Good, good. He would not cost much to feed; there would still be money for clothes. How mean one was. A sensuality to give pleasure welled in her again: one bringing gifts, a prostration.

Serge said: "Come with me. Van, whatever you want to do that we can do, we will try to do together."

They were close up, kissing one another, violently, repeatedly, tears running down, salting their lips. Hers she caught on her tongue, but his fell straight, lead plummets, and rolled off his chin, warm pearls, bitter to taste.

"Your tears are heavy." He nodded and shook his head. They walked together, slowly, to the broken sofa, and crept down onto it, side by side, into each other's arms.

CHAPTER 12

AN hour later, he stayed behind to draw while she went
out. He was so charmed, that what had been the burden of Judy shrank to a grain of discomfort, a speck on the
surface of his peace. The grain was the great parcel of sheets
in newspaper and brown paper which was to be completed
and taken back to her. Now the pain of his handling was
narcotised, there remained some half-memories he would not
disturb. And a grievance. The girl was a nuisance, a public
danger, probably murdering Peter Amburton now. Van, he
remembered, stressed the public significance of her efforts.
He did not understand. Wise girl, blessed girl.

It was amusing to think of those sheets stolen from Judy's
chest. When they had loved her, she had grudged them kippers and cream.

Van was worried because of Judy's evil prayer. These
things only hurt you if you let them. That parcel was the bold
answer to cursing witches. He laughed, a block of cartridge-
paper balanced on his knees. The wind lifted the curtains
and clattered the pictures on the walls. Along the streets, like
a dead tree blooming only with its disease, Judy hurried to
his door. He let her in as Morice Amburton had been let in.

"So I've found you here. I'm sorry, Serge, you've been ill."

His mind was still awash with its peace.

"That is all right now."

"How clean your room is. I think you have some property of mine. Here is a list. Would you check it and return
them as soon as you can?"

As he had let her in, his horror had come back to him

His knees melted. The relief of love, the pleasure of relief had no power then. A weak evocation. He stood up and threw back his head, preparation for death the only courage in him.

On a large easel was his painting of Van, naked, her knees drawn up, her elbows on her knees. The little, pointed breasts stuck out at them. He felt ashamed.

"Oh, so that's your last thing. It's quite good."

She went up to it. She was a good judge. Her red, pointed tongue passed over her lips. Serge said:

"Most of your things are here. Some are at the wash. I will see they are sent round. There is a parcel downstairs. It was good of you to lend them."

"You've found my successor quickly."

"In some ways you are a better model."

She was beginning to move about the room and to stop, shifting from foot to foot.

"I suppose—I suppose I've no right to mind. But you might have let me know that you were ill."

"Why should I? The last time I saw you—"

"My dear Serge, why do you make so much of my tempers?"

"I don't know—but, as Van says, why should you have it both ways?"

She was beginning to twist her hands about. He must help her. And what she said was true. He spoke in a low voice:

"Now you have come back, it is awfully good to see you."

"Serge, d'you mean that? Serge, I've missed you too. How are you now? Don't say you were very ill."

"Better. I was never very ill."

"What do you see in Van? I wouldn't have asked, but you said you were glad to see me back."

Evade. Toss your love in fragments to the she-wolf. The pictures were quiet on the walls. The people were quiet in the street. He felt his bare throat. A spot reddened by Van's firm lips. He said:

"I like her very much. What sort of a time did you have at Amburton?" (Had she got what she wanted at Amburton?) "Will you smoke?"

"Thanks, no. Your little whore has played me a trick."

"What trick?"

"She wrote anonymously to my fiancé's people. I'm getting the proofs."

"To tell them what?"

"That I am not good enough for their nephew."

He moved back against the wall.

"Don't be a fool. You have no proofs. You are engaged to him."

"His people were honey-sweet to me at first. They are not now."

"Why do you expect me to take so great an interest in the man you're going to marry?"

"I may not marry him."

"Then you'd better not quarrel with me. Laugh, Judy."

"I don't think I would if you had not found Van so quickly to take my place. But I suppose she told you that you were consumptive. When I found out that you were lying about that, I knew you'd find a successor to buy food. You're so greedy."

"I never said such a thing."

Inevitable now. He was watching a disease mount to its crisis, Judy's sick dream, inventing a drama that had not happened. What is truth but intensity of vision? This was better than truth because it had been more seen.

Judy said: "Morice Amburton was here to-day."

"She did not speak a word against you."

"That was what I wanted to know. Thank you."

"For God's sake tell me what you want."

"I want to marry that boy. That will re-establish my family also. Then I can rearrange my life as I please. He's a shell-shocked lump of carrion."

"Poor devil."

"Did I shock you, Serge? I'm sorry. When I think of you, on my honour, I have regrets. Don't sneer. That is quite true. You are dangerous to a nature like mine. I must have wealth and security. If I had them, I'd become nicer at once. I'm not your sort of adventurer. That's what you never will see. You are dangerous to me. As for Van, I'll have her turned out of Rings and the servants lined up to see her go."

Hill and the sea. Disks threaded on a sparkling wind. Bodies washed with it, and linen flying on a line. All the images of gentleness made fun of him.

"You don't mean, Serge, that you've been taken in by her? She's only a scheming, little liar. I met a man the other day who told me that she knew no Greek at all. They say at Amburton that she's the illegitimate child of old Anthony Ashe by a farm girl. She has told you these tales till you are turning against me. You are forcing me into this mercenary marriage. You are wonderful when you like. If you would work, I should not have to leave you for money. Some people must have money. But, for all our quarrels, you are the best thing I have ever known. Van wants you to further her ambition. When did I ask you for such a thing?"

True. A victim for Judy, Van's step up a throne. Judy was crying, fierce and upright. Not as Van had cried. Van crouched over the earth, breathing it, could do without him. Not Judy. Poor, blind lamb.

"Van's all right. Judy, you must leave her alone."

"It is so plain to me. She can take you in."

He did not follow the commonplace. He wanted to be touched by her and suddenly made whole.

"Anyhow, Serge, she allows you to paint her naked."

"She is accustomed to pose." Not even loyal to Van. This was being dragged over stones down an endless road. The pictures clicked on the walls, one after another, as the wind passed them. Stay with Judy. Yes. See it to the end. Submit to her. Exalt torture through hysteria to ecstacy. In the end he would turn her right about face, and there would be the end to the world.

Epicurus would have none of these things.

He didn't understand life. He thought: Van doesn't understand. There would be the awful pain, then anaesthesia, then vision. The skin grown over his wounds was torn off.

He watched it flake away, here and there, a little red.

He kissed Judy and pushed her gently into a chair. Her eyes relaxed and contracted again.

"I should like to know how many of my sheets you have actually lost."

"I have not lost any."

"Is there any scent left?"

"I'm afraid not; but Van has some money. She has gone to buy you another bottle."

"If I get a taxi now, will you bring the parcel round to my place?"

Van would be coming back. A nasturtium cap on a white stick past the carved doors. He closed his eyes and opened them to stare at Judy. A black stock round the cruel neck. A tiny frill of lawn. Tear it down. Sink the lips onto the stringed muscle under the warm skin. A bite into rubber and flexible glass. Draw your mouth down the iron breast-bone. As good as dead now. He would go through with it. Van would come back. She would knock and run back on to the pavement and cry up. He would be gone, away in Judy's shadowy room, flayed nerves reacting to vile words. At them he would break and plead, and fall away in anguish and silence, with a mounting fiend in his brain.

In the belief that if he endured it to the end, there would be a reversal into beauty and accomplishment Van could not achieve. That would bring about the end of this world.

Perhaps it was not like that at all. Perhaps, by his nature, he was drawn into a dance of death. At any rate he would go back with Judy. Van would understand. Judy had got up and was leaning out of the window. He saw that he was staring at the eye of the kettle handle made with scribble on the wall. A quiet god of indoors, watching him. He saw Judy's shoulder-blades moving under her shift. Why did she lean out and say nothing? Van, help me.

"Shall we go now, Serge?"

"I am not coming. I can't come now. I will bring them round to you to-night."

"Why not?"

"I have to go out to lunch."

"With Van?"

"Yes. I owed her that."

"Very well. I may tell you that I know what to do."

"Do what you like."

"You are driving me to it." She was grinding her palms with her nails. A bad sign.

"You've got to choose between Van and me. Van and your liberty. Van and your painting. While you have time to choose at all. And I know that you will choose, only it will be too late. I have power. I put out my will..." The voice was droning now. It rose to the thin whine of a gnat. He knelt against the table, his face against the wood. It smelt of Van. Hold very fast to her. He rose, afraid of some wound. Judy was gone. He sat down in the arm-chair. The high back reassured his shrinking spine. He waited, pride dawning, trying to light a cigarette.

There rose over the back of his head a distorted face, crimson, the mouth open and wet. It closed down on him snatching at his eyelids. The teeth bit down between eyes and nose. Fingers raked his throat. He was sobbing as he tore her off, his tears meeting blood, blinding him. Then, a moment later, Van had followed her back into the room.

"Get out, you filthy devil." The fear currents sucked and swerved. Judy was afraid.

"He drove me to it. He drove me —"

"God help you, you unspeakable thing."

She was taken out of the room. He heard the street door close. Van came back.

"I want to wash your face. There should be poison in those teeth."

CHAPTER 13

THEN she was ashamed to touch him. A flask of cologne stood on the table. She detested it. She would have kicked it into a corner, for being one of the causes of this trouble, but was afraid that the noise would trouble him. He turned from her passively, staring at the grey window. She looked out for the sun that would help her. The sun would not come out. He moved. What was she to do for him?

He was going away from her. She wanted him now. Quick to take him in her arms. They were numb at her sides. There was a kiss for each mark. Now this had happened, they could not be given. Hysterics might distract him. She could not show hysteria. Wait, wait on this frantic mood. Until one was bored.

He saw nothing. When she moved to him, he took the bowl and sponge from her, and wiped the blood from his face.

"Let us go out." He walked down the street, in utter quiet, like contentment. She could not judge. She grew angry. People stared at him. Leave him alone. Was this worth it, the pleasure of his company that had mounted so quietly in anticipation? She had run Judy out of the house, dumb, talking on her fingers; she had pushed her into the street and shut the door and leaned against it. The rest was a red smear. Get alone and cry it out. How could she leave him? He was in a most horrible case.

At first Serge had not seen her. Then he wished that she was not there. The pleasure he had had from her was now the hot memory of an incongruity. He was living in love's mystery. If his suffering needed pity, he would pity himself.

They walked on till they came to the restaurant.

Then she thought she might make him drunk. He ordered wine and told her to drink it. She got up and walked to the door. She went back and laid a five pound note on his plate under the bread. He did not move. She went away and sat in a cinema, and in the dark let the tears run down her face.

He went out into Shaftesbury Avenue. The sun hurried over the pavement, and its cloud, overtaking it, shook out a few drops of rain. He said to the wind "be quiet." His face and neck were very stiff and hurt at several places. There was blood on his collar. He sucked at the agony in his breast. An old pain, but never so keen before. He had been afraid at lunch that Van would tell him that he enjoyed it. She *had* said that. He imagined the flat edge on her voice. "I don't like the new sensuality." He clutched his throat and bent it back, to feel it swell against the cut of his nails. His mouth was like dust. The houses dissolved and reshaped. He began to cry. What had he done to Van? Little, blessed love. She had tried to wash his face, and been quiet, and stayed with him and gone away silent. Just before they had agreed to love one another. Now she was detestable because she had seen him.... She would not mind. It would not be ridiculous to Van. He turned and passed a shop that smelt of sugar. He went in and bought a pound of chocolates and walked out slowly, cramming his mouth.

In Soho Square the wind was loose and tore at the people and the trees. He leant against an area-railing, where he felt himself out of the wind. There came round again the idea of two female voices talking to him about himself.

"Played up the state of your lungs to get me to keep you."

That was Judy; now there was Van saying:

"Dear boy, you enjoy it. When you want to clear out you will." They skinned away at his mind, cutting till they met.

Why had Van said that to him? Lying little bitch. In his imagination, he struck her face and kept his open hand over her mouth. She cried. The wet lips closed on his palm and kissed it.

121

The first had been said. The other had been said differently.
The sugar mounted. It ran along his veins. A fine thing
sugar, like a noble wine. He became self-conscious because
of his face. He moved away. In a clouded window he tried to
judge it. Dark patches. He felt the raw pits under his eyes.
His fingers came away wet. There was a crust on his cheek.
Go and find Van. She had kissed his hand. But she had not.
She might not. Don't take that risk. Stick to one woman.
Give the rest what she gives you. Show them what love means
to a man.

He was going to Judy. It would be all right this time.

He must be there now. Taxi. Van's money. Good. Oh
Van, we'll laugh at this together on the green hills. O quickly,
quickly. He flung himself into one and then from side to side
on the slippery leather. *Gin love be bonny. A little time.* Quickly,
quickly. Get into her arms.

And Judy would be saying, "I am sorry. I was mad. Forgive me, Serge, my dear. But you were a beast too. Acknowl-
edge it." Assent slowly. She would be sorry about his face.
He would let her bathe it. And not Van.

It was infamous that she should touch him.

Quick, quick, into her arms.

Judy was saying:
"And you haven't brought my linen after all. Never mind.
My dear, I was beastly to-day. But you drove me to it. You
were rather a brute. And of course I'm furious about Van."

"But she never wrote the Amburtons a word. Acknowl-
edge that—"

"Well, then she talked to Morice."

"I was there. She did not."

"Well, something has happened. Listen to my adventures....'

Vanities and suspicions. Lies and counter lies. A keen
ambition, a mean outlook of mind, and rather witty.

She dressed his face, with little pats and touches.

—"And I got on with Morice Amburton. Peter is quite

mad and Melitta as bad as Van says. My finger is sore with making bandages. I don't really want you to be jealous of Peter. But he's rather pathetic. Oh Serge—that woman has a pelisse of ermine, and how can I make one out of rabbit scut and good intentions?"

"When it comes to clothes, you and Van are one as bad as the other."

"Only I've taught myself to sew, and she won't, the little slattern."

How long had he sat there? His mouth was foul with smoking, he was utterly fatigued; the delicate, convalescent vigour gone that was Van's evocation. The old melancholia had come back, the red moods, and the black.

A rancid crumb of Judy worth more than Van's cup of fruits? She was saying:

"Serge, shall we? Would you like to sleep with me once more? Before I marry Peter. If I ever do marry Peter. Sleep with me to-night? It must be late." He thought: Get into her bed. He had not taken Van into his. Lie close up against the steel and satin in the dark.

"Let's."

She was quiet. She might have been offended at his indifference. Had he frightened her? He got up and went into her bedroom under the roof.

"Should I waste the gas, or can I have a bath?"

"Don't be absurd. I'm not ungenerous. I'll turn it on."

The geyser roared. He pottered about her bedroom, playing with her scent bottles.

The imagination of danger rose. He licked his lips and his eyes sparkled. When they lay together would she attack him again? No, not there.

He went to his bath and rested in its hot fold. He dried himself slowly. As he put on his pyjamas, the water began to drain out with gasps and sucks. Covered by the sound, he went to the bedroom door.

She was there under the gas, in her rosy shift, stepping before the long glass, smiling, humming. To and away from the glass she slipped, delicately swinging and pointing a small sickle-knife. He remembered Atys. Then himself. In the arabesque, he watched the mine of her intention. Point and pass. Thrust up and turn down. She was dancing.

She bent and laid the knife carefully behind the pier glass on the floor, went to the dressing-tale and powdered her arms and her throat. He came in and flung her down on the bed. There lay behind her mirror a crooked, steel knife. He took her roughly.

"Serge, you hate me very much. You mustn't."

Silence.

"Don't. You are hurting me."

"Serge, forgive me." The dewy lips were sad. The great eyes stared mournfully and closed.

Ask her about it? No. Already the soul like a dog was burying its bone. Oh the marvel of it and the pain! If she could have loved him under any formula that permitted of life.

"It is all right, Judenka. I know all about you now."

Lie silent. Then he felt her body stiffen and stir on his outstretched arm.

"Are you beginning to hate me again?"

"Let me alone. I am going to sleep."

Let her be. Easy to lie on the back and think.

She lay on the outside of the bed. Would she slip out and cross the floor for that knife? He said:

"Wake up. I've not done with you yet."

"Serge, I'm so tired. Please, Serge. Days like we've had make me so tired. Serge, don't you know?"

"Stop shamming."

"I'm not shamming. Let me lie quiet beside you. I know you don't love me any more. I let you come to-night to give you your revenge."

"So. There is nothing more to be done about it. Go to sleep."

She gave a tiny movement and turned away her cheek. Too warm to stir again, he lay beside her, hanging over the mirror of sleep.

She lay in the dark beside him, licking her lips, trying to remember. She stirred, rose, and sank down. She dropped her arm across him and slept.

"Get up, you pair of imbeciles!"

Vile mouth, tight forehead. He heard the wind beating on the window. It was cold. There was Van at the foot of the bed.

"This is for you, Judy. Peter Amburton's in town. I saw him in Piccadilly. He came back last night. He'll be here any moment. The police, Serge, have been to your flat. They want your papers. Have you any?"

"I don't know." Judy cried:

"Serge, for God's sake get out of my flat." Van said:

"Judy, you sent the police."

"Van, on my soul of honour, I did not."

"Then it was Peter, on your information. I might have let him find you both."

"Go away, both of you, now."

"We are going. You have managed well."

"It wasn't me, I tell you. It wasn't me."

CHAPTER 14

SERGE dressed while they wrangled. Van taut and neat, Judy with swollen eyes and straggled hair. Van beat her with words. She had no reply but to entreat them to make haste. The wind whined and drove dust off the leads on to the panes. He glanced at Van. Would they go out together, set their teeth at the dust squalls, and in a quiet eddy let her laugh at him? Or, as seemed probable, would she never speak to him again? The bed was pulled back, the pillows beaten out. Van rolled his pyjamas round her hand.

"If Peter should come now, Judy, you can say we have come for breakfast."

"If you don't want to ruin me, quick, get out of this." Van stuck the pyjamas behind the mirror. He heard them brush down. There was a knife there. He tied his tie before it and followed Van out of the house.

"Tell me about the police. It is serious?"

"I don't think so."

"You saw them?"

"I was there."

"How?"

"I was there all night. I was afraid for you. When he came, it was to enquire about a gentleman who ought to have had his calling-up papers—he wasn't sure. I told the right sort of story. Have you any enemies in the house?"

"I don't think so."

"Then, unless you want to go to prison again, you had better move. Then I think you would be safe."

"But where can I go?"

"You could have my place, but then there is Judy. You

can't get out of the army on your health, and I don't suppose you would. If you don't mind, you must do what we arranged before; come down to Rings. We will stay at a farm where, under no circumstances, would any questions be asked."

Damnable charity. Divine toleration. Had she no passions? She had found him in bed with another woman. The dust stung in his nose. They were hurrying down an unnecessary street. He had supposed that they were going to her rooms.

She dived into a dairy and left him. Through the glass, he saw her buy a loaf. White dust under one's arms. It was easier to move about. He took the loaf from her.

"I've not been home at all, but the place was left clean. I borrowed Judy's char. We'll have a great fire, and a breakfast with eggs and toast."

Nothing but the ménage. He had heard that love took women that way. But how good. He was done for, and she built up life from its foundations. He trusted her. This was peace. For an instant he loved her. He walked off beside her.

In the flat, she went down on her knees, lighting a great fire.

"*Cook Marie.*

Kerosene.... I shan't be an angel yet."

"You are an angel now." She made a face at him.

So that was the revenge. To laugh at him. He would not have that. She should hear his confession. Too much playing for the cinema must be bad for the carnal passions. Fun to stir up her rage, a puppet-play after a reeking death. *Turn ye to me.*

She must know everything, believe, pity, or she would be no good to him.

Turn ye to me.

Time that had streamed past them, stopped and waited for them. Begin again. Be loved forever. Van lay in time's arms. Life in time. Life in eternity. She had told him. The double life....

"Bacon, and eggs to hide the bacon, and new broad beans. I like their bitter taste. It's all ready, come, Serge." He gulped at the tea, a thin, cleansing drink. A film skinned off his brain.

"Will you let me talk?" he said.

"Determined to enjoy yourself, aren't you?"

"One must get something out of it."

"I see that. Go on."

"Are you hiding a great disgust for me?"

"No. I'm not. Men don't have an emotional focus. I mean they have less than women. I mean that you are a painter, not a professional amorist. You love, or you are loved. You loved Judy."

"And you —"

"That's as may be; but from the first you ran on the knife."

"Exactly. This means nothing at all but that you think me a fool."

"Sir, we are in the presence of a mystery. Do you want me to enquire like a petulant female?"

"No."

"All I would want is to go on with you as best I can, and understand and even reduce to a formula, this last day and night. They have happened. I have no judgment. I shall call it myself 'the Russian touch.' I am terribly interested. But I am not you. I make no demands and am bound by none."

"So."

"How are you feeling now, Serge?"

"I'm sane. I mean that I never wish to approach Judy again, if that is what you mean by sanity. How long it will last, I can't say. But I don't remember, much less realise, all that has happened. Somewhere I can hear a high voice that never stops talking. I try not to listen. It's no good."

"I was a fool to let her know that the police had been to your place?"

"Why? She did not send them. People don't do these things."

"Such faith is not in character with the way you behave, Serge. Why will you have people honourable and keep such bad company?"

He thought:

Do not speak about Judy's dancing and the knife. Van will make too much of it. Stretch out over the fire. Squeeze

Van for tenderness. Turn to the fire. She stood behind him,
like a bird priestess, tight in folded wings.

"Van, what are you staring at?"

"A picture in my mind—A creek of the sea, and up it,
like a spear-head, the tide running in."

"Where did you see that?"

"I don't know. It rose."

"I thought I heard a knocking."

"On the door through which we both enter into time."—
He jumped at the phrase.

"I suppose my nerves are out of order."

"They are."

"What does one do?"

"Make your burden bear you. By that way comes health,
and the desire works itself free."

"You value health. It is an english fashion. But you indulge in extremes like the rest."

"How can you be free of the pair of opposites if you do
not know what they are?"

"That is all very well."

"You take it out in your painting, my son. That will teach
you."

Painting had not taught him. She had something good up
her sleeve. Self-sufficient. He disliked her. If he could despise
her, he might love her as he loved Judy. He wanted to love
her. So as to be rid of this business of loving, and go away,
wrapped in the warm pelt of accomplished love. Offering
himself to Judy, he had opened a trap-door for infernal powers. From Van he would receive the sanc-grail, and munch it
whole. She would give. Out of her riches she would miss
nothing. He would receive. That was best, that would make
it all right. And his secret walking place would be his own,
and Judy's mystery, and the white bees, her antithesis, and
her remembrancers. In fact, he could get rid of Van when he
wanted to. All the same, he had Van. He could pull out on
the grey seas with her. If he wanted to forget Judy, she would
find a way.

She raked at the fire. He made a face. "I'm sorry. I'm fretting you. Have some more tea." It was strong, the last depraved cup.

"Van, I am as sophrôn as you."

"So you say."

"I have led a more discreet life."

"The answer to that is Judy. I don't say anything about your conscience or your revolution. There you were a gentleman, and a man of heart and some sense. But Judy! You must get strong enough to paint again."

"Do you expect me to fall again into her bed?"

"Yes."

"When?"

"When she chooses?"

"But why? Haven't I had my lesson?"

"She learns as fast as you. My dear—I do not know, but I see a hollow room, quite empty that you have made with your reactions, and through it blows a stinking blast from hell.... I'm sorry I'm so restless and useless. Your cold is much worse. We must go away. We have had a bad time for too long."

"What will become of Judy?"

"She will go out of her mind."

That meant nothing. They were mad already, all three. His back ached. Then he began to want to get well.

Van did not know about his secret contemplation. Little street-by, fingers on nose. A creek of the sea, and the tide running up it. A net running through the sea for its fish. The net was their net and the tide was running in. They were fish in the net. Turned out and gutted. Van had a word of power. He would slip through the net. Up what beaches? Behind the beaches, there was marsh-land. Marsh-king's daughter. Van was speaking:

"Serge, there are two kinds of tragedy. When you can hear necessity tapping at the door; and another, when you are too busy trying to put things right to listen. For one there is no hope. For the other, the anguish of a good hope which is generally a lie."

He did not speak. She smiled. She rubbed his hand on her cheek. He drew up her hands and laid them on his face. "I love you very much."

"Serge. Serge."

He could hear the wind rustling into rain, the buses change gears in the street. Her mouth was on his hand, his palms were dry and grimy, which should be wet and red. She was kneeling between his knees She sprang up and went out of the room. Too weak to turn, he lay. Time was like crystal before the leaping fire.

She was singing. She stopped singing. She was talking, liquid bird-voice.

Parthenophil is lost and I would see him. For he is like to something I remember. A great while since, a long, long time ago.

He looked over the back of the chair. By the door she was kneeling, folding away clothes at the bottom of a trunk.

III

CHAPTER I

THE train smelt of varnish and soiled clothes, grease, metal, excrement and cold smoke. The dirt of moving armies was rubbed into every crack. A composition of grit and slime spread upon the floor made Van curl back the soles of her feet.

A child was sick. A man smoked a cigar. In opposite window-corners, Serge and Van sprawled down, worn out, feet stretched to feet. Silk ankles and lacquered shoes, he contemplated his own in great content. Half the price of a picture. He had sold two. Van looked out at the black roofs shining with rain, till they came to the monstrous area of un-planned streets and impure grass between the country and the town. Then she took out a ham sandwich, pulled it apart and gave half to Serge.

"There is only this, and a bun full of plaster of Paris."

In exchange he gave her two little slips of chocolate, worn at the edges. They thought of hot milk. Their great beauty made the mother of the sick baby stare at them, as she wiped it and handed it about.

Without looking at them, Serge was sorry for the people in the carriage. Van noted every gesture, placed them, and withdrew herself. They all looked at her, at her elegant limbs, the sorrows of her face, and at her eyes that followed Serge to comfort him. He said:

"Do you remember the parcel tied up with rope? Did it go in with the guard? I can't see it here."

"Time will show."

"I booked to Gulltown. Was that right?"

"No, but it does not matter. There is a station where we

135

change and crawl away on a side line. At no times were people encouraged to make this journey. Before we left, I boiled an egg hard. Pull down my trench coat. It's in the pocket."

Break down the gentle competence and understand her plan. He stood up, and the coat unrolled and fell like the heavens. A strange woman was under it, and Van and himself and the train smells were intensified, crossed with rubber and stale violets. Under the cloth, he knew the woman abnormally interested in them. He was thinking that it did not matter that she watched them. But suppose that the things you see and the people, even sick babies, curious women, fallen raincoats, eggs, are omens of what is about to be, or signatures of potencies who are watching man. And that now and then you are aware of it and afraid. Van had said something like that, and there were Strindberg's crossed sticks in the Rue Cardinal Lemoine. Another short cut to insanity? Would the train never stop for good?

They were sick from passive movement, and want of food. Serge found the egg and peeled it. Van cut it with a pin and they ate it, saltless.

Hours later the train stopped, exhausted, and he handed her out the luggage from the carriage-step. She took it from him, holding the topmost package under her chin.

The little station glittered with rain and sun. The air, still chill with winter and incredibly pure, refreshed them like water. A great labourer watched the train. The neck of a dead goose hung down from a basket on the platform. The asphalt was full of glittering specks. The farmer's son put the luggage on a trap. They followed him, the contacts of the train had left them feeling that a stone had been let into their foreheads, between their eyes. Van moved vaguely, swallowing the air. They drove three miles, to the mouth of a long valley in the downs. The rain had blown away inland, and the air was like an aquamarine. They came to a white farm, flanked with stacks and stables, and a tithe-barn like the nave of a church. Van shewed it to Serge with pride.

"On the other side of the hill, two miles as the bee flies, is Rings."

At the farm he had feared a reception, a definition of their position, but nothing was said. There was a parlour with two deep chairs, and, up a wide stair, two bedrooms trimmed with china dogs and texts. There was a rich tea. Night fell, a dark crystal. He remembered Russia, where his people had been landowners. It was strange to Van that he should take it as a matter of course.

"I want you to feel emotion for it."

"So I do; it is a pleasant thing."

But Van, last bee of her swarm, was hived.

"Are you going out?"

"Not to-night." But when it was quite dark, she grew restless because she could hear trees.

She sat on the sill. He thought he saw her body moving with the boughs.

The quiet struck his town-tuned nerves as sinister. He listened again, and heard the oak-trees rubbing their branches in the running air. How would this adventure modify their relations? She had let him come out of pity. If she had, that was his own fault.

He saw her judge him too tired for caresses. She kissed him good night. When he got into bed there was a hot water-bottle in the sheets. A very sensible alternative. He laughed.

He held it to his stomach and listened to the trees, and to a cow lowing. He was sliding down a dark road into a pit. The wind was feeling round the house. He heard Van get out of bed, and fling up a window-sash. She was sitting by the window, communicating with the chill fingers of the trees.

He wanted her to come to him. He had not wanted her so before. That night with Judy had been dilettante devil-worship. Van and he had been together in sad and terrible places. Together they should look for the garden, and turn the points of its swords.

It was no good. His life was like an overhanging bank he had fallen back in climbing, attempt after attempt. In a flash

137

and a flash, he had seen Van, and was left with a great kindness and affection. Then he fell into utmost misery because
he could not with another nature simplify his own. Judy pre-
vented Van. But he must have an answer to Judy. If there
was Judy, there must be a balm for her. For that evil will, an
equal good. It should be Van. It was Van. Van would not do.
He would not find another woman of her quality. If Van
would not do, he would die of his wounds. Why would not
Van do? *Fair and learned and good*—All right. She saw me when
I was abject. She is too wise. I need her wisdom. I'm spent
for love. I can only endure her for friend.

He was ashamed, questioning himself.

Have I hurt her? She will be too busy soon to bother about
me. Ah! He beat his head on the pillow, sleep staring at him
from a million miles off. Suppose she satisfied me. I should
only paint. She thinks that I am like her. She does not know
that we can be different, and have weight. She is too young.
She is holy. She will do the great work.

My little heart, what were you when you came and found
me? When you were hungry? When Amburton brought you
to your knees? I do not know what is wrong… No fault, but
that you came at the wrong time… He felt the sticky linen of
his pillow. He thought: That it should make me cry. No more
good than Judy's love. I am very stupid. He said aloud: "I am
being very stupid." He sat up and fell back. Sleep's head was
hanging over him. He could hear nothing in the next room.
His mind floated backwards. There rose an arrangement of
geometric shapes, which he knew stood for a simplification
of his imaginings. It often came. He could never remember
it. He slept for eleven hours. The tear-wetted linen when he
woke was stiff under his cheek.

CHAPTER 2

OH she got up in the morning, as white as any milk.
And he got up in the morning, as black as any silk.
Hullo!
Hullo!
Hullo!
Hullo!
You coal-blacksmith!
You never did me no harm;
But you shall not have my maidenhead, that I have kept so long.
A maiden I will die."

Serge thought: So that is how it takes us this morning. If women only kept to that. He flattened his plumy black hair, and left the window, while she was still singing. But out in the yard, in the warm sun, he said: "Van, look at the lambs." And when they sat down to breakfast he said: "You are a lamb, I think. This is a good place."

"Come out for a walk, my dear."

They went out along a sunk lane, across an uphill field, past a chalk-pit, into a wood. The shadowy earth was lit with wild hyacinths. She hurried him on until the wind-curled beeches ended and they came out on the down-top covered with flints.

They were at the head of a narrow valley, unsown, uncut for chalk, an empty shell of pebbles and grass. On the further side, below them, in the open country, they saw the house and precinct of Rings, its wood, its terrace, its orchard, its walled gardens and great lawn, its park that ran to the sea. Beyond it, the land rose again, planted with ragged firs, round whose edge the sea nibbled at the foot of a cliff. High away on their left, above the house, there was a hill crowned with a triple earth-work and a grove that stirred, answering the motion of the sea.

Van said: "There is Rings, and Rings Hill." She wanted to surprise him, and saw him bite his lip.

—"There is our nut. Let's crack it?"

"If you can."

"Melitta and the boy are there."

"How do you know?"

"It's the feudal touch before he goes to the war. Our chess board's set."

"Put out your pawns."

"*You're here and I'm here*, but I want the scaly wings of a dragon to sail down and flap them on the roof."

"Yes. Take me onto the Rings sometime."

"I will."

"If he is killed, do you inherit?"

"Of course."

"Do you want him to be?"

"No! Damn him."

The little valley was like a pig-trough, without angles. Half way along its bottom, there was a slimed tank for cattle, empty, the turf round it stamped into clay. Beside it a grey patch moved, dissolved, and got up. Where the spring sun struck, the air had already begun to dance. Van rubbed her eyes.

"There is someone down there."

"A shepherd?"

"Shepherds don't wear grey flannels. It is someone with nothing to do."

"Yes, there is. He is looking at us. Is it forbidden to come here?"

"On these hills? Even Melitta could not do that. He has turned. He is going away."

"Is he going to fetch the police because we may be spies?"

"He is going away to eat something. Give me a cigarette."

The wind blew his matches out. They climbed a barrow

and looked down again over Rings, a cluster of squares, variously figured on a pale field.

"There is the tower called Rings Root. The library leads run out of it towards us. Do you see a green spiked roof on the further side? That is the chapel. It has a vault, full of delicious smells and snails."

Apart from these familiarities, the shape of the place amused Serge.

"Was it built at one time?" he asked.

"Good Lord, no! Patched together for ages. It grew out of what we liked, each bit in terms of its time."

Amburton had said "your ghastly old manor." The walls had the wan brilliance of stone lit by a storm.

"Love it, Serge, love it. It loves me."

Pathetic fallacy. And what a request! Her eyes were on it, famished, she had hold of his arm. He felt her little breast under her sweater. This was ridiculously false. It might be his stupidity. Van's starved eyes were hard again, as she frowned over the empty grass. He shook himself free of her. The sun was creeping on his spine, a celestial masseur, working with warm, gold tips. They sat down side by side, not pleased with each other.

"Look here. You must not talk about Rings in that way—not so far as I am concerned."

"No."

"It may love you as you say. I do not feel it."

"I was only trying it on."

She laid her head on his lap, and stretched out flat, her feet rigid as on a grave. She folded her hands. The skin glittering in the hollows of her nose. He noticed the unfamiliar knobs of flesh a face makes, upside down. Then he looked out over the sea.

A stone clicked. A boy in grey flannels gave a side-spring on the silent turf and appeared beside them.

"I say." Van shut her eyes. Serge looked up.

—"You are my sister, Elizabeth Ashe." She did not move.

—"May I stay and talk to you?" Serge looked down and saw her lids shudder.

"Betty," said the boy, "why have you come down here?"

Her eyes opened for a second on the sky and rested there. They shut again.

"I am glad you have come. Melitta, our mother, however, will be mad. You don't mind that? No more do I.

—"My sister, won't you speak to me?

—"Sister, I mean us to be friends.

—"If I am killed in the war, you will be sorry.

—"I can see you are beautiful. I believe you kind.

—"I know you are wise.

—"Van, Florian, Ursula.

—"So you see, I know.

—"They told me you were our father's child by a farm-girl. Do you believe I am Melitta's son by Morice Amburton?

—"If you believe that of me. I shall believe it of you.

—"Why should we waste time?

—"We are the last children of Ashe.

—"I have always had what I wanted.

—"Who is this man with you?"

Serge answered hurriedly:

"My name is Sarantchoff. I am a painter, and Van's friend."

"You must be a very great friend to call her Vanna."

"Everyone calls her Van."

The girl was lying, stiff as death, her arms parted on the grass, white nails dug in the turf.

"Did you bring her down?"

"No. I came to keep her company. I've been ill."

The boy went on: "I see it is no good to-day, but I saw your mop, old Giroflée, from the valley's bottom.

—"If there was ever a time when you wanted me and I would not come to you, I am sorry for it.

—"I am coming to you again."

Serge looked at the boy. Valentine Ashe looked down at his sister, asking, without hint of supplication, while the girl lay with closed eyes.

The exquisite air stirred round them; he gave Serge a nod and went off.

As he turned, Van opened her eyes insolently. He did not stop, but at the sharp edge of the turf sat down and slid, working his hands and feet till he shot to the bottom.

She craned over. "The seat of his trousers will catch fire. He is my brother, sure enough. What do you say, Serge?"

"It seems like it. Unless they have coached him well."

"Morice? Melitta? Is it likely?"

At the bottom of the valley they saw him rubbing himself. He walked away down the valley trough; like a stepping butterfly, his whistle fluttering back.

CHAPTER 3

"TELL me all that you think of him, Serge."

A month before, Serge had been convinced of the insignificance of Valentine Ashe, and believed that the sight of him would correct Van's fantasies and bring her back to facts. Now the fact was there, it seemed likely to encourage them. Arrogant, sullen, stupid young man, he had hoped, and here was this attenuated exquisite. With his entrance, brother and sister would be running wild in a week, and anything might happen to Serge. One Van was enough, but duplicated.... Serge shook his previous creation. Nothing in the boy would fit it. Softly he abused him. Sophisticated, greedy child. He knew the type—heroics, a little wound, a little pacifism, side-whiskers, art-patronage. Punk.

"I don't know," he said. "He is rather charming."

Sitting on her heels, Van strained after the light motions.

"Look back, brother. Look back. Look back at me once." He did not look back.

"Feminine little toad." Then she laughed.

"I want my lunch," said Serge.

"It's not time for lunch."

He watched her, realised she was lovely and disliked it. She was exquisite, who had belonged to the bus and the street-market and the third floor back. She could not play the bohemian in those clothes, worn like her nudity, and enjoyed like a foretaste of Paradise. Violet wool and yellow, skirt pleated like knives, a jade tip to the lobe of each ear. Apple-pink and green. The boy smelt like a flower-walk at dusk.

Van was saying: "Kind boy, amusing boy. I like him. He'll wait because he must have us."

144

"That is what you said about the house, and, if you like him, why did you lie across the grass and refuse to speak?"

"It served my turn. Besides I remembered—he climbed on Melitta's knee and would not come and pick raspberries. And it has not been fair." She thought a little. "Come back and we'll go to the pub."

The hill rose up behind them. Last year's leaves were brisk under their feet. A blue sheet was spread between tree and tree, not picked out with flower heads, but a gauze, a ravishing décor.

"Here's wood-sorrel. Bite it. Those are lords and ladies."

Nonsense. He did not belong to this land. High wood or barrow, it was a pattern to him. She should understand that it was her show, not his. Damn that wood-sorrel! Hot stuff. He spat.

"Serge—I will do for you what we do sometimes. I will cut a turf-strip off the Rings, and we will stick our knives in it and you shall be seized of this country."

He was annoyed that he left his trade and its meditations for these local enthusiasms. He said nothing and hoped she would have some sense.

They came out of the wood. Her mouth crept into a smile. Her hand on his shoulder, she seemed taller.

"Never mind Serge. In Russia, here, or in London, it is the same sun."

"Of course."

"There is no reason why I should worry you."

"It is not that, Van. But one must be alone."

"Am I not alone?"

"You won't be for long, while that boy is about."

"Maybe. That is one way of looking at it."

In the afternoon she went out, and alone he began to enjoy himself. He sat on a wall and grouped and re-grouped enormous pigs, feeling his body on the edge of health again. His drawing had a quality he liked, he felt a little surprise and a great well-being. After a time, he slid off the wall, crossed the straw yard and turned down the lane. A quarter of a mile below, the lane joined the down-road. At the cross road, he climbed into the fork of a tree. A flock of sheep passed under him. He threw down a cigarette end to hear it fizzle in the wool.

They passed with their shepherd.

The situation was beaten down to work and quiet. Judy's image sank. He thought: Van you might come to me. Come to me quiet.

He heard the honk of a car, running slowly along the road from Amburton under the high downs. The bonnet crept up behind him. The wind-screen was marked with a red cross; in it were Judy and Peter Amburton. He drove, she showed him the road. Round the grass triangle, he backed the car.

At the moment she seemed to Serge remote, regarded as he would an unpleasant religion, or a theoretically poisonous antipodean fruit. They were going to the farm to ask for tea. Then he felt that he had no alternative but to run for his life and tell Van. He dropped from his branch. At the turn of the lane, he saw Judy, upright in the car, untying her veil. It blew out, verdigris strings in the air darkened by a grey cloud. He crept through a gap in the hedge and stalked the farmhouse from behind. Through the empty dairy he saw the open door. Judy stood in it. Now he had forgotten himself, transformed by utter loyalty to Van. These people must be kept away, not for his sake, but for Van's sake. Nothing now must come to hinder Van. There was such a thing as honour. He must stop them from getting at Van. The farmer's wife went through the house to speak to them, and he saw her look down the lane to see the driver of the car. Judy leaned on the door-post, her foot across the sill. Serge looked in at the kitchen window and beckoned the farmer's wife, who had retired thoughtfully.

"You must not let these people in," he said, his tongue throbbing and stammering.

"I told the young lady that we don't usually serve teas—that I'd go and see. Then she asked me if we had visitors. I didn't like to tell her a lie, so I didn't answer her. I thought

Miss Elizabeth might wish to be alone. It was Mr. Peter
Amburton in the car——"

"Tell her," said Serge——"anything. That you haven't got
any tea—that you have never heard of tea. Try and tell her
that there is no one here. They are both bad friends of Miss
Ashe's and of mine."

"Yes, I will, sir; but I'm afraid she'll have seen coats hanging inside that don't look like our things."

Damn these lonely countrysides! The woman went away,
but he could hear Judy's high voice:

"Oh, we know quite well whom you have staying here.
We only came to make sure." Pleased, vulgar malice. Then
he heard the car grunt and bump away down the grassy road.

Van sauntered in from the back, across the yard. When
Serge told her, she considered, scraping her caked shoes with
her stick.

"So she's come down here again," she said. "That's bad.
By herself, with Peter, at Amburton? It's hardly possible. If
she's done that, it means—what does it mean? That they're
married, perhaps. Anyway, it looks like funerals. Married or
not, they're after us."

"After us both?"

"After me, principally, down here. Come and have your
tea, Serge, there's cream."

He turned to the enjoyment of cream, and they ate till
they both felt sick. Then he wanted Van to say that she was
afraid of Judy, and she answered:

"I? No. What does it matter? I have other things to do."

Two days before, she had found him in bed with this girl.
Two days later, this was all she had to say. Arrogant little
brute. She was down here on her own concerns, and his position less of a consideration now. Very well. She would find
out whether she could despise Judy. Judy would shew her.
Very well. Then, for a second, his heart cleared, and he saw
Van, significant as the pigs had been significant, and a lovelier shape. If only she had not offered him too much. Starved
by Judy, she was too much. He would not confuse gratitude

and admiration with love. At the same time, it was joy to kiss her, so was the flashing movement that threw her onto his knees, and down into his arms. Poor kid: amusing little devil. And the monologue that pattered in his brain resumed its accompaniment. No good. She gave delightful kisses. Let her think that he wanted her.

For a moment, he wished that he had built up from their first intimacy, that he had not taken for an answer his refusal of her, a denial that he now recognised for a neurosis.

He had allowed himself to be spoilt. It saved a lot of trouble that he should be spoilt. He thought of the pigs and hugged Van close. Her body was the body of a four-limbed beast. Why should she want him to love her? She should know that she would be as well off without him. Women hang on to love's skirts because they need love more than men. But love goes, just the same. This is the whole truth of that section of erotics.

As an answer to his mind's whisper, she got up, vaguely kissed the top of his head, and left him. He stretched out his legs over the fire.

*   *   *   *   *

They are gone, they are gone,
The proud shall lie by the proud
Though we were bidden to speak—

"What's that you're whispering Van?"

"That's what Judy thinks of us in her heart. What she adores and persecutes in us."

"What is it?"

"Well, she is rather mistaken. So we won't discuss a mistake." She drank and filled her glass.

"They argue. She describes you to Peter, who can never understand. He is coarsely sceptical: he calls you a painting chap: she agrees softly. Let me go on." She emptied the common, green-bowled glass, and bit off a square of bread.

"In the world, Serge, the normal aim of its creatures, is towards birth or making things. Perhaps more are born at the end of old civilisations, but there are people whose impulse is abnormal, who are attracted to not-making and to spoiling; to the other side of life, to what we call death. What they are really after isn't clear. But these people happen. It's a terrible instinct, and man is afraid to talk about it.

"Consider the war. Have you known anyone who loves the war as Judy loves it? *Stoop then and wash.* She dips her tall, white body in the blood and rolls it in her mouth, and squeezes it out of her hair. She is a delicate woman of good family; I know nothing in her history to account for it.

"Am I clear? There is the war. There is Judy and her kind. The individual state bred the general state, that bred the catastrophe. Oh, I know tribal instincts and heroism, and love of a row, and coal and duty and obedience and too many people made the war; but this is different. Other people conduct a war, and suffer in it; get a man's job out of it or physical death. People like Judy live on the fact of it, and get spirit-nourishing food out of the ruin of so much life.

"There are no checks on such people now.

"*Childe Roland to the dark tower came.*

"That's an English poem.

"Now the dark tower is this: It is the vortex of death, or of life under a form absolutely inimical to man. When the human machine, and the soul—whatever that is—runs down. A room in a tower where a wheel spins against the course of the sun. Judy is your tower. She has brought you there. It was necessary to her life that you should come. *In our father's house are many mansions.*

"The qualities are mixed. The war is not all death, but she is purer than the war because she is tiny.

"She is a death-hound following us. I don't mean physical death. Money would cure your cough; the war's end free you. I am a girl, not to be taken for it. It is all in the mind. Peter may be another of her sort. He was a gloomy child. Wounds manufacture them. They whisper and they shriek their dreams. It is not that their wills are strong, though hers is. They are more driven than we are. But it is a fearful thing that they should have come down under Rings Hill."

"Why?"

"Because it is a place of evocation. Where the word is
made flesh. That's too poetical—I mean a place where the
shapes we make with our imagination find a body. Look at
them. They are saying: 'Why should that bitch and a shirker
from the Army come here and think themselves at ease? We
will have something waiting for them.' They do not know
what it is. They will not understand what they will do; but
they will work out a blind intention here more easily than in
another place."

"Your theory lets us in for old bogies."

"They were symbols for a correspondence in the mind of
those who believed in them. I am trying to explain Judy. If
you can do it better, tell me."

"I think that she is hysterical, and mad about men and
money and position."

"Is that all? But what do those things mean? My theory
fits the facts as I see them. When I have more I will revise it."

Serge was interested in this. He said: "If this is true we're
at a kind of vortex where extreme life—that's you—and extreme anti-life—if that is Judy, meet."

"Good for you, Serge. More drink." They touched glasses.
She laid her head on her arms stretched across the table, over
the plates. He kissed each finger-tip.

"Listen, Serge, they are talking." She drew up. "Do you
know I can follow them in the tapping of that thorn."

He looked, and through the window, in the last green glare
of evening, a naked bush beat the window with its twigs.

"The thorn is the Ashe tree. The ash is the tree of life.
Patter, patter, it's the were-wolves' night gallop. The tree will
work it for us. Oak, ash and thorn. Oaks are at Amburton.
Did they go out divining in the woods till they met old Morice
and frightened him?

"What do they do when they sleep together?"

"Ah, Serge, don't look like that. Was she ice over a core
of fire, or what? Those were fine sheets she had. I'm glad we

took them. We have made them into a bed we must sleep upon. We've got to sleep in Judy's bed. When the war came, I said—'Don't let me escape it, whatever it is.' I saw the cross of Ashe. But you, my Serge, you've had it both ways; war and its refusal. Judy strikes out blind. She smiles and shrugs. 'Aren't they soft?' she says of us, and then, 'They're soft because they're vicious.' And what she means, God knows. It is her conviction, you know, that we are lying and evil spirits.

"A dram more drink, Serge, and I'll get it."

She snatched the bottle, and turned it upside down over her glass: it fell sideways among the plates: a cold potato squashed against it. She drank.

—"I don't know what she is. I see what she has done. The delicate thing—that's you—she has dashed against a stone, has become raw. She draws her sharp nail across it. Nail. What did I say? A nail? Cold iron. That's it. She has kept us from each other, or the game would be ours, and hers the destruction. If you raise cold iron, things can't pass it. It's so delicate, the good impulse. She stopped it with a little knife, curved like the running stream the good people can't cross. *Things that scatter and flee*... What's the matter with you, Serge, you're green? Also, she has drawn your blood, and blood is the life. Mix it and you mix souls. A very silly ritual: she's opened a vein in you, a leak in the body of the world's peace. The infernal powers are loose, in a place of evocation.

—"That's a fish knife you've got. I mean cold iron.

—"Ready to dismount, Serge? We're at the tower. Must we be wicked to deserve it? That's one of her questions. Blow your horn. You're brave. I am Ashe of Rings. We shall not come back. We shall never have each other. We shall be different all our lives. Now we're for it. Blow your horn, I say. Under the door, time's running into eternity. Mount the Rings with me. Judy's past now, and I know this too—

"It was because of her you saw the bees. Remember, oh, remember them.

"Aren't a million bees better than one girl? The knife slits us up and opens a heart full of maggots, bred by her. We love the maggots breeding in our hearts. Not the bees."

She fell, face forward, on the table. He lifted her up and carried her up to her room. Carefully he put her to bed. She opened her eyes. Wonder and pity seized him.

He said: "Sleep, little one. Good night, little one. After all, perhaps we shall be able to make your life, not hers."

CHAPTER 4

SHE came into breakfast like a pale glass cup with a nasturtium in it. Serge ate his bacon. He did not remember what she had said; but that she had described, in horrible words, a most unpleasant secret which affected him; which seemed to mean that Judy was a female demon attached to some form of universal life. It was a lovely morning. He put the memory away. Let us wait its turn; like a drowned bird, the knowledge was there, ready to rise and corrupt the surface of his mind.

Then Van broke the silence and began to explain.

"I was not drunk last night. The wine made me pass through. I do that sometimes."

"You stared like you did when you lay on the hill across my knees on the grass."

"I shall lie out on the hill this morning and look at Rings."

They went out. She walked beside him, barefooted. Play acting the beggar maid. She told him to race her to a tree. She was behind him and ran round it seven times. She passed him on the wood path, with a side-springing dance-step. The skirts flew up over the polished knees. The red curls hung down, like a plunging calf's. She flung back her head, straining her neck. No sound. The rustle and click of sticks, the thud of her feet; but, from her throat, no sound. She snapped her fingers and stamped the earth, the pink heels rabbit-thudding. Her eyes were on the ground, or lifted up under the leaf-inlaid sky. She pirouetted and rolled in the blue flowers, snapping their stalks, their sap webbing her hands. She bounded up, and ran up the high wood to the barrow and plumped face down on a thyme patch, her soles in the air.

Serge followed her, dancing too, a step not remembered but felt, a race-evocation. He shot out his arms and legs, but at the wood's edge he looked round and began to walk. He saw her lying on her face, and ran up to her and tickled the soles raised like mushrooms on a stalk.

"I have danced, I have danced. I have set my stage."

He cuddled her.

A long way off on the turf, they heard a fast cantering horse. At the foot of the barrow they could not see what was coming. The sound deepened, coming up behind them fast. Panic seized them. The dead bird rose in the pool of Serge's mind and Van's words of the past night reeled off. They sat with their mouths open, stiff and separate from each other.

"It is Peter Amburton riding us down."

"Is Judy with him?"

"She was never across a horse."

Thump. Thump. Thump. Click.

"It's your brother."

She gave a vague cry and drew herself upright and laid her hands in her lap. Then she smiled, with cynical, tranquil assurance. A tall grey horse rose easily over their short horizon, a fly-away beauty with its rider. Valentine Ashe dismounted.

"Sister, sweet friend."

"Well?"

"May I sit down with you? Giselle will stand. Good day, Sarantchoff. Isn't that your name? If you are the kind of painter that draws people, may I say that you can draw me, the sooner the better, and get it over." Serge thought:

I am not that kind of painter. Unkind. Leave him to her. The boy passed his cigarette case. He had a long jade holder, like a green trumpet. Van said:

"Brother, may I suck?"

"Keep it, sister, it's for you."

She snatched it, then remembered her dignity, the feminine authority she must hold over the adolescent.

"I am not that sort of painter, Ashe," said Serge.

154

"Never mind." Van said: "Brother, you are like a wind-anemone, you are like a prawn."

"Sister, you are like a wallflower, you are like a violet."

"When I see you move, I see young leopards."

"And I see the Imperial Pekingese that is carried on a cushion under fans."

She ran her finger down his cheek. "Like the dry dew on a moth's wing—" They drew away, smiling. Her eyes swept the country, and stayed on the roofs of Rings.

Serge took a sketching block, and made notes of the dispersion of the long green hills. Brother and sister, their nature fluttered and rose like coupling butterflies. Their bodies followed side by side over the turf. Giselle trotted after them. He took off her bridle, and she nibbled among the shells. Valentine Ashe said:

"My little sister, where shall we go?"

"Where you like, we have time."

"They will kill me soon. I'm eighteen come Sunday."

"You are not going to be killed." She knew that. O tranquillity!

"Now that you have come, we will not leave each other again."

"Where shall we go?"

With the air of being a man, a state he had suddenly entered, he said:

"The first thing is to go down and settle ourselves at Rings. We shall find out what is happening, piece by piece, and then what we are to do."

"Melitta?"

"She is away in France with the Red Cross. She isn't expected back for three weeks—we have not got on lately."

"Go on," she said.

"What sort of a chap is your friend?"

"He has been very unhappy and ill. He is worth preserving for his painting."

"We'll preserve him then."

"When shall we go?"

155

"Now."

"I thought you were Amburton's son." She was thinking: Tell him that; it's quite safe too and a relief. She heard his answer. A splutter of laughter. Morice! He gave her tirade for tirade.

"Sister, I am thin, I am tall, but do I look like a manly man? I can dance thirty-two steps of the tango without stopping to think. I keep two tame ring-snakes and their family. I've been a vegetarian. I collect fans. I will not keep a bouncing chorus beauty in exchange for you. I shall vote Labour. I think conscientious objectors should have golden crowns."

"Then that is all right. How could I know what you would be like, or that you would want me—or him?"

"Your friends are my friends. We'll go down, and wake up the house together."

Van looked over the hills, and her contentment rose like a great pyramid of pride. She had given the earth a tiny shape that was pure. Three friends would go down the hill together. What were the snatchings of sexual love in comparison with this? She looked at her brother with hot eyes, and they kissed. They had walked a mile from the barrow that hid Serge. In a golden swirl the air washed them. Valentine said:

"You are too thin, sister."

"I shall get fat."

"I never saw a girl with such purple lids. You are the most beautiful girl I have ever seen."

"I never saw a boy like you." He hung his head.

"Where shall we go?"

"To Rings."

They hurried back. She longed for Serge, that she might lasso them both with the coil of her power.

Giselle trotted up. On the top of the barrow stood Serge, with the face of the dead. Chilled, she smiled at him.

"We are all three going down to Rings."

She put her arms round his neck. He gave a little snatch at her mouth.

—"Melitta's away."

"How will you manage with your bare feet?"

"Mount her," said Valentine.

"I can't sit on your saddle in this skirt."

"Sit sideways. I'll lead her. She's a bit fresh."

He passed the bridle through his arm. Serge mounted her. A squeeze on her warm foot. She rose again into her joy because of it. He settled her stirrup and walked beside her.

She lifted her eyes above the roofs and the hills and the sea. They went down the hill.

CHAPTER 5

CLAVEL came into the library to make up the fire. A small fire of apple-boughs, a silver flame mixed in a white smoke. They had eaten their tea. He had seen Van Ashe, in state, on a high chair. He had put the old footstool under her feet, and brought gold boots, from Melitta's room, lined with fur. He had seen her brother on his knees putting them on, his face overhanging its reflection in the floor. He remembered Anthony Ashe at the top of the seven stairs, and hanging once and for good over the well-pool.

He had spent several years alone, custodian of the house, its servant and its master. It was his amusement to turn his deep observation, his impersonal love into the formulae proper to his situation as butler. For that he was religious, subservient, a tyrant and patient with children. His enormous, pale body appeared like a djinn to the word of power. Melitta was afraid of him.

He put the furniture in place round the library fire, discreetly smiling, recalling his memories, memorising a new sight.

Here were the children of Ashe, warm round their hearth, a little fantastic, like peony-ghosts. He had waited a long time for this. A healthy hatred for the late Mrs. Ashe had been his previous food, but by now he had had enough of that. With great love and much quiet interest he served her children their tea, and, without being ordered, sent round to the farm for their clothes.

Van called Serge into her room to fasten her dress. Thick white silk, it hung straight as a shroud, covered with a black embroidery of flowers and birds. He marvelled. She must be

158

very sure to buy such things. She had a Spanish shawl, the colour of jade. He put on his old "frac". He had shaved and powdered his face. On his pale skin was a bloom, a lustre not of blood. His dark hair sprang back, his teeth glittered between the blood running in his lips.

Van had a back of satin. He rubbed his face between the shoulder-blades, where he had meant to pinch.

She sat at the head of the table, a peony in her hand repeated its colour in the curled threads of her hair. He listened to the sound of changing dishes, the feeble clatter of talk.

Both men were tired. Van folded herself into quiet. She beat her face with the peony-ball, a generous bunch of petals, a mother among flowers.

There were candles on the table, a sconce of eight. White crystal wax. Fastidious Valentine ate as fast as starved Serge.

"Is there any trouble here with food?"

"Officially, yes. But this is an occasion. Take some port to the servant's hall, Clavel, to drink Miss Elizabeth's health."

Candles have a more individual light than any flame but the flame of wood. A silent, innocent light shone above the roaring logs and fir-cones behind Serge's chair. A cone fell out. The flames mounted in a tiny leap.

Then they remembered that, outside, the moon would be blazing on the open chalk, on the distinct and tender outline of the hills. An old, white light, much older than the sun. Man burst out of the sun's yellow seed-ball; he cannot humanise the old moon's light. They thought they would walk out, all three together, across the hills. It occurred to Valentine for the first time, that he shared a general life; that, enclosing his beauties and opinions, there is a common warmth in man, a kind, sad, animal thing. He knew that he was lonely and that it was good to find that his sister and Serge and he were under the same yoke.

Clavel laid cherries and almonds on the table, and left the room for good.

The great painted curtain over the window was filled with air.

"Is the night clear?"

"Full moon."

"Let's go for a walk."

They went out. The light blazed from a compact, tranquil moon. A light that revealed a prick in the skin, but not one tint of the spectrum. Fifty yards across the park, they threw away their cigarettes to breathe the sweet air, flavoured with salt, a taste of almonds and curry. The footpaths ran under immense trees. The buds threw a shadow, an iron-dark pool.

They walked through them on to the open down.

They walked easily, pleased to be there, crying one to the other: "Good old earth. That's a Saint John's mushroom. Let it be. That's not poison. Bite. Bite. Look at the Rings. Count them. That means rain. What's a park to the sheep-walks? I don't want my shawl. I will roll. I will roll."

"Pick her up, Serge." The boy sang:

"Greensleeves is my joy,
Greensleeves is my delight,
Greensleeves is my heart of gold—

"An old song. Sing, Van, sing."

"I shall sing a proper song. *Iux helke ut tenon emon poti doma ton andra.*"

"Don't you dare be a witch. *Moon, moon, fascinating moon.*"

"Ring-a-ring of roses."

They all fell down.

"Ow, I've sat on a thistle."

"What's that bird?"

"That's a night-jar."

"Do you know what that is—Serge Fyodorvitch?" Valentine sang:

"Some of the time.
You love a girl on the stage
Some of the time
You love my sister,
One day you lost her,
But not for ever—"

"Heard him sing, Serge? Silver pencil on a glass slate. Your turn for a song. Then I shall sing the *Black Eyed Susans.*"

"Sister, you're vulgar. Serge why don't you refine her? Hunting a burr on your trousers? Who is that coming down the hill? Shepherd after late lambs? Old James Hobson lies a-mouldering in his grave, but his son goes marching on. Two people coming to cut us off, under the hill where I found you again. Two people. Sister, what is it?"

"It is Judy and Peter Amburton."

"That girl—what on earth are they doing here?"

"Come to meet us."

"Explain, you two. Why should they come? They are not amusing."

"Be quiet, Val. You haven't heard our story."

"You'd better tell it me."

"No time."

"Do you want us to turn back?"

"It is too late, I am afraid," said Serge. "They have seen us. In fact, I did not see them until they had seen us."

"How do you know that, Serge?—besides it's miles and miles to Amburton—"

"Quiet, my dears," said Van. "Walk straight up to them."

They put her in the middle and linked arms. She hurried them. A man and a woman with sticks ran across the grass on to their path. Valentine said:

"I can feel you're frightened of them. Must you meet them? I don't like that girl, and Peter's a scum—"

Van tucked his elbow into her side and forced him into step.

"Why don't they hail us?"

"You'll find out soon. Keep step."

No cover. Not a tree. Not a wind-tightened furze ball. Not a sheep. Too early for grasshoppers. A horned owl sailed up.

"The wise bird. It goes hunting."

A hundred yards ahead, a man and woman stood and waited for them. They walked up, three chins lifted, the pace

exact, two uncertain smiles, and Valentine with his mouth set.
"We could not see who it was," said Van. Serge thought:
That's her little, lying voice. Must women lie?
"We saw you some time ago," said Judy.
"We knew who it was," said Van. That was braver. That
was the girl for him. "What are you doing here?"
"Taking an evening walk."
"Twenty-four miles from here to Amburton and back,"
said Valentine. "A long way for an evening stroll."
Van said: "How did you manage it, Judy, in those shoes?"
Serge did not speak. There were wide bows on her feet's
arches, like a bridge. Peter Amburton said:
"I don't know what you people want to come here for. I
suppose you know, young Ashe, that your sister is a whore,
and this man a deserter."
Mangle the cub first, draw his blood for apéritif. She put
her arm round him.
"What d'you think of that, brother, for a start?"
Valentine Ashe stiffened.
" 'Tis pity…" Judy was murmuring. Peter Amburton thrust
in his shooting-stick, and sat on it. Judy moved about behind
his shoulder.
Van began to speak gently, piteously, trying to guard her
peace, not trusting to it.
"Judy and Peter, why do you torment us? Unless you killed
us, you could not have Rings. What would you do with Rings
if you had it? Isn't Amburton enough?"
"We want nothing of yours. It is enough for us to know
the sort of creatures you are."
"We are human beings—like yourselves."
I am humble. This is our trial. Sentence. Sentence. Quick.
Peter said:
"I went out to the war. There I saw what life is. When I
come back, I find you people still here."
"To reproach you, Peter?"
"We're going to clean you out of the world. That's what
the war's been for."

"That's one way of looking at it. But why did you let Judy teach you this?"

He glanced up at her. Judy said:

"He has given everything. You have given nothing. I suppose it is impossible for you to understand."

"Sister, sister—" Valentine was a little boy at her skirts again, whispering, "What is this? This is horrible."

"It is what we had not time to tell you. What I wanted you to know—what I wanted you to expect."

Judy said:

"Yes, you've got your brother into it now, to corrupt him. I tell you it would be better for you to kill yourselves now, straight away, on the grass."

This made Van giggle. She saw them at it, all in a row. Serge, hari-kari. Young boy, little sword. Me, swallow a pill.

Judy spoke.

"You might teach them a lesson, Peter. Make them understand that we mean—"

"Judy, stop!"

Serge dropped Van's arm, took a pace in front of them and said:

"Shut up. You're talking bloody rot. We've suffered as much as you, Amburton. You don't know what you're saying. You're repeating the phrases this woman taught you. You're under suggestion.

—"And what it all means is that you are both very unhappy."

"That's not all the truth of them, Serge!"

"It's enough to go on with." A faint joke, a whisper of sophrosynê.

"You have hunted us down to-night to insult two people, at least, who cannot be insulted. Your eyes can glitter their way into a madhouse before you can do us essential harm. Go and find your car, and go home. The peace you deny us go with you."

She felt his long hand in hers. Might be a beast's paw. How it pulsed. Then, Judy said:

"We thought it only fair to let Valentine know what people he was entertaining."

Adjourned. Adjourned. *To-morrow is another day.* Valentine was a tall young man again. He said:

"Your car is probably on the road over the hill. Or shall we send you home? My sister, and Mr. Sarantchoff are sleeping at Rings."

They turned their backs on them. Van stood behind Serge and followed him. It was a terrible thing to walk away.

Remember Lot's wife.

Under the stress she took their arms, and placed her hands in theirs. They whispered.

"My dears."

"Van, what were they?"

"Something very bad. Serge knows."

"Is it all right? Explain."

Van cried:

"*Love and man's unconquerable mind.* Say it over to yourself. Say it. Say it. You will evoke it. We did to-night. Serge did. We can do it again? We shall need to."

"I suppose we can," said Serge.

"We shall save ourselves. We shall save you."

"If we want to, we may."

"If we save ourselves, we save the world, and its peoples. Don't you know we bear up the pillars of it?"

The boy's hand tightened. Serge looked into the dark trees.

"You turned them, Serge, it was you who did the trick."

"We did it together, each of us," he said.

The boy cried: "We shall do it again. Every time we do it, the world comes more into peace. I understand everything now."

"If you like to think of it like that, you can," said Serge.

He led them into the house.

CHAPTER 6

R EBORN in the morning, they had the shame of youth
for their excesses of the night before. In the decent morning light, it seemed that they had been making too much of
a fuss.

At breakfast, Valentine poured tea into his saucer, and
drew it through his teeth.

"We did go it last night," he said.

"Yes, we did," said Van: "And, Serge, I do not see what
else we could have done. I mean those people are physically
dangerous. If we don't want to fight them, we have to frighten
them."

"It was a lofty altitude you took, Sarantchoff."

"Call it self-preservation. We want to live too."

"I expect they thought it bluff."

"So it was."

"Sister, if I get the gramophone, will you try some steps?"

"Yes. And you, Serge?"

"I'm rather exhausted, if you don't mind."

"Look here, Sis, you'll tell me what happened before, I
want to understand. We've got to talk about it."

"Yes, but let it come. O brother, the art of life is to let
things come."

Clavel found them in the library, dancing.

"Excuse me, Miss Elizabeth, but you have not forgotten
that you have a great deal to do?"

"You mean, Clavel?"

"You have not visited every place, Miss, yet. The people
on the estate have not seen you. You have not been over the
house. You have not been down to the sea. It has all got to be

165

done, Miss Elizabeth. It has to be cleared away before—"

"Before, yes. Before I go onto the Rings. I know." She screwed up her face. "It is all right, Clavel. I know it's a ceremony. Give me a little time."

"There may be very little time, Miss Elizabeth. But everything is ready."

"I am ready too. Only my eyes are getting accustomed to this light."

"Yes, yes, yes," Valentine was saying. "I'd forgotten. There is no time." She felt the panic that was all over the earth; and stood quite still, passing the fear out of her body by means of an image in her mind.

"There will be time enough."

The boy seemed to protest; but Clavel was satisfied.

She asked her brother.

"When will Melitta come back?"

"In three weeks."

"Where is she?"

"She is with a canteen in France. What's a war without Melitta? It might stop."

"We reckon without those two—Judy and Peter."

"Leave them to your Serge. What did you say last night? *Love and man's indomitable mind?*"

"Unconquerable."

"Thanks. Queer thing, memory."

"Don't forget."

"Not I."

On the terrace, in the sun, Serge watched the creeping plants between the stones, and decided that his confidence was in the mind.

He would not recognise what pure reason could not meet. Mystical vision compromises a man and in no social sense. Last night the mouse had fallen out of Judy's womb, the witch's nails out of his flesh. He felt his nose. A skin had peeled off. It ached when he pressed. He saw on the wall a funny little plant with a red tendril, like a centipede. *Better loved ye cannot be.* Go away, vile song. He squeezed the words out, as Van had squeezed her fear, her subjection to time.

Of course he could not love her. Judy had stopped that. He heard high voices from the library. *Keep a lot of ducks and geese an' neverything.* Noisy brats; and Van like a duck slid into a glass pond. He had liked her better before.

Last night he had acted on instinct. Judy and Peter had seemed pitiful. He had pitied them and frightened them. Done the right thing. Had it value, correspondence in Van's sense?

The brother and sister had believed in him, and followed his lead. Van had leapt at it, and the boy pondered. To-day, he didn't believe a word of what he had said. A bitch for the asking, and he'd have her again. That was it. He wanted her. Amburton? He must be jealous of him, so how could he judge him? Van and Valentine would force him now. How was he, without conviction, to keep the pace? No necessity; but they would cry if he deserted them. Say he had not played fair. That three loyalties were better than two. Problematical thing to say and rather mean. The little worm in his mind burrowed into a knot and curled up. He noticed the spirited sight of broken water, running in and out of the cove. Get it down to realistic fact. So that painting may be unrealistic and abstract. He began to feel well again, health stirring in his veins. He went in.

"Ashe, is there anything to ride?"

"If you understand horses, take Giselle."

Serge was pleased.

Brother and sister ran through the incidents of the past years. He told her that, on the lawn, among the stones where there had been a tower, an adder had bred. Melitta had opened the place in a hunt for treasure, had cut the turf and the hanging bush, flung out rubble and stones, and found nothing there. She had put the stones back again, and re-planted the top with a garden heath. It had run wild. Then the adder had appeared. Valentine had seen the snaklings among the purple bushes. The turf that had been cut out had been let into the lawn for a patch. It had neither merged

nor increased, but had grown long, a blue eye on the green
sods. He shewed Van the place, and she ran down and rubbed
her face on it. Returning to the house, he went on:

"They have moved the herm in the panel garden."

"Why?"

"Because, when the creepers were cut, his figure was too
distinct."

She did not quite remember how she had lain underneath
him in the first shock of conscious laughter. Melitta's score
stood one higher.

"Who has our father's room up the seven stairs?"

"No one. It is locked. I shall use it, if I come back."

Detail after detail, but nothing significant; nothing to show
from which quarter the wind would blow when it came. But
the adder was not disturbed, and had one bite to its credit.
That was pleasant.

A shepherd had died on the high downs in March, 1915.
The inside of his wheeled shed was covered with stylistic figures of Melitta. Valentine, at the time, had been distressed.
Morice Amburton, to propitiate his step-son, had shot a honey-
buzzard and had it stuffed; and had been taught to wish that
he had left it alone.

The Rings were quite well. He was discouraged from going there, but had made it a point of ritual to do so. But not at
the four cardinal points of the year. "I waited for you, my sister."

There had been a great night when Melitta had tried to
burn the winnow-corb in which Van had been christened.
Clavel had walked in, and snatched it off the fire. A Meleager
business. The basket was a bit singed, but intact. Now it was
back again in the gallery cupboard. You could see it through
a hole in the panel of the door.

"Nasty old basket," Melitta had said. "Let's burn it."

She had sent her son up to the gallery to fetch it, in the
dark. One candle, and he not really on terms with the place.
He felt that at the time, but not now. Van's name had not
been mentioned. He had never been able to make out Peter
Amburton.

"He used to be a decent kid; if I hadn't seen so much of him, I might have been like him. Van, what is your theory about the Rings?"

"How far have you got?"

"Our father thought of them as lovely ladies; bacchantes, oreads, dryads; or so I take it."

"That is how they thought in the 'nineties. It is no good for us."

"No. Well, then?"

"I don't know. By the living soul in us all, I don't know. I feel power, movement, a pattern. It goes and comes—my being able to think about it, I mean. No one can think about such things all the time. It is magic, whatever magic is; and magic is not a métier."

"Our father got out of it by making myths?"

"We can't. All the same, I know when that place of earthworks and trees, a place to picnic in and archeologise about, turns into a place of more than animal life, real by itself, without any reference to us. And there I stop; and when I see further, I can't tell it. There aren't any words, or shapes, or sounds, or gestures to tell it by—not directly."

"Art?" said Valentine.

"Art's there to be art, not patently to tell secrets about something else. The only sure thing is that sometimes we do see; that is we're servants of the caprice of Rings."

"And that is that," said Valentine—"but I wish I knew more about our cousin Peter. Something's happened to him. It began when he brought that girl Judy down to stay at Amburton. It put the lid on. Or took it off. I was uncomfortable all the time she was about the house. Imagine a grown-up flapper who pretends to want to play marbles with you. I took her for walks. Now and then she dropped the correct young woman of the world."

"Made love to you, chéri?"

"No. Let you look into her mind, like a queer, unpleasant room, half bedroom, full of stale bits of clothes and animals and a window that looked out on a bog. Then she was sad

too, sometimes, like a hopeless, tired beast. When she went
away, I found a lot of questions flying about my head. Why
don't I know my sister? I haven't known many women. That
girl is her friend. Is she like that girl? So, I had to find you.
Now for each question that is answered, a fresh one drops
out, like eggs out of a hen."

"Mother has done her best."

"You know I'm fond of her."

"Very right of you. You're her son. She is a disappointed
woman. How did she agree with Judy?"

"They seemed to like one another. They were always saying, 'I do so agree with you.' About the war and clothes and
hunting. She was so careful, I thought she must be a tart in
disguise. She said that her people had a place in Lancashire
which they sold."

"So they had."

"*By the pricking of my thumbs.* And so there did. Tell me how
you met Serge, and what happened to you in Town."

She told him, from the time when she had left Oxford to
sit before her boarding-house bedroom glass and observe her
meagre, milk-white nudity; and how the world had dealt with
her, coarsely, but not too dishonestly. Twice she had been
caught up in the terror of the world, and almost destroyed by
it. First in the war; and within that, burning wheel within
burning wheel, in the anguish of the Irish rebellion. While
these were breaking her heart, she had met Judy; and learned
that the passion in great events could be repeated, in miniature, in persons. Pity for the girl had consumed her; until disgust had strangled pity, and struck a formula. She tried to tell
the boy what she had told Serge that night at the farm. He
followed her, more moved than Serge had been, and with
greater understanding.

Then he asked:

"Where does Serge come into this?"

She told him.

"He's had it all and more. I tell you, Valentine, he was no
more than a fluttering ghost when I—"

"Let him love you. Never mind my innocence."

"We are not lovers in that sense. Or in any. I took what she left, and there's not much of it."

"How long had he known her?"

"Two years. If it had not been for his painting, he'd have died."

"Poor devil, he looks intelligent. And you, sister?"

"When the world got too much, I found, as he found, that I had life in my mind. And there was fun in the dressing-room and rags at night. I danced, oh, I danced.

"—The arts don't fail you, nor things to do with your body and your head together, nor learning, nor contemplation. The rest of life is to make the best of a bad business. The business is not permanent. When it is love, the business is sometimes an excellent best.

"—I've lost a lot to find that out, and cried a bath full of tears. Brother, if it makes you cry—"

"I am crying for myself."

CHAPTER 7

THE years sliding by had polished Melitta and the country townswoman had become a great lady. For fears, distastes, uncertainties, were replaced ambitions, bitterness, formulae. With it all, she was a sad woman, angry yet speculative over the forms of life that were beyond her.

Her impatience raced on her journey back from France. She was a powerful woman; on a porterless station, she carried a heavy dressing-case out of Charing Cross, pinning herself down to the details of travel. Find a taxi. Oh, she was mad to be home! Say Waterloo. Eat there. Never mind the disgusting food. Ask about your train. Remember the refreshment-room clock is five minutes fast. How Anthony hated missing a train. Let the crowd see who you are. Hold a white ticket at the barrier. Then there's nothing can prevent your getting back. Thus she had made her way from Boulogne.

Peter and Judy had wired to her. At the information, she had turned, imagining herself wounded, and charged home from the war's only half-personal occupation.

Back to the deep life of personalities, a blood film behind the eyes. The machinery of war ground on behind her diminishing back. Solitary, immaculate bodies would quiver at her approach.

She flung her dressing-case onto the rack; her furs slipped off, her great arms sank. The train jerked. She staggered, her knees touching the blue-padded seat.

The purple seas that swell and roll over are a similitude for bodies like Melitta Ashe. She lay back, a wine-coloured sweater of curled wool tight over her breast and moving with

172

it; two rings of gold on her hand. She took off her hat and her coarse veil. Her skin was heavy, her energy laboured. She let go of her possessions.

A stranger sat down in the opposite seat. She moved and closed her large, sparkling eyes. The train crept out of the station as though it were afraid of her.

She had left Amburton and Rings to serve her country. While she was away, this had happened. Through a slit in her armour the poisoned needle had run in. She was like a great whale harpooned, the will behind the shaft, the will of her own child, stabbing her into madness.

A woman of will and energy were her arrangements not to be final? Was she to see the gutter and the chorus capering in her house?

"*Think you should know your daughter at Rings with Valentine and young man.*"

The worst was in the penultimate. The unknown, and a young man. Like the third person of the Trinity. No rest for her at her journey's end. The train was rocking fast, and the trees flashed by.

All that I have done, I have done for the best.

A little dark spot remained in her mind over Van. I could have been kinder to her. Yes. I have made mistakes. We all learn. What do I mean to do? What have they counted on? My Saviour, how did this ever come to be? It was quite simple. She was unmanageable. Hopelessly wild. Suspicious. Some-one poisoned her mind. I had my little son. I had my duty to Morice. My own son was a duck of a baby. Then there was that thin, plain child. Unwholesome beauty. Not good style. Soulful, pert miss—I know I'm an ignorant woman, but I could have taught her a thing or two...

...Now if we had not been mother and daughter, we might have got on. I might have admired. She would have toler-ated. Why does God allow this?... I shall find them against me in my own house. They can say what they like. I mean to have respect. Until Valentine comes of age. If Valentine lives to come of age.

She shook her head. A huge tear burst out under her lid.

Oh, my son, it may be natural for you to follow your father and not your mother. But my own daughter. She should have taken my part. I've never had anyone to take my part. It wasn't fair. Their heathen gods did what they wanted them to do. Impious to believe that. God forgive me.

I will be mistress in my own house.

They can go packing to town by the night train. She wasn't pleased with the bureau I gave her when she was fifteen. It was good enough for a school-girl.

There are things I'm sorry about—things I shouldn't have said. The day I found her in the loft with Morice. It was her all over to mind my temper so much. I told her I was sorry, but the servants might gossip, and it was my duty to protect her, and she didn't believe me. I hurt her, I suppose, and she'd no sense. An awful pride she had, never satsified with a simple way of looking at things. Amusing things she said sometimes, but she meant them....

And whether they like it or not, I'm their mother.

It's a pity I'm so tired.

She measured her slackened energy, her charge home pulled up into a sad walk. No bite but bark for the wicked cubs.

Adorable, detestable Vanna Elizabeth Ashe. Secret wisdom laughing in its sleeve. Weeping there too.... Sceptic, infidel, unchaste. She's had an interesting life. I should like to hear her talk about it.

'Tis pity—Dreadful old play. Be quiet. *Lest haply ye be found to have fought against God.* Oh, I don't know what I ought to think.

She recognised her impetus gone, whistled it with a smile.

Perhaps she had been rash to come back. Her easy powerful years forbade her to consider that. She thought: You accept or rid yourself. They will not have you. She remembered the humiliations each remembered. Her dulled anger was whipped. She thought of her son. He is my little boy, he loves me. She shan't have him....

Disarm him first. Her forces began to return to her. She brooded down in her corner seat, as a wide, malicious hen might sink upon a tiny hawk.

The restaurant-car tea revived her. Van was down with a young man at Rings. Young man? In God's name, what sort of young man?

She may have married him. Maidens do that. This wire may mean anything. Peter had telegraphed. Why had not Peter's telegram said more? He had not met Van since they were children. It was that girl Juliet who had sent it, of course. Her mind contracted round a dislike. Ambitious slut. Dangerous girl. She might do for Amburton. Someone would have to marry Peter. What were her children doing at Rings? They are my children. I must go and see what my children are doing. I must hear what Juliet has to say.

There was no illusion as to the alliance in her mind.

At this point of meditation, she reached the journey's end.

The train crept in and lay down between the sheds, and barred the short cut to the road. She could not see the old cab, huddled away from the sea wind, under a wall. There would be no car. She must find a cab. The cedar-green block of her dressing-case scraped the asphalt, ridged, waxed skin on sand crystals, opening thin wounds.

The train did not move. A strange child-porter stared at her, and picked it up.

"You must find me a cab."

"'Tain't easy."

She climbed over the bridge. Vile, blood-pink paint. Lifted up into the wind. Uneasy night sea—*I will lift up mine eyes unto the hills.* They ached.

"I am Lady Amburton. You must find me a cab."

He took no notice. At the bottom of the steps, she saw an old man scramble onto his box, and there was more abominable vehicular sound.

She looked down the road. Not a light on the pale road to the downs. Not a light all the way to Rings. The end of the day and a cold sea-wind. A finger of winter laid on spring's mouth. Dark fir-trees on the road to Rings. Night coming fast. A bank of torn cloud rising. A star upside down in a puddle. A full ditch gurgling along the hedge to Rings.

Iron wheels grinding in the mud, the smell of old leather. She sat upright, very sick.

There was no one but Clavel left in the world who remembered that Anthony Ashe had returned, twenty-five years before, along that road, quietly, in a cab.

Clavel received her.

"We did not know what train to expect, my lady."

"My telegram must have miscarried."

But she had not wired. Had Peter told them she was coming? She was dog-weary, and the house bleak as a rock. A very old rock of sacrifice: an altar, almost a temple: not a house: no lights: no gold fires in its eyes. Trees tossing in the park, uneasy gestures answering the sea.

Clavel was on the children's side. She should have dismissed him when she turned out Elizabeth. Mrs. Beeton's Book of Household Management. *How to give the butler notice.* Why had she not done that? Now she was over the threshold, the damp rising from the flags.

"Where are they? It is long past eight."

"Miss Elizabeth, Master Valentine and the Russian gentleman, Mr. Sarantchoff, are gone up to the Rings, my lady. They put off dinner till nine, as they did not know what time you might arrive."

"I do not know what led them to expect me."

"They informed me that we might expect you, my lady."

"Why did they go to the Rings?" (What am I talking to him for?)

"They made picnic of it, my lady. They wished to go for lunch, but the rain was heavy. It lifted at five o'clock. Miss Elizabeth thought it time to go."

"The hall fire should have been lit. You know that I dislike sitting in the library."

"There is very little coal, my lady, and the new logs are only just dry."

A strange, stout girl, creeping with shyness, crossed the hall and knelt before the chimney-piece. Huge stones, hung low, and climbing up the wall. In the steel basket, the paper smoked. A cold blue flame shot out of it. A maid came in with candles. Outside it was night.

"The carbide has been on order for a month, my lady."

The war again! She turned away, and the servants left her. Clavel went in at his pantry door, in a green-washed passage, lit by a single candle, like a corridor under the sea.

The high roof of the hall was an open vial, pouring down mist. It fell like a gauze about Melitta, from the invisible hollow of the roof. She sat by the thin fire, which was like a bouquet of white flowers. White candles in silver sticks. High walls and a stair to a gallery. She thought: It is a dark night, and there are one or two stars. They will be back at any moment. It is half-past eight. Then she heard three voices.

Clavel knew. All these years she had forgotten that. The house laughed at her, the house had been kind. Since then it had not laughed once or been kind. Up the wide stairway, its daimon was standing to draw the children in, to wrap them in colourless nimbi, to pour out vapour for their aureoles. Three children at the stair-head, like God's choir. Poor me.

The fire was biting on the wood. Don't face them like this. Who told them I was coming? She yawned. Outside the wind broke against the house.

What were the servants thinking of to leave no light on the gallery wall? She threw her fur coat over her arm, grasped a candlestick and started. Half-way up she heard voices. She ran up and along the gallery, turned and reached her room and shut the door. In her room, the glass and gold blazed; her dressing-table had turned altar, its mirror a sun-disk. With rising heart, she marched into its light.

Clavel said:

"Yes, Miss Vanna. And she was surprised to be expected."

"And we even got the train right."

"What do we do now?" said Serge.

"Dinner in half an hour. Dress, you fools. Shave. Powder your faces. Be exotic. Be damned. Grow side-whiskers. Be anything you like. But be chic."

CHAPTER 8

MELITTA looked at her sagged neck in the mirror. Hand some still, like a fine hound. In another room, young beauty was skipping into its scandalous, bright clothes.

She'd a hole in her stocking,
And eyes that were mocking.

Melitta thought: Poor old Morice. Poor old me. What do they care about us? Or about the chance teams of young and old, which are as hard pulling for the old as for the young? She dragged herself upright, a heavy gown clinging to her back, pricked bags of skin under the eyes, drenched with loose powder-dust. She fought for time against the dinner gong. In her room she imagined her daughter, pulling on and off her stockings, serenely, like a witch.

The men dressed, the noise of Rings hummed in their skulls.

They struggled through white shirts, and came out at the necks, clown-faced through the crackling linen; their minds hurrying ahead of their dressing, in the world of the next event, which is like a mirror flashed and withdrawn.

Van pulled on her dress, delicately, from the feet up; and on her skin, moist with wind, laid a little powder and a little scent.

Melitta came down first and sat in the hall. Nothing could give her the shape of youth, but she had the shape of power. Like a crescent moon, the children came to the stair-head, first Van; Serge and Valentine carrying candles behind her.

"Are we late, Mother? Are you there? I can't see you. The candles carry such a little way."

Melitta thought: Step by step they are coming down the stair. Rise and go to them. Until they are close to you, they will be above your head. She rose stiffly, gathering her train.

"I am very pleased to see you here. You did not let me know that you were coming."

"You did not let us know when to expect you back. But we guessed it right. This is Serge Sarantchoff."

Serge kissed her hand.

There was a faint rubbing on the gong. That was Clavel, leaning on the helm.

"Let us go in. I'm sure we want our dinners."

Serge gave her his arm. Led across the hall, she heard the light, broken steps that followed her. She thought: Like the noise of a brook under a hedge. Patter, tumble, break. They are changelings, of course, mushroom babies, spawn out of the Rings. Moon babies rolled down the hill into her candle. Some dinner would do her good. A very attentive young man, with wolf's eyes. Three hungry children, and Betty beating the air as she used to do with her spoon. Valentine copying her. What would the servants think?

Clavel was a father to Betty. He looks like Anthony tonight.

"Do you drink milk, Elizabeth?"

"Yes. We both do, because of Serge. His lungs need it. He does not like it, so we keep him company."

"It is very scarce now."

"The cows are giving fair milk, aren't they?"

"Has your friend been ill?"

"Very ill. But he is getting better here. That's why I brought him."

"So long as the milk is not wasted. I am very glad for you to have it."

Then she sighed, as she saw that they could not be at ease, and she could not permit them to be at ease. They were here on business of their own, and she was in the way, to be propitiated, and, if possible, tamed.

Serge saw her great shoulders rise in a sigh and sink. He

pitied her, and gave her his whole attention, while the brother and sister chattered together over their plates. Serge made her speak of the crossing from France, the halts, the officials, the food, the want of food, the porters, the taxis, the officers. He adjusted its incidents until it was shaped into a female Odyssey. She saw that he was managing her, but he re-evoked the adventures that had amused her. He was a man. She acquiesced.

But, when she had gone up to bed, they began to quarrel together, with the exasperated nerves of the nursery at the end of a wet day. Serge was the imperfect philosopher, Valentine his mother's son, Van a scold.

"Told us not to sit up long because it keeps Clavel about. It doesn't."

"Asked us when the war would finish, and was surprised when I said never."

"Played up to her, didn't you, Serge?"

"I don't see what you're crying about. She was quite decent."

"Wait. In the morning she will come down snapping her teeth."

"It is difficult for her."

"It is meant to be. I hate this house. I can only remember how unhappy I have been here."

It roofed them, a dark coop and no hen in it, a coop that might become a prison. A nursery, swollen till it filled the house. Their frail command over their lives unchallenged, but non-existent. The house would not help. In London they had at least a room each. Go back.

Clock after clock struck eleven.

Van said:

"I hate this place. She's poisoned it."

"Clear out of it then," said Serge. "I tell you it will be your nursery until you master it."

"It is not your business, Serge."

"My dear chap, it is easier said than done."

"He means," said Van, "that we are not worthy of it.

181

The house is ashamed of us. He won't explain. He has gone away yawning."

Serge looked back over his shoulder.

"I should go to bed. You forget where we have been this afternoon."

"What did you think of it?"

"I noticed an uproar of wind and a lot of wet undergrowth. But if this place is an annexe of that, what you want will come from up there. Not from down here. And don't worry for miracles. Good night."

He walked into the shadow, into the dark that hid his face, into the solitude wherein he could lick his wounds till morning. Nor more light till next day. Thank God for the hiding-place of the dark.

They followed him.

In Van's room, the candles glittered. She picked off a shroud and rubbed the sticks in her palms. Grey wax to rub the skin pink. She moved about wretchedly. There seemed to be no meaning left in anything they had seen, except that in her mother's room was sleeping an almost infernal power. They were back again in the formulas of childhood; escapade, defiance, fear; forgetting what they had come for, teased out of thought. She sat on her bed, staring till the thoughts came.

Melitta's afraid of the Rings. Remember that, Van Ashe. You're not. They won't feed her, but they're milky for you. Pretty Valentine. I must remember the things that feed me. I would like to say my prayers.

What should I pray?

To remember that we are all children of one father. That's all right. But I do not want to think that Mother is.

I wish I had not come.

We're miserable little kids. She's playing with us. Give her a day, and she'll rub her smeary finger along our good. She's right with her sentimental venom that winds up our good. She'll have her laugh in the end; once or twice I've seen her do that. This is what Serge has seen; I understand him now.

There are our catch-phrases and her power. The Good, the Beautiful, and the True. Poor Serge. Poor Serge. *Hand God back the ticket.* Wish I'd the pluck.

She tried to remember old lovers, old victories, good things she had done. They did not seem to matter. Melitta had sucked the life out of them. They were hardly clean now.

Mothers ought not to be like that; not with a war on. They should be proper mothers who comfort their children. But she'd have us dead; me really dead, and Valentine alive, but dead to his job, whatever his job is.

And she's not a bad sort, but the bad power uses her. She doesn't know it; but Judy knows and uses her. It's a tight knot in hell for us to cut. The good daimon won't answer me any more. I can't evoke. I can't say my prayers. Try a few names. Sophocles: Synge: Cézanne. A rotten lot; and rotten they are in the world whose creation she is. Suppose I fall on the bed now and sleep. Sleep as I did when I was growing up, ignoble, afraid sleep—Hunt in your dreams, Van Ashe. Good old Freud!

If one of us had the strength of mind to go into her room and kill her, then I should forgive her, and that would be ease of mind. Oh dear, working up to classical tragedy point. We would.

Then she decided that a walk would shake the horror and the nonsense out of her; and, like a schoolgirl, afraid of being caught, blew out her candles and crept downstairs.

CHAPTER 9

UNDER the old stairs there hung her school cloak with its hood, and a belted rag that had been Valentine's. She buckled it tight, and stepped out of the pantry window into a border of soft earth, light as a down bed. She stood in it, eased, and the pressed up earth filling her shoes. She dragged herself out. She thought: You've got the boy. He's more than you deserve and will be more than you bargain for. You've got Serge. You may go to bed with him yet. I don't feel like that just now.

You came back to let a god into this house. For a god, you've got intrigue and subjection. The house, the great adorable house, is an ugly schoolyard. Your blood bubbles with little disgraces. This is Melitta's answer to Ashe of Rings. And all that has happened is this; that I'm letting a suspicious, embarrassed old woman frighten me.

I shan't win because the world belongs to her. *They that are of the flesh*. Prig! I'm in a cul-de-sac, and I see the end of it and it's a wall hung with nailed-up bodies. One of them is Serge's, and there's room for mine. All this because I have a mother, and that is the burden we all share.

One should be allowed to choose one's burden. She fell over a wheelbarrow, rolled over and lay on the wet gravel, crying and sick.

I dare not look into Serge's mind. He is sick. We're all sick. We do not know how sick we are. I've left him alone. I did his body good. I've left his mind. He sent me away. I told him the truth. Whoever told you to come bothering him with the truth?

A roller of warm air poured up from the sea and curled

over her, where she was still lying, in the night-rustling garden. She turned on her back, and her head struck a turf border. A worm slipped under the arch of her neck, a red tube for the excretion of earth, tolerable as a machine. But it was not a machine, and further distressed her. A white bubble, the moon sprang out and fell back into a cloud. Rings was a stage, set with all the properties of tragic mystery, and no play. Van got up. Her stocking stuck to her raw skin. It was a straight line to the Rings. Half-an-hour's tramp and back again. She thought: Let yourself go. Don't be afraid. This place is true; and the truth never hurt anyone. Bird of life, drop out of the heavens, fly to my lips. She went through the kitchen garden and out by the old door, where, eighteen years before, Melitta and her lover had stood and been given a key. Outside she thought she saw an old man, and then that it was a wild apple tree. A sheep dog barked. She felt the earth, a mosaic of large pieces, opening, relocking, carrying her. Trees ran up and down. The ground was like a moving staircase. She walked fast, her body obeying her, without reference to her distorted perception. The light, firm, elegant step carried her up the hill.

There were people on the Rings. Damn that moon. It dipped. Her shoes clicked on the flints. The ground drew together and stood still. There were two people on the Rings. Not poachers. One was a woman. Some of its fearful stories played visibly at last? She doubled to it and ran, until, with her blood mounting, she reached the foot of the outer ring. Two people came out of the wood. From the wall of the outer ring, they looked down on her, thirty feet above her head. They disappeared. She clawed her way up the wet chalk steps, with broken finger-tips. It was very odd. She stood up leisurely, sucking her hands. They were on the next ring. She ran down the fosse. Up again. They were on the third bank at the edge of the wood.

"Hi! there. What are you doing on the Rings at night, Judy and Peter Amburton?" They answered:

"Here she comes."

She waited an instant, her mind working, as usual, to a double measure. It was not possible. It was most surprising. It was fantastic that they should be there, on a wet night in spring. What about Judy's reputation? What a tale to tell Melitta. And then, instantaneous with this, broken and low-toned, the terror that they should be there. They have drawn me out. They have wound up a charm. On the Rings we meet in the dark night. *Must we be wicked to deserve such pain?* Think yourself inside a ring of pure light.

They were standing by the grove now. The grove was squat, like a dark tower. She ran to the dew pond and up the barrow beside it.

"Come out, you two!"

The moon slid under a cloud. They were like dwarfs in the immense grey night. She had walked straight into them. Her own place had betrayed her. Fear rose out of the barrow and climbed up her.

Judy came running and shouted at Van.

"We've found out all about your filthy, mystery-mongering place. It drinks blood. Give it a drink, and it works. We've given it a drink." Peter came up behind her. He said: "You might call it drunk." She thought:

I must speak to them, but my throat is like a little whistle. Lovely Rings. Dancing place. Which one of you has betrayed me?

"We've given it Peter's dog. There's lots of blood in an Airedale."

A large Airedale. Lots of blood. There would be. Beastly to drag a decent dog into this.

"You are fools to have come here."

And they said:

"Ask and it shall be given you. That's the stuff."

"You pair of maniacs, come off it!"

The wolves have galloped a long way since the night we turned them. Shall I run away? Faster than Judy. Not Peter. She pressed her palms down her body to her knees, stroking out fear. The ancient sanctity, the moon, appeared. An enor-

mous cloud slid past. The wood lost its solidity, and was a
tower with a thousand doors. Peter and Judy were moving out.
She was playing king of the castle over a pair of wolves. She
said from the top of the barrow: "Why do you hate me so?"
"Because you're rotten with your ideas."
"What do you want with me, now I am here?"
"You'll find out. You can get a lot out of this place if you
give it a drink."
Was this death? One tightened oneself to meet it like any
other event. A relief to find it one of life's series, important,
but substantially the same. Are they going to kill me? Not if I
can help it. They're only mad; but madness is madness. Fear
began to pull again at her knees.
"I know more about magic than you," she tried. "I'm on
a circle. You can't touch me." (Maybe they'll believe that.)
Peter lurched forward. Judy pulled him back. They
whispered. She thought: How long till morning? Very long.
Sanctuary of my race, have you nothing for me?
"It is one thing to kill in war," she cried again. "It is slightly
worse to kill me here. If you take my blood, it won't give you
power for ever, and it will be very difficult to explain the
corpse. The Rings will betray you, you amateur invocators!"
We are like rival magicians. Ridiculous life! Don't go away,
moon, I want light.
A stoat squeaked under a blackberry bush—the night life
of the earth, running its course. Judy's frock swung with her
restless movements.
They may be more afraid of you than you are of them.
Fly into the wood.
"I am going to the place itself." She sprang down and
rushed past them. The undergrowth parted, easily, or with
nightmare locking. She fell across the stone in the centre of
the grove, now filled with the tranquil spears of the moon. In
her skull there were noises like bells. There was blood on the
stone. She scrubbed it off with fern. O loveliness, O quiet.
They who were following her were her friends, bound by an
abnormal need to envy and not pleasure. Well, that's death's

short cut, and a dark accident. Not like the friendly people
who kill or are killed in war.

She was good enough to die with the great dog which
had been so strong.

She lay back on the stone and opened her palms to the
moon. They were slow in following her. Afraid perhaps. Innocence did not guess their terror's pit; their desire measured by
their impotence. They crept in, where she had beaten her way.

They were looking at her, long before she saw them, from
the shadow of a tree. They had thought to kill her, but they
had meant to annihilate; and out of their fury another idea
came to them. Judy whispered and Peter stared. She shouted
from under the trees.

"Van, we won't kill you, but Peter can do what he likes to
you. You won't mind after the life you've led." Peter was
lighting a cigarette.

Van lay on the stone. He was like a stage villain lighting
that cigarette. Move? Run? Run away? Double round the
moon-shafts? That's no good. I'll not play blind-man's-buff
for my virtue. Wrap up in the light and lie still. Become part
of this place, and they will only find a stone. Anyhow, they
can't hurt my soul. Later she heard them talking.

"Go on. It's the best thing to do. Not a thing she can tell.
I'll go away. Mind? No, I know you love me."

Van sat up. Was she a corpse, safe for ever in a glass box?
No, not at all. She was to let everything go. She lay flat on the
stone again.

Florian and Ursula, my father and my mother in Ashe.
Her mind ran on. Peter can't see far. The stone is white. The
moon is white. I'm white when I have no clothes. He mightn't
see me at all. Judy would have to go away. They are whispering in the trees. My overcoat, my shoes and stockings and
frock. I can keep my shift. She pulled them off, and lay flat on
the stone. I think I would sooner be dead; but I'm not sure.
She heard the bushes part. Peter came out, by himself, into
the open space round the stone. He looked back, and began
talking in a low voice.

"If I leave you alone, will you clear off with the Russian chap, and leave Rings alone? Judy can't hear. I know you're there. Answer me."

Don't answer him. Wait.

"Little Ashe, listen. I'm afraid of that girl, Judy. She wants something deep, too deep for me. My head's queer since my eyes got like this. If you don't answer me, I'll have to do what she says. Must obey orders."

"You can't even see me."

"I can see you. You're there, somewhere, on the stone. Near my dead dog. I'm coming to you."

"You can't get at me. I'm in the cradle of Rings. Come nearer. Then you'll know."

"The cradle of Rings is a rotten, old basket. Your mother told us. If you won't promise—"

"I do not promise. You must do what you can."

She heard him moving round the stone, behind her head. There his voice:

"You are lying in something. It's like a white cup, full of you. Little Ashe, let me come nearer. I like you better than I like her. My mind's raw. I'll do what I said I'd do. It'll make Judy jealous. You wouldn't mind. I'll marry you. The war's going to do your brother in. *She* says so. What do you say to that?"

He was right over her. Self-bound in iron. She shut her eyes, and made knuckled lumps of her hands.

"I don't care one way or the other; but it would be grand to double-cross Judy. Listen to me, Van. I've had a rotten time."

She thought: If he touches me and finds I'm warm, God knows which way it will work. I should be cold by now. There was a long run of silence. Harp noises began in the tree-tops and ceased. She heard Peter saying:

"Where the devil have you got to? I won't touch that stone. It's alive—we woke it up earlier. I remember. The dog's blood turning into a white poison and moving the stone. Oh, God!"

She heard him crashing back, and wondered how she could ever have been afraid of him. She folded her hands on her breasts and watched the moon.

CHAPTER 10

PETER crawled away into the bushes, dragging with him the body of his dog. There was time for her to run away, before Judy came. The dew stung her feet. She put on her shoes, adding, piece by piece, her dress. She put her stockings in her overcoat pocket, belted it tight and stole away. On the other side of the grove, the serene miles lay, twelve empty, glittering miles to Amburton in its woods. Judy would be waiting across the valley, by the car. It was all right. Round the outer fosse she ran lightly, till at the opening she could look down. In Rings, a light was burning. Another light sprang out and another. She ran down and walked out of the cutting that was the entrance of the outer ring. Judy was sitting there, on a stone. She got up.

"Hullo. That you, Van."

"You'll find Peter in the bushes." She tried to pass; it was hard to have her mind ready for this.

"Not so fast. What did he do to you?"

"D'you think he could harm me there?"

"Oh well, we'll have a fine story to tell."

"Judy—" It was difficult not to cry.

"You poor little object. I told you I'd show you what I can do. I had to show you. You're finished. Now we'll let you alone."

"I'd like your blood, but I'll not take it."

"You have wanted a lot of things you'll never have. I am going to find Peter. He'll tell me."

She saw Judy's face, her crazed eyes, her tongue wetting her lips. She made a face at her, and at her own fear. Her head was light.

MARY BUTTS

"Judy, if you go near him now, you will have a child, and it will be a monster."

"Speak for yourself."

"Do you suppose he has hurt me?"

How silly we are, really; like servant girls. Why servant girls? The only sort of poor we are supposed to know. I know lots. Tarts and machine-hands, and typists, and girls at college, and girls in the theatre....

Judy was running a thorned bramble sucker into her palms, she drew it out and whirled it at Van. It caught in her hair and tore her forehead.

Do not be touched by those palms full of blood. She pulled out the thorns, but she did not think she could go away. She wanted to stay there and argue, till their conversation should reach an indescribable climax, and the question should be finally answered—for whom was Judy understudy? Answered, the rôle would cease.

People were coming up the hill. Coming to take care of her. Coming to hit Judy and hurt her. What shall I say? The truth?

The boys were coming. She would put up her hurt face to them to be kissed.

"Judy, run away. You are safer with Peter than with my brother."

She ran to meet them.

"Thank the Lord, we've found you."

"Van, what has happened?"

"My little sister—"

"I'll tell you. Take me away down the hill. What were the lights in the house?"

"Clavel got the wind up. What's that girl doing here? She's hurt your face. Now I'm going to spoil hers. It's been something vile. Let go my arm. My God, I know."

"Quiet, Val. You must send her away."

He went up to her stammering. Judy edged away.

Serge said: "Ashe, let her go. We can't do anything: only the sort of thing she does. It is all right. We must take Van home."

192

"It is not all right."

"It won't be made better by touching her. Why, Van, there is blood on your face."

"You're mistaken. It's dew." She sneered at him, believing him to be afraid, and so pretending that she had not suffered.

Judy turned away. Valentine put his arms around her.

"Sister, tell us, for God's sake."

"Take me home."

"I must follow her. You must let me. Where is she going? We'll take you home and put you to bed and go straight to Amburton."

"No. Serge is right. He's detestable, but he's right. I will tell you. Settle nothing to-night."

"Does Melitta know?"

"We think not. We have no idea how Clavel knew that you were gone."

"I left the pantry window open. Don't let Melitta know."

"Why not? I know now what they've tried to do. It was the vilest thing ever attempted. She's our mother. She must care. Serge, you've guessed?" He nodded.

"You'll find she'll be decent."

"Little optimist. Oh, that's bad of me. Sorry, brother. I'm so tired."

"Sedan chair, my own sister. And you mustn't think."

"Or let it give you a complex or anything—"

They lifted her.

"You won't let Melitta know?"

"Isn't it too good to waste?"

"Perhaps you're right."

There was her bed, and milk bubbling in a glass, doped by Clavel, a sweet burn in it. This was home. Lie safe for one night. A lot of trouble to buy one night's peace.

She slept till eleven o'clock, and lay in bed, drinking tea till lunch. Valentine sat with her talking about himself. When the gong rang, he walked in to lunch beside her, holding her arm. It was a wretched meal. They could not speak. When it was over, Serge pulled her aside.

"Can you stand a scene? Your mother means to have one. She's found out about last night. This morning, she tried to question me."

Van thought that this would be bad. She would have to tell Melitta. What could she tell Melitta that Melitta would understand? Last night she had put shame in its place, but not what makes shame contemptible. Neither shame nor its solution mattered to the boys; they were too young and not women; Valentine too excited, and Serge too detached. To the boy it was part of an amazing game. His game was her game. Well, she would play too.

"I'll have coffee with her in the library."

She followed her mother. She thought: How many times have I had to face her? If I can make this clear, I am free of her for ever. Free of my fear of her. I must be truthful. I shouldn't be rude. I'm pleased with myself, really. I think I shall show I'm pleased.

Melitta began: "I only want, Betty, to say one thing. I gather from Clavel—in fact I heard the noises outside my door—that you were out last night, at an exceedingly late hour. Neither your brother nor Mr. Sarantchoff were with you. You returned, or, it seems, they fetched you, long after midnight. Now, I ask, is that seemly? While you are here? I know you have led an independent life, but you must see?"

Drum. Drum. Drum. Spit. Squirt. Tinkle. Tick. She speaks to me like that. Last night I was out with the powers on Rings hill. The next day, I am rated for the event. Poor old woman who could see no further into life. The girl sat up in a stiff frock, sprigged with flowers, folded into her conceit.

Valentine followed them in. It was all plain to him. These people had insulted his sister. Suggest, insist if necessary, on his mother's connivance. He knew no details. He did not want to know them. Melitta went on.

"For you to stay in bed so late gives more work to the servants. We are understaffed as it is. If you come here without invitation—" Oh, the detestable girl! Feet like small mice. Ineffable air. Always naughty like that, when did she not cry, or make a speech. Grey lids. Had she quarrelled with the young man? "I do not want you to think that I am not perfectly willing—it might have been in better taste for you to have let me know." Eyes. Eyes. Anthony's eyes. This place is awash with ghosts.

Valentine began: "Mother! I do not think it right of you to talk like that."

"And why not, my son?"

"You do not know about last night. She went for a walk. They were waiting for her; your precious Peter, and that girl you encourage, Juliet. They dragged her out of the grounds and insulted her. You know as well as I what they intended. What they would have done, if she was so not pure that they were afraid. Look at the mark on her forehead. My sister. Our Vanna."

He thought:

This is the goods. Put her in the wrong. Much better than putting ourselves in the right.

"Valentine, what do you mean? Betty, explain. A decent woman does not understand—"

"If you want it plain then—they—I mean Peter, threatened to outrage her."

"Valentine! Elizabeth, is this true?"

"Yes, Mother, it is true."

"I do not believe it. Nothing shall make me believe it."

"Do you want to know all about it?"

You bet she will.

"What you are saying is obviously the delusion of an unclean mind. A girl who runs about a lonely garden after dark is liable to misconstruction."

The fire sat down on itself. The door at the top of the seven stairs swung open. A pale sun opened over the garden. The library's dim rainbow turned to full, white, crystal day.

The house was roaring with laughter. Laugh too, Ashe-children.

They sat still, while the extreme transparency closed on them. Van got up.

195

"So that is what you think of it?" she said. "Is my word nothing beside your fancies?"

Valentine, opposite his mother, shewed a buoyant rage.

"They let you know that my sister had come here," he said. "You came tearing home. One can guess what their communication with you has been. All my life you have lied to me about my sister. When you find that game's up, you try this on her. She's your first child."

Melitta thought: My terrible son. He doesn't understand. He doesn't know what he is saying. She hesitated: she thought: that sort of thing does happen. She has become a heroine to the boy. If I am unjust, God will be angry. My son will hate me. I was wrong to have shewn that I suspected her. Haven't they both run wild? Clavel was watching out last night. Have they invented this between them?

While Van thought: We've done it. We're turning her. She's running. Let her race. The wall's rumbling down that keeps us out of paradise. The house is laughing. I am beautiful. I have the Rings to play with. I have power. I have done better than I understand. Magnificat.

She rang the bell.

Clavel had been there, all the time, by the door, Serge beside him, the two men judging together.

Van said:

"Clavel, send Hilda to pack for me. I am going to town by the night train."

"Mother, you are to understand that, if she goes, I go with her."

O wise and silly brother. Kick away, old cow. Clavel stood again by Serge at the door. What would Melitta do? She was angry now, her mouth was like a crooked hole. Get up and bully your male servant, you great lady.

She heard the low wounded rage in Melitta's voice.

"Clavel, I want the carriage for Amburton at once. Miss Elizabeth can have the trap. You need none of you ask me where I am going. It is to clear the honour of my husband's family."

"You've forgotten the honour of your first husband's family. You had children by him."

Melitta, troubled with her exit, saw Serge just about to smile, very gently. She thought he was sorry for her, and passed him, her eyes full of tears.

They saw him smile, and called him to them.

"What were you smiling at her for?"

Serge said: "My fancies about all you passionate people. But you could guide her, as well as drive her, you know."

The boy considered and agreed. Van, rapt, had no interest.

"Look, friends, at the room," she said. "It knows. It is blessing us. Look at our father's room up the seven stairs. There is the hour-glass full of red sand. Fetch it, Val. Keep it on the table, and let it measure them."

"Sister, what happened last night?"

"*Never ask this week, fair lord—*"

"If we don't want to quarrel, we had better go out."

"We'll ride. Tell Clavel."

"What about our luggage—?"

"*We won't go home to-night.*

We won't go home to-night—"

They went out, a chorus.

CHAPTER II

THE heavy carriage strained up the hills to Amburton, out of Rings.

Melitta tightened her furs, and sorted her alarms and disgusts. If the girl Juliet were staying at Amburton, it would be without a chaperone. That was impossible. Then her own child was a liar. A point to be cleared up, when she saw the young woman. See the young woman. "It" could be said so as not to hurt her feelings. Horrible. She felt a fool. The girl is not one of us. I shall speak to Peter.

I must see Peter. Odious enquiry. Simpler to have believed, to have taken her children's part? Suppose it was the girl who had made Peter telegraph?

That is unfair. I don't much like her; but I have nothing against her. If Peter wants her, he can have her. She brooded over her nephew; sulky, male cub; satisfying her as her exotic had not done. It had been anguish to see him maimed. No son by Amburton, and the Rings boy a memory and a threat. A wonder and a great admiration. We shall have more rain. The clouds were sinking in the valleys, lower and lower down the grass hills. The glass was covered with minute beads. She rubbed away her breath with a suède finger. The bloom went off the leather. There is a tiny discomfort in seeing a surface spoiled. The coachman pulled up to put on his white macintosh. The strong horses were quiet in the rain. Her mind ran on: God wishes me to be patient. I have tried to do my duty. We shall drive into that cloud. Whisps were flying down the hill, the cloud's body pouring slowy behind. How many more hills to walk up? I want to move fast.

It rained hard. A streak of water ran beside the cheese-coloured road. The mist opened over the steep grass into the valley on her left. She looked down into a copse.

Lords and ladies, I picked them there when I was a girl. I loved their name. I'm a lady now, among lords and ladies.

Down hill now, all the way to Amburton, too steep either way to go fast. She was bumped into the air over a dressing of flints.

In the valley, the rain poured straight. There was a noise of a full watercourse, deep and pleasant. On the hills, there had been a reedy whistle of sea-wind, following them, like a little voice trying to get inside the glass. Here the deep gurgle from the stream and rain drumming from the sky. She lay back.

Amburton's woods lay folded round its drive, immense trees, half a mile from the lodge to the house.

Men had cleared round the huge trees, and exposed the structure of woods, leaving no brushwood round their columns for people to hide in. The branches threw off their rain with a patter as Melitta drove by. She sat bolt upright, her mirror-box in her hand, her veil beaded with fog. She saw the dark brick of Amburton; a swimming, yellow, gravel sweep; ivy, oiled and dripping. On the mounting-block, a robin sputtered the water over his wings.

A servant told her that Mr. Peter had gone out to look for rabbits, and that it had been too wet for the young lady.

She found Judy in the smoking room, her long chin tucked into her lawn stock, her black head smooth as a pebble. Good style, thought Melitta, but she can't be here alone. Suppose they are all a fast lot. Oh, dear.

Judy got up. Melitta saw her arrange her smile.

"My dear Juliet, I have just got back from France, and I went down to Rings. It was all so hurried, or I would have let you know when to expect me." But the girl knows about the wire. I am a fool. She is uneasy. What is she uneasy about? What is going on?

"I think that Peter said you might be coming. I hope you'll forgive me for being here."

"Of course. It is very natural."

"I'm staying at the farm with a friend. We come up and take Peter for walks."

"How do you think he is?"

"His nerves are bad, but he is very fond of this place."

"I am sure that it is a good thing for him to have you with him." If they had anything to be ashamed of, would they have wired to me? "Will you give me tea? I ordered it as I came in." Then, with the élan of the first cup—"My dear Juliet, I hope you'll forgive me. I came over here to-day on some rather disagreeable business."

Judy tried to supple herself and grew more rigid. Melitta felt that her teeth were locked behind her bright lips.

—"I know she is a friend of yours, but my daughter, Betty—forgive me if I speak frankly—"

"Of course—but I know Betty so well."

"That makes it easier, doesn't it?"

Judy considered, nodded and said: "I'm afraid I ought to tell you that I know about Peter's telegram."

"Well, that simplifies matters, doesn't it? I expect you know that my daughter and I did not get on well in the past. In fact, I had practically to forbid her the house. Now I find her there, uninvited, with a Mr. Saratchoff. They are both very intimate with her brother. Please, please, tell me anything you can. Is there anything in her life which would make her an unsuitable companion for a young man's innocence?"

Judy thought: So she'd come for that. Not about last night. What a chance. Breathe quietly. Besides, what did it amount to, last night? If I tell her, what business had I to know? Can I? Better not. Tell her about Betty. Tell her about Serge. Tell her some truth and a lot more like it. The woman's looking at me.

Melitta, looking at her, said:

"I'm sorry if I've said anything to vex you." Why doesn't she speak. "You see—with Peter's shell-shock. I know it is difficult. Betty has come to me with a revolting story, no mother would believe. That Peter insulted her. Out on the downs last night. Of course she should never have gone there, but she says that you and he were out for a walk. I'm sure it is all nonsense."

"Lady Amburton—"

"Let me explain first. You see, a word from you and it would be all right. As a child Betty had delusions—that we were not her friends—that her step-father and I did not love her. There was a mark this morning on her cheek. I had to come here. It is only fair to you. I have known, you see, Peter do some dreadful things when he was ill. Tell me—you look so worried. Of course you couldn't have been there—you were neither of you there. Does he go out much alone?"

"He goes for long walks."

"By himself?"

"Yes."

"Then you think that there might possibly be something in it?" (She's a nice girl. I shan't have to explain. Is she nice? Is she thinking out a lie?)

Judy said: "Betty is a very extraordinary girl."

Now what does she mean. "Can you explain?"

"I really don't know. Peter is in a morbid state of health. He does not like her."

"Then you mean, you mean, you mean—?"

"Of course not. I know nothing at all. All I could think is that he may have met Betty on the Rings and frightened her."

"Miss Marston, you must explain instantly."

"I really can't explain. I don't know. But I have often noticed that Betty has a strange effect on people who are ill. She is dreadful with them. She can drive them mad. She does not mean to… There is something about her—I mean that unless this story is made up, she may have brought on one of Peter's attacks." That's it. Confuse her. She'll never get it clear. "As to last night, I can't say. I was in bed. He may have gone out."

"You have known Betty in London. Do you believe her a liar?"

"Don't you know, Lady Amburton, that it's impossible to be sure of anything with her?"

Melitta thought: Now that doesn't mean anything. Why am I frightened? This girl has been quite straight. I ought to thank her. She said:

"No. I won't have another cup. One thing before I go. Would you mind ringing for the carriage? Would it be any good if I saw Peter? I see that you can't tell me any more. No? You think it would be unwise? I feel that we have not quite got to the bottom of this story. Don't shake your head at me. What are you doing here?"

Judy rose, and stood restlessly, picking at the tiny buttons on her cuff. Melitta crossed to the window and stared at the park and the marching walls of rain. By the window, an old, round mirror hung in a panel, and in its spotted glass, she saw Judy behind her. She saw her make a face, opening her mouth and turning her eyes down into slits.

And Melitta thought: She's making a face behind my back. That's what she's like when I'm not looking. There is my Vanna with her head so high.

It is true then. They tried to hurt her together. Betty, I'm your mother. I'm coming to you.

They mouth at me like that when they think I can't see them. I will see Peter. I must have the car. I am going back to my children.

I dare not turn round. She's seen me watching her. She is mad.

She swung roung. Judy stood there, holding her furs. Melitta thought:

I'll turn and see if she does it again.

"I'm sorry. You must have thought me very abrupt, but you don't know how worried I am. Wait for me a moment. I want something from the bureau."

Fumble, run through the papers, give her a moment. Look up. She is doing it again. She has her tongue out like an idiot. Her eyes have fallen into her head. There is an apple of blood in her cheek. It is spreading, it will drip over her chin. If she gets what she wants, my children will be dead. There's Peter in the hall.

She rushed out.

" "Lady Amburton, your bag—"

"Peter, what have you been doing to my children?"

"My God, Aunt. I meant nothing. She put me up to it. Betty's all right. The Rings looked after her."

"Send for the car. I shall wire for your uncle. Don't come near me. I will drive myself." She went down the steps, to the stables, in the slackening rain.

Sweet rush home between the trees, along the river's bank, up into the hills. Sea-wind over Encombe, away from those trees, rustling profundities, talking, talking in bad dreams. Over to Rings. Rings that made me. Rings that gave me clean children. It doesn't matter that they are different. I am going back to my children.

We are all children of one father. Tony, forgive me. Tony, you really love me now for the first time. Morice come home. My children shall do what they like.

CHAPTER 12

IN the hall at Amburton, Peter turned to Judy.
"Rotten dirty trick you made me play last night."
"Well, Peter, you asked me to do my worst."
"They're my own people after all, not yours."
"Why remember that now? Do you mean to say that you don't want us to go on?"
"What is there to do?"
There was always the police for Serge; but Peter had disliked that. She thought of other ways. Now she could hardly remember what she wanted to do. A satisfaction, half gratified, had gone stale. Dreary, malignant place, Amburton. She realised the empty hall, the sick, evading man in it, the chill from the stone, the coming night. She snapped on the switches. The hall glittered with gold pears. Rings would be under candle light.
"Peter, what's the good of our going on like this?"
"I don't know; and I tell you I don't want to quarrel with all my people because of you."
"Your shell-shock will get you out of it. Melitta will soon find it had better be that. It's me they'll turn on."
"She doesn't know anything about you."
"I shall be in it. I shall lose my reputation. I shall—"
"I am going to have a bath."
"Shall I rub your arm?"
"Yes, you might. I'll call when I'm ready."
She thought: Rotten cub he is. Far worse than Serge. Ugly shrapnel wounds. Pits of drawn skin, tight and blue.
"I will do your arm. To-morrow, I shall go back to Town. To-night, I'll have dinner at the farm and pack."

"All right."

"Call me when you are ready. I'll come up to the bath-room."

Lying in the hot water, Peter hoped that she would not come near him, because she had such ugly hands.

She moved about the fireless, brilliant hall, where the cold glittered over the damp, thinking of the tranquil earth lights at Rings. They'll have it now. I'm tired. I don't care. Why did I care? I wish the trees would step. There, they dance. Here they breathe and sob. I'm going back to Town. Peter's played out and he's such a bore. I'd sooner work again. He'll follow if he's keen. No need to do his arm. His man will see to it.

They've done us. They've distinctly done us. Let it stop at that. Some day I'll get hold of them again. Now, I don't quite remember them. There is always Serge. I must do my hair.

She went into the smoking room and sat before the old glass, arranging her hair. A bad glass, but the damp had made her hair curl.

I'm forgetting. Some day I'll get a proper revenge on Ashe. They've got away this time. I don't want to see them again. I shan't see them again for a long time. *We have lit a candle that by God's grace...* So that's all right. I must go away. I'll go to-night. Leave Peter a note.

"Dear Peter, I can see that you don't want me any more. I have gone back to Town. We both know that it would be better for me to go away. Judy."

She leaned on the bureau, writing precisely, and staring across the park.

That will do. It means nothing at all, and it will do. I'll take a book. Useful to have something to return. He won't follow us to-night. He won't go out in the dark alone. The servants mustn't know. Servants must never know. Fun to be a servant. They find out. I shall be a servant some day. There is always Serge.

Quick and quiet she crossed the hall, and turned out the

lights. Immediately the rain could be heard, falling softly between the sighs of wind rising to blow it away. She went out down the water-soaked steps. At the third she fell, and lay face down on the yellow gravel. She got up, dumb, with amazed, sad eyes, wiped her face and walked down the avenue in the rain.

CHAPTER 13

SO the spell of Rings was wound up and worked out; and the Rings children received the rewards of warriors. Everything was over, everything was beginning again, in the flight of their race and age. Life had justified itself of Melitta, Vanna and Valentine Ashe; made a clean job of it, which is the beginning of wisdom. Melitta was not the woman to say: I married without love, and suffered, and was corrupted by a good that I did not understand; spoilt my second love through fear; drove away my children. Nothing can alter what I have done, or what I have suffered.

Nor the girl say: Remember my insulted childhood, my exile, the aptness now for sorrow which will be characteristic of me. Were these necessary?

Nor the boy say: Who will give me back the years when I did not know my sister?

Or each one say of two: What will undo what has been done to them? The question occurred to Van, who rejected it as a piece of discipline and common sense. That would be Serge's line of country; to make pain valid for ever and unforgivable; with great contempt for the cosy earth-animals who licked their sores and forget. He would say: "If you can forgive for yourself, how can you forgive for other people?— What bloody right have you to forgive for other people?" And, in action, he had been more pitiful than she had been. She said to herself:

"Serge, let me rest. Serge, isn't it enough that I shall never have you? Shan't I? I'll try one more fall. That means back again into more life. But he shan't corrupt me. He shall never make me stop enjoying myself. I'll try one more fall with him."

This was a month later. She went into the library to find him.

"We have been here for a month," she said. "The sun has moved into another sign."

"What about it?"

"Several things have happened, Serge."

"You have had things to do, and years of time to catch up. When does Valentine join his regiment?"

"He goes in a few days."

"I shall go too. Shall we leave you here?"

"God forbid. Why should you?"

"I thought you might have done with London for a time."

"Why? She has settled money on me. I've even had an offer of decent work once the war's over. If it ever is."

"Will you get more when she dies?"

"Yes. You are very practical, Serge."

"Sometimes, for others."

"Serge, tell me, why do you grudge me these weeks? They've been so good. Honour, security, pleasantness. My complexes analysed out flat. Do I cry as I used to? I've got the boy and the place, and a bewildered mother, but kind. But these last days, I've seen you come out of your dream to despise me. I was burying my bones and forgetting their grave. Are you turned ghost. Remember that you sent me away."

"Did I really?"

"You know you did. I told you all the truth I could. Do you remember the night at the farm? Now Peter's gone to Brighton, and Judy's in town. We've turned their tail. Come out of your dream now, and take up our acquaintance where she broke it off."

"Those two are still in the world, and what they stand for, and what they have done."

"Not in our world. Get up. Come for a walk."

They went out over the lawns, and turned towards the planting and the firs above the sea.

Serge said: "Would you mind if I went on alone?"

"No. That would be amusing for me," and stared at the

unmoved young face, stony with more than fatigue.

"Serge, you helped me to this triumph. It is high spring. Won't you share a minute of it?"

"My part is over."

She thought: Sense it, Van, sense it. Tease it out.

*"Your breast shall not lie by the breast
Of your beloved, in sleep."*

He is my beloved. For him I trod out our jungle. I levelled it and set it for love. He is a grey, maimed, young man walking away. Be cheerful. Why should you embarrass him?

"Go on for your walk."

He had got up and gone away. She sat on the red needles, burning her tongue as she bit them, holding up her wounded senses till she could understand. She thought: Remember, I met him when he has been under torture for a long time. It was more than I can manage. We sank together. When we were drowned, we kissed. Poor girl, you wanted him so. We came here. What else could we have done?

Van, you saw what Judy and Peter meant. You faced them. It's done and we're alive. Life has come out with its triumph. This is the triumph of life. I have money, and the freedom of this place: Val and I have each other. Melitta is reconciled to us. She knows that she is righteous, and that life is more amusing because of us. Morice has flown down in a staff car to embrace us, and whistle *Home Sweet Home* while he shaves. A most honest gentleman. For three weeks I've had peace; on a foundation of wisdom I have laid another stone; in the secret book of my house I have turned a page. It is done. It is done. It is not done for Serge. I look at him and say "Come." He gets up and goes away. I do not see him lying close to me. Never. I want that. I shall die if I do not get that. She rolled over, biting her wrists. Be quiet, Van. You will feel this for other men. Oh yes, you will. You will meet him when you are both famous and rag each other. In the years to come. Not now. Not now.

She sat up, sucking the needles she had bitten. Her senses came back. She smelt the earth, the smoky air sucked by the first strong sun. She thought of Melitta in the garden, cutting hyacinths; Valentine and Morice in a cool pantry, making cup; that they were going to dance that night.

They are coming to see me. They shall see me the devil of a lot.

Is Judy doing this to him from a long way off? Nonsense, you know she's not. It sounds a neat continuation; but she's human. One brush with the dark powers, and we're back in the life of the five senses.

To-night we shall be dancing. I'll try once more to show love to him. Don't love him too much. Be free, be exquisite; make a perfect job of the return of Ashe of Rings. That is the way to do it. Can I do it? Oh, Serge, I want you, not for the sake of a finale or a prelude; but because you are my dear.

She went back to the house. The coloured spring had turned to lead. On the terrace, Melitta took her arm.

"How much better your charming Serge is looking. I never saw a man more changed. Aren't these blue hyacinths a dream? I don't know, my dear, if he says anything, but I can't help wondering why he is not in the army."

Van thought: At it again. The world's common skeleton popping out of its cupboard. Julia with her teeth under his eyes had been more honest than this. Is our mother going to play Judy's game, after all? Nonsense, she was bound to ask that.

All the same, she was afraid and answered from a contracted throat: "He's not English; I suppose they will send for him if they want him." Again she turned Melitta out of her intimacy, easily this time, like a child she had let in to play.

"We must go back to London for a bit when Val goes. We have lots of work to do."

Melitta sighed, not quite conventionally. The gong rang, and they paced in like two women who had been together a lifetime, at a routine.

The day went out, curtseying through light clouds that tinted and turned grey. The garden was grey, the little birds confused their chatter; the spiced, sharp smells were blended and sad.

* * * * *

Valentine said: "Why do pink girls wear yellow? Now that one ought to be pretty."

"Brother, go and dance with her."

"I have the first dance with you...."

The tune poured out:

> *I'm so happy, oh so happy,*
> *Don't you envy me?*
> *I'm going back, you see,*
> *Down home in Tennessee.*

She tapped her heels into step. The walls began to move past.

"Brother, what do you think is wrong with Serge?"

"He goes out all day alone. He has found a ridiculous creature, all muscles and no chin, and is dancing with her. Playing Christ like Russians do."

"He is a kind of Christ."

"In a way, perhaps. Ikon-style—you know what I mean. But you're looking marvellous to-night, like a Kirchner Madonna."

It was good enough to dance with him, in the brilliant intimacy of brother and sister. They were a double-branched flame, joined at root, parallel at crest; one fire and two.

> *At the stations*
> *My relations.*

She thought: Dance with him, dance: Make it perfect: Break it up, ever such a little after the beat: Our heads pass in the mirrors: I can see Serge being very kind: I'll have a drink, and try my luck. Melitta will say—"Aren't you going to dance with Serge? How well he dances." I shall say, "Do you know, we put each other out of step." Later, I shall dance with him: To be sure it is no good: And work up my feelings till they break. The truth shall make you free: Time that it did something for the living....

"I have ordered the drinks to be served at once. That will start them off."

"Thank you, Mother. They need it."

"How beautifully Serge dances. I love to see you together."
Van thought:

Whispering dowagers, and she wants to announce an
engagement. I'd like to please her.

"Val, get me a drink." I met his devils for him: I broke
their heads: my head aches. "Had a good walk, Serge?"

"Very. I went up to the Rings."

"Is there anyone here you don't know and like the
look of?"

"No, I've got the next dance with your mother."

"So."

An hour later he came over, flushed, his hair standing
up.

"Clavel's got some marvellous drink up his sleeve, sub-
lime stuff of your father's. Just for us. Come in."

"Clavel, give me a drink."

"You look tired, Miss Vanna."

"Yes, Clavel."

"It's all in your day's work, Miss Vanna."

"Can I stand this drink, Clavel?"

"There is nothing, Miss Vanna, that you cannot stand."

"It won't change Mr. Serge, Clavel."

"I'm afraid not. I've done my best with the wine; but he is
even more tired than you, Miss Vanna. He will always be
more tired.

"Be quiet, Clavel. You are breaking my heart."
Serge came back.

"This is great stuff. Van, will you dance this?"

Try again now, and get it over. "Come out on the terrace
with me, don't let's dance."

"But I want to dance. Are you tired?"

"Have it your own way."

They danced. Plenty of mana round him to keep her away.
He has been up to the Rings? What had he got from them?
If Judy could tap them, why not he?...

It's no good. Dance the evening out. There was Clavel's

wine for a witness of God. Leave him alone. Truth had popped up through the wine. She looked up at him He was enjoying himself. A dead man might so dance, once death was over. When had he died? Now that was very curious. Duck into the sweet tune. Drink your father's wine.

CHAPTER 14

SERGE rode back from the station to Rings. He thought:
Get rid of her. Get rid of her. Get rid of her. That's what
the little train said, chuffing out of the station. Tell Melitta
there was no carbide. Two hours to lunch. Oh, this land of
the morning calm!

He turned his horse into a lane.

Ride alone, look down from your horse. Set her towards
the hills. There's a crab on your back, pricking your waist.
It'll never drop off. Try and forget. *And they rest not day or night.*
You shall rest, but not yet. Not till you have quite given it up.
You're sighing. You shall soon have something to sigh for.
Get rid of Van.

Won't that do? She'll go at a word. You wanted to want
her, but you don't. Go back to your painting. Of course I
shall go back and paint. God can have his ticket back. That's
not his ticket, it's mine. I've been to the Rings too. Day after day I've been. They might have blessed me. Only Van
gets that. Not even the boy. I've heard wind drumming in
wet grass and high trees, found it a cold place, drearier than
Praed Street. I've chewed wet leaves and lain on the stone.

Be honest. That's English, that's the ethical phrase. Van'd
say that. I wouldn't take her, though she's a gift. I don't like
her. There's peace in knowing that. I found that out last night
with the wine.

If I say nothing, she'll speak to me of love again. I'll tell
her then. She'll squirm and swallow it, and stick up her head.
She's too generous, too well-bred to whimper. That's her
stunt. Get rid of her. Get rid of her. Get rid of her. Giselle's
saying it now.

214

It has gone light in my head. I can deal with her. Why did this happen? Once I was keen enough. She'll have a theory. I shall listen to it. It may be true; but it won't matter.

She's the opposite of Judy. I don't like life worshippers. I'm not having any more of it.

I've not done with Judy yet.

He saw her on a green sofa, waiting for him to come in, with money from his family, and a spiked tortoiseshell comb for her thin head.

Dreadful images from history rose in his mind. Elephants with shorn trunks; muzzled slaves at the mill. Punic lords, legs broken in a pit; Barca in the ergastulum. Judy had been born for him. Credo.

Van had marched in, and said that she was real also. Sobbed at him to believe it. No. He walked his horse, uplifted in his mind, sustained by truth. He would have been wholly sure, but he remembered his previous love for her, and that made his present unbelief less convincing. There was a flaw somewhere, but he was right on the main point. He was going back to London, to Judy. He heard himself speaking to himself. Must I? Must I? Yes. Why? Because it's the most dangerous thing. And the most perverse? Who could choose Judy, who had Van offered? I would, possibly because I have been offered Van.

Shall I ride up to the Rings; try them for the last time for the Ashe-blessing. Suppose I meet those two children, out on foot, squalling like young gulls. What shall I say? Hullo, and ride away. They leave me alone now.

He left the sunk lane and rode over a field, to a low wall giving onto the open turf. He put Giselle to it, and they cantered away.

A mile off there was a barn, in a valley full of young corn, its stones patched with mustard-lichen on a strip of liquid blue. He looked at it. Ride to that barn and not to the Rings. *Maria Martin,* famous English spook-story. It looks a small, wicked house and quiet. All the evil on earth is contained in a small house, built anywhere. Once you go in, you pass from

curiosity to curiosity; you find something and then you sit
down and watch yourself disappear. So when the wind-up of
souls comes, yours won't be there. That barn looks likely. Go
and sit in it. D'you see that red harrow and through it the
young blades? And the cushions in Judy's room are those
colours, that are waiting for me. Get along with you into that
barn. Not that it matters; you've been there all the time. No
need to externalise. All you've got to do is to notice what you've
been doing all the time.

He rode away, looking back constantly at the barn, frowning at it. Not to have externalised an impulse like that, was
that weakness or strength?

Giselle carried him to the house. The Rings hung their
sullen crown behind him.

He considered the rest of the day.

Lunch well. Pack Valentine for the wars. Might come in
for some old clothes. The house was a great pod, ripe to split,
and spit them over the world. Where to this time? There's
little of the world I haven't seen. Prosperity, poverty, prison.
Prison for sedition. Prison for conscience, group pacifism at
its worst. At its best. Poverty. He pitied himself. Back again
on the poverty-stunt, bean-food, and kippers and tea. The
food you do not eat enough of when you have enough of it to
eat. It had been a good month, and a charming boy Valentine to lend his own horse. He did not want to leave her. He
patted her neck and felt a new edge to pain. Leave Giselle.
Leave Giselle and Van. Courage. Twenty pounds from Russia to pay the back rent. Tell Melitta there was no carbide at
the station.

They clattered over the stable cobbles, a noise of shelled
almonds and ivory.

After lunch Valentine said:
"Come and stick the first torch in the funeral pyre."
"Where? In your room?"
"That's it. Baldur's not in it. I suggested Giselle for finale.
Lots of blood in a horse... Revolvers complete with tooth-

brush and shaving mirror. Morphia injection. Melitta's last pick-me-up. D'you remember the wine and cheese in the Iliad?

"By the way, Serge, I've heaps and heaps of kit I'll never wear again. Would you care to take any of it away? As a kindness. It'll spoil, you know—

—"You will, of course, you will. Suits—spare trousers. Ties and shoes and shirts and socks an *everything*." Serge said warily:

"Why won't you want them again? You won't necessarily be killed."

"I'm growing. Serge, stop looking like a marble idol with a lamp inside. Serge, I say—" The boy was thinking: As a sign that we do not forget. For Van's sake.

He held up a suit.

"Most distinguished, intriguing and discreetly cut. See Vogue, Van's chief delight."

"Leave Van alone."

"Why? I thought you two were lovers."

"We're not and never likely to be."

"Why not?"

"I don't know. It's my fault."

Shall I tell him? Why not? Give her away? While I'm about it, I'll be disloyal as well. Van won't mind.

Valentine said: "If you don't mind my saying so she is very fond of you. Bad luck, and not your fault."

But all Serge said was:

"Van's not a masochist, to bother her head about me."

"Are you?"

"I suppose I am. I may be after Judy again. I don't know."

"Oh, that's what it means. God help you. I wish she were dead." The boy thought that it explained a lot.

"I suppose you'll start painting again."

"I may do peace propaganda. There's more money in it. Might try an office."

"Or a bomb?"

"Too old at twenty-eight."

217

Valentine saw the sorrows of being a man, and they impressed him. Van's love had not been enough for this man, but anything was better than Judy. He must make a gesture to indicate the continuance of intimacy. He made a cache of trinkets in a cigarette box.

"Take these—in case I'm killed. They'll last when the clothes wear out. Also, they'll pawn."

A ring among them for his paint-cracked hands.

He saw Serge's lip tremble. He had moved him then. He said softly:

"Change names with me, Serge, as people used before going into danger, to remember each other by." He heard a wounded voice. Voice of the mutilated, incapable of death. "Serge." "Valentine." And Serge had for second thought how Van would have seized him of her country, and that this was even sillier.

She came in heavy, blue-lidded, yawning.

"There you are, Serge. Had a good ride?"

He thought: Now I needn't speak.

Go away.

Go away.

"Oh! Tea will be in the library."

She went away.

CHAPTER 15

SERGE came into his room, where a black scarab with coral tipped horns was dipping in his portmanteau. Clavel stood up, looking mildly at him.

"The train goes at ten to-morrow, sir. I thought I had better pack for you to-night."

Serge saw Valentine's cigarette box stuffed with socks.

"I don't think Mr. Valentine meant me to have that."

"He did, sir. You see, Mr. Serge, it's for a remembrance of your being here, and what you all have done here. It may remind you, sir, that nothing comes to an end."

"Suppose I only want to go away, and forget this place utterly."

"You would not say that, Mr. Serge, if it hadn't power; nor hate it if you did not feel yourself nearer to loving it than you dare love. What Miss Vanna wanted to do for you can't be done; but the Rings are here for ever; and odds and ends of jewellry may remind you."

"Why should this place and these people insist on following me?"

"They have the right, sir, to keep themselves remembered. Mr. Anthony Ashe told me that Memory was the mother of the Muses from whom all good things come."

"You mean that the war may not have ruined everything?"

"We have tried to reverse its operations, Mr. Serge."

"My God, Clavel, you believe all this, and talk about it with the propriety of a butler."

"It's like this, sir. Every situation has its formula. Every person has his situation. I have mine. I've found the formula for my situation, sir."

"And yet we are your children?"

"Yes, sir."

"I could not help it."

"No, sir."

"Miss Vanna had the Rings to help her. They're no good to me."

"Perhaps you haven't got what Mr. Anthony Ashe called the words of power, Mr. Serge."

"Magic is no good unless you believe in it, Clavel."

"Quite, sir. The only good in it is to take out of you what is already there. Inside out is the rule."

"Well—I mean the business has come to an end." In his mind he saw rail lines running into a point. When you reach it, they are as far away? When you see them joined, are they joined? Ancient speculation. Pack away, tall man, the future up in boxes. *One far-off, divine event.* Balls. Clavel went on:

"Some good has come out of this, sir. Miss Vanna and her brother are friends now. They've joined up in their own place; and done what they should have done; and got what they needed out of it. The place stands fast. Once I thought I should be the one to see the end of Ashe of Rings."

"Lady Amburton won't turn against them again?"

"It would not make any difference now, sir, if she did: and you will see more of Mr. Valentine when he goes into the world."

They stopped talking because of a stirring in the place; not of doors and windows and old floors in the wind; but a throbbing of stones.

"She does that, sir, at the turn of the event."

"The house moves?"

"Yes, sir."

"If I went up to the Rings now I would find"

"Bushes and wet grass, sir, and wind."

"And a cold stone. I'm going to town."

"The train gets in at 1:15, sir. I should go to some old street you know—"

"They're dark—too dark to tell the difference."

"Then, sir, go to your flat and light the fire. You'll find it not so bad."

Damn these people. Sit in the barn under the hill and feel. A dark hole, and round it the unthwarted air running for ever. "Thanks, Clavel. Do you mind? It's the formula."

"Not at all, sir, thank you, Mr. Serge."

They heard the gong humming the call to late tea. Serge went along the corridor laid with green carpet, lustered like a strip of sea; past the white wall panels and square-paned windows. On the third sill, there was a dead bee, a last year's bee fallen out of a crack. The sun fell dully through a blight rising from the sea.

As the sun at noon-day to illustrate all shadows. That is what I never see. Come.

In the library, the fire was too hot. Valentine said:

"Butter's out." Melitta bit a coral lip.

"If you had said nothing about it, Valentine, Serge mightn't have noticed."

He turned sweetly to Melitta.

"When you have eaten as much margarine as I have, you prefer it," and she believed him.

Van came in, and poured sugar from the bowl into her cup.

"My daughter, to sweeten, not to thicken."

Serge said:

"I was going to put marmalade in mine."

"I don't mind Russian customs. It's waste that's wrong. I should have thought you would remember, Betty, that the poor have to do without."

"Whose fault was it that I was poor?"

"Betty."

"Van."

"Van."

"I only meant that with your interest in social questions…"

"I see. I'm sorry, all. I thought you were throwing old shabbiness in my teeth."

"You talk as though poverty was something to be ashamed of. Now Serge here—"

"It's easier for a man, Lady Amburton. I never felt it so much as Van." Van tried to smile.

"Won't someone else say something handsome?"

Melitta kissed her. "For goodness sake, let there be no more quarrels in this house. What train are you catching to-morrow, Serge?"

Van answered for him:

"The morning one—and that reminds me. I promised to shew him the old gallery. Serge, will you come up before it is dark?"

She took him up to the gallery, where there were no candles set, no chairs but two, carved and gilt, dusty fleur-de-lys on the velvet that had been green.

"Don't sit on them, Serge. Sit in the window seat. Look at the sea whitening. It will blow to-night."

He saw great presses on the inside wall. "What's in them?"

"Ancient junk."

"Why did you bring me up here, Van?"

"Only for this, friend, before you go. I know that you have ceased to wish to have anything to do with me. I want to know why."

"I thought you would be sure to have a theory."

"That's beastly of you, Serge. Go back to your sadistic female friend."

"I suppose I am not behaving like a gentleman?"

"I hadn't thought of it, Serge, like that."

"Little liar." He felt like pulling her hair.

"Why call me that?"

"It is the first thing you would think since you came down here, and picked up your caste ideas again."

"You're hurting me. They sit lightly enough."

"I know I am."

"You like to do it."

"Yes."

She thought it her duty to understand, and answer steadily.

"We'll take it for granted that we have done with. But let me know why it has happened."

"I don't know. I have wanted to love you. I can't. I'm sorry. I don't know why?" (Bad. If you can't think of something better, she'll go on.) "Van, I don't want you to think it is Judy."

"Why?"

"It might be rather horrible for you."

"I didn't. There should be a limit to idiocy. But now—"

"Oh, I shall clear off. Go into a monastery. Join the army."

"I see you're fed up." She thought: I've left it too long. Throw yourself out, Van Ashe. Not Judy. Why not? She said: "When I was drawn up that night on to the Rings, and lay outstretched on the stone, I though that I had done it for us both."

"How could you save another?"

"I see that know. But Serge, when we met those two in the park, it was you who got us out of it. Were you acting, or did you mean it?"

"I tell you, I bluffed. Said what one would like to be true. They were stupider."

"If Judy is stupider than us, why are you afraid of her? Is it your will she has corrupted?"

"I don't know what you mean? Oh, Van, if you had asked me even three weeks ago I should have said that I wanted you. Van can't you see that you are watching a weak young man growing into a bad, stupid man? But I tried to want you."

"You might even have married me. Now?"

"I should say that I am spoiled, for you, or for anyone."

"Do you want to go back and live with Judy?"

"Not exactly. At times. I feel I may in the future. You see, you could never stand that."

"Hush."

They sat opposite, on the horns of the casement seat, their hands loose between their knees. It was nearly dark. The floor creaked. Serge said:

"I dislike this place."

"How could I dislike it or fear it? But come back to Judy."

223

"Listen then, if you will have it explained. I grant you, she is what we call an evil thing. The point is that she's real. Or she seems real to me. With what you would call infamous images, she has distorted my mind."

"You think them the whole of truth?"

"I don't know. But for me they are. They're real. They're effective. They have weight.

"Or she has, if you like, an hysterical effect on me.

"There is a quality about her of reality. She loved her thoughts. She put them out to breed. They are not true of themselves. They become true because of her nature and her will. They are alive. They are following me about.

"She called you vile, Van. Now, it is not because she *called* you vile that I think you are. I do now, intently, as I sit here. She has made me *want* you vile. In the last quarter of an hour I've found that you are. See? Before I only hoped.

"She stuck a maggot in my heart, and it's breeding. I shall say the most filthy things to you if you don't go away." Van said:

"Isn't it possible, Serge, that this hating of me is an excuse you have to make to yourself for ceasing to care for me. Which might have happened anyhow?" Mother of God, what have I found out?

"It is not that. I've been fighting it for years. Then I met Judy. It came through. I shan't live long. I mean, I shall change. I can feel the change moving. Another soul is changing with the one that was mine."

Where did that one go to, 'Erbert
Where did that one go?

"Serge, my dear."

"I know, Van, you're a decent creature, but you're like a weak drawing."

"Why won't you live long?"

"You won't recognise me. I shall be another person, and a nasty one."

"It's an hysteria."

"You can psycho-analyse it. Only I know. I didn't know exactly till you brought me up here to this abominable gallery in the dark. It's quite dark now, isn't it? There's a blaze over my eyes."

"Quite dark, Serge. Will you join the army?"

"No, because I want to paint."

"Are you going straight back to Judy?"

"I don't suppose so." And then: "I want her to be what you once were—"

"Oh, my son—"

"What?"

"You can't have it both ways. If she has made you understand life from a new point of view, why do you break down and want her changed to me?"

"I don't know. I suppose I can't stand it. It's the inside knowledge that life is evil—"

"Damn you with your good and evil. But I know the thing you mean. To talk to you is like a person with a cold talking to a person in consumption. It may pass. I can't say anything more. I'm gone dead." He thought:

I knew it would do that to her. It is strong. Sucked her up, and left her under the window, a little heap of white bones. Dead a hundred years. Little bones and rags stirring in the draught. Dead, red tags of hair. I can hardly see her. Don't like this passage in the dark. Perhaps she's dead. I've killed her. A hundred years later, and they've not found us yet. What's that tapped the window? "Van, Van, where's there a light?"

"There is no light. I'll take you down."

Tell him there is a way to save the mind from this. He would not listen, and I could not say it. I am not sure of it now. She said:

"Put your hand on my shoulder, Serge. The stairs are queerly placed." Ah, pain.… Dark. Let it out in your face. He won't see. Suppose my hair went white, I can feel my scalp turning. I'm dying, dead up to my knees.

"Careful, Serge. That's a cupboard door. What's inside?

Old musical instruments. Here are the stairs. They twist."
I've got his wrist. Kiss it. Cold and hairy. If I could leave my
mouth on it, it would warm. Run two fingers up his sleeve.
Breathe without a sound. My mouth's full of salt. This is the
last thing you will do for him. Let it kill you. Daddy, take
notice of me. This man doesn't.

Put your arm round me, Serge. Say we will find out together. Don't go. Love you, my bird. Love you.

We're down, that's over, there's the light.

"That's all right, Serge. Do you know your way now?
Good luck to you. If you ever want me, ring me up at the
club. Straight along there to your room.... Say something
before you go."

"Are you very sick with me, Van?"

"No."

"After all, when we're famous, you can tell this affair—"

"It will make a play for me to act in. Thank you for
reminding me of that."

CHAPTER 16

"VAL, what are you doing to-night?"

"I promised Serge I'd ride with him. We'd better go early to bed. It will be a long day to-morrow."

"All right. Valentine, will you look after Serge? You will, you must, you promise."

"Can't you see I mean to? Van, I know."

"Do you understand what is wrong with him?"

"Not exactly, but I've done what could be done. Is it so bad with you?"

"Bad enough; but I'm good at going without."

"You have other things. I go to-morrow to a filthy depôt. He's going to a filthy studio. What the devil has happened to him?"

"Brother, I don't know. He is having an experience. It has made him turn me out. Now it's your turn. Cuddle me."

"Nothing shall alter us. I'm not going to die. When I come of age, we'll share the world."

"There is that. That's more than Serge."

"He is still in the family, after all."

"I must find a flat."

"And take care of yourself. It might be as well to devote your spare time to settling Judy. She started this."

"Conducted it. God knows where it came from."

"I won't ride with Serge if you'd rather not."

"No, but let me watch you mount."

"Wait till I kick off these things."

She drew back the curtain. "The moon, she's dim. Be careful."

He tied his stock.

"How often I've done this before. Like the ladies in the Cenci.

—"Van, how funny you'd look with your head on a block, like a King Charles spaniel. By Jove, Van, were you ever executed? I can see you kneeling in a dirty shift and red stockings, squinting at a shiny block. D'you believe in reincarnation?"

"What's the period?"

"Couldn't say."

"Are you ready?"

"Coming."

Serge was sitting with Melitta in the hall. He stared between his knees at the stones. Melitta said:

"I think I hear the horses. What a good thing the rain has kept off for your last ride."

They mounted. The women stood on the steps. The horses fidgeted. The moon revealed a shapeless world. They smacked down the wet gravel towards the sea. Melitta said:

"Do you mind his going off with your brother like that on your last night?"

Damn her impudence. If she had said "with Valentine." Save yourself.

"No. He's a queer bird. At one time we were nearly in love with one another. That came to nothing. But I'm glad he gets on with Val."

"Yes. I'm glad it's all right."

"It's quite all right." What would it be like to have a mother who would stand the truth? There are no such mothers.

Melitta said:

"Betty dear, while they are out for a ride, I want you to see something I have found."

"Yes."

"Come up to my room with me then."

"What is it?"

"It is curious. I am not quite sure. That girl Judy seems to have left it behind. A knife. There's something nasty."

Your are in the hand of God. Follow her up. The room's like Waring and Gillow. Block crystal and gilt. Mirror in my mother's room, reflect the truth for me. Let me through. Hide me. Confuse her. Hide me if I cry.

—"Here are some amber beads I want you to wear. You know that girl Judy was a bad lot. I hope you'll have nothing more to do with her. I don't believe even Peter will marry her. He certainly won't if he gets better and I won't receive her here. She's not a friend for any decent girl."

"She is not."

"Do you know, my dearest, she actually tried to set me against you. She was so convincing. I never let her see it, of course; but there were times when I half believed her."

"But what is it, Mother?"

"This afternoon I found this."

Melitta gave her a knife with a sickle-blade of plain steel.

"My daughter, what was that doing in the basket which holds the first-born of this house?"

"Up there in the cupboards? It's too fantastic."

"I consider it a great impertinence."

"It's that sure enough. How did you find it?"

"I had occasion to look for something in the gallery. In the basket, which I guard very carefully—it is centuries old, and I hope some day to see in it your children and Valentine's —I found this."

"When was Judy here?"

"For a few days last Christmas."

"Yes." The boys are riding by the sea, under the moon. Grey waves are tumbling in the gap. Strong beasts between their thighs, moving so easily.

"It was there in the basket, by itself—stuck right through."

"I can't explain it. She's rather mad, Mother. It's so irrelevant."

"In what way could it be relevant?"

"She was an evil brute. But what has that to do with it? Let's have a look. Handle of copper wire. Nice grip. Sharp. Sort of knife you could do hari-kari with."

"I remember now. She showed it us one night, and asked where it had come from."

"Did anyone know?"

"No one seemed to know, and we'd several old soldiers here. I felt at the time that it must be something unpleasant."

"Look here, Mother. Be a sport. Let me fetch ink, and pour a little out. I'll make a few passes over you, and we'll find out what you'll see."

"Vanna! The Bible forbids such things."

"All right. But she used to do such things, in a dirty, emotional way."

"All the more reason we should not."

"Good, we won't."

"Promise me you'll leave her alone."

"I will, if she'll leave us."

"Do you think she will marry Peter?"

"Yes, I do." She thought: My dears have pulled up, and sit talking, their heads close together in a little veil of raining fog. For a moment Valentine is driving out Judy. That's a lick of sweetness; not enough, not enough.

"But, Betty, how do you suppose the knife got here?"

"The explanation is that she put it. How did she know about the basket?"

"I'm afraid I may have shown it her. As one of the antiquities of the house. But why did she do it?"

"One form of insanity is a weakness for symbolic actions."

"But what did it symbolise?"

"I suppose her vile intentions."

"But, Betty, I must know more than that. This has frightened me. I don't like to think what may have been meant. If she's mad, I must stop any marriage with Peter at once.—

—"Oh, I don't know that I even care about that. I want to stop wickedness, and I don't know how."

"None of us know how. Look here, Mother, you know the story of Florian Ashe?"

"Your father told it me, in this room, when you were a week old."

"Take the knife, and stick it in the stone of his tower, and leave it there. Hang a cocoanut on its handle for the birds,

and if ever I find out the whole truth, I'll let you know."
"That is a very good idea. Shall we go out and do it now?"
Get it done. Will my body go so far? They have not found
it cold by the open sea. I'm cold. The doors of this house are
open. A door in London for Serge. Shut, but he will open it
to-morrow. O Rings!

The stairs fell, shallow, pale. Down, drop down the heavens, through the star-circles hanging in the dark air; down to
the great fire that is the earth, bloody with heat and pain.

Look up where the candles climb your stair. Three at the
head, six along the gallery rail.

Up and down the ladder of my race. There is Melitta
coming down. The knife's not under her cloak. I've got it.

O Rings! The candelabra's over-run its cups. Plop. Plop.
The wax drips on the stone. We must go out into the dark.
There's a rose of lights, and from them wax is dropping. On
her knees, in the morning, a girl will be scratching it up.

Melitta said:
"I'll get a cocoanut to-morrow."
"Good, Mother. Come out." The boys are riding home.
Valentine has given him a ring. Rings. Rings. *Upon the bells of
your horses. Pray for the peace.*

I can hear bits clicking, hoofs drumming on the soundless
turf. Come home, you two. Go away again and come home.

"Mother, take my arm. Yes, they may be back any time.
The rain is nothing."

Let's get this done. Left, down the lawn. Nothing to fall
over. There is the tower.

"Here we are. Stick it in. On the side facing the sea."
Spear in Christ's side. Oh damn analogies.

—"Yes. I hear them tearing up the park. It's all right,
Mother."

"It is rather frightening to hear such great living things
coming so fast."

"There they are. Hullo, there, Valentine! Serge! —They
have not heard us. We'll come home. Come away, Mother,
from that knife."

They are home before us. They are in the hall by now, drying fog beads off their hair.

Serge said, flushed: "We rode to the sea."

"Along the cliffs and home," said Valentine.

"Now you're ready for bed?" said Melitta.

"We are all ready," said Van.

"Good night, Serge, good night, Betty. My son, come and talk to me while I do my hair."

They went up. Serge followed, lighting a cigarette. Van came last, rising through the light points to the head of the stair:

In her room was a red fire; the air in suspense, like the veil over a cradle.

She went to bed and fell immediately asleep.

As the fire died, the sea wind poured in over her.

Cornwall—London 1918-1919.

AFTERWORD

To see one's first novel appear, after fourteen years, in one's own country, gives the writer a slight shock. Twelve years ago, through the kindness of that good friend to young writers, Mr. Robert McAlmon, it was printed in Paris. Shortly after, in America. Now, looking at it again, it seems necessary to add a note to it, in an attempt to explain a book one had almost forgotten all about.

One sees now what it is—a fairy story, a War-fairy-tale, occasioned by the way life was presented to the imaginative children of my generation. Also by the overwhelming influence of Dostoievsky. As a story, it is entirely an invention; yet one finds that one had good reason for everything that one put in.

Some very curious things went on, in London and elsewhere, about that time; a tension of life and a sense of living in at least two worlds at once. Though it may be hard to believe now that respectable young women practised evil witchcraft. Or that, apart from the chances of battle, young men felt themselves devoted to death. Yet they did. Or even that other women, though this perhaps was more common, remembered their antique priesthood of life.

While, because it is a fairy-story, it had to end happily, with the reconciliation of "lost princesses and insufferable kings". Yet one sees now that this would not necessarily have been the true end; that, as things are, there would have been far less chance of peace for the Ashe-children; nor would the mother have so easily accepted the magical leading, or her dead husband's will. The essential triumph, with which the book ends, would very likely not have happened. One can think of any number of grim alternatives.

Yet, after thinking it over for months, one found it impossible to alter this; and only one word with which to send the book back to the printer—stet.

M.B. Sennen. Spring, 1933.

Imaginary Letters

We must not expect all the virtues. We should even be satisfied if there is something odd enough to be interesting.
—ALFRED NORTH WHITEHEAD
Science and the Modern World

I

Chere Madame,

I do not know what you think about being a mother; it's an odd department of one's existence, but I suspect that you love your son. And you are more than naturally cut off from the very little a mother can know. And I expect your curiosity has not weakened. While mine has been gratified, so that without knowing enough, I may even know too much.

(God forbid that I should give away the young to the old; but as you will never read this, written in Paris, you, a Russian exile at Yalta, who knows no English, still less mine, I do not think it will be impertinent of me to talk to you, as if you were a living ghost.)

Boris, your son, will be—one might say, he is—the cause of art in others. "C'est la poésie," as our friend Claude says. And there is something displeasing in new poetry. It is like new wine, the difference being that we are not fit for it, not it for us. Translate that again into the body of a young man, and you will see that it becomes difficult, because he is neither poetry or drink, but incalculable flesh and blood. I have said: "Your son Boris is poetry." (I have not said that he is a poet.) A monster of vanity and pride. A high-bred, honourable boy. Capricious, selfish, insensitive. *Shy as a rabbit, helpful and shy.* Lecherous, drunken, bold and chaste. He arouses equally unconquerable affection and despair.

As one person stands for the West of Scotland, *black rock and skerry,* another for the green wood, another for ragged vines and split soil; one for the Hotel Foyot, and another for the British Museum, so he is Russia to us. And you must take that sentence for much more than I said in the last. He has a fine intelligence, which it pleases us to see at last in use. He has led us a pretty dance. He is cruel, devoted, jealous, double-willed, capable of every perversion of sentiment. He is a gentleman, a saint, a cad, and a child who should not be let out alone. Our friend Claude has a good saying for him: "Another of these arrested developments," and there is a riddle in our set, "What is the difference between a cocatrice and a basilisk?" I asked it, and the beautiful American, who will always stand him a drink and a dinner, answered it: "Why, that's Boris Polteratsky"; the laugh that followed had now a touch of discomfort in it.

I suppose I should explain what Russia means to us. Apart from what your son has taught me, I mean—I believe I mean enough. Dostoevski, Turgenev, Sologub, Chekhov. Every variation of the Ballet, and what I have seen during my life of your people. Your first batch of exiles and their successors in such remarkable opposition. Odd by-product of the victory of principles, this crowd of émigré boys.

And this tradition as well; when I was a child, my father once said: "I fought them in the Crimea, but when you are grown up and meet many races, I think you will find that it is only the Russians whom you will understand. They are children, and gentlemen, and mad. Add to them tenacity and control and you have us."

Your son has just left my flat to call on some compatriots. His clothes I took away from a friend, are the clothes he would have always worn, and become him neither more or less than the rags that hung on him in days of his bitterest poverty. (The epoch just preceding this.) He is flushed to a tint like warm gold. A jay-feather picked up this summer in the high woods is a tiny heraldic bar in his hat. He is carrying a pair of my driving gloves, and for good luck a ring, a wheel in silver and enamel, on the last finger of his right hand.

You will see, with less cynicism than I, the tall bird-grace, the face tilted a little off the throat, the unspoiled green eyes glancing, the delicate body, a trifle too thin, the uniting principle harmonious and strange.

Brightness falls from the air. One of the responses of Claude's and my litany for him.

Never mind at once how we came to know him, nor the year or so we watched his career, until I decided that I had better attend to it myself. I did not start without encouragement, and now I neither rejoice about it, or regret; but have a certain pleasure because I have been of use to him.

He was created to make people regret and rejoice:

> *Brightness falls from the air,*
> *Queens have died, young and fair.*

And I am the type that knows when it is beaten, and perhaps not sufficiently when I am not beaten.

He has gone, and however much you may love him, he is better out of the house. Or out of my house. For the people who love him are too gentle, and who dislike him, too stupid. And most of what I write is false, because I describe him as a person grown-up, a young man set, a coherent personality.

There is one thing I would like to know, and I do not see how I can find out. What did his father do to him? Did he beat him, sneer at him, lie to him? Boris won't tell, but somewhere your son is checked by his memories of your husband, Madame. There can hardly exist a father less esteemed, nor one whose vices live more in his child, who repudiates them. And does not understand. And the result is a check on the expansion of his nature. He is a picture cut in bits; the parts slide up and down each; shoot, crawl round, dart and chase each other. To his torment, certainly to ours, who greatly love what we have guessed of the design. On the other hand, I quote from Claude's litany:

"My dear, his eyes. They are not the eyes of a fool, they are not the eyes of a man who has seen what he has. They're the eyes of a baby." He is as innocent as the night when he was dressed as Cupid, and frightened by the lights, jumped down from his pillar to burrow in your skirts.

From this you will see that: "Il nous a beaucoup troublé." If I could know what his father had done to him, I might know what would give him power. What you seem to have done are most things becoming to a mother. A woman older than your son and much younger than you, will tell you more about it another night.

Adieu.

II

Madame,

Brightness falls from the air,
Queens have died, young and fair.

Alter that to "queens survive," and I can begin to tell you what may alarm you, but will interest you most, what he is as a lover. Well, he is not mine. If he had been, these letters would not have been written in a more lyrical and less accurate key.

Did I want him? That's another story—kept, what there is to tell of it, for another letter.

"Queens survive, young and fair." Not that he is what a "queen" has come to mean now, but the line indicates his fanatical pédérastie.

When the day comes when my looks are finally gone, and my appetites (I hope) with them, I shall write the best book that has ever been done on the half vital reality, half fashionable snobbery of our age, the romantic and sensual passions of men for men.

Think that it is romantic, is sensual; is mixed with the will towards the creative life at the needle point where it pricks the unknown. Is sensual, jealous, angry, preoccupied with rendezvous and beds; in hotels, apartments, parks, bars; will follow the fleets to ports, scour the 'grand magasins,' prowl the suburbs for roughs, if dangerous the better. Is a recognized medium for advancing the career. Is comic, detestable, admirable. Has its prostitutes, its ascetics, its victims, its saints. I think I may add with justice, its dupes.

You will want to know in which category your son is. I think in all except the first. Which is the only one—until perhaps lately—that the world, outside his friends would have placed him. And you cannot say now, as you might if you were an English mother, with the proud love I am sure you have: "then, as regards my son. *None ever lived more just, none more abused.*" That is not it at all. He told me once: "My dear, if it had not been impossible for me to bear to be interfered with for even half an hour of my life, I should have become a tapette long ago."

So you see. And it is perhaps a better protection than principles.

He has just come in. A little late, even for Paris bedtime. In the middle of the morning. Whisking like a kitten after the tail of last night's amusements. He had left me ill, with the promise to come home and look after me before two, as a sign of a now amended life, and perfect 'sagesse'. (The steps by which we arrived at the idea of this do me both credit and discredit. I ran through every direction of emotion, from effective teasing, to a perfectly useless martyrdom of grief.) I suppose I should be pleased. I think I am. He had been out with princes, not the gutter; had been drunk gaily on champagne, not malevolently on 'fine'. Thoroughly refreshed by contacts with his race and oddly critical of them. Surprisingly kind to me. I was not allowed to finish a letter or visit a friend in peace, but coming back in the stony Paris cold, he wrapped me up in his arms, saying "Comme nons sommes deus orphelins, n'est-ce pas, ma cherie?"

And after lunch, he telephoned cleverly for me, forgot to buy a dressing for my hand, and sent me home to mind the cold I had only got because he forced me out at night and let me stand in the wind because he was afraid of Claude's concierge.

And tried to get me to send out my old servant, whom I did not want to send out again because of the awful cold, and found out that I supposed I could endure it if two of his boy friends came to tea. And saw I was working and stopped talking. And is asleep on my bed now, practically sucking his thumh.

That was all right. He woke up and went out and bought a dressing, and by the time his little friends arrived, I was gigling at his jokes. They were Americans. They were drnnk. They brought three bottles with them, Calvados, a carafe of vin ordinaire, some restaurant must have parted from under compulsion, and a bottle of scotch whiskey. I liked them, but the evening developed curiously. Shy and bold in turns, they were full of an inexplicable fourth dimensional fear. They loved me and each other and your son, and they were equally prepared to hate us both. They shook out their bodies in Charlestons, and seemed to be listening to something that was not being said. Later, one of them alarmed me, when he followed me into another room, and told me that a friend I expected had not come because he had pushed a cigarette into his eye to blind him, and had succeeded. Which was not true.

And your son lay on a heap of cushions and laughed at everything, his mouth drawn up to his wicked eyes, and said irrelevant things, relevantly and backwards, and kept me laughing, which is not so easy to do as it used to be. Nothing burning mad in his folly that night, only grace; *brightness falls from the air;* until I sent him away on parole with all that was left of my fortune because he had wakened up the laughter he had often killed.

I hope you slept that night as well as I slept, in a dark full of gold sparks glancing, memory of your son, memory of a presence, but even more of a state of the imagination whose reality is only found *east of the sun, west of the moon.*

III

Madame,

He has not come back today with, nor, as I have reason to fear, without the money, which is not his at all and is not really mine. He has not come back to dress my hand or take my ticket to England. (Perhaps I shall not be able to go to England.) It is not likely that he has gone to his work, and very likely that he has got off, and slept with some sailor, the fashionable excitement just now, in a little gilt and fog hotel; and is still asleep, his small, unshaven chin stuck up on the pillow, my ring with its wheel of blue and red gleaming in the sheets. Once when he had wanted money for an orgy (and got it as he was carrying my note-case) a pneumatique came for me next morning by cyclist. Much too early. Waking me, dry and unrefreshed in the dust of late summer, in a bare room. "Come to me at once, because I can think of nothing but you." And I went across Paris to him, instantly. Calling at the Bank on the way. And he did not need money, but he clung to me. I was not to go away, ever, because without me he would do worse things and mind them less.

This time there has been no pneumatique, and he may be all right. Warm in one of your lost prince's makeshift palaces. Outside the streets are iron-dark with pure cold, and inside my flat the lights are reflected like an interior under the sea. A mirror would be a miracle of decoration in a world that did not know how to make glass, or any reflecting surface. They would have bowls of water, wine, ink; the round shapes that suit reflections. I have shaken up a glass snowstorm ball round a Russian ship. It has settled now, and I will tell you about how this began to happen, last summer, a strong memory, but right away in the past, without much sense of continuity between that time and this.

Now I remember, the time began exactly like this—a procession of cold days. I had not seen your son for a year. When we met next day for lunch, after a moment in a bar, I said: "He will be sweeping the streets unless he dies." And wondered if he would hurry up and die, and how ghastly the little Paris funeral would be with Claude and me for the procession. And as I watched him across the table, the sense came back of stars jumpingt about in a ball with the paint off. Or the electrons dancing round their atom. At any rate, a constellation sweeping past my system to alter its course. My course was altered; instincts were aroused, homely, exalted, ridiculous, violent.

Reluctantly, I went back to the old discipline, part sweet, now more than half intolerable of going without. Of making money for one serve two. Of contriving, planning. To create through him. To create him. In his own image.

That is work. Or rather that is a life. A life hardly possible except for a lover. Once, like a creature in a dream, making explicit an instinct it will deny once awake, he suggested, I might be his. "Sauvons nous de cette pédérastie—" Then, once we were away, above the trees like green fire torches, under the high apple-land, where they are twisted and drop stones for fruit, I was told, with averted head, quickly, that it was impossible. "You are my only friend, and you are all the world. You would be like the men I go with; I should hate you afterwards. Besides, you are the only woman I have ever knwon."

Pure pride, and the sentiment half weakness, half strength which cannot bear to increase suffering, held me to our friendship bargain. With results I will try and show to you. Well, one thing has come out of those country months, when I did my duty, and hoped a little, and fretted. Was envious and unjust. When there was no self-regulating balance, and I was ten times more than ordinarily alone. That time has hurried

243

into the past. I will try and show you what has come out of it.

What has come of it is a physical grace restored, and a future nearly assured at work he likes and does well. An intelligence developing within its own pattern at a speed that is enchanting. (Half with assurance that amazes me, half like a graceful savage, casually occupied with 'big thinks.') For the rest, he is what he was before, the romantic properties polished up which have served him so well with our English set who, when the worst came to the worst, were the only friends he had. We'll grant him, too, his descent, noble and hieratic, from you, Madame; and from your husband, who strikes me more and more as a sinister figure in your saga. We'll give him the air, the lightness, the cutting balanced between sensibility and strength. Then, remember what I said about a ball. Think of it as green glass the mud of the underworld caked; it is now washed off, and in it stars are dancing. And you can think also that I am describing his eyes. Eyes of a baby, I said before. No, wicked eyes. Eyes of a wicked baby? A baby can't be wicked. And we know he is our child. All I can say is, that, after my careful restoring, 'brightness fell from the air.' *Dust has dimmed Helen's eyes.*

IV

My last letter was not a successful attempt to describe to you the side of his personality that has driven me through so many varieties of distress. A cycle of miseries now known by heart, with cynicism the only moderator. Or, in our usual phrase, why he drives us all mad.

I remember, for ordinary people often hit a truth in a dull way, a little garcon de promenoir once said to me, earnestly: "Don't have too much to do with him. There is something bad about Boris." And questioned: "I don't know what it is. It's in the way he gets tight. Like when he's dancing, something violent, as if it was made of something cold." From a remark like that how many things have been lived through, grouped and sorted? From that also you see the power in the word, the descending logos, which is often humble, and escapes through common, silly lips (he was a deplorable little boy) on its way in and out of brains, lives, actions. Altering them. By hazard? Inevitably? When he said: "Bad about Boris," I wondered. Before he had been a boy to me who had amused me. Now, I became anxious about him. I have never taken him seriously, but the flick of curiosity (while I was saying that I did not believe anything much against him), turned me, and so it began.

What the remark has come to mean can be described by the 'stanzas written in a moment of dejection.' Written when we were leaving the village; when I was over-worked and under-played and over-tired.

> *Give bread and drink*
> *To soap: even to prayers,*

245

for the surprise it prepares.
Give scent, give fire
Everything to restore,
You will not find it a bore.

Hang out a wire from the stars
To the Banks, for a friend,
Notice where it will end.

It will not end where you think.
You have set something going.
DO NOT TAKE TO DRINK.

A sailor has a parrot
A barman has a bar.
The human heart is unpredictable
LIKE GOD.

Restore life
To its capacity for beauty
That sounds
An order to make pleasure out of duty.
BUT,

Watch the surprise in your eyes
Waiting for the moon to rise
A surprise moon for the wise moon,
the sight for sore eyes.
A lean moon for the serene moon of peace.
CULTIVATE PLEASURE IN SURPRISE.

When
You set a feather in a cap
A feather in another's cap
(A feather up in Russia's cap)
If the cap slips the moon flits
If the cap sits the moon flits

IF THIS CAP FITS, PUT IT ON.

V

Madame,

This correspondence seems to be dwindling into an account of nothing but your son's crimes and misdemeanours. They have perhaps obsessed me too much, arrested me from the study of his character. So, because of the obsession, I will devote this letter to a typical and exaggerated example of his badness which has driven me deep but confusedly into my estimate of him.

I will tell it to you exactly; for it is, with cyclic variations, all there is that is wrong in him and that makes him and his friends unhappy. Which destroys his life, and exasperates theirs.

Variations on this theme give it all. The childish, appetite-swayed egotism, and irresponsibility, with consequences from the tragic to the ludicrous; which always are finally ludicrous, and earn him our easy forgiveness (giving practice for a virtue, which has almost disappeared).

Part of my plan for him was to get him back to the company of his own kind. So, I was pleased when an unequivocal princess invited him, sent him off with praise. And with something that is worth less to him than praise (you must always remember that) a thousand franc note I had buried in a jar of rice against a final evil day.

I knew I could trust him. I knew I could not trust him. I so needed to trust him. I gambled.

He came back next day, bright and sweet. Again I left the money with him, when he went out with them that night. Again he came back. The next day I was going to England. I wanted that evening with him to myself, and he agreed as a lover might, and rested my heart with confidence and peace.

We had a Russian dinner, with vodka, and meat cakes baked with herbs, and went to our dancing place off the Place de la Concorde. He is sometimes surprised when I want a little fun for myself, and disconcerted with I find it.

At midnight, with my journey before me, I said: "I must go home. Coming, mon ami?" "No," he said, glancing sideways, "there is something I must do. I can't tell you about that. It will be worse if I don't go. It is not love, it is not money. It is something disagreeable. Go home, and I will come in an hour. This is your evening, I know. Trust me. You must have trust in me."

It is on occasions like this that my cynicism and my sentimentality clash. I had no trust in him, and as ever, I needed to trust him. And arguments about money are not gracious, or wise at a bar that is three parts club. I went home, and built up the fire in my room to warm him, and lay down till he should come in, and, over a final drink we would run up to that point of understanding when our play together becomes reality, the prince and princess walking in the wood.

My invention. Described by him: "As if we had lost our way, but would soon find it again."

And how many times have I thought it found, to find it had not been found? I fell asleep, and when I woke it was just morning, and there was no sign of him. I suffered my disappointment until I slept again. Woke. Went to his room to see him flung across the bed, drunk to stupor; and when I woke him to say good-bye, the money was gone. I cried out at him and recollected myself most unwillingly, and said: "It is not the money, little one. It is that you should do things like that." And he said: "Do not make me suffer double." And I went away with a lead weight on the pace of my journey.

When I came back, balanced again by contact with my race, I was adjusted to any little surprises he might spring. He had had a week to miss me in. I was going to enjoy his pleasure in my return. Agreeable thoughts tuned up, as I saw him hurrying on the platform. His walk is one of his charms. It gives a suspicion of instability, because his feet, a repetition of his hands, are too small for the hard, tall body, advancing to kiss me on both cheeks and take me away. I was taken away, but I could feel something like a small, iced wind threading the tenderness and the chatter. I did not know from where it blew—it may have followed me from England, a quality in me from my contacts there. And next day I was awfully tired. I should have gone to tea at the Ritz, and I could not get there. It was disgraceful weakness, but I had no hat that I had confidence in; and, instead of telling me that I looked well, he said it did not matter, because I ought to go.

So, I did not go. I stayed in and found out all that there was wrong with the house, examined the natural law by which one's possessions, left in the care of an impeccable 'bonne,' look on one's return as if they had been left out in the rain. I spent a wretched, active time restoring, and after dinner, I went into my room, warmed with logs and scented with wood ashes. He followed me. 'Abrutie,' I fell on my bed like an old-ish child and slept. Without a word, he curled up at my feet.

Later, I woke up. There he was, as tired as I. And I meditated, with the perception that follows a short, sharp sleep, that our position was absurd; this pederasty nonsense, and in his case, a lie. That there we were, young man and woman, *beaux and bien nés et bien faits*. With every link but the link of bodies. The living intimacy that resolved all differences not allowed. Every relation of lovers but that. Every quarrel to be made cerebral. And every pleasure.

The quarrels are the worst. Their only answer is an embrace and quiet. Clarté comes after, and the intellectual love of God. When I had slept, I had dreamed of another love that had not turned out well, and woke to see your son sprawled at my feet. Sleeping a pinched, uneasy sleep. We should have been sleeping in each other's arms, and I woke up to tell him about my dream; let go the iron spring I had wound too tight; talked a little nonsense; heard a little peace.

I put out the hand I had burned and took his. Hoping

that he would take it simply and let me rest. He woke up and put his finger hard down on the burn, and I tore it away; and still half asleep, went out to look for something, and a moment later found tears pouring down my face. Tears I could not help, not about him, but about everything that was too hard because of him.

Not noisy grief. Just crying. A little later, he said:
"Why are your crying?"
"For nothing."
"Why?"
"Because I'm tired. Take no notice."
"Je trouve ça ignoble."
"Why?"

I do not quite remember all that happened then. Remember that I was being sorry for myself. He screamed and raved at me, and I did not understand. Pain waved on and off, and a good deal of sense and laughter, but rather wild. For a moment I was afraid of his gestures, of the green eyes glaring out of the chalk-white mask and chinese-pitched cheekbones. But innocent with an animal's stupid innocence, I was making up verses that began with lines like: "O bird-troika," "De Tranquillitate," "To have a real friend," "True love, true love, true love, true love."

He was screaming at me: "I am going away from you to see my freinds." "To get drunk," said I, "that's no news," and then, "Boris, explain. What have I done?" He said: "What do you want?" "I thought—I thought," (I tried to think what I thought—) "that I was unhappy, and perhaps you would ask me why. And then I could tell you, and it would not hurt so much. I have something to cry about, you know. If I could only have told you about what I saw when I was asleep." He screamed at me again, laughing; and went away. I had quite a long cry, until blessed Nature asserted herself in rage.

When he was a child, were you accustomed to this? And to its sequel? I was determined not to see him again. Wrote him a dry, delicate letter. The judgment that one makes at the beginning of joy and the end of pain.

I was working in my room when he came in, listened to the fire whistling in the wet wood while I read. He came in, very drawn and black:

"You don't wish to speak to me?—Why did you insult me last night?"

I should like to know why it is necessary to tell people that you will not speak to them again in order to make them talk.

I listened to incoherence, but I was surprised when he said as if he was dragging it from some agonized recess in his huge skull: "Why do you pity me? I know I am pitiable, and that makes it worse."

I said: "I didn't. I was not thinking of you—I told you I was pitying myself, and wanted, if you like, an echo."

"I thought your little equivocal smile meant me."

"And my tears?"

So great is english sentimentality, that I even felt guilty because I had not been sorry for him, and uneasy because I *was* sorry for him now, and that did not seem to please.

There seemed to be no way out of it.

"I am beginning to be sorry for you now" (de vous plaindre). "You have been living in a nightmare." He had stayed up all night drinking, was sick and bruised with exhausting rage. Had come home to curse me again. Had come home to be cured. My letter, it appeared, had done it. He said:

"When I read that, I saw you. You wrote like a man would. Not personally. What you said was true. I am an intolerable character." We then indulged in a reconciliation, from which I drew three sentences to comfort me.

"I was like this apartment before you came. A closed up chaos of furniture. And look at it now. That is what you are doing. I tell you that is a miracle."

"Yes," said I, "and while I am in a corner waxing a parquet, you are in the kitchen, breaking the glass." He said:

"You said: 'There is not enough light' and you have made glass doors that open onto a garden. All kinds of flowers. Don't think I don't know."

A sort of thanksgiving after that, the mysterious sense of what used to be called spiritual victory. Of which, I suppose one can say that it is one's strongest impulse realized impersonally. And what, on the other hand, was it all about? Also, three days later, we ran through a milder arrangement; but I have given you a typical cycle of his crime and punishment, and for six months, I have endured variations of it.

VI

There, Madame, I have told you in haste a number of things about the male cub you have produced, and I have looked after. We mothers must hang together. Indeed, these letters are rather like a 'ballade des pendues'. I am sure your life at Yalta is not gay and rather mad, but I doubt if it matches for insanity our life in Paris. We are all abnormally sensitive to pain, and people are getting their fun out of torture, a habit I mistrust. To prefer 'crises de nerfs', agonised reactions, brutal scenes not by contrast, but instead of harmony, gaiety, accomplishment. Consider the experiences, the inexperience that makes such a state possible. It is no good getting out of it by saying to me: "You must know a very odd set, my dear." Of course, anything said is partially true. I could redescribe your son as the tragic russian aristocrat, fighting a losing battle here, pure among the debauch of spirit, helped by a disinterested woman — that might do. In fact, it would do, for a number of silly women who think starvation, with its attendant vices, romantic. I have a little nonsense about him too, when I sing, changing an old song:

> *Jeune homme sans mélancolie,*
> *Beau comme le soleil de la Russie.*
> *Garde bien ta belle folie.*

And when we play at dragons, and the prince and princess in the wood.

Voi che sapete che cosé è l'amor. That is the song of songs, and in it is all the difference there is between us. I know a little what love is, and he with his fiery pretensions knows nothing whatever; is like a man in danger of death for want of what he needs, is offered and will not touch. It's not his pédérastie that makes him ignorant; that can carry love (I've seen it do it), but the state of our society. Boris has a heart. If he had not, should I have taken such pains with him? Even his exile has not killed a princely spirit out of which a lover might be made. In a way, I am his only 'education sentimentale', and that as much for love's sake as for his. Also, apart from him, there is the crown of his little fancy-boys who have the run of my house.

I like most of them very much. If they are french they are intelligent, self-contained, and quick to bed (which is more than Boris is. Through timidity, through mischief, through malice, he is as elusive as any female minx). If they are english, they are generous and sentimental. If americans—well, amateurs of the impossible.

Well, he has a rendez-vous with one of them, and off he goes. And the other one does not turn up. On the other hand, he usually calls here later and presses cautious enquiries. Your son is lost, and I know quite well where he is, dead asleep again in some hotel that takes the throwouts of the 'boites de nuit.' They run round again for a bit, until Boris charges at him like a young bull, and they run off for the night, and your son drags him off the dancing floor and hits him; and then there strolls in out of blazing, car-running Montmartre a sailor, in uniform, and your son goes to the bar, and smiles shyly and wickedly at him, and runs back a little later and tells his friend to give him a hundred francs so that he can go off and sleep with the sailor, and he either does or doesn't, but your son gets it somehow; and after that the affair ends up in re-crimination. (I've had this happen to me, and I know—but he did not get the hundred francs out of me. I am sure he has never quite understood why.)

But what is going to be the end of this pédérastie that depends on women, which asks everything and gives nothing in return? I know (and Boris knows, for I told him) that what he exacts from me are the attentions, devotion, sacrifices of an adored mistress. What will be the end of it, for most of them, when their boy's beauty has hardened out into a man's beauty that has not quite come off, and there is no recompensing principle of work or passion to organise their lives? Will they marry when they are forty to have the children they most of them want; and insult and plague their women with the sentimental rape of the next generations' boys? It is too soon to see—the fruits of Wilde's tragic, tiresome martyrdom; only this much, that the choicest men of our time are turned that way, and the women like them; to be chosen or not chosen; and the spiritual fertilizations, the chief fruit of love does not come off, is aborted and wasted in scenes and injuries...

Enough of that: he is asleep on my bed again. Told me I could make a poem because our life was the same as it was in the Greek cities (I had amused him, reconstructing a day with Alcibiades). He said: "It's a question of style. We are as poor as you say they were, and we have some of their things which aren't priced. And one set of fine clothes apiece, and gramophone discs from Mozart to jazz. And the honey and the eggs and fish, and the bath room sponges, and the piece of jade that pins your scarf. Your ear-rings are the only gold in the house, and we have to stand the weather, but we don't miss much."

He had an enchanting facility for playing with a conversation; developing, never resolving it. I sometimes try to do that; change for a moment *into the condition of fire, when there is all music and all rest.* I believe, I shall always believe, that, if you can do that, when you can do it, you must. You risk everything to attain that condition, the false, the sentimental, the banal, a state of interior uncleanness worse than disease. I will however tell you this as another example of our life. I was resting when he came in, furious, and I don't blame him, for they were trying to get his work for nothing, trading on his poverty. He wanted me to run out to a bar across the bridges, and though the gold rhetoric of the pont Alexandre III, would have done me good, I would not go. Too quick a way out, and rather a bore now. Instead we went out to a little "bistro" near which was Italy. Right off the French map; the patron's head narrowed by black whiskers. Blue lights and a feeling of Florence.

I watched him snap up a raw steak, blind with rage. Ready to turn it on me. Afraid again; discouraged. I had tried the usual shifts, to be furiously contradicted, but food and wine do their business in their own time, and quite soon we were practicing eating spaghetti without ignoble cuts with the fork. Then I repeated the formula which has certainly lost the freshness of its pleasure: "Don't worry. It will be harder for a time but our help will turn up." He said:

"Do you think it is so agreeable always to be helped?"

I said: "It must be perfectly beastly; you have all my sympathy." He said:

"Besides, I wanted to help you."

That warmed me, and I knew that a series of events were coming together to make a new arrangement, eliminated, selected, made significant, like a work of art. The patron who was serving us kindly, the tiny room, the tallness of the black bottle, our audience, three old Frenchwomen, idiotically curious. And others unknown.

"It's time for magic," I said. Because it *was* magic. (I could write you a treatise on your son's superstitions, his faith that I can *do* things.)

"What now?" he said, cocking his little head sideways.

I knew that what we must do was to stick together, endure a crazy, cruel earth, a situation half agonizing because half glorious, repeated in another way by the falseness of our personal relation. Remembered a doubtful poem of my youth.

They have taken the oath of brother-in-blood on leavened bread and salt.

That might catch his attention. The 'pain' would do. Unleavened is biscuits. I broke off a piece, and noticed him very excited, and a startling sentence in what he believes is English: "Don wan doz wummans to see."

"Does it matter if the cows in the field stare?"

"No."

I broke a piece of bread, sprinkled it with salt, and dipped it in wine. Halved it and gave it to him and to myself.

"What is that?"

"Sign that we can bear it, that we'll see things through," and tried to translate brother-in-blood. Then added what I suddenly saw, "It is also the *'saint sacrement'*."

He was all eyes. Went away to meet some friends, and next day, when I was discouraged, instead of point out what a nuisance I was, encouraged me. I said what one should never say: "You're all right to-day. Did I get you through last night?"

Like a child asked if it has posted a letter, he said: "But, of course you did."

One way of managing the unmanageable. And of managing oneself. Like a little bread to go on with.

So we live from day to day.

I wonder how you live at Yalta.

I am exceedingly curious also to know what produced your general situation, shot an aristocracy on to the streets, dispersed the singularly vivid illusion we had of your vigour and tenacity. The cross-relations, the forces, the calculables, and the incalculables. How far you and your son are the microcosm—but one must start from somewhere.

Good night, russian mother, separated from part of yourself. Good night, russian son, who seem to carry two continents in your shell of a body, from the pale Baltic to China, in whom the east and west play pitch and toss.

I hope this means something, but I don't like his cruelty. His fatalism does not appear noble, only daft. It is only tolerable because his qualities are twisted on a string of poetry, the only string that is never broken.

VII

Madame,

I know that these notes on the personality of a naughty boy, on poverty, change, and the "sexual life of our time" are ways of looking at something else, a partially understood category. Snap at a huge cherry in the dark. A fruit I should like to see, and the tree no less than the life-earth-tree itself.

A Russian wrote a sentence I find of profound importance: *It is necessary to understand that all objects known to us exist not only in those categories in which they are perceived by us, but in an indefinite number of others in which we do not and cannot sense them. And we must learn first to think things in other categories, and then, so far as we are able, imagine them therein.*

My categories have been obvious and personal; local, and all the time I was looking for somewhere to put your son. A system where he shall be sun and smallest star, where he shall dance round, and there shall dance round him all that I feel is related to him. Principally and at the moment his race history.

That category would include the Tsardom and the Third International, the westward drive of the east, trek of the Tartars and the Chosen People, and the emptying out here of your disinherited. How it all happened and eternally *where*. When there was too little food in one place, and too many people in another; down to the events which turned on a match-head that snapped, so that a word was not said or said differently; or a car passed in the street that altered the inflection of a voice saying "no" or "yes" or "you" or "I".

There we should find your son, and his fierce, childish ways and high manners; there why Marx's historic materialism should have become a workable religion. And the category that includes this category in a speck of its dust?

Again, to take a secular survey of what seems to be the downfall of your civilisation, and more subtly of our own, what do we see? I said before that people are getting their fun out of torture, and I want a historical study of parties and persons who have deliberately made the unpleasant their pleasure. It is not as if we were so surfeited with joy. It is not for contrast, which would be clear enough, if a little unimaginative; still less, in this riot of appetites, for deliverance from the pairs of opposites. It seems to be from want of experience (I speak of the boys of our set) of anything but pain.

This is not fair to your son, whose spirit is the least sceptic I know; who has kept his fun which is half his enchantment. All he does is to accept his ruin, even to death's point. Or did until I flew at him. Asleep again, (I have written half these letters watching him asleep) his head on a cushion covered with silk stripped from an old frock. Oh, the days when we had some clothes. I am writing this from the heart of Paris, dressed for a shooting lodge. And our life is like that, of danger, sport and fatigue.

The purpose of a good revolutionary is not personal heroism or martyrdom; but the creation of a happier world. Well, well. Again: *Stripped of their camouflage and regarded as a national government and as successors to Peter the Great, the Bolsheviks are performing a necessary through unenviable task. They are introducing, as far as they can, american efficiency among a lazy and undisciplined population.*

No one has a greater respect for Mr. Bertrand Russell than I, but it would be interesting to know what would happen if I tried that on your son. Economic pressure in pleasant Paris landed him in the gutter. And american efficiency, whatever that is, may not be every nation's meat. And who wants Russia americanised (or any other country russianised)?

Discipline a lazy, irresponsible boy? I wish I knew how. What for? To make an american patch in north-eastern Europe? Or to turn you east again, reversing the road of Ghenghis Khan?

What is it all about?

The springs of these actions are to be found in one of the unknown categories. Cheap fiction about hidden hands may correct the theories of the great mathematician, the enthusiast for the liberty of man.

Do you remember, in a novel called "Peter the Great," the young courtier who comes back from Europe to Russia, re-examines, takes part in affairs, and finally disappears across the eastern frontier to look for God in those two likely places, the sunrise and his own navel?

Merejkowski insists on that as a proper end, of which nothing could convince me. But it seems that you are turning east again not for contemplation, but the Imperial game.

And what has that to do with Communism? 'Very like our rule in India' your administration is described. 'Very like Plato's' your reconstruction of society, who call Plato middleclass. And how is Marx's economic determinism swallowed in exchange for your rich, magical rituals? (Boris would believe in a miracle-working dried bat.) What are you? What is he? I swing from Petrograd to Paris, from the communist party to one boy. Penitent, he said, once: "Chérie, je sais que j'ai tous les défauts du caractère slave." I added: "And all the qualities," ever wishful to please. But what will his new life make of him? A good painter, a young man about Paris? In fact, a success? And after that?

The business of the good revolutionary is to create a happier world.

A happier world—an uncorrupt and efficient form of government, by preference a democracy? Good. Unlimited produciton and enjoyment of the fruits of the earth? Excellent. Less babies? Sure. Better babies? Right. Extension in every direction of man's curiosity, and command over nature? Most certainly. Best of all.

And after that? The question mark that rises like a ghost after every triumph. Only to negate them, I think, when its interrogation is not admitted, and man runs back to the game of futile apologia for what he has done, instead of search for

the category where all facts exist together with the answers to
the ghosts they raise:

The thing-in-itself is demonstrated by the pairs of opposites:
To be weighed, to be divided, to be chosen.
To be illustrated by the possibilities of cities,
And the notable vagaries of Oriental kings.

Back again to Boris for another series. —Boris so busy
playing at work, and working at play, and making a good job
of it. I suppose that I have been the good revolutionary, and
am a little disillusioned about it because the happier world
does not seem, so far, to have affected me. I wanted a friend
out of it, the friend he might have been and is not. I think
now that I have almost done with him. That he has not in the
least done with me. In fact, that I shall have to get rid of him.

Now I am quite sure that once you asked the same questions and came to the same conclusion about the man by
whom you had Boris.

"How shall I get rid of him?" you said.

And you only did when he went to prison, and as he is out
again that question has never been settled. Boris told me once
that there had been divisions between you and his father,
hinted at uneasiness over him, which may have been like mine.
Admiratiion and despair because the lovely, living thing had
slipped through your fingers, and its brightness the glitter of a
fish, which would rather not be a fish.

The father is the key to this business. Here the shadow of
Freud seems to have a body behind it. You married for love,
it seems, against advice; and your son is like your husband,
and hates him: thinks too much about him. Loves you: is a
bad son. Do you ever get a letter from him with more in it
than: "I hope this finds you well as it leaves me?" Can't love
me. Neither loves nor is loved as he should be. Only Claude
and I have seen the brightness, the innocence, the shred of
moon riding a cruel sky.

The noise of horses a long way off, riding in from Asia, a
black company. The dancing, the rising power. Ruriks and

fair men from the Baltic. Romanoffs, and the race pressing West into lands with practicable histories. Vienna. Paris.

Then the war that confounded all shores spat out these children. *For ever* written in steel on the walls of the Third International.

No one knows why. Not for american administration. Not for innate disgust with shiftless orgies. Not for order, justice and peace. Above all, not for a turning of the soul against cruelty, cruelty of ignorance, cruelty of sadism. Through no descent of the spirit "pour faire aimer l'amour." In north Asia the commissars are galloping back. And you are an old lady down at Yalta taking in sewing, I think he said; and Nadia teaches girls to play the piano; and your young boys don't care much so long as they can knock up some commonplace fun.

Only Claude and I have asked questions, loved and troubled ourselves; sent a ripple to break on your beach at Yalta, in Iphigenia's country. And I see neither brother nor son coming to fetch you away.

VIII

Madame,

It is over now. It is exceedingly difficult to describe to you how. Against my real will, and, I think his; against our practical interest, our romantic interests, against what we might have realised out of them, we have come to the end (which, for all I know, may be a beginning, and is certainly the beginning of something else).

We are walking backwards away from each other, a little chorus of short barks from our friends accompanying us.

Every history of every love-affair is important. For one reason that it reflects the exact states of emotional tension in its age and its group. Your son and I are making a duty out of what might have been a pleasure, our spirits so parted that he seems to be a charitable societies' case for tolerance and self-control.

> *A certain pain,*
> *Hung on a steel chain.*
> *And never, never, loose that dog again.*

I know how it happened. I hope the one thing I have made plain in these letters is the cyclic nature of our relations, the recurrence of crises. And one of the main points why they should have been crises of suffering and aversion, which might just as well have been of pasison and joy. Passion indeed! We've had enough of it. Always the wrong kind; and it is here that the enquiry broadens again, because, pederasty apart, that is the scale with the magnet in it. And the last time it was too typical. The last time we had a row, it lost even the element of surprise. Left me incurious. Fell flat. He only came in drunk

and abused me; and after it, I took away his key, which he
had the grace not to try and get back. He has been broke
since and I've helped him, sick and I've visited him. What has
been a pleasure has become a duty. Which means that it should
stop. And I've had the luck to have had the pleasure. To see
him restored and taking life. Life at my hands and what matter
if he bit them? Or rather dropped them once they were tired.

He has only himself to thank now if he fails. But it occurs
to me that he may, and for the same reasons which, from his
side, have separated us.

A man once said about him, a long time ago. (That man
was cutting down his meals by half to feed him, out of an idle
passion to develop him and see things grow.) "After all," he
said, "you never see Boris about with anyone but himself. If
he had a little boy he ran round after and went without his
meals for and adored, I'd say 'good boy, I've twenty francs,
here's ten'! But does he?" And there was nobody among us
who could say that he did. He hasn't altered, which means
that he has only himself to think about, and so, on the rules of
what he calls magic, he is not free enough from himself to
judge that self's way.

Manque d'amour—better a little hypocrisy and the pretence
of it than this blind scuttle after the tail of his own appetites.

He has gone a long way from me, the friend I might have
had, if the dark head had turned itself gently to me. In this
world of steel and strain, where there are no more troikas
with bells jangling, and the Paris trams an iron-crawling substitute. No more smooth furs smelling of scented beasts. No
more soundless carpets and quiet servants to receive us home.
No more mothers, the lovely mothers our imaginations construct out of the surprising realities, as I have constructed you.
No more following the sun and our fancy. No more toys to
play with, while the rough edges of our wounds draw together.
And the perpetual fret of those toys displayed for who can
pay, for bodies less fine than ours. And who have finer bodies
than ours when not too hard-driven, allowed to take on their
lustre, not asked to be more virtuous than they can be?

This winter is like one long storm over a black heath. There is not much distinction between night and day. In our cabins we keep some sort of fires alight. Fire is the sign of enduring life. One would have thought they should be banked now with every generosity of sentiment. I am putting it the wrong way. This life has been too hard for the green plant, love wasting itself like flowers, the generosity of strength. I am as anxious and as generous as a cat with ten kittens, and no milk.

No, it is only by an imagination half false which made me look to him as a friend, and regret, and ask what might have happened if he had come to me, even for a short time, with heart and spirit full. What he could have got from me. What I could have done with him.

The short way out of the wood, closed by a barrier that is not there. Pederasty born out of aversion to his father, and devotion to you, confirmed by his life of poverty and strain, thwarted by it into a condition which makes him incapable of any directed and expressed love. A chance with me he could not take, a chance for creation raté, and a lot of information gained. There is always that. There is always the long way out of the wood, the cast round when you have made a map of it. The way that implies the patience I am without, and the only pleasure, the satisfaction of the mind when it is on the track of what *is*.

Both good ways and equal, the long with the short. I have made a virtue where I have had no choice. Have written these letters to you.

Mysteriously, I am almost happy now it is said. Not quite purely. Not quite cynically. Hurled a storm of letters to you, unknown, of whom I have not an idea that is not conventional; letters that are not for you to read. What they have done, I know, is to fix a little in this flying world your fleshly and my ghostly son, the black and green boy, who comes less and less often to see me now. The ray, the shadow, the memory, the mirror in which I have looked, seen and understood, imperfectly, many things.

Paris. Hotel Foyot. Autumn, 1924.

Warning to Hikers

I

AMONG other disquieting features of the situation, people in England are beginning to notice that the separation from nature and from country-life which began a century or more ago, is now in a phase of reaction. With the ever increasing aid of mechanical transport, the people who have passed their youth without any direct contact with it, are rediscovering the country-side. With the result that there threatens soon to be no country-side left for them to discover. The subject is curious, painful and mysterious. Until quite lately we have been writing the greatest poetry about nature, all kinds of nature, our own and other people's; we are still admirable at prose descriptions of life out of doors. While the horrible story of the progressive ruin of our landscape is told and retold, shown as a public menace, become part of public instruction, held up as public disgrace. It is a hideous story, a dirty story, in every sense a vulgar story. If the machine of civilisation were to break down, it would cease to be told and the wild land come into its own again. And there are moments, when one sees what is being done to green shaw and hill-side and harbour, when one imagines that there are worse things that could happen, even to a disintegration of present society, which would give us back virgin earth.

Meanwhile with the defilement of every natural object from a blade of grass to a rock, the cult of nature goes on, and one sees no power likely to put an end to it that is not catastrophic. For as in many situations whose real nature is abominable and full of danger, a veil of illusion hangs over the relations of the country and the town. All men need fresh air; a great many English people live in towns from necessity,

not choice. We are a sporting people. The enemy is the demo-
cratic enemy, in a country where people have lost their sta-
tions and like badly-trained chidren can neither keep to their
own places nor respect other peoples'. It is not the better-
bred or even the better-off who are most at fault. In this case,
the more a man belongs to that minority, the less guilty he is
likely to be. Meanwhile something very bad has happened.
One would like to understand it a little more, when understanding is all one has to set against despair.

I have never heard a satisfactory answer to the question
why, about a hundred years ago, for the first time, man began
to manufacture every object in common use, from houses to
boots, upon unvarying patterns of ugly vulgarity. He had attained a new technical skill and he had not lost his sight. Something had happened to him. The accepted reason that it came
with the invention of wholesale production which necessitated
bad design is not the whole answer. That rat won't do all the
fighting. Why did he make his machines do that? Machines
are in use to-day, much the same machines, and the common
run of things in ordinary use, when they have escaped the
blight of art, are often quite agreeable to look at again. Still we
do not know what happened to man. Machines will not cover
all the ground. Houses, for example, have always been built
with hands. Compare a sober, unpretentious eighteenth-century brick façade with the same kind of house built after the
Great Exhibition. Compare the dress of a man in 1800 and
1880. The problem to-day may be about to solve itself, but
that is no answer as to its origin. Blame has been thrown right
and left; on the machines, on Queen Victoria and the middle
classes; ideas to be witty about, not an examination of something sinister, as when a whole people has lost its power to
distinguish between what is ugly and what is beautiful, that is
to say has lost one of the chief characteristics of man.

The first thing to find out would be if it has ever happened before. Public and private collections give an answer,
reassuring or not, according to taste. It is possible however to
go to the Louvre for one kind of consolation for there you

will find a frieze from the palace of Darius the Persian in blue and yellow glazed tiles, equal to anything a modern ceramic factory could do for us. While among the ruins of Rome— spend an hour reconstructing the Baths of Diocletian. Something between Balmoral and the Savoy.

There is not much left of Susa under the Archaemenidae, and plenty of late imperial Rome. This gives us two bad periods, but even then what is left is more or less the work of millionaries, or an example of public rather than private taste. It is difficult to know how far they are separable, but one doubts if even at the worst of such times every single object in use by every citizen was vile in shape and ostentatious in ornament. This is what happened to the English peoples and to most of the peoples of Europe during the last century. A change in the visual and aesthetic faculties for which no satisfactory explanation has ever been given; and which corresponds in time with the enlargement of ancient towns, often round a nucleus of serene original beauty, an enlargement either pretentious or squalid, but wholly hideous. While at the same time, there began the self-conscious awareness of nature at the very moment when it was passing out of the lives of a great part of living men.

Everyone knows this: no one understands it. Every sensitive person spends much more of his life than he knows avoiding this; surrounding himself with reasonably agreeable objects, lodging himself, even inconveniently, in a tolerable— that is to say in an old or a very new—house; putting good stuffs on his body, spending any money he has on one dish or on one good bottle of wine. He may be quite successful, even if he is poor, even because he is poor, if his taste is innate and his training has elicited it. What he does not always reckon on is a kind of psychic shock or rather strain he will suffer once he leaves his own house or those of his friends or the out surroundings he may have picked, and is forced inside the majority-home of England, in a town or a suburb of a town. He may be conscious of nothing worse than a new sort of fatigue and a horrible staleness in the eyes. But things will go wrong with him, psychic balances will be upset, and he will leave with a sense of escape as from something deathly. I have known children—not spoiled or precious children—from a beautiful home, kept weather-bound in seaside lodgings, miserably affected, in spite of all our efforts, by the ugliness of shape and colour that surrounded them.

One imagines that people, even people who through ignorance and familiarity have grown up half blind, suffer from these conditions more than they know; those who do know, more than even they understand; and that everyone, in the effort either to change or endure, becomes unconsciously strained and sapped. Modified also, and this must be particularly true of children. If it has been one's fortune to be brought up among physical beauties, natural and created, if one's senses and tastes have been formed on them; if also one was taught their use as a standard and to reject passionately all that was not like them, adult life becomes a greatly enchanced but not an easier thing. With such training goes contempt and anger; a snobbery but a powerful one; and with the sensibility, a capacity for nervous exhaustion, until such a person is positively healthier on insufficient food than in pretentious surroundings.

There must be one profound difference between the men of the country and the town, that the most ragged village child who ever went egg-smashing in spring, sleeping in the dirtiest cottage, has not had his sight and smell and touch and hearing corrupted from without. For unless he was born already with a life in his imagination, there is next to nothing in a town for a growing animal to *do*, if it is to grow according to human animal capacity. A training in "movies" and "last across" is no substitute for the various experiences in growth and pleasure and hardihood and danger the hillside gives, the shore, the tree and the stream and the weather, handled by a country child and by which he is handled. A country child has his decent dangers, things to fight and circumvent and endure. He has his endless pleasures which he shares with princes, pleasures for which there is no substitute and no price.

It was Gibbon who said with elegant confidence that with

the exploration of the earth, the advancement of the power of European man and the subjugation of native peoples the world over, we had now no more to fear from invasion by barbarians. While it was H. G. Wells who pointed out that Gibbon as he wrote this, congratulating himself and the scholars and gentlemen of the eighteenth-century, had not been able to forsee the infinitely greater number of barbarians who were to be bred, in groups, with every great city in Europe for nucleus. A different sort of barbarian, not called by that name, and to become by familiarity less and less thought of as such. A partly trained barbarian, trained to do one thing or two. A lettered barbarian, lightly washed with information. A necessary, a re-christened barbarian; and finally a barbarian for whom there would be a cult. For his baptism had been a sacramental act, where he was named citizen; and his society, now become ours, a democracy; and at that baptism it was decided, without distinction of character or gifts, that every man alive is in a state of grace.

When it is felt that a thing should be true which is patently not true, it is the way of mankind to begin by pretending, usually for moral reasons, that it is, reinforcing the conviction, often by a ceremonial act. Hence the baptism. Then the belief, for the effect of the original act must be strengthened. This is the most dangerous of all the games of spoof man plays with himself—until it becomes impossible or inconvenient to play it any longer, and there is a general return, often unjust and in panic, to what appears to be the original facts of the case. It is unpleasant to think that before this essay is finished, the future of England is to be decided by a majority vote of the barbarians; that because the minority of un-savage men have been in love with the fair ideas of liberty and opportuinty and the absurd idea of equality; because they were out of love with snobbery, and honourably ashamed of physical wretchedness, they should have magicked themselves into a belief that all men could be equally magicked—into the likeness of the Ideal Citizen, into the image created by aristocratic and humanitarian minds.

II

England is very much a countryman's country: not too large, not too up and down, delicately various, inequable within a pleasant mean. Private, bird-haunted, a land to perfection types of beasts; sturdy, companionable, exceedingly mysterious; balanced between giving and exacting; exacting and giving what breeds as good a man as has ever been bred on earth. And on this land has been written the history of that man, stone times and bronze times, his little cities and small houses and great; his beautiful and terrible works, his conquests of nature and his compromises with her; his worship and service and rivalry with her. Until to-day, after the last hundred years, his denial of her has spread like a nest of sores.

One result of this denial, the breeding and isolating of millions of industrial workers in large towns for the sole purpose of this industry or that, is to have done a thing which has hardly ever been done before. We do not know or cannot visualise adequately what a similar life must have been like in the great slave-owning empires of antiquity. That is one of the things people definitely prefer not to think about. It is within the proper meaning of the awful, a hideous awe. On the one hand we say: "It can't have been as base as all that"; on the other that it is best not thought about now it is over. Yet there is a historical novel of the first importance waiting to be written about a man who became a slave; who, perhaps, had a foster-brother born a slave; and how they went down into the world where there were no more human rights, outside the legal and social sanctions which belong now to each child at birth: what they found there, who had nothing to rely on but human virtue; and how that virtue stood the

274

strain; and what happened to the character of the freeman who became a slave.

It is perhaps the best thing man has done to have erased that arbitrary division. If only he had not proceeded to intoxicate himself on the equally unnatural idea of equality, not of opportunity, but of nature. What is to be done about this error, which may threaten our whole civilisation? Nothing, it seems, but to correct our enthusiasms, unchristen our barbarians and return to the facts of the case—the unequal nature of man as he is—with as little brutality and as little panic as possible.

While we can. Can we? If we can. Magic is magic. May we not have given our god-child our civilisation to tear to pieces? It was once supposed impossible to undo a sacramental act.

Still, there is a point about our barbarian at home which can hardly be paralleled in the condition of the ancient slave; that our man, for what must actually be for the first time in history, has been growing up and spending his whole life away from any natural surroundings whatever. This must be unique. Think of the kind of animals we are. The condition of our existence was that from the hour of our birth we coped with life out of doors, wet and stony, green and dark, dry and glittering; beautiful with corn or in "the meadows mad with horses," treacherous with snakes or perilous with wolves. Whatever the weather was, we had to do more than bear it; actually to make the best of it, become modified into temperate or tropic or arctic man. The end of that story, at least in any possible climate, has been a version of the song the Three Children sang in the fire: *"Oh! ye fire and heat, Oh! ye ice and snow, bless ye the Lord, Praise Him and magnify Him for ever. Oh! ye waters that be above the firmament.... Oh! ye whales and all that move in the waters.... Oh, let the Earth bless the Lord; yea, let it praise Him and magnify Him for ever."* A nearly exhaustive paean in praise of natural phenomena, as they are and for what they are.

But in our cities we have done what man has never done before, almost manufactured a weather, a climate, a whole

environment, in which there is little amelioration as possible
and every curse. For light we have substituted smoke, for
blue air or silver or gold or white or dark crystal, a partially
solidified brown-grey. For the scent-box of nature, a smell,
curiously compounded of burnt carbon, oils and dust and
our own sweat. For the interesting variations of earth under
our feet, a monotony of iron pavements, whose impact trav-
els up the spine, until at the back of the skull there is a pain.
While a walk, which is, after all, the original way we move
about, becomes a quick source of fatigue. The accompani-
ments to sleep are rain, wind, the tides, a tree creaking, the
squeak of a hedgehog, the delicate bark of a fox. To these we
slept, and awoke with birds to encourage us. For these we
have substituted a distant roar, which, whatever it is custom-
ary to say, *is not in the least* like the roar of the sea. And with
the roar, a vibration, mechanical, implacable. Now this is
equally true for the distinguished part of cities (that is to say
when a large english city, outside London, has a distinguished
part). The residential parts of such industrial towns as I have
seen, the homes of their chief citizens, were masterpieces of
graceless comfort and self-satisfaction. Still, London, at least,
is tempered with gardens and fine buildings, with privacy
and proportion, where delicate clothes are worn and interesting things are done; where the inhabitants steal away in
their cars to the country, which is still their principal home.
It is not tempered at all for the majority of homes, where
men have been grown for several generations under conditions for which I can find no parallel. There were slums in
Rome and Babylon, one could make out a case and say that
mediaeval cities were mostly slum, but never before were the
works and wealth of man based on coal, and the largest cities
were easy to get out of. While no one had as yet discovered
Nature. Very simply, because one does not easily discover
what has not been lost. In the past, it was to points of nature
that men were sensitive; spring's return, daisies white on dark
grass, the "klangê" of cranes that fly across the sunrise; but
these are noticed with the kind of surprise that comes when

the attention is caught by a detail of the familiar. Gilbert Murray, in contrasting our nature sensibility with the Greek says in effect that we rhapsodise about the state they breathed: that "we talk about worshipping a sunrise, while they trudged to the top of a mountain and did sacrifice."

This awareness of all nature is beginning to be spoken of as though natural life was an antithetic condition to the life now lived by half the world. If our taking to town life was not the cause of the cult of nature, it must have enhanced it, speeded it up, been responsible for its exaggerations, its snobberies, its absurdities, its morbid variations; and for certain recent developments it may be well to examine.

There is no quarrel with the extended scope of poetry. The poet knows his own business, and any artist who is in love with nature. It is their business to be conscious and to make men conscious. In this case, to-day, of something they have lost. Perhaps the preoccupation of Wordsworth or of Shelley was an impulse (*"Hell is a city much like London"*) forseeing what was coming, an instinct for what man was about to lose, about whose loss he might yet be warned.

The trouble seems to be that in a sense the writers have done their work too well; that while they have had the maximum of their proper effect as artists, their readers have gone one better. Going one better usually means going something else. It implies a reversal—often a very subtle reversal—of the original intention. We have been landed, not in nature, but in a cult of nature; not in the country brought to our towns again, but in our sort of town running wild over the countryside for an escape from towns. And all the time, our new barbarians, bred inside that hideously fabricated world, under conditions that man has never known before, without experience, conscious or unconscious, of man's original life, and until quite recently without any cult for it, have lately heard of the cult. It is their way to help themselves to what is going. They have now heard that there is something to be had free.

III

The middle classes began it. In our society, the upper classes, and what is left of our aristocracy have never left the land. Professions might call them away or capital cities for their "seasons," but the country was their home as it was the peasants'. Several homes in different parts—too many homes —but homes. Not week-end cottages, not rural villas with a garden and no land, within easy reach of Manchester or Newcastle, with a daily train-load of city neighbours for company.

Nature or country life, life on a mountain, beside the sea, in a wood or between fields is not like Wordsworth or Shelley or an Elizabethan lyric. Art is not Nature. It is something more or less. Anyhow, it is Art. Wilde pointed out that when a poet or a painter took hold of nature and extracted from her some powerful beauty, that she seemed often to follow him up with an imitation of his invention. But there her complaisance ends. Love of nature is the Bunk. You are either used to it, part of it and generally unconscious of it, except for some detail or of your own well-being, or you are an outsider. People, even of true sensibility, who "love" the country, who leave for a holiday full of rapture and anticipation, are not insincere, but they are treating it as an opera or a picture-gallery, with the extra advantages of a first-class nursing home. They are treating it as a mixture of régime and art. This is unavoidable, natural, not dishonourable, but still the cult widens down until it reaches the people of fake sensibility; the people who have discovered that the country is good for children; all the people who think they should like something which they have never learned. Until the cult be-

come craze reaches the mass of our people, the unique barbarian we have been breeding for generations, and who are
beginning to stream out at the tail of our motor-cars.... Out
where, exactly? Not very far yet, and only in nice weather;
and round London at least the land is as green and safe as it
ever is, and piteously downtrodden and over-picnicked; and
there are art tea-shops and pretentious public houses and old
tudor garages and petrol pumps in clumps. Shall we have a
tree grown in mimicry of them? Is nature grim enough for
that? These they find reassuring: "Convenient, ain't it?"
"Friendly, that's what it is." One knows what they mean.
Beauty, or even pure air, is not a friendly thing, not until it
has passed into you so completely that you cease to notice it;
so that when your consciousness of it returns, it will be like
the sight of a lover who has never gone away.

No chance of that for the working-class boy and girl gone
hiking. One is beginning to wonder if there may not be a
town-consciousness developing somewhere, an identification
with the cities we have made. Not of their stately parts, for
these imply open spaces, parterres and fountains and trees,
but with the double ranks of grey houses and the clanging
lumbering trams; with the public house and its smell and its
shiny wooden fittings; with the wide garage courtyard, the
bright metals and woods lacquered in colours; with the tobacconist and the sweetshop, and the fruit-stalls, which are
beautiful; with the public library and the hospital with its
fire-escapes; with the wretched, blackened Victorian-gothic
church; with the tasty air and the vibrating roar; with the
street shrieks, and even with the pneumatic drill. If this seems
unthinkable, remember that we are growing more than half
our people to be aware of very little else.

As an environment it has been tested, grown our new
barbarians, who may quite possibly invalidate the whole effort
of man. A curious revenge, for they would destroy their own
protection, the only protection they have, who would be left
to face the nature they have not been able to know; who is
waiting outside upon the rim of cities, patient, indifferent,

ready to come in. Such men, trained only in the use of machines, would find the only machine left for them to work the natural one; the tricky, intricate, sure and unsure, slow and dangerous and delightful mechanism of the earth, which cannot be hurried or learned quickly; which demands of a man all patience, every adaptability and technique. Mr. Wells gave a picture of such a catastrophe. It was not pretty. There were slums in the woods and a folklore about bicycles and dead trams. There was fear at night, and religion about an old man called God and a silk hat. In that book Mr. Wells gave no solution. Nor in any other, of exactly that state of things. Is there a solution of the whole question? There seems to be only a faith that if we find some way to do what we ought, find out where to interfere and where to let alone, it may solve itself.

It is implied or taken for granted or advertised that what drives the hikers out over the country-side is a half-articulate wish in the soul of man to return to the earth. Nothing seems to be more unlikely. Curiosity, a proper love of exercise, a chance to be alone with your boy or girl friend, a new stunt, mass suggestion by the Press, which has its own reasons. That is how it began. How it will go on (if it goes on) is another matter; but if it does, it would be interesting to show something of what will happen, something which has not been calculated on, something there for them which is waiting, something whose nature is attention, which waits and always waits.

IV

The earth is indifferent always. The earth has its eye open night and day, an infinite number of eyes. Utterly observant, utterly indifferent eyes. Under that watch and that carelessness, these ribbon-streams of people run out and sub-divide and waver; hesitate and dart back; withdraw like tentacles, arms of a squid pulled in and wrapped again about its mass. They set out by foot or train or car, so far; but what is going to happen when they get further? There is one thing that is true about the earth, not often noticed or obviously true, how quickly, in the friendliest country, the most loved, described, harvested or defiled, the land will become again a no-man's land. A stone's throw from the ploughed field, the orchard, the vicarage garden there will be the strangeness of the unharvested, and patches of wilderness dividing field and field.

Two steams meet at the top of an orchard in Kent. The left branch ran out of a tiny gorge, clay and moss banks, but moulded like boulders and dark as the entrance to Alph's caves. Wooded too, but not with copse, spidery pale withies, lean rods clashing, and underneath a wet starring of flowers opening with the sun and dying with the moon. The stream is choked with a corrupt matting of dead wood. Is it wood? It is corrupt, anyhow; and at the head of the gorge there is a sandstone rock stained with moss, and down its face the water drips, milky with clay; and there is neither pace nor sparkle, only wetness, in the twilight of a secret desolation. No birds.

Nor does one return willingly down that stream. To get out one climbs its side, to be thrown out on rough turf, on the flank of a wilk hill; where, sunk like a stone in a tangle of strong-smelling herbs, a very small dwelling has gone wild.

This in a part of the country become a garden of orchards and hop fields; true wilderness. Round a corner, round any corner: it is the same.

Quiet in the woods is like no other quiet. High wind in the tree-tops and the groaning, pitching branches is not an easy thing. Tides play tricks, and the hours—perhaps above all the hours—of the day and night, whose each hour has its rhythm and quality. No one knows anything at all about the out of doors who has not passed beyond the lovely and the sensational, through the conditions imposed by fine weather and order and cultivation, into the quiet of the ordinary untouched; the workshops of the perfected, and for the man-perfected thing. Rubbish heaps of Nature and burial grounds and try-outs and rankness. It is possible to see that in a town, where a house has been pulled down and not rebuilt, and if you look in between the builders' boards, you will find a savage wilderness for version of the waste-land, dock and elder and sorrel, a mixed coarseness it is sometimes hard to name separately; not lovely, chiefly alarming. One asks: "How did it get in?"

Havelock Ellis wrote a book called *The Dance of Life*. A very great book about the rhythms in each person and thing, and in each kind of person and in each kind of thing; each separate dance and each group-dance making the Dance, the Ballet of the world. Of these group-dances are the weather, the star changes, the tides, the history of each egg and leaf. Each feather, apple and stone. Man was trained to his dance; man's dance and each man's dance; in and out, with and against those patterns. They trained his sight, and all his senses and his body's ability, conditioned his nervous system and the whole range of his responses. There is no substitute for these experiences; our inventions at best are no more than a repetition of them, miserably limited; at best a forcing of the intelligence and the imagination, without the basis of physical and sensual experience, pre-eminently necessary in childhood, and without which—well we are beginning, and only beginning, to see what happens without them.

Whether there is a new "town-awareness," an unconscious reaction to the city rhythm, as universal as the reaction to nature was once—one does not know. But there seems to be a new kind of person about, the latest development of the "city-bred." (It is to be noticed, that, in Victorian literature, where he first appears, he is not very significant. He is ignorant, a man in a minor position; towns were smaller; the richer classes still could and did live in the country; and the assumption seems to have been that nobody worth much attention would possibly live anywhere else.) It may not be possible to speak accurately for any time but one's own. (Or even for any time at all.) But surely, to-day, one is able to observe the product of the town who has had all that the town can give. Education and physical care, athletics, and holidays, and almost certainly a dash of the nature cult. He is intelligent, our town-born, and often intelligent about the right things. He is skillful and diligent and short-sighted. He is reasonably good and there is no sap in him. He is not a barbarian, but it is said that some savages speak of a man who is dying, or a man who is outside tabu, as a man who has lost his dance. This man has no dance. Dance comes out through the body by way of the imagination. The other way round won't do. Or, perhaps he has a dance, is making a dance, a machine and indoor dance, a *pas d'acier*. He is preponderant among the "intellectuals," the "red" intellectuals. If he has vitality it is there. If he dances, it will be to that tune. There is something uncomfortable in these attempts at observation.

This man is an assemblage of correct parts, of good details, with something weak about the mainspring or the ignition. We are only concerned with England, but for a great number of Americans this is an understatement. There, there seems to be a principal that is definitely insane, actually against the running of the whole, loose among their works.

Our variety does not go "hiking" in crowds. He does himself fairly well; week-end tramps with an ordnance map, or a cottage shared with friends and lots of intelligent fun, which *is* fun. But wherever he goes, he brings the town with him, an abstract of the cerebral life of towns. He enjoys himself, he does himself good; he is not a part. It does not matter. He does not destroy or litter or make a mess. He has an eye for period and for what is fitting, and generally not enough money to try improvements. His morals scandalise, but it is good for people to be shocked. He does not matter. He does not go, and on principle, where the crowds stream and defile. Ribbon-houses are not built for him, who wants his place off the map. Nor does he want a cinema, nor County Council lighting down the lane to his house. He is the model for something which is pretty good or really fine. But the model, even the working model, is not the thing. Not the whole living body, fully *incorporated* into the intricacies of nature, the in-and-out shiftings of the seasons and the weather, the variations between the speed of light and the quiet of a stone, the activities whose forms are harvest and war and sport and sleep and love and death.

"Life is a pure flame and we live by an invisible sun within us." With these men of the towns it is as though their invisible light were not derived from the sun or from any star. Synthetic fire; fire without heat; not fire at all.

It may be objected that all the intelligent men from cities are not like this, any more than all countrymen have the pure instinctive fire within them. *Of course* there are exceptions. One is attempting an observation, a new classification. Something like this is happening, which would not have happened, so far as it is possible to see, if man had not recently altered the essential character of his living arrangements. He must be modified by such a change. The modification would be startlingly visible if a great number of the observers were not themselves a product of the thing observed.

Town life in certain directions sharpens the wits, makes them not reflective but self-conscious. Hence the passion for self-expression in the better taught, the craze for forgetfulness, for escape, from self or any other kind of reality; the need to find a bolt-hole from urban reality and unreality into the extreme reality of the land.

V

I once read a description of cholera at Naples, when the sanitary authorities smoked out from the sewers, where they had lived from Roman times, the countless rats of an ancient city. The writer who described them, their rushes along the streets and quays and into the houses, said that they were mad, and that he had never before been so afraid. More afraid than of the plague and of the people falling in the streets. Rats, let alone mad rats, is not a fair comparison. But if the rats were mad, it was through fear, and human beings are very easily made afraid.

Last summer I was out alone, "hiking" myself, in the Northumberland hills, on the moors above Chesters, near Tower Ty. I had left the road and sruck across country in the grey keen air, and among the boulders and bright wet grass, the drip of water running underground and the debris of the wall, with innumerable curlews for company, I caught myself glancing back over my shoulder, as if something which I had hardly ever noticed in myself was awake at some touch, and telling a different part of me to look out. There was everything to see and nothing much to look out for, until I remembered that I was on the Picts' side of the wall, in the wolf-country and the country of little men who had much to fear from wolves. And I knew that until I had brought it to light, I had been living in the fear of a past age. Wolves spring at your shoulder, break it, and pull you down from behind. I was alone with wolf-memories and shapes. A little further on, a tall weathered countryman appeared from nowhere. We said good day pleasantly, and he looked hard at me, and in his eyes there was an extraordinary reassurance. I went on over a long bony ledge.

Then, as happened last summer, clouds began to stream over from the north, from the Cheviot Hills, and the rain began. I fitted myself in between two boulders, into a stone chair, and began to eat sandwiches and ginger nuts. I do not like picnics with people, but I enjoyed that one. Then, round somewhere to the left of me, invisible, I heard voices; harsh, Tyneside voices, whose every other sentence ends with the word "bugger," a wholly non-commital endearment. A few moments later, about fifty yards beneath me, through the mist travelling in torn veils, there trailed across a "hiking" party. Youths and their girls from Newcastle or South Shields or Gateshead. I had seen such parties before, going out noisy or returning drenched and sullen, but not before on the high moors. They were not noisy now or indefatigable or resolute or at ease. Or even happy or unhappy. They were there. And from their movements they did not seem to know where they were or how they had got there; what they meant to do or what there was to do; how to stay or how to get back. They were a very long way from anywhere. Two thousand feet below were the enormous trees, the flowering grasses, the bright quick rivers of the valleys of the north and south Tyne. We were above them, sitting on the top of the world. They drifted past, less articulate than the curlews, the girls treading over in their ridiculous shoes. An arm of the sun wheeled like a searchlight over the moor. A scarf of mist spun in and extinguished it. They seemed to take no notice. *To what green altars, O mysterious priest?* It got darker. Like Lord Peter Wimsey's Bunter I remembered that "the phenomenon had habits" and thought I had better get back. Looking at them, I saw the pace of their slow scramble lessen as they crossed over below me to the right, to a rock face and a fall of scree. Into that most unfriendly hill-pen they drew, like sheep out of the wind; and like sheep they stood, turned all in one direction, more quiet than sheep. A mist blew across them, every minute it got darker, but once through the darkness the sun stood out with a terrible glance, then wrapped itself again in blackness against them; and as I struck out, in an interval of the rain now beginning to pelt, in a moment of flying quiet, there was blown across to me a whisper of their fear.

No one who has seen the Tyneside, perhaps especially during the present industrial depression, could wish any form of human or any other animate life to stay in it a moment longer than it could help. Newcastle-on-Tyne and the group of towns which extend down the river to Tynemouth are a condemnation of man, a permanent public catastrophe, so obvious, so recognised by every kind of sane observer, that it is hardly necessary to insist. London by comparison is some dream city of the soul. From old maps Newcastle was once a pleasant place for tudor shipping, with high-pitched houses down to the broad quays. While man was never given a better place from whence to enlarge his city. A valley in a stately countryside, wide but high, on which to build in descending terraces the approach to his wealth on the river's back. Instead, between Newcastle and Tynemouth, he has thrown down, in a chaos of filth, eleven miles of smoke-blackened brick and stone. Over whose roofs hangs stench and blackness; in whose streets there is nothing for the eye, but for the ear a fury of sound. (Traffic is not regulated in Newcastle, except to allow for the quick transit of cars coming up through England to Scotland by the Great North Road.) Inside the town it is possible to recognise six objects that are not abominable to the sight. It is not possible to ruin a river, spanned there at one bend by a bridge, a single green arc, the crosswork of whose stresses, imposed by the nature of its construction and nothing else, being strictly beautiful. A cathedral, whose curious spire, supported by the lightest of flying buttresses. Wren copied for St. Dunstan's-in-the-East. The castle keep, now no more than a burnt-out stump of blackened wood; the soot-black doric front of an old public library. A new electric-light building, and in the centre of the town, where, in about 1840, Richard Grainger, a local architect who died young, was allowed to construct in a façade of "pure and noble classicism," a street and a part of a street. Buildings which one is told are about to be pulled down, to be replaced by a North of England town gone Regent Street.

The boys and girls go "hiking" out of this. The better-off migrate, like a snail with its house on its back, up the valley to the west. Where, on the grey Northumbrian hills, they are setting their shells, not built of the grey stone nature has everywhere provided and man has previously used, making for himself the traditional grey cubes roofed with slate, but of gaudy, imported, cottage-renaissance red brick.

Get away from this the young artisan must, but what do they find when they have got out? Either they destroy what they find or are lost in it, driven like the party I watched on the moors like quite mindless sheep. Lost and mindless and in fear. In some slight physical peril, and in another peril, which is not slight, nor physical as we are used to reckon physical things. A danger which is in nature and of the essence of nature. I said before that the town-bred run out into the country to escape from themselves and from reality. Or from town-reality. From himself and from town-reality into another reality to which he has not been tuned. For which he is now essentially not fitted. (The countryman may reverse the process, but he has something to which he can return, which can never be lost; which does not change or question or strain or fret; equable as the city can never be alike to the just and the unjust.)

One supposes that since building began, the perils and temptations, especially the temptations of town life, have been impressed upon the young. The Girl Who Lost Her Character did it in London; "When she left the village she was shy." It is a common assumption that the Girl Who Left Home was a country girl, and the wrong turning led straight to Piccadilly. But if this sort of thing goes on, we may look forward to a new school of thought, in which the innocent town-girl leaves home and is exposed to all the terrors and temptations of the country-side. Her return to the old street and the corner tobacconist will move us to tears. This may well be the first city-myth, the beginning of a town folklore, which in some form or another must develop, and of which the Cinema is an earnest.

VI

The return of the city native may make us weep; the stones of the pavements may cry out with joy; but the country-side which has betrayed her will not care. Nature is a divinity usually seen as a goddess, who has hardly ever lacked for recognition throughout time. Like the Catholic Church "she has never had the reputation of being an institution to be trifled with." It is only within the last century that we have begun to take liberties with her.

There are conquests and familiarities which honour and those which dishonour. In nature there seems to be a power latent to turn our triumphs against us, re-strike the balance of power when we have prevailed against her in our wars. The wars we have had to fight; which she has imposed; which are part of what can be called the game, and occasionally the sacred game. Our first and our best and possibly our last cities are a part of that game and that war, whose triumph is to put a feather in nature's cap, nature, our adversary, not our enemy. It is not Rome or Florence or Seville or Edinburgh or Alexandria, or even Moscow or Paris which are an attempt to live outside her. It is the industrial town, the unplanned overgrown capital or provincial capital city, the flung-down suburban box of bricks which are their extension, the creeping ribbons of toy slum which corrupt the country-side without bringing to it the centralised amenities of the town— these are our last move against nature, against that potency, that great daimon, who is masculine as well as feminine, father as well as mother.

The "bosom" of Nature. "She" has a breast, but that is not the way to find it. Contact with nature is very much what a man has when he participates in any rite or sacrament. Rites and sacraments are a kind of drama, a ritual play taken from universal natural events. They are about the health and ill-health of the soul, about marriage and birth and death. Things which happen. I think it was J. E. Harrison who said that the point of their efficacy, writing of the ancient world, at least, was that a man took out of them in proportion to what he put in. Properly understood, this may be altogether true. It is also true that in relation to nature generally and the life of the country-side, you get what you ask for; you take out what you are capable of putting in; you get your desire, whatever that desire is. There are certain forces there in motion, innumerable forces, all the forces. The further you get away from pure man and group and house and mechanical force, even country house unit and machine, the more you are alone in a new arrangement of life, of forces, and what will happen will depend on you primarily, it seems, but not altogether. A tree may fall down on you, the tide may get you, you may "come off" your mountain, the earth may open and swallow you up. These fates depend largely on your common sense, which depends on your experience and your judgment. Largely but not altogether. Luck comes in, and no man knows what Luck is. Certainly, in comparison with town life, physical risks are less. Nature may have invented the bacillus, but it went to town for company. Wild beasts have not the spring of our traffic or the appetite of our machines. If in some parts of the globe, even over great tracts, there are local and special risks, they are in no way comparable with the risks from your fellow-beings, who become more dangerous the more they know, the more they resemble yourself.

Wherever a man goes, whatever he does, Luck has its way with him, Luck whose true meaning has something to do with Grace. Mr. Huxley, among others, has written about Grace. The image of nature is the Leviathan, the vision of whose monstrous splendour has disquieted many souls since Job. Mr. Huxley says: "In the final chapter of the Book of Job, God is justified, not by His goodness, not by the reasonableness of what He ordains, but because as if His strange, enigmatic, and often sinister creations attest, He is powerful and dangerous and gloriously inventive beyond all human comprehension; because he is at once so glorious and so admirable that we cannot sufficiently love and fear Him; because in the last resort, He is utterly incomprehensible." For God in this passage, read Nature.... "The wild horse and the untamable unicorn, the war-horse laughing among the trumpets, the hawk and the fierce eagle, 'whose young also suck up blood,' these are the heraldic beasts emblazoned on the banners of heaven." And on the banners of Nature. To follow Mr. Huxley's argument, where Justice is shown, opposed and complementary to the fact of Grace, man elaborated his life in cities in his war with nature which was to make Justice absolute, make Grace serviceable to Justice, bind the Leviathan, set the Behemoth to work for man. It has not succeeded; neither Christianity nor Humanitarianism nor Materialism has altered the facts; but that war is a war of the pairs of opposites, which must go on for ever, a part of the sacred game in action.

Meanwhile our city-justice has resulted in a subtlety of injustice without parallel, now that we have begun to breed a race outside, or thinking itself outside, the experience of grace in the true nature of things. "We are all equal, and, if we are not, it is our neighbour's fault." That is a town-cry. It has been pointed out before that it is not apathy but a true instinct that keeps the countryman indifferent to that aspiration. Out of doors all day, he has found out that there is no such nonsense about nature, whose sun shines equally upon that familiar pair, the just and the unjust.

The people of the towns, of whom so large a proportion form our new kind of barbarian, are beginning to go out into the country where neither they nor their fathers were born. They are going here to escape from themselves, going into a place and a state and a complex of forces which are all real as we reckon reality. And the unavoidable realities of nature, birth and death and change of state, are of the same nature as the offices and dramas we call sacraments. While the people have lost the use of formal sacraments in their daily lives, and will go to participate in them without knowing what they are about. In such observances a man takes out what he puts in; that is why people were once taught that it was possible to eat and drink damnation to themselves.

VII

It would seem also that there are times when the indifference of nature is no more than a mask, and the patience of it more that of a mouse with a cat, than the majestic play of forces we have been taught to conceive. I remember the full-dress production some years ago of *A Midsummer Night's Dream*. The most memorable thing about it was the transformation of the wood. At night, a most imaginatively conceived place for dance and magic, with an undertone which was not in Shakespeare's mind—not in that play—of the awful and mysterious; fading out at dawn, to one old oak-tree in an open copse, grey with dew and colourless dawn-light.

There is not a field or a copse or a bay where these transformations are not carried out, almost as many times as there are hours in the day or night. The primrose and violet-sewn hedge in spring, on a winter night with the wind shrieking and cracking the elms, can be a place of furious exaltation, full of that potency which made gods of the winds.

In India to build bridges over the Ganges was held to be impious. The Mother River, they said, would sweep them away. Kipling has a fine story about it. And there were times when it looked as if she tried to, floods would come down before the piers could stand them; and man, western man, had to fight for his works. But for a work that was neither small nor contemptible nor easy nor safe.

It is to-day as if the lovers of England, or of any land, saw the beloved thrown down and bound and trampled on and wounded, called by dirty names and false names of adoration; and all they are able to do is to call down curses and weep; half mad with anger and contempt which fester in their

293

uselessness, or drug themselves with common sense about inevitable developments and other people's rights. Until there rises that faint hope, that suspicion that comes to the lover, that the beloved, as is often the nature of objects to whom eternal love is given, can, finally, look after itself.

To-day the worst of men are going about, leaving a dirty little trail through a sanctuary, a sanctuary which can also renew and rebuild itself. Man's baseness can renew itself also, but not inside the precinct of the sanctuary. It must be withdrawn for that into its own breeding-place. Nature lies like a hand open with the fingers loose for man to run about the palm; dig into the pure flesh and build a palace or sewer or a desolation of his contrivance. The palm is his earth, the fingers are what he does not see, nor understand that they can move, curve in and grasp him and make the palm a gulf, and all his works no more than a fertiliser for its flesh.

In nature a universal catastrophe is latent in the shifting of her finger, and man has a buried terror in himself of earthquakes and tidal waves, of the dreadful works he calls God's act or hand. The great catastrophes force themselves on his attention. He takes less notice of the subtler forms, the piece-by-piece destructions and readjustments by which nature defends herself, and ultimately man. Changes and transformations and vengeances appropriate to the situation, to what has happened, unforseen and in keeping, often strangely subtle and still.

Last August I heard it suggested that the absence of last summer, when the flowering, gathering months combined in themselves the more disagreeable features of November and March, was no more than nature's hint to "hikers" to turn home again. A hint to be followed up by a winter to be endured by bodies starved of their reserves of sunlight. Drastic? Unjust? Nature is both. Ineffective? Possibly, when in the spring—if the spring ever gets here—fresh hoards start out. Unnecessary? I think so.

For once they have taken one step across the line of protection, the belt of urban needs and values each of them carry strapped tight about them, they will find themselves in a world as tricky and uncertain, as full of strangeness, as any wood near Athens. No friendly greenwood, fixed by poets; no wise gnome-tapped mountain; no gracious sea. *The dragon-green, the luminous, the dark, the serpent-haunted.* Will they face it? When the Sirens are back at their business, sisters of the Harpies, the Snatchers? When the tripper-steamer—her bows to the sun—turns into the boat called Millions-of-Years?

Quiet in the woods. They can be very quiet when a wind from nowhere lifts in the tree-tops and through the pine-needles clashing the noise of a harp runs down the trunks into the earth. *And no birds sing.*

[1932]

Traps for Unbelievers

I

IT is being continually brought to our notice, by different people in various ways, that for about the first time in history, the Western World is going about its business, to a great measure, without the belief or practice of religion, organised or private. We are told this in various ways, from different standpoints; several *qualities* of men rejoice or deplore this, or merely observe. Explanations, chiefly tiresome, abound. Books are beginning to pour out about this; by people who believe that men should believe—this or that, but at all costs believe. By people who believe that men ought not to believe; though what they are not to believe is not so simple as it sounds; there is a forest of negative disbeliefs and superstitions, a hitherto pathless jungle. All, or nearly all, are agreed that if man is to believe anything, he must only believe what is true, and then the truths begin to pop out like a fleet of rabbits.

It would be interesting to observe a little more what is really happening. *Something* is happening—or has happened—right through society, a change observable in contrast with one's childhood, not a change in practice, but in sensibility. A moral temperature, not a protest, but an indifference. An indifference to the forms as well as to the spirit of every variety of Christianity; an indifference which sometimes seems to mask an uneasiness, for it is often a strident indifference. Strident indifference often breaks down in panic—that is to say, it is not indifference at all. Panic is the invariable short cut to the false, or to the septic statement of truth.

A part of what has happened is obvious, obvious enough to be reconsidered a little. Clemenceau says: *"Ce qui donne du courage, ce sont les idées."* Somebody else said that up to now mankind had been investing the great part of their spiritual and imaginative energy in church securities, all fundamentally and indissolubly bound up in the personal immortality of the soul, and what was going to happen to it once it had left the body. While, for the two or three generations, people have been asking to see their securities, securities which have been shown to be by no means gilt-edged stock.

For suppose that the doctrines of any one of the religions of man were discovered to be true (or all the doctrines of all the religions at once to be a way of saying what is true) *except* the survival of the individual soul, the bottom would fall out of that market. Men would put up with a round of incarnations—the Tibetans have a proverb "the man who knows his way about will be comfortable even in hell." He might make the New Jerusalem habitable; provided that at his death he is not going to stop; which means, finally have a chance to make a better job of it. For the more a man is, the more he feels that there is something in him which would take more than one stretch of life to make clear and handle significantly.

"Now a religion which is scientifically preposterous may have a long and comfortable life before it; any man can suspend the scientific side of his nature when he is worshipping." Professor Murray then points out that it is when a faith, any faith, becomes ethically untrustworthy that its day is over, not because ethics are the same thing as religion, but because they have always been found eventually to be mixed up in it, though their relation is often by no means an obvious thing.

In the same way as the religious securities for the personal continuance of the soul after death are no longer felt to be sure, men have found out that none of the schemes of conduct so largely advertised in all the religions, and on which depend his favourable transit from his body, quite meet the case, all the cases, in which he has to make up his mind what is best to do. (For, after all, whether he is a devil-worshipper or a militant atheist—a type among the educated now almost extinct—man does, in practice and on one scheme or another, spend his life on deciding what is "best" to do.) The activity may consist in provoking a vendetta in which the innocent family of his enemy may be senselessly destroyed. His idea of "best" may suppose that his "best" will be "worst" for other people, and he may enquire no further. But always for himself it will be "best." No man has ever yet set out to do the worst for himself.

Now, to-day, all over the earth, every literate man knows something about every other man's competing and contrasting faiths. Gone is the blessed ignorance which called the worshipper of Allah "the beastly devil-worshipper of the false prophet Mahound." *False* prophet indeed! All prophets are false. What is a prophet? There never was a prophet. *"Ce qui donne du courage, ce sont les idées."* Clemenceau should know what courage is. Prophecy is now dead, part of the stock-in-trade of all religions, and the Western World is finding itself short of an enormous number of energy-giving ideas, ideas which it is singularly feeble in its efforts to replace.

I once spent a week-end, cut off by floods, in an inn in the Alps, with an old and militant Baptist lady, and used to think of her asleep next door, quite happy, because once in the past she had got wet all over in a large tank with several others; and between that and a discipline of life which included not drinking such things as Bénédictine, she had spun her thread of contact with the tremendous mysteries man has felt encompassing him since the beginning of his time. It is rather too easy to make fun of her. Baptism by immersion is not as good fun as bathing; Bénédictine is pleasant to drink. The point is that she had a working idea, had gone through life with conviction, conviction which had given her courage, focused and released her energy. A conviction people have become by this time more and more indifferent about. Preoccupation with the "unseen," with the whole complex of emotions we call the religious attitude, has vanished from our world as a straight reaction. People would as soon confess to a personal Saviour as to personal dirt, to hereditary syphilis than to original sin. They are not interested in their sins, and do not call them that. Do not want a Saviour. And occasionally go raving mad for want of its equivalent. So it happens that psycho-analysis is one of the lambs of God who is taking away the sins of the world just now. Aldous Huxley says: "There are comparatively few men and women in the contemporary West who unquestionably rationalise their feelings in terms of Christian philosophy and Christian ethics, few who find in the old Christian ideas a source of comfort and determination, and a motive for prolonged and effective action." And again in another essay he has traced what he calls Substitutes for Religion: Art, Antiseptics, Democracy, Success, and the Suppression of Sex; adding on their inadequacy a few pointed notes.

One can spend a good deal too much time watching such specific interests, sources and vehicles for energy, being overloaded and worked to death. Loaded with more than they can carry, being asked to do more than they were ever intended to do; being blamed for their natural inadequacy and abandoned—to be replaced by the stupidest form of scepticism, when every activity had been "found out," and all are equally mistrusted, subject to the shallowest rationalisation, the ugliest sneers. Or if persisted in, are used, not as a means of achieving a full and satisfactory life, but as a kind of drug, taken for its own sake and for one's own sake, until detachment is impossible. While the rule is that without detachment, without a certain fundamental indifference, no occupation or belief will work out satisfactorily at all. The rule is very ancient, and we did not make it. It seems inherent in the structure of things; that for the proper achievement of any given purpose, to the person who pursues it, it should matter everything and nothing. Strictly everything and strictly nothing. As a Buddhist once explained that in order to attain Nirvana it is necessary to put away the desire for it.

Understanding and activity of this order is not what the world is busy with just now. It is busier to-day, perhaps with more things to do than it has ever had before. With this variety: that now men in common are without the one preoccupation, the unifying thing called religion, which once, under whatever form they took part in it, even when they fought about it and beat up each other's gods, they shared.

They are getting along quite nicely about it in the West. So they say; but one would like to look at the situation a little more. One of man's major preoccupations does not pass in the night. Some gaps, some suppressions even must remain. The old militant atheism which was once a form of belief, an idea that released energy, is gone. The present indifference seems something a little more than ignorance, a little more than genuine unawareness. It is delicate work taking psychic temperatures, but if the religious impulse has been so perfectly sublimated, examined, and resolved into all its constituents, and its energies sublimated into strictly accountable activities, would people be so shy, so shy and so offended and so offensive at the word? The other day, after a lecture at London University, I heard the word casually introduced. "Religion," repeated one young man, and shied as though some one had made him an indecent proposition. Another, less modish and intelligent, was noticeably uncomfortable: "What a word to say here!" he said.

The point was, that for separate reasons neither could bear the mention of it. The word Religion, with its vast connotations, is working its way into the category of the shame-making or obscene. It is the same again with a certain class of abstractions, the abstractions of moral qualities our ancestors used to personify, or try to represent in great works of plastic art. Faith and Hope and Charity. Prudence, Justice, Fortitude, Temperance. Try one of these in conversation. You will get the pause, the averted eye, the slight gasp of embarrassment, and the instant reputation for insanity or worse.

Now that is not the way to behave about a complex for which one has been successfully treated, from which one has been finally delivered. One remembers one's own release from the dogmatisms of one's youth. That was a cheerful affair, and one was only too anxious to talk about it.

"He is not loved, He is not feared,"
The man with the receding beard."

303

So much for God the Father, we told the world. We were frequently silly, but we were not shy about it.

But with all this discarding, man, whether he likes it or not, whether he thinks about it or not, has been forced back (and that was the last thing he bargained for) onto the final, inescapable, and implacable question: "Is there anything there or not?" Anything at all? Or has the whole vast various structure been built out of nothing but my misunderstandings of phenomena and my suppressed wishes? Is there anything there at all? That vague, crude, inescapable question is being asked everywhere, and answered or re-answered nowhere.

Nor is it any use to point out that the conclusions of nineteenth-century materialistic science have been just discovered by the mass of the people, and that nineteenth-century materialistic science is dead. True enough, but the new physics and the new psychology, whose conclusions, it is assumed, will reach the people in time, offers nothing at present to replace the beliefs a century of brilliant discoveries destroyed. No convincing re-statement, no inclusive or original development.

It is pretentious of man to pretend that he does not care what happens to him when he dies; that he prefers that nothing should happen to him once he is dead. He may embrace death like a lover or fear it like the devil, or be exceedingly interested to know what will happen next. Indifferent, unless there is something wrong with his works, he is not and should not pretend to be.

Meanwhile the question is as undecided as ever, though possibly in a hopeful state of suspense. But it is *the* question, and on its answer depends man's whole reaction to life.

People now do not pray for the souls of their dead any more than they pray for their own, but Queen Victoria's rite in the bedroom of the Prince Consort is not quite extinct. I have seen a pair of riding-boots, the photograph of a hunter, grouped on the table of a locked study, with two of the horse's hoofs set as inkstands and two as candlesticks. Candlesticks that were lit.

II

An old ghost accompanies the advances and speculations of man, inexorcisable, inexorable, materialising at will. Neither fashionable nor unfashionable, with us like the seasons or the weather, asking in a whisper, as Tennyson put it, if the stars run blind. There is no way out of that statement, they either do or they don't. Every little boy in a bar, with friends and his gay clothes, has that whisper jazzing in his head. And most of the girls. All that they have by way of critical understanding is that Science has shown up the universe, put an end to the moral compulsion not to get drunk or go to church on Sundays. Shown morals up. There is no need to be good any more, and they don't try. And it seems quite simple to see why it is no longer necessary to be good, when the only bill that is likely to come in for any kind of behaviour is some slight social blame or some physical disaster. And science again is being useful about that. So, "Why be good any more?" they ask; and the answer is, "Why?" What answer is there that cuts any ice which does not depend ultimately on unproved premises, and surmises whose very sound is "unscientific"? Suggest to a boy the advantages of reasonable chastity, and the answer is: "What on earth for, so long as I don't catch anything?" Tell him that he should be chaste for the sake of other people or for the sake of the race, and he will repeat, if he is that sort of boy, that so long as he does not catch ...etc....the race will come to no harm. And for any views implying emotional subtlety, he will not have an idea what you are trying to talk about. He is not looking forward, as people twenty years older once did, to any more perfected state of society. So far as he fears anything, he fears want of success. And his sister dreads the new disease, the Repression, which would modify her towards the type of the Baptist lady, whose energy-releasing ideas are unintelligible to her; who is unlovely, self-satisfied, and timorous, with only the memory of a bath taken under peculiar circumstances to stand by; kind but ineffectual. Who has failed to please men. The deepest of the life-instincts is uneasy there.

In practice there seems only one line to take, the suggestion that, in the past, the best men and women have been reasonable in such matters; that there are other things to do; and that some control makes for better fun than the four- to four-thousand-footed mating of the animal creation. An appeal which may or may not work. There are so many exciting exceptions. For youth is getting on pretty well. It was never freer, lovelier, more joyful. Never did it know more accurately how many beans make five.

Then the time arrives when something disagreeable happens, quickening often, with secret and horrible vitality, into tragedy; and one begins to notice what happens to natures who have only human nature to fall back on; not strengthened to meet pain by any of the old receipts, and for whom no new ones are available. Receipts which linked the phenomenal world to an eternal, condemned events by reference to concepts not affected by change or by any of the vicissitudes of man.

Thus, when the trouble has started, the substitutes described by Mr. Huxley begin their useful life. The artist, if he feels up to it, falls back on his art, or on an aesthetic justification of life; the man of affairs, on his business; each to an over-worked Rock of Ages which, put to a use for which it was not intended, subsides under the burden. Each substitute, then, can be seen taking its revenge; art in the lives of the aesthetes, or in the artist who is a cad in practice, of whom Mr. Shaw disapproved so much.

While, refuges apart, the troubles of existence come and go; and in their intervals, "every violent, emotion-producing sensation" is tried for its own sake. Then a malaise sets in, a melancholy and want of balance equal to anything that the Romantic period offered, and without its consolations. This is particularly to be seen in America. Young men of good fortune and conspicuous looks and elaborate education come over to Europe, already surrendered to a sense of chaos and illogical destiny. One has seen it afflict them like a nightmare. It can appear sometimes that when one is looking oneself at a road leading to a town with a tower, hills, and the sea, a well-proportioned mixing of man and nature, these young men are conscious only of a chaos of unrelated objects and a field for despair. Something like this also is responsible for the fierce, steady drinking, the eagerness for pointless and often ferocious adventures, as though the order seen through intoxication were preferable to the view seen sober, of an irrational disorder lit by stray flames of fear.

All this is very peculiar, suggestive, or alarming, and one's instinct—which would probably be the common instinct— is that something will have to be done about it. If any one knew what to do. It is no longer a question of re-establishing Christianity, or of an attempt to replace it. All faiths, except perhaps pure fetish-worship, which is flourishing, are under the same weather. An enormous, fundamental need and occupation of man is out of work. It is the fault of the stars. Something like it seems to have happened before.

Once before, in a well-recorded period, in a time of uncertain faith, men had begun to find out enough about the world to be frightened by it—not only of its disagreeable details, plague, pestilence, and famine—but of the whole of existence, with its ambiguity and injustice, its hints of invariable and indifferent laws. Of these the men of that time had found out less than we have; but it was an age, the first of whose speculations we have an intelligible account, whose interests were critical and scientific; an age of great public works and administration, of trading and learning and increase of public and individual wealth. We called it the Hellenistic Age, and were taught to underrate its importance, coming as it did between the short miracle of Hellas, and the

rise of the Roman Empire to world power. It was definitely
an age which had found its traditional beliefs inadequate;
"found out" Zeus—and, except in some monotheistic or
mystic sense tending to become more and more abstract—
Apollo and Osiris, Bel and Ashtaroth, and Our Ladies of
Athens and Ephesus and Mount Eryx. It was full of great
names in science and philosophy whose works are lost. It was
an age like our own, of wide and superficial education; of
lively curiosity, political uncertainty; of battle, murder, and
sudden death.

It was not, in our sense, an irreligious age. Gods there
were and the idea of God; only a few people, and unpopular,
were prepared to go so far as to say there were none. The
Epicureans, one of the chief schools, were drastic enough to
admit of the existence of the Gods, and then go on to explain
that by no means could they hear any one or do anything to
anybody.

As in our own age, there was no religious persecution—
an invention which, when all is said and done, seems to be a
speciality of Christianity, a legacy from its Jewish origins. As
in our own time, the organised ceremonial of religion, the
building of temples, the dedication of cities, and in Egypt the
deification of the last line of the Pharaohs, the Lagidae, the
fair, North-Europe mountaineers, borne south on Alexander's
shield to rule a land of sacerdotal mysticism—went on by its
own momentum. In all, from Persia to Marseilles, you had a
society which, the more one notices it, seems to have repro-
duced some of the unpleasantest features of our own. With
the exception that it was still felt necessary to pray to something. And it is a commonplace to say that what they finally
prayed to was Luck—whom the philosopher-snobs and the
better-off called Destiny.

Luck is one of the oldest of the Gods, perhaps the only
one to whom worship has never gone quite out of fashion.
Whose nature is unknown and unknowable, who has nothing to do with morals, who favours the just and the unjust,
who is here, there, and everywhere; and yet not seen at any

time. The exquisite film, "Running after Luck" is the neatest attempt to catch and make visible Luck's essence; Luck, Tychê, of whom one actor in that age said that he would as soon be a slave to one of the old gods as to the Destiny of the philosophers.

Professor Murray, in his *Four Stages of Greek Religion*, has given an account of that time, so searching and so brilliant, that a few sentences stolen out of it could be enlarged into many books. It is the fashion to-day to underrate him, and though his point of view is too gentle for us, or even too sentimental, that fashion is the Bunk. More than any Hellenist of our time, he has given pointers for the use of the historic imagination. He calls the religious temper of that time "the Failure of Nerve," and though writing before the war, has drawn parallels from it by intuition with what is happening to us now.

The hellenistic world was like the Western World to-day, the West that includes America. A collection of races, "superficially enlightened," in touch with one another, and with a common stock of half-assimilated ideas. Ideas that had been imposed on them from without. As Professor Murray explains, it was Alexander the Great's fault: "Had Alexander and his generals practised some severely orthodox form of Macedonian religion, it would have been easy to see that their gods were the true gods...but they most markedly did not." They hospitably entertained every god whose path they crossed. (Though there is some evidence that they tried to put down grosser acts of cruelty and superstition.) Meanwhile the peoples of Greece, Egypt, and Near Asia saw their gods powerless against Alexander, and "faithful servants of Apollo come to a bad end." Then the hero Alexander died, of fever or poison, at thirty-two, and his companions started to murder one another. Two founded empires. His luck had given out, who had had all the luck, and still the world went on, and what was more powerful than Chance, Tychê, Luck? Perhaps it was all written on the stars, whatever the stars are, and then it is called Destiny. But who knows? The "effective protest of real science" was already audible, but not very effective. And where has that protest carried us to-day?

For the next few hundred years the protest of the human mind was not with science but with mysticism, mysticism of an astounding variety of symbolism and quality, or else, as with the Stoics, a rule of conduct too stern for the common temper. To-day the "effective protest of science" discourages mysticism, while there is nothing remotely resembling the stoic temper about in the world to-day. While what has repeated itself is a respectful eye on Chance, especially the main chance. Luck flits in and out, flicks on and off our screen, the projection of our temper—Luck and its attendant imps, the charm and the mascot and the fetish up-to-date; the little objects we will not part with, which we feel to be tabu; or else charged-up with mana, as they have always been; the ring that a lover has worn, the medal that a Pope has blessed.

One step more the hellenistic world took, when its nerve broke, running after Luck. Having had a good look at Alexander, who may be called a Greek, since he represented Hellas, it re-introduced what the hellenic mind had explicitly denied, one of the chief of the antiseptics it applied to human thought—the worship of the God-Man, or, as it usually works out, the God-King. He had come to enlighten the world, hellenise it. It is easy to see how it happened. Kings had often been gods, until the Greeks persuaded man that he was not, and never had been. Then Alexander appeared in Asia, a man more like God than had ever been seen before. He became infected there, in the swamp of that old muddle about the nature of things. It is easy to see one reason why he did not deny his divinity: "…it was not good policy to do so…and self-depreciation is not usually the mark of a born ruler." Besides, there was in him a strong and violent and not sufficiently examined mysticism. Not, perhaps, mysticism of a high quality, and allied with a common-sense without parallel. For he was a man with the power of exploiting and making serviceable to his purpose every excess. Not of moderation and patience and cool temper were his glories, but triumphs of temper, of passion, all the passions; such a triumph that what he did was permanent, and Rome a continuation of it, and european civilisation its fruit. Odd luck for the son of a generous king with no nonsense about him, and a princess who was a medicine-woman and a priestess, a lover and a murderess, whose son became king of the world and a god. Here it seems more respectable to call Luck, Destiny, but what exactly do we think that they are? No man has ever found out. All he knows is that something like them is there. While it has always been impossible to catch them, Luck on the wing, Destiny in its stride. And this has been sufficient to preserve their divinity.

III

Old habits of mind die hard, if they die at all. To say that religions are derived from magic is not true; to say that magic preceded religion, as we know it, is probably true enough. Magic has not yet been properly defined. In its *practice* it is, of course, very largely primitive science, misunderstandings by false analogy of the way things work, of natural law. But behind that there seems to remain a very peculiar kind of awareness, an awareness modified and sometimes lost by people whose life has been passed in towns. It is most difficult to describe. It has something to do with a sense of the invisible, the non-existent in a scientific sense, relations between things of a different order: the moon and a stone, the sea and a piece of wood, women and fish. Its *application* by means of primitive guess-work is one of the most shocking records of human trial-and-error in history, but it is by no means quite so sure that all of the original guesses were unscientific, or the original "awareness" quite such nonsense.

This perception has no more died in man than has his sight or any other of his senses; only he does not now try it out, or at least not often, on agriculture or the construction of motor-cars. If he has it, it may make an artist of him, probably the best—that is, the most extroverted—use he has made of it. If he is not that kind of man, it may make some kind of crank of him, in the world we live in; give him a one-track preoccupation with the prophetic structure of the Great Pyramid or the Number of the Beast. I have seen a man who was a distinguished soldier making an anagram out of what he thought was the hebrew word for the Abomination of Desolation, and the name of Lenin, all done in cowrie shells, worked into an imaginative ground-plan of Karnac in Brittany. At least, that is what I think he was doing. He was certainly playing with magic objects, at a kind of personal map-making of the movements of Destiny in unrelated terms.

It is curious. Books and books are being written about Primitive Animism, holes and corners of the earth are visited at great difficulty and expense to find out what one sort or another of primitive man feels about his totem-pole, his bunch of holy feathers, his reaction to a king cobra; antiquity is searched for the driving-out of pharmakoi, the peculiar behaviour of the Capitol chickens; while it is insufficiently admitted and never properly observed that, in an unco-ordinated and furtive manner, we are behaving in exactly the same way all our enlightened lives. At one time, half-way along the development of this primitive "awareness," you fitted that sort of thing into the whole scheme of your life, because it was pleasing to the gods, because they had given you that way of getting to know their will and of helping yourself. Or you did it out of pure devilry, because your gods or God had forbidden such misleading short cuts. To-day it looks as if we were back where we started, with a pure primitive instinct, unexamined, trained not even to a misleading use. Not banished where it should be banished or rationalised where it is capable of rationalisation. Or accepted for what it is. One even wonders if the whole process of magic is not going to repeat itself again from the beginning, whether, now religion is out of fashion, we shall not work out some pseudo-scientific terminology to sanction it. Madder things have happened, but not drearier, than when man overstrains a part of his perception, puts it to uses for which it was never intended, for which it is not fit. Until he has to deny it, which means in practice, since he cannot wholly ignore it, put it only to superstitious uses and to his own loss.

If anything like this is happening, if Luck, the incalculable, is our guiding star, and primitive "awareness" is again running wild, without even illegitimate employment, used furtively or restated in terms of pseudo-science for our misguidance, as in hellenistic days, it will be interesting to see how far our re-statement will carry us. Shall we, for example, devise a suitable formula for that most reasonable of magical conclusions, the worship of the God-Man? I cannot see at the moment how it is to be done. The early greek mind has carried its point there, and Christianity would have none of it. With the Roman Empire, "the worship was in some way thought to be symbolical...a means of testing the loyalty of distant Oriental provinces.... In Caligula's case, the divine horse was an admitted eccentricity...." But to-day Mussolini might not object to it, while it is to be remembered what they did in Russia to the body of Lenin.

With human divinity about, human sacrifice is never far away. That might come in again if, O profoundly magical process!, the right word could be discovered to describe it.

Lacking these, there are some very curious practices about. Backstair rites and credulities which seem like spontaneous inspirations, reincarnations of old theories, sane or insane. The antique world believed in a set of entities called the Kêrês, a sort of cross between a bacillus and a ghost. They were represented in swarms, like tiny winged figures or like flies, in times of battle and sickness; little clouds of them about a grave or about the dead. (Like many collective imaginations, some of the Kêrês left their swarm, separated and developed, became, first bogies, then figures — sometimes beautiful figures — of doom. There was a Kêr of old age and death, a harpy or a siren, even Eros, in some aspects, began life as a Kêr.) But to-day, as Aldous Huxley has pointed out, the preoccupation with physical infection, now often become a rite, and particularly a transatlantic and a women's rite, in its irrational aspects, is no more than the same belief dressed up with a little science. One has seen perfectly healthy young men rush home after an evening at a cinema to fight the Kêrês of sore throat with a gargle in the bathroom in the same spirit as their ancestors at a ceremony of riddance from a tribal curse. Who has not met an american matron stranded with the sanitary arrangements of a french or italian inn?

Who has not known them fuss about their children's small adventures and mishaps, until the child has to be taken to a psycho-analyst? It is the old fear of the unclean, the opposite of the holy, on a better technique, but again got out of hand; not primarily for disinfection from physical entities; but rites of avoidance and propitiation, the tendence and hoped-for expulsion of the wicked Kêrês. *Plus ça change...*

IV

What is the Religion, and who are the Gods of the Western World, the European and Near-Asia Gods who, since
our civilisation began to shape, for the last three thousand
years have been the synthesis, the abstraction, the incarna-
tion, and the mask; our opinion, not only about the final, but
of the immediate, practical, necessary-for-man nature of
things? Two sets have dominated us; classic polytheism and
christian monotheism, a very tempered monotheism, divided
at its core into three; scandinavian polytheism, with no monotheism about it, and a common heritage which seems to belong to man everywhere, of folk-belief, little potencies in a
series of common forms, often with the most agreeable local
variations, small gods, often exquisite, of in- and out-of-doors.

In groups of tens and twos and threes and twenties or
hundreds of thousands man has discovered and invented and
adored and propitiated, and fused and separated and believed
and disbelieved in these Gods. He has given them his life
and his labour and his time and his money, his learning, his
imagination, his fear and his love; stitching and unstitching
the fabric of his societies to fit his conception of them, and
his re-conception. Until to-day he has decided to dispense
with the lot, in the name of scientific truth, an activity which,
for all its overwhelming importance, was not designed to deal
with the emotion behind the experience of religion.

You cannot have been thinking of a thing or a set of things
or of a sequence of ideas, on and off, all the time, you and
your ancestors before you; you cannot have left tangible signs
of what you have thought in Art and Architecture and language and habit and social arrangements, and then carry on

as though you had never done so, and your century-in, century-out creation was not there. In this case of religion we are trying to do what we have never tried to do before; trying to do without what has up to now been considered as necessary as air. No drastic change of faith, no puritan house-cleaning, no revival, no militant atheism even, but a tacit understanding to ignore the whole occurrence. In comparison, the russian slogan, "Religion is the opium of the people," has far more reason behind it.

A habit or an attitude of mind is the hardest thing to change, whatever tricks or suppressions you may play with its projection. Change your formula, the words, the names, the acts, and the idea will remain, either changed for the worst, with less effective power, or with the incalculable powers of a new creation, if the restatement represents truth more accurately. Or you may change it to something dangerous, or, as in the theory, so popular just now, that you can invent *new* morals, merely idiotic.

Gods. And Goddesses. God. The Ones. The Threes. The Nines. The Twelves. Think of a number; double it; add six to it; halve it. Take away the number you first thought of—and Three remains. It is remarkable how often in this arithmetic three has remained, and the idea of the divine fallen into three. Lucky at the start, the number three has had a transcendental history. "Holy, holy, holy," sang our fathers, and felt better. What they were doing was very ancient magic. But if a person in conversation to-day, unless it were in reference to a gnostic heresy or a question of psycho-analysis were to mention the Trinity, he would be given to understand that his behaviour had been unbearably foolish at best. Try it and see.

A little time ago, I found a most curious ritual being observed in a country house. An off-shoot from an earlier preoccupation with Christian Science, a true heresy in the making, whose principle was that for the effective attraction of the benign powers everything must be done in threes. A room had been devoted to Threeness. Lights in three groups, three

lights in each. ("Three candles burning in the room, father
will be Lord Mayor of London next year," was my nurse's
folk-version of this.) There were three jars of three sorts of
flowers; three kinds of jam on the table. The normal number
of fire-irons is three, but action must suit arrangement, and
in that room it was considered good manners to feed the fire
in three shots. Good wishes were repeated three times, the
number of people invited, three, nine, or six. There was great
difficulty about things which fell naturally into one-ness or
two-ness; milk and sugar, indian or china tea. Every act and
situation which implies an alternative or the use of the word
"or." Our ingenuity was exercised in trinity-making, and there
were propitious moments when a curious harmony was the
result.

V

So far as christian theology is concerned, it is all a question of date. We are still only emerging from its forms, the bones of them sticking up all about us, still dripping wet from that sea; and determined, or presumably determined, to get dry as soon as possible. Like all lately rejected things, about which we still feel self-conscious, Christianity is going through a period of tabu, of being one of the things which are not done. A little difficult to explain away or deny effectively as a whole, but in that delicate state of transition when it is no longer a mark of distinction to renounce it, even brilliantly, let alone with passion. It is not "chic" or the mark of a distinguished mind to attack the faith of our fathers just now.

I do not think the story is quite finished, but that is another matter. The point is that it is felt that to-day the christian symbolism of the divine is one to be ignored. The less half-conscious reaction, let alone speech or argument, the better.

Fortunately we have another religious inheritance, another set of symbols, inextricably worked into our culture, and definitely taught, at least until quite lately, to every person with a pretence of education, the profound, fruitful, and entertaining beliefs of Greece and Rome. Every one knows something about them, their gods have worked themselves symbolically into every subject under the sun; and if it would be harder to-day to find a person who could pass an examination in Lemprière, we are gaining a better idea of the historical growth and inner content of those faiths by a comparison with every other religion there has ever been. There is even a new delicate god-snobbery about, a spot-the-god game played in certain circles.

("That fascinating little fellow from Cochin China — Quite too phallic.") Every one to-day knows something about the beastly devices of the heathen. (Note that the word "heathen," with its christian implications, has gone out of use, to be replaced by the classic "pagan." While even "pagan," implying as it does a contrast, is felt to be a little didactic, a little wanting in taste, and it is now no longer the fashion to refer to any religion by a word which implies a comparative standard of truth.)

Jung has something to say about the value, the possibly unexhausted value, of classic religious symbolism and myth. It used to be fashionable to think that they had survived because of the motifs they supplied to the arts; we know now that it is more true to say that it was the quality of the belief which produced the works, and that each religion gets the art it deserves.

What sort of religion was it? We all know, or think we know, what it looked like, as there passes across our minds the images of a series of statues, or, in most cases, copies of copies of statues, with a *risqué* story attached to each. This was felt to be generally satisfactory from the Renaissance to our fathers' time (who, incidentally, had the advantage of knowing something about both languages). Then came the rise of anthropology and the science of comparative religions, and we have learned how to take fresh stock, compare Zeus with Jehovah, Aphrodite with Ashtaroth, and the pair of them with the Virgin; re-state Athene as a "functional daimon," as a vegetation spirit, as a totem, as a Luck; as an owl, as a feminist, as a wish-fulfillment; compare Orpheus and Osiris as Saviours, and both with Christ. It was a re-examination of extraordinary possibilities and value. Its exaggeration came from a desire to be primitive at all costs, to scour the cults and ceremonies for traces of totem-worship and fetish, for cannibalism and human sacrifice, for orgies and black magic, for exogamy and endogamy, and all the "gay science" of the anthropologist. An impatience sprung from satiety with the polished shapes, and stories retold and repainted in the spirit of the *Decameron*.

As a test of education or as the mark of a gentleman,

after an unquestioned reign of five hundred years, classical education is losing its prestige to-day. For one thing, there are so many other things to learn, or rather so many new and elaborate techniques, such a mass of information on all old subjects and some new ones. Every one knows the controversy. While part of the truth is that classical knowledge, like christian rites, has got so worked into the scheme of education as to go on still by its own momentum, whether people want to acquire it or not.

That will not last much longer. It is a kind of learning, except for some pure enthusiasts, wholly dependent on leisure, and a taste for it, which is as much a gift as any other gift. Also on the prestige it once gave to a man, and that once all liberal employments were dependent on it. That one might as well learn the classical languages as anything else, because once you have learned them you can learn anything else, is neither a true nor at all a popular statement. For it can be pointed out that people who have learned them often do not want to learn anything else. While it is a study that goes with a kind of simplicity and order and propriety of life which does not agree with the way existence is shaping itself to-day.

So it would seem that the Gods, who for two thousand years have survived the organised forces of Christianity, are about to descend into a final twilight with their conqueror. As we have seen, they have not, like Christianity, become tabu, merely more and more symbolic, and what is more at the moment, artistically suspect, the good with the bad, the Parthenon marbles along with the copy, at five removes, of a detestable late Venus from a gentleman's private house.

But the God to look out for is the God who does not put up a fight. His successes may not be spectacular, he has no hell up his sleeve, nor even much of a heaven. He is himself, for what his is worth. Take him or leave him, he makes no protest. Takes himself off, manifests himself in other ways, is called by another name. Until one is suddenly aware of him again, that his departure has been a feint, a trick that has been played on one by oneself.

The survival of the Olympians has been something like this; the Olympians and their relations, who were notably broad-minded, who made few promises, who surprise us by their demand for ritual acts rather than for a pure heart. The Olympians, and if one is curious to look further, their near cousins, another aryan set, Thor, Tyr and Baldur, and all the Gods of Scandinavia, whose grouping is a repetition of their own.

From what came their vitality, their adaptability to all situations from the homeliest to the most dramatic; to all the arts from the mystical to the gayest? Why have they not been forgotten with Seb and Thoth and Hathor, who is remembered because her Cow-Head was touched by the passion of Io, a Greek girl enchanted; who, like her, wore between her horns the moon? Who can dramatise Siva and Vishnu, or in the West, without feeling that he is doing some essential violence to his nature, adopt the Buddhist way?

I think that there is one fairly satisfying and complete answer to this: *"Ce qui donne du courage, ce sont les idées,"* and these Gods are the most successful projection of the ideas of man —not about the nature of the universe, not about good and evil, not about what has happened or is going to happen; but about himself.

These Gods, "to whom a doubtful philosopher can pray, …as to so many radiant and heart-searching hypotheses," are no more and no less than so many descriptions man has made of himself. Descriptions that cover the ground pretty fully, the "subtle knot" retied, thread by thread. Man as an animal, as a prince, as a saviour, as a lover, as a phallos, as a warrior, as an artist, as a "magic," a flash of the hidden forces in nature. The sub-divisions are often exceedingly delicate. Put together it is difficult to find one aspect of human nature or occupation or desire which is not personated. And always, as Professor Murray points out, the trivial or base, the obscene or irrational, the mysterious or the merely obscure and tiresome elements, are subordinated and kept within bounds. Which is, after all, what man likes to think about himself and do with himself.

Man has a pattern about himself, of what he would like to do and to be, which, with all its local variations, has never changed much. Or at least, whatever changes he is prepared to make, whatever disciplines or experiments, they must not be allowed to affect a very few old things, qualities or a quality so assumed, so taken for granted, that he has never troubled much to reason about them, not enough even to give them common names. What a man or a woman will, if put to it, have no nonsense about, is the question of the "virtus" common and proper to both, their virility, courage, the source of each of their separate virtues. The best name for it is "Mana," the word which science has taken from the Polynesians; that which gives a man or a woman potency in every act or situation. It is not easy to write about the all-prevalent. Mana has been taken for granted since man became man. It is what Chaucer meant by the "law of kind," that which makes a horse a horse and a sword a sword, a man a man, and each man the kind of man he is up to the limit of his expression in individual terms; and so on with every object, animate and inanimate throughout nature. If something poisonous were to sap this, the biologic pressure under which each man lives, that which keeps him man, would become unendurable. He feels that he would fly apart, that one part of his nature or one aptitude would grow at the expense of the rest. Not an over-development or an over-specialisation which would leave the whole of him essentially intact, but a growth of cells become hostile, a malignant cancer. That in the eye of some lonely creator, it would not matter, makes no difference. He has never seen God on those terms. The image of himself as a man that he has made, has been in some measure the divine image.

It is this, I think, that gives the horror to such books as Mr. Wells's *First Men in the Moon*, where intellect has been developed through the evolution of insect life, or in *The Island of Doctor Moreau*, where the pig and the leopard have been made man. While all the stress a nation lays on individualism and on its racial type, the frenchness of a Frenchman, the nature proper to an Englishman, or on spanish, german, chinese mana or "virtus," comes from the same instinct. And the core of our reaction to the russian experiment, the meaning behind the panic and the prejudice and the moral indignation and the horror at its cruelty, is the sense that with their doctrinaire idealism turned inside out and their sudden command of science, they may *alter man* too much, alter him out of something which is essentially man. There is a danger there, I think, but such an instinct as this must have its blind side, or rather its blind application. In itself it is not a tabu instinct; sets no check on variation and experiment, so long as that something which is felt to be the essence of the human contract, the nature of the human knot, is left alone. And to keep this knot intact, at a particularly lively period of his story, he made his gods directly in his own image, projections of ideal human mana, "virtus," and virility. Not gods, with one or two exceptions, of sacramental mysticism, not gods come down to man, but gods who were man and God.

Man has rarely been accused of not loving himself enough. Religions which put that affection to too great a strain have in practice to compromise. Worms and dust may be the theory of us, but we do not believe it. The mana-instinct comes in to correct the exaggeration of any such belief. It has always been the reproach of Christianity that it has been felt to lay insufficient stress on the power instinct, on the ruling, shaping, riding and over-riding, experimental instinct in man. Its origins partly account for it, origins it forgot all about in its struggle with the Roman State. And one has only to think of the concentration of mana in the person of every Pope and every priest.

Mana is not religion. It is the "virtue" or part of the virtue, behind every religion, the law of kind in action, and, with the classic gods, the law of human kind. (For their worshippers had even constructed a ladder, a kind of moving staircase, by which the hero and heroine, the man or woman of mana, whose working-out in action is usually some form of the heroic, could ascend to the company of the gods. And even at times descend again, as human values shifted.)

VI

There is plenty of sense of mana about to-day, though perhaps it is only in moments when the mana supply threatens to fail that people become so preoccupied with it. Great prosperous or great creative ages were too charged to feel sensitive about it. But always, at the least threat to it, the world becomes uneasy, and is showing it to-day in its fantasies about robots, and all the children of the far-seeing of Samuel Butler. For each machine has its mana, its law of kind, while there is more than a chance that machine-mana may come to dominate human mana. (Consider an American praying to his typewriter.) There is uneasiness about, which might grow into terror, which may develop equally into constructive reaction or collapse.

It was something the same in the Hellenistic Age, when Luck and Fate, with their incalculables, pervaded the whole of life, sprouting and seeding like wild plants in the choice order of the garden of Olympus. Names of the Titans were heard again, shapeless potencies of chaos and old night thrust their way back. Old names for undifferentiated mana, like Kratos and Bia, raw force, got a stranglehold on men's imaginations, tuned up their courage and did nothing for their fears.

It is much the same now, when "every violent, emotion-compelling sensation is pursued for its own sake." For the sake of its mana. Mana now that tabu has weakened; tabu, the check, often the ridiculous and superstitious check, but also a technique for dealing with crude power, the dangers inherent in the law of kind.

Mana worship is of the nature of things. No one in fact, at however many removes, has ever worshipped anything else.

MARY BUTTS

It is a profoundly primitive conception, handled, differenti-
ated, made serviceable to man in every religion he has ever
conceived. What is happening to-day is a return to its most
primitive form—not to it defined or idealised in any shape,
christian or classic, but to the raw thing.

One can learn a great deal of the essence of any religion
from its art. The most convincing expression of savage religion that I know comes from Central America, where in those
ghastly images men found the skill to represent their gods,
those terrible fetishes of whom Roger Fry once said that their
makers could not have taken a better way if they had wished
to convince us of the objective reality of their belief.

Those idols, concentrations of mana, were tabu also.
Tabu, which in our christian origins was used differently, as
in the case of the graven image which "thou shalt not make
to thyself."

I knew a collector once, all that was most civilised in french
atheism, who for aesthetic reasons, the fashion being then at
its height, made a collection of african cult-images and mana-
projections which was his friends' envy and delight. (Little
parties used to be given for them at which every one used to
say the right thing—such right things.)

So I was all the more astonished when I called there,
unexpectedly one night, to find him at his devotions, which
included offerings to them of pure wax, honey, semen and
blood. It was tiresome, because one knew he did not believe
in anything else. And they were not all of them good potencies, *agathoi daimones*, not sufficient, one felt, to be the unique
objects of belief. And it was particularly disconcerting to find
such worship in that neat, fashionable, hard-bitten man of
high french civilisation, clear and bright in his latin convention, the outward epitome of its tastes and of its habit of
mind.

There is a good deal of this sort of thing going on, *and* in
the educated parts of society. What the bulk of the people
are up to is a vaguer, more passionate affair. But with people
of culture to-day a religious revival, when it is a definite cult,

326

is for something queer, exotic and out of the way. The gods of Africa are not indigenous to France. (Any more than the vast religious structures of Asia are native to the soil of England or America. These, under their theosophic transplantations, have a larger aspect, and something of the appearance of a real movement.) But the cults of the small exotic are always variations on one theme of exceedingly primitive religion, almost of that magic which, if you like, was before religion, under its grimmest and oddest shape. Return to classic paganism it is not. At least to nothing that the pagan we know of, the Greek or the Roman, or the inhabitant of the graeco-roman world, would have recognised. "These people," says Apollo, in Dr. Garnett's story of the demons who were tempting a hermit, "weren't about in our day. Or, if they were, they knew their places."

Pious exercises to-day in the demonology of all the demons, the folk-spirits each land has invented and repeated and re-dressed for itself, from the innocent mascot, the luck-bringing trinket, to the rediscovery of the power latent in other peoples' idols, influence all classes behind the mask of scepticism. What one never hears about, never has seen and is never likely to see, is the man or woman, in private, lacking public facilities, who bows the knee to Neptune, whose life is the result of his obedience to the commands of aegis-bearing Zeus. That would need too great a quality of self-deception, too great an effort of imagination, too realistic a morality, impose too great a strain. Rebecca West says, taking us far into that part of the subject, and perhaps into the most important part, since what she has to say concerns the people as a whole: "A new body of simple people has been created to-day, by the heaping of races pell-mell in some territories, and by the changing of country-folk into towns-folk. They have the old need for polytheism; all that is new about them is their inability to satisfy this need by inventing supernatural beings."

VII

We have seen the universal discredit of christian monotheism. In an age of violent transition and discovery its old
weakness has appeared again, its insufficient insistence on
the wild, enchanting, incalculable force in nature, the mana
of things, the non-moral, beautiful, subtle energy in man and
in everything else, on which the virtue of everything depends.

It can be well argued that its Founder had no such weakness, but some such unstrung temper worked its way into his
followers. And by some malign trick, inherent also it would
seem in the nature of things, whenever the Church lost that
weakness it was to enter on the struggle for earthly power,
and in so doing immediately lost or corrupted that in its
Founder's mind which had made it unique.

Meanwhile, men have not changed. If Christianity satisfies
them less, what about the gods who were there before it,
whose understanding they have never lost, for they are the
projections of themselves. It is not aestheticism which demands the restoration at Piccadilly Circus of Eros.

"They have to call forth from the eating-houses of Brook-
lyn, from farmsteads in Kansas, from shepherds' huts in the
Puszta in Hungary, flesh that can bear the weight of the
world's imaginings about Aphrodite." Aphrodite and Hermes,
Ares and Artemis, Apollo and Heracles and Dionysos. (Call
them more coarsely, Venus and Mars, Mercury and Diana,
Hercules and Bacchus, and you have the commoner evocation, that is all. No change but the change implied in a
vulgarisation.) All the young gods, of sex and war, of art and
sport and maidenhood; of drink and the mysteries of excitement and moving about. Not, it may be observed, the older

328

and soberer incarnations; not the Father or the Grandfather or the Intellect; not Zeus Chronides or Athene; not "Zeus of the Underworld and dread Persephone," gods of the dead; nor, as we press closer into towns, Our Lord and Lady of the Sun and Moon, the Mistress of Wild Beasts or Poseidon of the sea. Only what their polytheism created, and Catholic Christianity to some extent allowed for, the gods of ourselves, in the order we most want them; forms that will never change unless man changes, a statement, perhaps the most satisfying for such values that has ever been conceived; which we have handed down among ourselves and never forgotten.

Only it is men and women now who have to bear the burden of that desire: the movie star and the athlete, the flying man and woman, the speedboat racer and the boxer. It is in books about Hollywood, of all curious testaments, you will read how passionately and how hardly that cult presses to-day. (And with these must be counted the artist, the doer of a specially creative act, not with his actual body, but by his mind, creating objects which have a separate existence, and in a certain sense are outside the limitations of time and space.)

$$* \quad * \quad * \quad * \quad *$$

We are back in the historical situation which Nietszche described of a people "for whom God is dead, and for whom no baby-god is yet lying in his cradle." Back where we were at Alexander's death, with an instinct that is more than an instinct, a habit of life and a necessity for us, unsatisfied. Back in the blind and primitive assertion of that instinct; running after Luck and awaiting Destiny, or indulging ourselves in an orgy of mana, stripped of the morals and even of the tabus which once made it serviceable. Or, if we must specialise, back with certain people of the Hellenistic Age, in "chic" cults of the least of other men's divinities.

Until the way may be open for the last extravagances of the failure of nerve. When it comes we are only too certain to have our attention called to it.

In common with the christian, the classic mind at its best

insisted that, though it was possible for the divine and the human to mix, "man is not God, and it is no use pretending that he is." When they weakened on that position, the way was open again for the practice and the conception we can read of, in all its idiocy and all its monstrosity, as well as all its splendour, in the pages of *The Golden Bough*. The belief that man is God, a special man a special god, which works out in practice as the glorification of kings by right of birth, and millionaires by the ways by which men become millionaires, may quite possibly happen among us again. What happens when it does can be read in the history of the kings of Persia; in the ptolemaic inscriptions; in the fate of roman emperors, when the hardest-headed of the world's races, their natural beliefs bankrupt, succumbed to that temptation. Whatever may have happened in remote Egypt, it is not an edifying story, not in great states in the full blaze of history; nor in the little cults and private magic-makings of savage peoples, from which we are, by another time measurement, not further than half an hour away. Something not very far off the deification of man is on us now, not, or not yet, of the kings and millionaires, but, and again, and this is primitive, of the conspicuous young men and women, our sexually desirable ones, whose nature it is to wax and wane and be replaced. Our Year-in-Year-out spirits, *eniautoi daimones*, "whose beauty is no stronger than a flower."

Human nature was not meant for that strain. The stardust at Hollywood is full of dead stars. For the potency of the human god wanes, and his end is horror; rebirth, but for their human nature, terror. That is a story told in the Gospels as well as in *The Golden Bough*.

[1932]

"Ghosties and Ghoulies"

Uses of the Supernatural
in English Fiction

TO-DAY one form of popular writing—the detective story—has been developed on the lines proper to a new form of art. It has shape, rhythm and its own kind of epiphany. It has also become an elaborate craft; and for the reader an intricate, intelligent and enthralling game, allied to chess, insight into the spirit *in extremis,* a battle; crime-at-home in an arm-chair, with no after regrets, complications or visits from the police. (So far from being an incentive to bad contact, as the cinemas are often called, one wonders if the perfection to which stories about sudden death are being brought, may not act as some sort of equivalent for adventurous wrongdoing to the blameless citizen, deep in the story of Death in the Train, the Tram, the Hotel, the Home, the Bath, the Bed.) A book, for example, like *The Murder of Roger Ackroyd,* with its pace and balance, the surprises and resolution of its theme, has qualities which are precisely those of a work of art; with its living characters, the well-locked joints of its events, like some old cabinet, opening and shutting smoothly and filled with secret drawers.

The subject of this essay is not the detective story, used only as an illustration that it is possible for the artist to handle any theme for the purposes of art, once he understands its limitations and its conditions. There is another form of letters, less popular, of longer descent, whose public is more anonymous and, so far as the writer knows, without its "fans" —the stories commonly called "psychic" or "on the supernatural." These, compared with the detective story, form a very small literature to-day; yet they continue to be written and by many of our best writers. This in an age when the accepted view is that anything may be true, "that anything may happen," while that none of the explanations—espe-

333

cially the religious explanations—we were once taught, *can* be the right one. A point of view which is a legacy from the dogmatic materialism of the last century and still unconsciously powerful; whose influence to-day leads us to describe the beliefs and faiths of our ancestors as science misunderstood; or the visions of saint or artist, profound or fruitful, curious or bizarre, as nothing *more* than a way of externalizing the unconscious. Yet in spite of this—in itself a half-conscious process and the common man's partial submission to it—people still write and turn out tolerable or even excellent work on the subjects they are not supposed to believe in at all—the old motif of ghost and spirit; and of our occasional sense of awareness of other forms of life other than those shown us by our senses.

It is curious, along with the sheikh story and other folk themes, this class of work exists, without erotic or detective attractions. At the end of a ghost-story there is no one to be married and no one to be hung. Neither beds nor blood occur much in them. Their problems are not for ingenuity to solve. Their scope is wide, and for the worst demands some imagination. They range from sheer silliness to real literature. Even the greatest of poets has touched on witchcraft and the elemental powers, evil or exquisite.

It would even seem that writers are more and more making use of the "supernatural" *conte*. Anthologies are devoted to it, and omnibus volumes. From conviction that there is "something in it"? From pleasure at the material? But if the matter pleases, it should contain a minimum of truth. What sort of truth? Would a story—to take Professor Bury's suggestion of a hypothesis which can hardly be proved false—of a race of donkeys, alive on Sirius, who speak English and spend their time discussing eugenics—make a story of any interest or value? Only if the donkeys were really there, and another state of existence shown. Or if they were used symbolically, as a criticism on the life of man. Ghost-stories cannot fall into the last class. Their common business is "to make our flesh creep." And by that we mean, not simple horror or terror at a new and generally evil world, usually invisible but interlocked with ours; we mean also a stirring, a touching of nerves not usually sensitive, an awakening to more than fear —but to something like awareness and conviction or even memory. A touching of nerves inherited from our savage ancestors? Well, that is one explanation, drawn from the lately discovered fact that, like savages to-day, our forefathers thought "animistically," endowed everything that lives with life, like or unlike his own. (All artists still do.) The kind of life depending on what piece of nature they were looking at, alive or dead; and on the *quality* each individual brought to his contemplation.

There is a tree, a scarred pine, in the park at Azay les Rideaux, which might inspire another *Golden Bough*. Any "savage ancestor" of mine would have sworn that it pounced, when I stared at it (though it instantly frightened me), and talked about Van Gogh, instead of placating and adoring; and that the ring that slipped out of my ear and rolled through the only crack in the plank bridge, was the offering it had taken, since I had not made one; and that the sickness that came on me an hour or so later was the tree asserting its power....

Like taxi-windows, stories of the supernatural fall into two classes. Their borders are sometimes indistinct, but the first order, implicitly or explicitly, assume theories of life existing beyond, or generally beyond our perception; theories which, in different makes-up—some hideous, some lively, some awful, some idiotic—are immeasurably old; and not *all* accounted for by our increased scientific knowledge of the world. Theories which suppose laws, a range of beings from gods and bogies to daimones and God, an atlas of unknown worlds, physically existing regions beyond the senses of man. This is the first class. The second class are tales, well or ill told, about things happening which do not happen, all theory ignored. Their success depends on their getting the reader into a state, varying from desire to get into bed quickly and, most irrationally, not to sleep face to the wall and give horror a chance to creep up behind, to a sudden quickening of mind to a sense that it is the bed, the book, the body that are shadows; or at least that there is a "real" outside them, tangible as "an army with banners." While both classes unite in trying to persuade us that *millions of spiritual creatures walk the earth unseen.*

There is a third class that we can leave out altogether — the vulgar stuff, the sniggerers in the cheap magazines at stories of the appearance of the dead. Afraid of the dead and of what they call "science"; doubly false, either by a cheap finale where Science is called in and patted on the back because it has declared such phenomena impossible. Or derided because it has shown man the way to such knowledge and his infinite capacity for error — above all, in a field where his five senses are not all that he needs to arrive at truth. Such work need not be considered, except for the light it throws on modern imbecility and superstition *á rebours.* Though now and again there is valuable material to be found in popular books which propose to tell of historical visions and hauntings; valuable either as story-material or as evidence; one notably in a volume in wide circulation, a rehash of appearances "alleged to have been seen" in an Irish castle to-day.

A singular intelligence and a writer of degraded English assembled that book. Quotations from eighteenth century anonymities are admitted as evidence; along with letters fifty years old from a Mrs. X in India, who dreamed that her daughter was dead. And dead she was. A girl forgets the name of a flower; dreams that she meets a woman called by its name. This is tabulated under "occult" in 1923, by an author who drags in a quotation from Zeno that "not until we study our dreams shall we reach truth."

Yet the story, or rather the series of stories of things seen in that castle, culminating in one unspeakable apparition, is of sober and awful interest. The story is a well-known one, apart from this version. A number of people — of whom several died soon after — wrote out their account of it. This evidence apart, there is some quality in the description that rings true, masters the commonplace eyes that saw it, the trashy English in which it is written up. If the whole business is a fabrication, it is one that moved an abominable writer to the use of simple and convincing words. It is the story of an animal-thing, seen, heard and smelt, but impervious to touch and infecting like a poison. If true at all, it comes under the class of creatures called "Elementals"—a very ancient belief and a name old enough to be decent. Ariel was one and Caliban another, in the antique supposed order of such natures, outside the skins, furs, shells and feathers of our earth.

But to leave this lowest class of our age's half shamefaced interest in supernatural beliefs, there is a considerable and variously entertaining literature worth examination. We have divided it into two classes; authors with a psychic axe to grind, who wish to persuade us that current materialism and credulity are alike insufficient; or those who seek only to produce horror and wonder; or at best, and without explanation, the consciousness of a universe enlarged. Starting with the first, the stories of Professor Montagu James are in a class alone. He has no psychic axe to grind, no theory of which he wishes to persuade us. Cheerfully he says in each preface that he hopes these idle little tales will entertain, before proceeding to frighten us out of our wits. A master of plain style like plain-chant, a humanist, a scholar and an observer of men, half the force of his stories lies in the simplicity of their setting. The wailing, luminous nun in the ruined abbey may or may not wail and shine? Who cares? We rarely pass the night there. But no one can be quite sure that what happens in Professor James's tales may not happen to him. His "terrain" is Trollope's, and as familiar. The garden, the library, the cathedral, the country hotel. The terror, in essence, that comes upon his agreeable humanist gentlemen is the fear of a life, believed to be dead and buried, returning and rising to the contemporary surface like a bubble from some foul bottom, breaking on some clear pool where men usually whip for fish. The stories are without theory, pure evocations of man's still latent fear that there is an animal life outside the animals he knows, less than human life and more, and infinitely malignant. Such is the theory of the evil elemental spirits, implicit in Professor James, making him the principal master in our second classification; where the object is not theory or persuasion, but telling the tale and, with luck, evocation.

His second theme is the pleasant fancy of a body that is not properly dead. Not decently haunting in a luminous transparency, but hideously changed, and charged with a vitality due to its evil life on earth; in one form or another, beast, pest and ghost.

On these he rings hideous and awful changes, culminating in that masterpiece, "The Mezzotint," sober little Cambridge episode, persuading us by the sheer perfection of its invention; forcing one to say: "If this sort of thing can happen, it happens like this."

While, for all his kind, sceptical disclaimers of any intention but to amuse, there are implications in Professor James. It would not surprise me if once — and he will never own to it — he has met something uncommonly like the presence or the work of an evil spirit. Or that there has been but one episode in his life which gave him a psychic "turn," left an impress on his imagination. Even that someone underground once came up, and made him aware of it in no easy shape; and that this one encounter gave him the material for five books. Some experience, apart from his immense scholarship, he must have had. Or it is also possible that the belief and the experience in some old book came through and stamped itself on him and persuaded him.

As to the possible existence of such creatures, it is curious to note that men's gods have come and gone, but that the belief in "them" (and in the evil far more than in the good) has not changed much. The last is inevitable and human enough. Isis and Osiris have passed from our devotions or, if evoked, not by name; but the kêrês of sickness and destruction seem as long-lived as the amoeba. Demons in short. And all nonsense and misunderstanding of natural phenomena apart, when imaginative writing reaches a certain degree of precision, produces such an effect of reality, it is difficult to see how this is done if the observation implied in the writing is without *some* foundation in experience. A love-song may not be about one particular love-affair but, if it is a good one, it is about love. A writer must, if only half consciously, believe in what he is writing about. Details he can invent, and setting; terror and wonder he must have known and may have reflected on; at least putting the question if their origin was only in himself. There is a Dutch Primitive of the mockers of Christ; faces, one hopes, that never have been seen on earth—their quality of bestial cruelty is not of this world. Where did the painter find them?

There are moments when one remembers Lecky. In his *History of Rationalism,* writing on the kindred subject of witchcraft, he says: "In our day…it would be altogether impossible for such an amount of evidence to accumulate round a conception which had no substantial basis in fact." And that, "When we consider the multitudes of strange statements that were sworn and registered in legal documents," the way to a wholly rationalistic explanation is hard. (Lecky went on to explain it by saying that fashions have changed; the persecution for witchcraft ceased, more because the belief in it went out of fashion, than for any failure of evidence.)

Still, granting every ghost story ever written a lie, and that each phenomena examined by the Society for Psychical Research to mean, not what it is supposed to mean but, as Mr. Aldous Huxley suggests, something else—a question remains, more easy to feel than to ask. Professor James can say as often as he likes that he only does it for fun, but through his masterpieces like "The Mezzotint" and "Casting the Runes," through all his books, the same theme repeats. Something called his attention to them; turned the mind of the archaeologist and ex-Provost of Eton to "ghosties and ghoulies and long-leggity beasties and things that go bump in the night"; from which the Scots Litany prayed that the Lord would deliver us.

Leaving Professor James to his fun, there is Mr. E. F. Benson, who can write gaily and wittily about people of fashion; soberly and well about things which are supposed never to happen at all. He can go to the length of a novel about it, and it is not a subject which usually lends itself to full-dress. Lytton's *Zanoni* is written round a full-fledged theory, and would to-day I think be found unreadable, though the idea of it is interesting—and very ancient. Lytton was a serious student. Mr. Benson's *Image in the Sand* is also a bad novel, tiresome and padded. Apart from the earlier chapters, in which he said all he had to say, the reader finds himself insisting: "If any part of this business happened, and I feel rather that the beginning did, it did not develop and, above all, *end* like this." But his collection of short stories, *The Room in the Tower,* has in it as good work as has ever been done. Brick kilns remain the brick kiln which could be seen from that house. A kiln with a man going in and out, with nothing particular about him but his hands, one of which carried a knife; and his wrists, round which played a small light, dirty and impure.

It is Mr. Benson's attitude to his subject, to-day almost improper, as though one of the arts had had an illegitimate baby, which gives his work a great part of its charm. His sharp contempt for spiritualist humbugs and illusions; his pleasure in the more comforting kind of story (he is one of the few who deal with good spirits); his reasonable wish to convince us that our world, whether we like it or not, has more in it and more comfort for our spirits than it is fashionable to-day to admit; the belief that certain incredulities impoverish us, and are no more truly scientific than past superstitions; that change is the true name of death.

As in the story of the Long Gallery, where the tortured baby ghosts, who innocently bring death, lose their power to destroy when the girl masters her fear enough to sit beside them on the floor and bless them. It would be hard to find fault with Mr. Benson's attitude, his impatience with the sentimentality and shameless credulity and wish-fulfillments of most popular spiritualism; whose follies hinder research by disgusting people capable of weighing the evidence; and aware how far a desire for personal immortality is responsible for the "revelations" given under most conditions of trance. His "Spinach" is a gay story of two young professional mediums , who by chance strike the "real thing"—contact with a boy struck by lightning, with something on his mind he is forced to tell; this and his slow fading-out into their usual subconscious fabrications about white robes and further shores. He knows the worst of fraudulent and silly psychism, the handle it gives to the materialist, the instrument he would have been called, in any age but our own, of despair. Immortality apart, a word none of us can realise, if there is no continuance after death for those who die when they should live, at ten years or two months, or young of disease or accident, or young in battle, nothing can make this earth rational for the only rational animal known to it.

Mr. Benson knows too the narrowness that confines the question to that of survival after death. With James, his stories pass in settings we know, are often obvious *contes,* arrangements of what might happen, whether it did actually or not. But now and then his story turns on what he obviously and passionately believes to have happened—our possession by the powers of good and evil, our logical blessedness or punishment after death. It is here chiefly that he wished to persuade or even to teach. (It is curious. Up to our age a writer, even the most detached artist, was allowed to teach. Having special love or knowledge of something, he was supposed to hand it on. The present world, its majority suddenly become literate, unless the subject is technical, faints at the thought. Until it is noticed that, having read any imaginative work from Aristophanes to Ronald Firbank, and taken pleasure in it, something of its quality has entered in and become part of oneself. Has made one more aware and *sensible,* using the writer's eyes. So that one finds out that, after all, one has learned.) But the present theory seems to be that one can learn about engineering or beetles from a book; not fortitude and faith from Marcus Aurelius. Even Wilde, founder, abroad at least, of so much of modern aestheticism, set out, in *De Profundis* and *The Soul of Man,* to persuade at least.

341

To return to the subject: it is also curious that, over all
this field of letters, the opposite idea to that implied by "possession" should be so little used. If man can be in contact
with more than human intelligences, as Plotinus thought he
was, and Socrates and Saint Joan of Arc, why are there so
few stories about the man delivered by death after a life well
spent, or of earthly contact with some spirit of life and grace?
Ariel instead of Caliban. If the business of such writing is to
awaken consciousness, why should horror be the form preferred? Is it that, without a shudder, interest is lost? But why
should it be? Apart from Mr. Benson, there is only one writer
of distinction who has seen beyond this. Her place is later. In
the past Hogg found an answer; but he comes at the end of a
series, begun in the Middle Ages—the Scottish and Border
magic poems, almost the only poems *on* magic which *are* magic.
That no one can write now, unless one must count Mr. de la
Mare.

Thomas the Rhymer, whose prophecy quoted in the six-
teenth century seems to have come rather accurately true in
the beginning of the nineteenth, met on Huntley Bank a
woman he took for the Virgin Mary. She told him that she
was not, but queen of those people the Irish call the Sidhe.
He followed her, and they went off together on the Border
Hills. There the transition took place, which has been observed before and after, when a place becomes another place;
and you know what you have suspected before—that all the
time it has been two places at once.

> It was mirk, mirk night, there was nae starlight,
> They waded through red blood to the knee;
> For all the blood that's shed on airth
> Runs through the springs of that country.

> It was mirk, mirk night, there was nae starlight,
> They waded through rivers abune the knee;
> And they saw neither sun nor moon,
> But they heard the roaring of the sea.

That is one description of a state evoked, of consciousness enlarged. Thomas came out of it all right in the end, with his future as prophet and as poet made. His adventure has a certain relation with Plutarch's young man, and what happened to him in the cave of Triphonius. Variations on an initiation rite, public and sacerdotal, or accidental. And few people would dare to say that these experiences and these rites did not sometimes initiate. Remember E. M. Forster's definition of blasphemy, to the Northern mind a question of bad taste; to the Latin or Mediterranean, "the incorrect performance of certain acts, especially sacramental acts." Why? Because such acts were in their essence automatic receipts for taking a man out of his body and putting him, and even it, into another state of existence. The rules of the game, the natural laws set in motion, or even their existence, were and are imperfectly stated and never understood. While Heaven alone knew the consequences of tampering with them. Hence the danger of amateur meddling.

*   *   *   *   *

After the ballads, "Lulli, Lulli," the "Lyke Wake Dirge," even "Tam Lyn" and the "Wife of Usher's Well," who saw her sons' ghosts in hats of bark that

> Neither grew not in syke nor ditch,
>   Nor yet in an sheugh;
> But at the gates of Paradise
>   That bark grew fair eneugh.

After these, there is little good writing about such things; though Shakespeare believed in his witches; he had seen in Warwickshire similar country hags. And Caliban, so it seems inevitable, is more convincing than Ariel. For the seventeenth century, one can say that Milton's preoccupation is chiefly with the supernatural. But what a supernatural! An educated and intelligent man—take the classic Chinaman—but entirely ignorant of our civilisation, what would he make of our religion and our theology from the study of "Paradise

343

Lost"? How fantastic, how insanely improbable it would appear to him, wanting our saturation in its assumptions. While from what one reads of chinese folk and mystery tales, "Tam Lyn," to Professor James and even Mr. Benson, would be familiar country to him, old hauntings newly set.

The Scots ballads died, came to life once and have stayed dead ever since Hogg published "Kilmeny." His best poem, variations on the theme that is the theme of "True Thomas," which haunts in infinite varieties the imagination of man:

> Late in the gloamin' Kilmeny came hoam,
> For Kilmeny had been she knew not where,
> And Kilmeny had seen what she could not declare.

Here he manages to persuade us, but from point of treatment, most of the poem is as objective and unsuggestive as a novel by Mrs. Radcliffe; the girl's vision and adventures being no more than a translation of a translation of something half forgotten. Except for one verse, on which the whole poem depends:

> In yon green wood there is a wake,
> And in that wake there is a wene,
> And by that wene there is a make
> That neither has flesh nor blood nor bane:
> And down yon green wood he walks his lane.

Kilmeny's lover came from that place, where the bark was cut that shone round the heads of the sons of the wife of Usher's Well.

Scotland after that stayed mute, except for George Macdonald, who picked up the trail to that land by way of *At the Back of the North Wind*. Strange company for Apollo on his winter journey there. After him, Fiona Macleod, probably unreadable to us to-day. Then, in the full light of soldiering and Parliament, the easy writing of the finest adventure stories, Colonel James Buchan, in the books which have earned him least praise, writes with reserve and reverence, but with conviction, on his race's traditional material.

It is noticeable that men with a *flair* for life as it is lived—war and adventure and social relations—have often their mystical preoccupations as well. The more thoroughgoing the worldly activities, the public life, the deeper the preoccupation would seem. (The other way round, Desmond Macarthy has something to say about the hard-headedness of the mystic.) Colonel Buchan can be called Rider Haggard's successor. Mr. Benson knows his pre-War world. Colonel Buchan sets his stories up north, but not always in Scotland. There is one about the agony of the Emperor Justinian, transmitted through a bust of him, brought to a country house and setting loose forces of destruction there. Another of a stream called Fawn, and a hunting that went with it from classic times. A scholar, antique civilisation haunts his work also; as in a recent novel, *The Dancing Floor*. Colonel Buchan is a man with many of Kipling's prejudices about strong men and his distrust of the arts. This with real scholarship and love of life; the natural beauty of his land assimilated until his descriptions have a classic beauty. His *Dancing Floor* is one of the first novels to owe its origin to *The Golden Bough*. There, in an obscure greek island, owned by a girl the peasants hate on account of her father's sham obscene sorceries, the ritual of the Kouros and Korê is evoked by them against her. Colonel Buchan knows the first law—for whatever it may mean, the law is there—of the interaction of other worlds with ours; that it can be somehow described by a parallel with the knight's move in chess. The other moves are comparable with ordinary activities. Only the knights move two squares and a diagonal, on and sideways and can jump. The young man in the book, has had all his life a recurrent dream to show that an adventure of profound significance is on its way. Mistranslates its nature, and yet is there in time to play Kouros to her Korê and save her. And the dress she wore when they passed through the fire, which had shocked him in a London night club, was the one the maiden would have worn twenty-five centuries back. But it is in the young man's dream that the kernel of significance lies.

The *conception* of *Brushwood Boy* is exquisite. Variation on the significant theme of *The Dancing Floor*, the realisation of a dream-sequence, shared by a "gentle girl and boy"; Freud ignored, but not without parallel in one's experience, as in many folk-tales also. There is a tradition, old as humanity, that sometimes in sleep, instead of hanging about the body and play-acting its desires, we leave it, and go off on an adventure where no body can go; visit a country whose relation to this world is like that of our world to the stage set, with it painted trees and sky.

"What does it mean?" the girl asks the boy, another Korê with another Kouros, as they draw up their horses after the ride, which was not unlike the Thirty-Mile Ride they had taken together in sleep. "If it means anything, it means this," he answered. "This" being marriage, India, children, a country house. They had done better in sleep, and had the sense to take this world as they found it. In this story there runs through what Paracelsus, I think, and Swedenborg called the "signatures." The law of signatures or correspondences is familiar to everyone in experience, but usually hustled out of consideration under the name of coincidence. What the mediaeval mystic, and perhaps the Cambridge Platonist, meant by it was this: that every significant event or happening which quickens the individual life is, as it were, announced by trivial physical accidents, fortuitous, unconnected, a kind of pun on the event in progress or to be.

You see in a shop and buy a ship in a glass snowstorm, or fill a glass wine-jar from the Midi with water, and call it the "sea-at-home." Then comes the event itself—a friend returns, a sailor, after years, and a friendship is very deeply renewed. You turn up the Encyclopaedia for the name of a Siennese primitive, and in a parallel column see the name of the man who has come back—but this time he has only some oblique connection with the sea. After that, the sea gets loose all about the house. A jug of salt water is served in mistake for sweet; a small child, who has not heard about the sailor, will talk about nothing but boats. A friend arrives who can eat nothing but fish. These go on until they die out. But they can reach a point past coincidence, the important incident signing itself a dozen ways in different varieties of matter. Observed by early man, they account for divination becoming official, part of the state. While to-day the pursuit of their significance is a thing to be wary of, if one would escape Strindberg's haunted walks through Paris, driven by imaginary enemies to crazy terror—fear which came out again in illuminated prose—as he trod on the crossed sticks in the Rue Cardinal le Moine.

If the test of these stories is evocation, no trick of technique is more useful than the use of "signatures." In the "Finest Story," the finest moment is when Charlie, the bank clerk, once a viking with Thorfin Karlsefne, once a galley-slave, crosses London Bridge and heard a cow bellowing, with a book-bill chained to him.

It is not in Mr. Kipling to indulge in theory; his gift is a unique eye for what things look like. All his "uncanny" stories —including an extraordinary one in his last book, being closely allied to the strictest scientific experiment—carry, if not in the denouement, but by some beauty of detail, as in the "Basara of Poree," profound knowledge, and the necessary kind of physical awareness in Mr. Kipling's own nature. This sensitiveness is unique in kind, and absolutely necessary for this sort of work. Its absence makes D. G. Rosetti and his attempts to handle magical material outside the scope of this essay. The success of those works, such as "Rose-Mary" and the "Ballad of the King's Tragedy," is the success proper to poetry; as evocation of the supernatural they are of no use.

There are stories by Mr. Kipling which have had children by Lord Dunsany and Mr. Metcalf. The last published, not long ago, "The Smoking Leg." Well-written tales, if rather too sensational, at least for one whose taste is all for the lovely sobriety of Professor James, for the rational hope for Mr. Benson. Still, the story "Nightmare Jack" is ghastly—too ghastly for sober telling. And it is perhaps not impossible that the stories, so outrageously ill-gotten, saturated in the rites of an East Indian god of priest-paederasty, charged with the

347

ritual, the cult, the desire, may have had peculiar effects on men who did not know what they were handling, whose hands were bloody, and who were mortally afraid.

What a man can conceive, he can become "like." Meditate on Apollo and on Artemis—in the right way—and concepts of radiance and swiftness will possess even the body; until, with luck, a young man or woman may become not entirely unlike the Twins "whom Fair-haired Leto bare." This is the truth about the gods. Give yourself up to your conception of them, and you will become in some sense a repetition, an image of them. Many a testy, fussy, vengeful, rather righteous old gentleman is the direct responsibility of the Protestant Jehovah. From where do they come, these objects of contemplation, changing and developing down the centuries, of whom our conception, Christian or pagan, seems, at certain moments of intensity, to be outside normal experience? We know their geography, their ritual, hardly their vitality's source. What is it in the universe which gave to the tribal gods of the Achaeans something like immortal life? Developed the tribal mascot of the primitive Jews? Vitality which seems to shift and draw new power, out of each and to each of the generations of men. Artemis and Apollo show signs of lasting longer than Jehovah. He began as a small godling, as humble as they. The Second Isaiah exalted him: Greek speculation or taste arranged him in a group of three. Join him with Ammon, Zeus and later Odin, and you get God the Father. The Brother and Sister crystallised earlier, never claimed universality and remain *"Gods to whom the doubtful philosopher can pray … as to so many radiant and heart-searching hypotheses."* It is infinitely subtle, this making-over of vision by generations of minds. Visions that harden and slowly lose their quality; become dull, stucco and plaster: stages of the Cheshire Cat: that flash out again and repossess men's minds by means of some brilliant restatement: *"Queen and Huntress, chaste and fair…"*

Mr. Metcalf's "Smoking Leg" is one of our last "occult" additions and an original one. But it is the story that the reviewers passed by which has the most value, the soundest of originality—a quiet little tale, without properties, but curiously persuasive; variation on the antique motion that a place can be two places at once.

In the past certain holy spots, caves and "temenoi" were, at one and the same time, a place on this earth; a place where once a supernatural event had happened; and a place where, by luck or devotion or the *quality* of the initiate, it might happen again. The cave on Mount Ida was a cave and the birthplace of Zeus. Also, if one is not mistaken, a place where a supernatural event could happen again, and man "become God." At Eleusis, at certain times and in different ways— during a play, "mime" of a "sacred marriage," or in the dark, by an *"ear of corn, reaped in silence,"* upheld in a beam of light, an even physical change came over man; he was translated, "converted," initiated, "saved." So far as these were ceremonies and the rites symbolical, any Church may be counted in the same order. By such circumstances men profited; drew out in proportion to what they put in. The crux of the business carries us a step farther when, as in the case of Triphonius in the cave, things happened to you whether you liked it or not. No doubt mechanism was used—"Sometimes, I do not say always, very simple and innocent contrivances whereby the priest fortifies the faith of his flock." But outside what may be called the regular places where men went for initiation, to have their souls strengthened by contact with reality outside the observation of their senses, man has kept a belief and a tradition that certain places exist, of themselves and quite unofficially, charged with mana and tabu. Not always places you would expect. Explanation or theory apart, a good many sensitive persons have a list of their own. For instance there is a neolithic earthwork in the south of England. It is better not to say where. The fewer people who pollute that holy and delectable ground the better. No shepherd, no farmhand will go there after dark. In mediaeval romance, a place identified with it was a "temenos" of Morgan le Fay. (The country people have forgotten her.) But there are other earthworks nearby, including Stonehenge, where they will camp out all night at lambing time. Not that one. It is, or was until lately, mana of high potency and, at the same time, strictly tabu. The writer of this essay discovered it when young; and it is no exaggeration to say that a great part of her imaginative life was elicited by it and rests there. Archaeology had begun to interest me, but I knew none of its stories then. It entered into me, "accepted" me. That was all at first; but through the years, what was begun there has continued; where one grew decades of imaginative life in an hour. Returning from there once, I fell into an abnormal sleep, caused probably by the may in full bloom with which my room was filled. I found myself there again, but in mid-winter. It is difficult to find words to describe what I saw. I can only speak of part of it as a seeing of what was really there, the true nature of the place. Hanging above the grove that crowns the earthworks was a face. Fifteen years later I met the owner of the face; or rather the translation of its unthinkable loveliness into flesh and blood. We stared and immediately recognised each other. And with that began another sequence.

This story is as true as I can make it, but a personal digression, and so not very satisfactory. (Though it is hard to say why in this respect alone personal experience should be suspect.) It is an attempt to explain what is meant by the experience, so often used by writers on the supernatural, that a place can be more than its assembly of wood and leaf and stone visible to us; more than the atomic structure common to all things. Ossandovsky writes of a barrow in Asiatic Russia, one of the tumuli which mark the road of Genghis Khan, which the peasants do not like. He saw it, once a round grass mound, and once as whirling grey mist. Apparently his camera saw it also. Sometimes he could photograph it, sometimes he could not. His evidence is called suspect, but a big-game hunter and mining engineer is not usually over-fanciful. To quote again one's own experience: there is a part of Lincoln's Inn which does not always "stay put." Also Great Russell Street. But that, whatever it is, is something projected *out* of the British Museum. Mr. Metcalf's story, "The Bad Lands," makes the most of this. A man, a confessed neurotic, takes a walk each day in a countryside most perfectly described. Each day the walk gets worse; until one day he goes to the house that is not there, to burn it; because of the downstairs room he has looked in at, bare but for the table and the infernal spinning-wheel. He is arrested for arson and the attempted destruction of a barn. The spoke of the wheel, he had put into his pocket for evidence, is the handle of the patent separator, marked with the angry farmer's name.

*   *   *   *   *

So far we have divided the literature of the occult into two classes—those which are written round a theory of the nature of matter, space or time, and those which ask us to believe in no theory. We have observed a few of the second, and that their success depends on evocation, a state (to which "bogy" fear is only the accompaniment) of wonder in its rarest sense, of *clarté*, of a universe enlarged. The first class is more elaborate—exposition of a theory which has to appeal by its interest, by its reasonableness; and we have to be persuaded or half persuaded that our three-dimension space and time arrangements are no more than an arrangement of our senses, a setting for our play; a conception to which science itself, as even the newspapers are beginning to remind us, gives more and more its authority.

Here we are a long way from Professor James and his sheer skill; the divine trick by which the artist draws tales out of anything, raw fish on a plate, a piece of common sentiment; from a god men have long since ceased to pray to; or from things which are not supposed to happen at all. (Or if they ever do happen, make doubly sure of the existence in nature of hideous evil and fear.)

We have glanced at his work, and at the earliest, purest, least theoretic origins of all such work, in the ballads and in the practices of antiquity. While writers such as Hogg and Mr. Wells, Kipling and Mr. Metcalf—to take a few names at

351

hazard—may sometimes assume theory, but they have no
theory to back up. It is now time to consider the writers of
distinction who have set out to prove a case.

In modern letters, Bulwer Lytton began it. His long short
story, "Haunters and Haunter," is a classic, and is reprinted
to-day when boys and girls refuse to read *The Last Days of
Pompeii* any more. His theory is explicit. The old London
house is what might be called a "mixed haunt." Ghosts of
the evil woman, the drowned man and the child. A host of
light balls and elemental shapes. These are set in motion
and in different patterns of horror because Cagliostro once
lived there, and left behind some sort of focusing and materialising mechanism, closely described, in a space between
the walls. A kind of compass, I think, in vibration, which by
troubling the atmosphere made the phenomena visible. The
word "vibration" starts an old theory—the utility in the
Middle Ages of the ringing of bells, whose ringing purified
the air, released the holiness stored at the altar for the driving out of evil spirits. Such were the sistra of Isis, descended
to-day to the bell-strokes before the Elevation; the drums
and flutes of the Bacchantes degraded to the Salvation Army.
And many people know what a sudden bell will do. So we
arrive at the whole range of the effects of music, from
Beethoven to jazz.

Zanoni is a full-dress novel. A young man, so far as I
remember, wishes to acquire supernatural powers, and ac-
cepts the long initiation period supposed necessary for their
safe use. Got bored—and no wonder, with the amount of
fasting and prayer considered obligatory—for he was to be a
respectable magician. Finally, mastered by his impatience—
for a young woman, I think, who he hoped to get out of
it—he tries a short cut and expires. For the theory go to
Dogme et Rituel de la Haute Magie, by Eliphas Lévi; *magnum opus*
of the cold Latin-Jewish mind; where the history of the descent of the Logos into matter is described as if Lévi was
writing a treatise on cookery. William Butler Yeats said he
was a man who would have said anything; though his huge

book reads plausibly, not as though he wished to deceive other people, let alone himself. Did any of the experiments, so seriously vouched for, ever come off? Perhaps, but never in the way he expected. On the analogy of the knight's move, one can say that his work bore fruit, indirectly and successfully, in Huysman's great novel, *Là-bas*.

After Bulwer Lytton came a writer to whom Colonel Buchan is again in some sort the successor, Rider Haggard, famous in one's childhood as Dumas, father in letters to them both. One wrote *King Solomon's Mines*, the other *Mr. Standfast* and the *The Thirty-nine Steps*. But already in *King Solomon's Mines* there is a hint of the author's chief preoccupation, which was to be the theme for his other great success, our youth's bestseller and even now reprinted—*She* and its sequel, *Ayesha*. Even now in memory they seem to me to be very good books, great illuminators for adolescence; and they are written round theories, so precise and so strongly held as to be the essential structure of the tale and of the writer's conception of what is most important in life. Moreover one was left at the end sure that Mr. Haggard knew very much more than he cared to write down; that some experience of no common order lay behind the country gentleman turned popular novelist; who laid that aside in turn to become an agricultural expert—like another man of the same order, the Irishman, "Æ."

This essay is not the place to examine the Celtic field. Ancient or modern, there is too much of it. To-day it can be smug. Can assume, without so much as a polite gesture in the direction of evidence, that it is the mind of the debased Saxon, lost in materialism, which questions the stories of a supernaturally enlightened peasantry on the existence and nature of the Sidhe. Who exist in Ireland for the Irish; sole inspiration of the only art worth mentioning in Europe. I have heard a young woman nationalist, on what philological grounds I know not, that the Tuatha da Danaan were Homer's Danaans, come there to repeat Hellenic civilisation....

It is cult that is fatal. And the Irish to-day seem to make of their folk-mythology a national asset. This with admirable exceptions—Lady Gregory's sober classic, *Visions and Beliefs in the West of Ireland*; Mr. Yeats, Mr. Stephens and "Æ," at their best. But in most literature that is specifically "Celtic" there seems to be a shapelessness. Things happen as we know they do not happen, and as we do not want them to happen. The magic princesses—for this is just as explicit in their earliest epics—are too magic. Thirty invincible knights fight thirty invincible giants for thirty nights and days; without, as Professor Murray points out, any interval for meals. Not only do these things not happen; we do not care to pretend that they happen. Nor are they made symbolic for any of the invisible tides in human affairs. Very different are the true countrymen's stories, of a small, green, strange, gay, earthy, child-stealing folk. Moreover it will be found that an overdose of Celtic "magic" can give one a sense of something very like a special kind of evil, a spiritual quickening that soon turns to poison, as it might from some drug.

Compare some of those stories with True Thomas's sober tale, stirring a hope in most hearts that in some way it might be possible to share that adventure, to go on that ride.

Compare them again with a supernatural story so good that I have seen it reprinted in a recent anthology, side by side with Bulwer Lytton and Mr. Benson—"Glam's Ghost," Chapters XXII to XXV of the Grettir Saga. It is sober, awful and precise. There is "something wrong" up at Thorkall's sheep pens, and with incomparable skill it is suggested that there is "something wrong" also—though Thorkall does not know it—with the shepherd he has got in to deal with it. The shepherd is found hideously dead. Then *his* ghost begins to trouble Thorkall's dwelling and the whole settlement. The description reads like that of a "poltergeist" turned dangerous. Then Grettir arrives to see what he can do. Meets Glam's ghost in the stables at night, fights with it and destroys it. But the fight has drawn him out under the cold Icelandic moon. It is the saga's turning-point to tragedy. For the evil spirit, about to be made to depart, speaks; tells Grettir that the encounter has been fatal for him; that he shall grow no stronger; that what he has done, his looking on the ghost's face, shall bring him early to defeat and death. And Grettir, when he has heard that and seen the creature's eyes, kills it. But ever after he fears the dark, and suffers pitifully on account of that fear. Until, not many years later, he is killed—and this time by plain witchcraft—on Drangey.

Observe the knight's move again. While it is impossible to give any idea of the sober precision of the telling. It might be a report written by an imaginative, simple and accurate person for the Society of Psychical Research. *If it happened at all, it happened like that.*

One of Dr. Hyde's stories, in his classic collection of the best Irish fairy-tales, is on the same matter—an evil corpse, which makes a man carry him on his back, all night, running over stone walls. And there is pure evocation in another, on witches, who come visiting a woman nightly, until a voice out of a well tells her how to be rid of them. "And they departed to Slievennamon which is their chief abode."

*   *   *   *   *

Rider Haggard has written more books than people are ever likely to remember again, and of priceless value for adolescence. Apart from some of the African series, they are forgotten. Who to-day reads *Stella Fregilius, Cleopatra* or *The World's Desire?* One hopes never to read them again. Many of us have an excellent version of them written in our heads, which we do not want disturbed by a tactless reference to the text. Perhaps the best thing that can be said about them is that they awoke imagination and curiosity in children; *Stella Fregelius* about love, sacred and profane; *Cleopatra* about a great moment in history, where his evocation of the goddess Isis was a "variety of religious experience" to children about to become sensitive to such things.

From these and other forgotten books one learned also the rules of mysticism, the sentences which crystallise the mystic's experience and belief. An exciting story illustrated them; and if Victorian morals and certain historical ignorance made him condemn Cleapatra for not being married to Antony, his portrait of the queen is not vulgar. He had a sense of the mysterious links and repetitions of history— Cleopatra strung like her own pearl on a thread of beauty and disturbing power running through man's history, opening at its dawn with "Heaven-born Helen, Sparta's queen." Reborn, now here and now there, making one feel sure that such happenings and such repetitions are not fortuitous.

He made the ancient religions live; re-evoked Isis; led one into the heart of the Pyramid to the grave of Menkau-Ra. In *The World's Desire* he invented a small materialised form of the evil forces in nature; a motif used neatly in *The High Places* by Mr. Branch Cabell. In Mr. Haggard it is a kind of animal, not described—almost a foretaste of Professor James. Mr. Cabell too can evoke when he likes—the only American writer outside Poe and Henry James who can. And some tastes find Poe, especially in his much-praised "House of Usher," too lyrical by half. The state set is over life-size— if one's preference is for small, neat wonders in a familiar world. Or if they must pass in a grandiose setting, let it be in a pyramid we all know to be there, or in a cathedral where we can hear evensong.

In *The World's Desire* the scene is bold enough, but not unfamiliar. Odysseus's second wanderings, Penelope dead, to find Troy's Helen, his first love. Then his death at the hands of Telegonus, Circe's son. Interesting to youth, just alive to Homer, and made acquainted on the way with Plato's theory of the division of souls. This is really Mr. Haggard's theme. Even in his Zulu tales he wrote about little else but a piece of some absolute beauty, divided up, usually into three, bodies of men and women; trying again to unite, slipping through each others' fingers; and according to their quality, realising or destroying themselves.

Throughout the adventures and the big-game hunting, the battles, the lost treasures, he made it understood that here we are no more than shadows, working out a play on our true existence, and aware of it as shadows might be of their body. His little preachings are those of a Victorian gentleman. His vision persists, if my memory does not fail me, of a singular breadth and exaltation. It also civilised. His Zulu chiefs are men like ourselves. In one book, written round T'chaka, his "nigger" tribesmen contain princely boys. One of them, who had suffered greatly, hunted with a pack of ghost-wolves.

There were once words, cut on an emerald, whose understanding would deliver mankind. The emerald is lost. Some of the words are remembered. He told them. There were other things like that. A distant cousin, though I never met him, there came from his mind to the mind of a child, wandering and reading in a Dorsetshire garden, the first idea of an earth "one great city of gods and men."

If it is difficult to end this study, it is harder to draw conclusions from it. So many names occur, and there is no space in which to deal with them. Ghost-anthologies have become popular, and contain such names as Conrad, Ethel Coburn Mayne and Violet Hunt. Œnone Somerville and Martin Ross slip in, between their hunting and shooting comedies, the story, here and there, of a ghost. Not on the traditional Irish material, but what one may call "plain ghost," the sober kind, fit for the ears of the Secretary of the Society for Psychical Research, and no less convincing for that. While Miss Somerville in her memoirs tells simply how once she heard a ghost-pack hunting on the Irish shore.

Marion Crawford, with his plain, deep love of the sea, wrote two classic sea-horrors—"The Upper Berth," story of a cabin on a line which each night smelt of stale seawater; and there was a port-hole no one could keep shut, and a berth which had in it the body of a man long-drowned. With that there is "The Screaming Skull," a tale worked up from that object, supposed still to be seen in a south-country farmhouse, high and dry on the rafters, and better left there, because it squeaked if you displaced it and invariably found its way back.

With him, though in very different keys, are Mr. Tomlinson and Conrad. In another style and content altogether,

357

Mr. Barry Pain. In the Victorian past there was Mrs. Oliphant, who wrote one masterpiece of sober loveliness, "The Library Window." Dickens and Wilkie Collins, neither very successful; and Le Fanu, sole example of an author who rarely wrote about anything else. It is curious; the rest of his work for us to-day is practically unreadable, but his short stories, like "Mr. Justice Harbottle," are fresh and enduring. There are many of them; it is becoming the fashion to include them in anthologies; and they were written from his heart. Dreadful tales, chiefly about the evil and unresting dead.

At this moment new authors are appearing—Mr. Harvey, Mr. L. White, Miss Lawrence and Miss Naomi Royde-Smith. Certain of these have a peculiar quality, which will be noticed later; but if they have one thing in common, it is an absence of the facetiousness or stressed scepticism, which the Victorians thought essential, and which has lasted in the least distinguished of this work till to-day. A class which I have left out of account, to be dismissed now in a paragraph—the books which say that they are not fiction, which profess to describe hauntings and disturbances, traditional in certain houses, known of from generation to generation. It is a pity. I do not know of a single even tolerably good writer who has devoted himself to this. These accounts seem to be written by persons whose style has not developed beyond the commonest journalese; whose ability to judge between fiction and possible fact, hardly exists at all. The evidence for such stories is suspect enough, yet it is of the greatest importance that it should be tested. For if it is all rubbish, the sooner that it is known to be rubbish the better. While if there is any truth in these traditions, the sooner that it is determined *what* truth, the better. At least the business is one that should not be left to third-rate journalists.

Outside "Kilmeny" and the Ballads, we have not spoken of poetry—poetry one of whose qualities is the evocation of the invisible. It would be agreeable to compose a "magic" anthology—it would not be a large one—of English "supernatural" verse.

There is still another attitude of mind before this subject, best left to the end, so that there may not be time to say all the rude things that occur to one—the class of story whose writers set out, not to evoke or examine, or to frighten us into a fit, but to prove a case; who have a theory of the unseen and set out to insist on it. One knows no surer source for a pettish scepticism than some books I read once, issuing from some theosophical association in America, in which the most preposterous things happened—to the dismay of unbelievers in reincarnation, auras and the ecclesiastical possibilities of Tibet. But better writers than the authors of those books have fallen into the same trap, and out of pure good-will. There is Mr. Algernon Blackwood, who may be quite right about his nature potencies. But he—except on occasions—so wishes to persuade us, so multiplies his presences, that it becomes difficult to be sure what he is writing about. In actual experience, the exasperating point is that, to us, there is often no discernable point. While Mr. Blackwood, in trying to tie down the elusive reasons, seems only to succeed in obscuring it further. His contact with nature is deep, his reactions and his reverence stimulating, but it is often all reiteration, all multiplication of effect. So long-drawn-out that one thinks of Miss May Sinclair's God of Pantheism—"as though He had sat down on the piano, on all the notes at once."

There seems to be a new school in these stories, the newest school of all—at least the most recently printed. In them is developed what may almost be called a novel horror, descended perhaps from Professor James in its detachment and absence of theory, but without either his faultless style or lucidity of mind. But Mr. Metcalf in "The Smoking Leg," Mr. Harvey in "The Beast With Five Fingers," and Mr. E. L. White in "Lukundo" have given a turn to horror which is hardly tolerable. Perhaps Poe is their master, but to some minds he is too literary to be convincing. With infinitely less accomplishment, what they have to "put over" may actually carry more persuasion. The beastliness of those stories, handed out, without so much as a comma to indicate a pos-

359

sible explanation, may have affinities with something that is appearing in our society, a wantonness, a want of standard, an acceptance of unreason, which may not be without parallel, but has a quite peculiar flavour about it. Until lately, it would hardly have occurred to anyone to invent such things for their own sake, and without much literary excuse. No one would have thought them up; or if they had, the point, in part at least, would have lain in their explanation.

There is one writer of great reputation who in these matters has gone further than most others in our time—Miss May Sinclair who, round variations of pure theory, has written one very remarkable book. With assurance enough to be banal, she called it *Uncanny Tales*. It came out some years ago and has been reissued lately in a cheap edition. I do not know if Miss Sinclair has written many other stories like these, nor what prompted the book. Only that she is a metaphysician and, I believe, the usual open-minded, sceptical member of the Society for Psychical Research. Some of these stories have a most persuasive enchantment. They are chiefly on the reappearance of the dead or the conditions of life after death. Miss Sinclair is one of the few who can make the return of blessed spirits to their loved ones as interesting as the horrible thing Mr. Landon thought of—the dried body of a tortured nun at the foot of a bed, whose rags and bones, tangible and finally broken up, seemed to have collected themselves together and gone back to wherever such things go. At least the people, whose agony of terror is as convincing as one's own would be, hear steps outside the room where they have taken refuge, and, on going out, there were no rags and no bones. Miss Sinclair has none of these terrors. On her theory, they would depend on the will of the dead. And her dead are young wives and tender mothers and wise old men; who even though his chauffeur murders him and cuts him up, comes back to forgive him and advise him in a shape of radiant old age; with only a hint as to the form he might have taken had he wished for revenge. That story, "The Victim," is well known. It deserves to be. There is a perfect charity about it, understanding and reasonable hope. No one who as read it could find anything to say but—"If there is a life after death, and it is not a leap into a logic unknown to us, this is what it should be."

Even better done, and more valuable because there Miss Sinclair explains her metaphysics, is "The Finding of the Absolute," the realisation by several spirits, to whom death has been a deliverance, of their lands of the heart's desire. A high-spirited tale. One "got in" to the reality he had desired by love of beauty, one by the service of love, two by the love of truth; each by more than the love of pleasantness, or being well-thought-of or by virtues instead of virtue.

Perhaps in the story "Where Their Fire is Not Quenched," Miss Sinclair is too hard on her poor ghosts, giving way to a prejudice Mr. Strachey has quoted from Newman on "the high, severe ideal of the intrinsic excellence of virginity." One of them had never pretended to love other than coarsely; the other had been mistaken in thinking that she had. It is not "pitched" quite right for a sermon on pretension in love. Which should open hell, if hell there be—the hell that is implicit in the nature of things.

After Miss Sinclair there remains Mr. E. M. Forster, whose special sensibility, curiosity and faith makes him indifferent to any ultimate distinction between pagan and Christian supernatural values. Capable of observing "one form under many names," for him it is "all Hermes, all Aphrodite." This is explicit in some of his short stories and implicit in his *Passage to India,* perhaps the chief novel of our generation, where many varieties of "magic" are shown or suggested or described —with scepticism, with faith. While the whole book is shot through with a light—that radiance so incalculable, so recurrent, so variously described, whose power of suggestion is greater than any other; light of the stuff that grows

> Not in holt or heath,
> Nor yet in any sheugh...

but always in that country man has never been able to mark

on any map, yet is the ambiguous place of origin for his most durable works.

Mr. Forster knows the knight's move, its oblique turns in human adventure. He is also the historian on Alexandria, and in *Pharos and Pharillon* he describes the adventures of its founder in the oasis of Ammon. That story and Mr. Forster's query on it will serve to end, illustrate and sum up the subject of this essay. We all know what happened, the little event on which so much depended, and which has so impressed itself on the imagination of the world.

In the temple at the oasis the priest, who was not supposed to know who he was, saluted Mr. Forster's "young tourist" as "Son of God." As he points out, there are two or three explanations to this. One is that the priest spoke bad Greek, and said "O Paidios" ("Son of God") for "O Paidion," which means "my child." Or that the supernatural salutation, however correct it afterwards proved to be, was a put-up job on the part of the Egyptian authorities, anxious for the young man's favour. Or, finally, that the priest meant what he said. For at least, so far as humanity can judge, he was right. There is no such thing as a divine man, or, more exactly, a divine in man, if Alexander was not such a man, had not something of a divine nature in him. Or if there is no such thing as a divine nature anywhere, what is Alexander? (Alexander or Buddha; Plato or St. John of the Cross; Akbar or Asoka. Or…or…?) To-day the balance of powerful thought is inclining, not to a change of definition for the Divine, with the supernatural that accompanies it—we are used to that—but to a denial of Divinity as a whole, or else of its effective existence in terms conceivable to man. (Not unlike Epicurus who, if one has understood him properly, admitted the gods of antiquity, but on the understanding that they could not affect, in any way, any person or any circumstance or any thing.) This last seems about as far as anyone outside the religious professions is willing to go to-day. While the men in power who still profess belief are easy to drive into a corner, and somehow do not put up a very satisfactory fight with their backs to the wall.

To the common man of intelligence, neither party in this most fundamental of all controversies manages to convince. He feels that both sides profess either too little or too much, and his chief hope to lie in the study of religious origins; and there less where faiths have differed than where they have agreed. Meanwhile he continues to read and to write, according to his vision, taste or imagination, about any sort of supernatural that may conceivably be true. There was never more curiosity than there is to-day about "the uncanny" or "strange things"—"things" that even in our fathers' day it was improper to believe in at all. Things of which the smallest proof would prove very much more than the actual event. "Things," from the appalling horrors of Professor James to the exquisite and delivered spirits of Miss May Sinclair; to the bright and dark thread running through the world scene of Mr. Forster. *"Brightness falls from the air..."* Very tentative, very inventive, wisely theoretical or mercifully untheoretical happenings, that so many writers are trying to invent, to display, to evoke for us.

After them all, there is no better book than the late Miss Harrison's *Prolegomena to the Study of Greek Religion,* or Miss Weston's *From Ritual to Romance,* the work to which T.S. Eliot owes to much. There is set out the *natural* history of so many of our beliefs, in bogy, ghost, daimon, demon, angel or god. Some were absorbed direct into Christianity; all have affected our culture; not one of which has not been, in its time, material for the finer orders of men to see more deeply into the structure of reality, and to make others see also.

So perhaps we shall find ourselves back again where our "savage ancestors" began—back again to initiation rites that really initiated, so long as you brought something to them: good health; faith; knowledge and goodwill—to whose men peace was promised. That conception may come round again —a great wheel turned and ground gained—to initiations which will really initiate; not by haphazard; not by fraud or hypnosis or superstition, but inevitably. Because we shall know to what further fields of veridical experience they take us.

Even now old formulae haunt and stir:

> LOVE: I have fallen upon the breast of Despoina, Queen of the Underworld.
>
> DEATH: You shall find on the left of the House of Hades a well-spring. Beside it is a white cypress. Say: "I am a child of earth and the starry heavens. But my race is of the stars."

Formulae that are very old. The time may be coming when, their ritual origins traced, their risings and settings chased through our subconscious, we shall know what powers we have evoked exterior to us. How far also it depends on man which he choses; who, at his word, from among the seraphim, the angels, the demons, the daimones will come.

If we do not find out, we had better look out for ourselves. We have been careless lately what spiritual company we have kept; in our choice of ghostly guests. The results are observable.

Paris—Sennen. 1928-1932

A NOTE ON THIS EDITION

THE FIVE WORKS contained in this collection have not appeared before in a single volume. For this edition, orthography has been established in general conformity with our other editions of Mary Butts's novels and stories. Obvious spelling errors have been corrected, and internal consistency has been enforced whenever the author's intention could be adduced. Clear idiosyncrasies of style are maintained.

The first edition of *Ashe of Rings* appeared from the Paris house of Contact Editions in 1925. The following year, the American firm of Albert & Charles Boni issued an edition either based on the Contact one or employing the same manuscript. Differences between these texts are slight. In 1933, a revised edition was issued by Wishart & Company in London. All three texts were compared for this new edition, which is based on the Boni. Several clarifying elaborations to the text have been accepted from the Wishart; these usually entail no more than a few words. The Wishart also deleted an unarticulated plotline, and we have followed suit.

Imaginary Letters was privately printed in 1928 in an edition of 250 deluxe copies, containing line drawings by Jean Cocteau, by the press of Edward Titus in Paris. In 1979, Talonbooks of Vancouver reset and issued a paperback edition with an afterword by Robin Blaser. *Warning to Hikers* was issued by Wishart in 1932 as No. 6 of "The Here & Now Pamphlets." *Traps for Unbelievers* appeared also in 1932 as a pamphlet from Desmond Harmsworth, London. "Ghosties and Ghoulies" was serialized in four issues of *The Bookman* in 1933.

Thanks are due to Camilla Bagg, Harvey Pekar, and Lawrence Rainey for loaning copies of the three editions of *Ashe of Rings*; to Nathalie Blondel for a photocopy of the 1928 *Imaginary Letters*; to Camilla Bagg for photocopies of the *Traps* and *Warning* pamphlets; and to Gerrit Lansing and Nathalie Blondel for photocopies of the "Ghosties and Ghoulies" essay.

The text of this book has been set in Monotype Baskerville at the studios of McPherson & Company. The design is by Bruce McPherson. The book is printed on pH neutral paper and sewn into signatures. The first printing consists of 1200 copies bound in cloth over boards and jacketed.